MORTAL REMAINS

MORTAL REMAINS

Peter Clement

BALLANTINE BOOKS • NEW YORK

Mortal Remains is a work of fiction. Names, places, and incidents either are a product of the author's imagination or are used fictitiously.

A Ballantine Book
Published by The Random House Publishing Group

Copyright © 2003 by Peter Clement Duffy

All rights reserved under International and Pan-American Copyright Conventions. Published in the United States by The Random House Publishing Group, a division of Random House, Inc., New York, and simultaneously in Canada by Random House of Canada Limited, Toronto.

The author wishes to gratefully acknowledge the following: "Stand By Me" by Jerry Lieber, Mike Stoller, Ben E. King © 1961 Mike & Jerry Music, LLC, Jerry Lieber Music, Mike Stoller Music. Copyright renewed. All Rights Reserved. Used by permission. "Most Likely You'll Go Your Way and I'll Go Mine" by Bob Dylan © copyright 1966 by Dwarf Music. All rights reserved. International copyright secured. Reprinted by permission.

Ballantine and colophon are registered trademarks of Random House, Inc.

www.ballantinebooks.com

Book design by Susan Turner

The Cataloging-in-Publication Data for this title is available from the Library of Congress.

ISBN 0-345-45778-1

Manufactured in the United States of America

First Edition: September 2003

10   9   8   7   6   5   4   3   2   1

To Vyta, Sean, and James

Acknowledgments

My thanks to Dr. Brian Connolly and Dr. Jennifer Frank for their consults on the clinical story line.

To Dr. DeWolfe Miller for his tutoring on the darkness and techniques of deep mountain lake dives.

To Dr. Yasmine Ayroud for her advice on the state of a body after it spent twenty-seven years in the mud of a deep mountain lake.

To Johanna, Betty, Connie, Anne, and Arnie for their editorial comments.

To my agent Denise and her staff Maura and Joy for all their support.

To publicist Nancy Berland for her enthusiastic encouragement.

And to my marvelous editor at Ballantine, Pat Peters.

MORTAL REMAINS

Chapter 1

Mark Roper followed sheriff Dan Evans down, staying so close to the man's flippers that they occasionally brushed his face mask. But he didn't want to get too far behind the tunnel of light from Dan's headlamp, which led them ever deeper into the darkness. Unable to see anything but black outside its range, Mark couldn't tell up, down, or sideways unless he focused on the illuminated streams of algae streaking at them. Like snow against a windshield, they heightened his sense of speed.

The cold penetrated his hood, giving him a doozy of an ice-cream headache; it burrowed through the vulcanized rubber of his dry suit and a double layer of thermal underwear, then through skin, muscle, and bone to settle directly into his marrow. Despite diving gloves, even his fingers threatened to freeze up, but he kept his grip on the safety line, kicking and propelling himself ever lower, moving hand over hand. God, when would they get there? he wondered, repeatedly having to pinch his nose through his mask, then blow to relieve the painful pressure in his ears.

He'd been down this deep before, but in the warm blue ocean off Hawaii. Here he might as well have been swimming in ink. Though the water was clear, the mountain lake, nestled in a steep gorge, was so narrow and deep that it swallowed most of the sunshine from the surface.

Other dives they'd made in the district were shallow, but with this one claustrophobia pressed in with smothering force. He couldn't let himself get far from Dan, who carried the big handheld spotlight. If he ended up alone, his own headlamp would be too feeble at this depth, and Mark wasn't at all sure that he'd be able to hold panic at bay. A dangerous situation, because down here cold and disorientation were killers. Already he was breathing too hard, the sound rushing loudly through his ears, and he made a conscious effort to slow it down.

A white cord trailed out in front of them to nothingness. If it hadn't been there, the end abruptly marking where the bottom lay, they might have hit the thick layer of silt and muck that covered the lake's floor and thrown up such a cloud of debris they'd be in a virtual blackout that not even a lamp could penetrate. As it was, their arrival kicked up plumes of dirt that hung suspended around them like giant gray fronds.

Dan looked at the dive computer on his sleeve. Mark did the same, barely able to read the screen. According to the numbers—measurements of the cold, the pressure, the depth, the altitude of the lake—the calculation told him they could only stay about fifteen minutes before having to head back. Their ascent would be no faster than a half foot per second, and they would have to make a three-minute safety stop fifteen feet from the surface to allow the release of excess nitrogen from their bloodstreams. The clinical consequences if he got it wrong—multiple emboli, pneumothoraces, mediastinal emphysema, subcutaneous emphysema, all of them air bubbles where they shouldn't be—were nasty enough that he'd die screaming. As county coroner, in the last four years Mark had seen three dive victims with just such injuries, and he sure as hell was going to be careful.

With so little time, he wanted to get going. But the silt remained—in fact, seemed to grow worse—making it impossible to see at all, cutting him off from Dan. Waiting for it to settle felt like an eternity, and he began to doubt his senses, unable to make out even his own bubbles or tell if the rope in his hand led to the surface or the bottom.

Stop! Think! Act! he said to himself. It was the diver's credo to stay out of trouble. He breathed deeply, slowly, to gain control. Then he adjusted the pressure in his suit with a small squirt of compressed air to maintain neutral buoyancy.

Dan came into view, floating just below. Mark suspected that he, too, was trying to conquer a sense of panic and probably regretting the day they'd flown off to Hawaii together for the week of scuba training that would qualify them for these forensic dives. But Mark had pushed the idea so they'd no longer have to wait around for an outside team every time someone drowned.

Finally, the particles in the water cleared.

The area around them hadn't so much as a strand of seaweed on it. But it wouldn't be easy to spot what they were after, he decided, surveying the little he could see of the barren landscape. The hooks from the search-and-rescue boat must have snagged their catch deep within this soft mush because anything of any weight would have buried itself under its surface.

Unless the pulling had rooted up the rest of the remains before the limb tore off, he knew they'd never find them.

Dan slowly turned and swept the surrounding area with the probe of his lamp. It barely penetrated ten feet before the thick, absolute darkness sucked it up.

Hopeless, Mark thought.

Indeed, after a complete rotation, they had seen nothing.

Mark took a reading from his compass. The draggers had told him the target should lie approximately north to northeast from the anchor line. He oriented himself so that what they were looking for should be in front of him, if the men above had been right in their guesstimates. He handed Dan his headlamp, took the powerful handheld light, and started forward.

He'd gone only twenty feet when it loomed up before him.

A headless thorax, rib cage included, protruded out of the soft mud, resting at a slight angle. The left humerus and a more or less intact right arm trailed into the black sediment, making it seem as if the skeleton were trying to push itself up out of its grave. The bottom half, the pelvis and legs, remained out of sight. There was no sign of the skull.

Earlier that morning Dan's volunteers had been dragging the lake for the body of a seventy-nine-year-old man with Alzheimer's disease who'd wandered off the previous weekend. Retrieval should have meant a simple transfer to the undertakers in Saratoga Springs, the paperwork to follow. Instead they hauled up the bones of a left forearm barely attached to the remnants of a fingerless hand. They called Dan and Mark, but not before dropping an anchor with a line attached.

Up top Dan had shown Mark the limb as they prepared for the dive. It was pretty well stripped of flesh, but enough cartilage and connective tissue held it together that one of the grapple prongs had caught the space between the ulna and radius, the long bones running from the elbow to the wrist.

To Mark's amazement, the bones' owner appeared equally intact. Except down here the strands of remaining tissue waved in the water like tattered clothing. Using the beam, he signaled Dan to swim over.

Everything had been colored brownish green by a heavy overgrowth of algae. That the flesh and organs were otherwise mostly gone certainly meant many years had passed since this person went in the water. That some of the bones were still connected at all, he thought, had to be from the preservative effects of cold and mud on gristle. Certainly the absence of a head was no surprise. The bony portion that joined a skull atop a spine was a small peg no bigger than the end phalanx of the little finger. In life it took a neckful of muscle, sinew, and cartilage to hold everything together, more than for any other joint in the body. No amount of cold mud could preserve that much connective tissue and keep everything in one piece. The skull would have detached from the spine and stayed in the sludge at the first yank of the grappling hooks. Better not go rummaging about for it either. There'd be other much smaller bones scattered about in the sediment, such as the fingers. One of them might have a ring on it that would help with identification. They'd have to get a forensic dive team with specially insulated suits to sift through the gunk and, using a modified scopes basket, do a proper retrieval. And they'd have to do it pronto—or wait until next spring to finish. Freeze-up could occur by late October, early November around here, and no one in his right mind would go diving for a skeleton once it meant cutting through ice with a chain saw.

Mark got down to basics.

After returning the lamp to Dan, he took an underwater slate from his belt and made a primitive sketch of the find, indicating its distance from the marker. He then used his favorite tool for gathering underwater evidence, an Olympus camera in a light-and-motion housing with a built-in strobe. The blast of light firing once every second animated the skeleton, making it appear to move and shift position as if it were posing for him while he drifted around taking shots at different angles.

He looked at the spot where the pelvis disappeared into the dirt. He'd better confirm that the lower half was all there, not wanting to miss the outside chance he was dealing with a cut-up body.

He drifted gently over the top of the hipbones and dipped a hand down either side to where the legs should be.

The sand beneath him exploded to life, and a six-foot ribbon of black undulated out of the murk. He screamed into his mouthpiece and jerked backward, crashing into Evans, who'd been floating a foot above him. The shape writhed between his arms and shot into the darkness.

An eel.

Normal in the lakes around here. Even known to wrap around the legs of swimmers at night. But harmless.

Tell my pounding heart that, he thought, peering into the thick silt the creature had stirred up.

He could make out his watch only by holding it up to his faceplate. Less than five minutes left before they'd have to head up. No time to wait for this latest disturbance to clear. But unable to see his nearest surroundings, he'd lost all sense of direction again, and felt a nauseating swirl of vertigo.

Stop! Think! Act! he once more reminded himself, slowing his breathing, then expelling a few bubbles from the side of his mouthpiece. Before they disappeared in the gloom he glimpsed enough of their passage toward the surface to orient himself, and, trying not to think of the eel circling somewhere out there, reached toward the bottom.

Once more passing his hands through the silt, he found the long shafts of both femurs and palpated along them. The tibiae and fibulae of the lower legs came next. He slid his hands farther down to confirm the presence of feet—and his finger caught on something that felt like thick chains.

What the hell?

They were looped around the ankles.

Oh, shit!

Running his fingers along them he came to what must be a padlock. A few links more led to a smooth hard surface that felt like a metal shaft about six inches in diameter. Following its shape deeper, both his arms up to the shoulder in muck, he made out the double-pointed flanges of an anchor.

He reached up to grab Dan, who hovered just above and, drawing him closer so they floated faceplate to faceplate, guided the sheriff's hand into the ooze. Dan's eyes grew wide behind his mask, and he immediately signaled for them to start up.

Mark agreed. This was now a crime scene, which they must not further disturb. The forensic team would have to sift through the muck not just for parts of the body, but also for evidence that might help them determine who had sent it to the bottom.

They rose slowly, no faster than the proscribed one-half foot per second. Mark felt they weren't even moving. Any quicker, however, and the nitrogen bubbles would appear in their bloodstreams, blocking every tiny artery in their bodies. So they hung there, two specks suspended in a horizonless, charcoal world, the surface still invisible beyond an infinity of gray twilight.

Mark's thoughts slid to the scene below, and thinking about their find unnerved him more than when he'd actually seen and touched it. The idea that they were swimming in water steeped with the remains of human rot didn't bother him. His head knew that that part of the process had mostly ended long ago. It was the possibility the person went into the lake alive and conscious that made his skin crawl. The image of someone plummeting through this nether world, struggling round-mouthed to scream, nothing but bubbles streaming out, filled his head. From the way Dan kept staring down, pupils magnified big as dimes behind the Plexiglas, he, too, appeared to have trouble keeping his imagination in check.

Who could it be? Mark wondered. No one had been reported missing from the Hampton Junction area since he'd started general practice seven years ago. The ten years before that, while in New York at the university, med school, and during his residency, he'd gotten home often enough he would have heard about anyone who'd disappeared. It was possible, of course, that someone had brought the corpse here to dump it. Might be Jimmy Hoffa down there for all he knew. Everybody from the Northeast came here to party and play. Why wouldn't they import their murders as well?

Chapter 2

"**D**addy, look! It's drooped."

Earl Garnet turned from the stove where he'd been hastily making oatmeal and saw his four-year-old, Brendan, running toward him minus the bottoms of his pajamas. "Drooped?" he said, bending his six-foot frame at the waist to scoop the youngster into his arms and sweep him up near the ceiling. "What's drooped?"

The little boy grinned with delight. "My penis! It was big, then I peed, and it got little."

Earl tried not to laugh. "That's normal for boys."

"Does yours do that?"

"Sometimes." He brought him in for a landing on the kitchen table. "How about a bowl of this delicious hot cereal I'm making?"

"Where's Mommy? I like hers better." He climbed down to the chair where he always sat.

Mommy was Dr. Janet Graceton, obstetrician, lover, friend, and wife. "Off delivering a baby."

"Again? How come she has to deliver so many? She does it every day."

"That's right. It's her job."

"Do you deliver babies?"

"Only when I have to. Here." He plopped the bowl of steaming cereal in front of Brendan, doctored it with brown sugar and milk, then glanced at his watch. Sign-off rounds with the night shift started at eight, but he liked to be in ER by seven-thirty to have a coffee, do a walk-through, and pick up any loose ends before the day shift got busy. *What the hell,* he thought. Chief's prerogative. Let the staff tie up their own cases. He wasn't about to pass up this father-son breakfast.

"Wanna' know what I'm making at school?"

"What?"

"A statue of Muffy."

Muffy was the family dog, a standard poodle. Getting on in years, she'd taken to sleeping late, especially when Janet took off in the middle of the night and left a nice warm spot in the bed. More than once Earl had sleepily awakened and draped his arm around what he thought would be his wife, only to get a wet slurp and a cold nose in the face.

"A statue of Muffy! How big?"

"Big!" Brendan's little hand shot over his head to indicate great height.

"Wow, we'll have to get twice as much dog food in the house."

He giggled. "It's a statue, Daddy."

"But will you feed her and walk her and play with her?"

The giggles grew louder.

*   *   *

During the twenty-minute drive to St. Paul's Hospital, the sun rising at his back, he found himself still grinning. As did most men who became fathers late in life, Earl relished moments like those he'd just spent with Brendan. Every day he savored a deep sense of happiness, carefully secreted within him where it wouldn't tempt his lucky stars, the gods, or the fates. With Janet and Brendan he really did have it all.

"Hi, Dr. G.," the triage nurse called out just as he entered his department. Her name tag said JANE SIMMONS R.N. Earl always called her J.S. In her early twenties, three rings piercing her right nostril, J.S. was a bright, cheerful, sometimes zany presence in the ER. Now she hovered over an ashen-faced, middle-aged man lying on a stretcher. Without looking up she slid a large-bore needle the size of a three-inch nail into his arm.

Stepping to her side, Earl asked, "What have we got?"

She hooked her patient to a bag of saline and thumbed the valve wide open. "Bleeding from both ends—coffee grounds up top, both black tarry stool and bright red blood by rectum. Vitals, ninety over sixty and pulse one-ten."

"Coffee grounds" meant blood turned dark brown by stomach acids. "Tarry stools" indicated blood also originating in the stomach, but rendered black by those same acids during their longer passage through the intestines. "Bright red blood" meant either a second source of bleeding below the stomach, which was unlikely, or that the hemorrhage was so severe the blood ran through the gut too fast for the digestive juices to work the color change. Bottom line, the man would soon slip into shock. "Name?" he asked.

"Dr. Garnet, meet Mr. Brady," she said, the worry in her eyes belying her reassuring smile.

"Hi, Doc."

"Well, Mr. Brady, looks like I'm your host, and you are our VIP patient this morning. Hang on. We're going for a ride. Don't worry, J.S. here and I just passed stretcher-driving school."

Together they rushed him down the hall to a resuscitation room, picking up help on the way. Earl kept up the banter so everyone would stay loose.

"How many metal detectors did your nose set off today, J.S.?"

"Hey, I'm a one-woman security check. You should pay me extra." They skidded to a stop, and she immediately started to secure another IV line, this one in the groin.

"Okay, people, listen up," said Earl. "Who's got the head? Who's on the tail? We need full monitoring, bloods, type and cross for six units, and hang up two of O-negative stat."

"Tails," an orderly said.

"Heads!" called a tall, model-thin woman with a boyish haircut as she pushed through to the table and applied oxygen prongs to the man's nose. Her name tag read SUSANNE ROBERTS, NURSING DIRECTOR. "Morning, Dr. Garnet."

"Glad to see you here, Susanne."

"What happened? You were late at being early this morning." She'd been director of nursing for as long as he'd been chief, and knew his routine as well as her own.

"Breakfast with Brendan." Gloving up, he swabbed Mr. Brady below the right collarbone.

"With competition like that, we're lucky to see you at all." She ripped the wrapper off a coiled green catheter, anointed one end with a glob of sterile jelly, and stood ready to pass it down the back of Mr. Brady's throat into his stomach, but through a nostril.

"Don't worry. The nanny always throws me out by seven-twenty-five." He draped a sterile towel over their patient's chest and explained as he worked. "Now I'm injecting a bit of freezing, and then we'll put a central line through the vein under your clavicle to better replace the volume of blood you lost with normal saline."

A young medical student hastily joined him, obviously eager to try the procedure. Seconds later, under Earl's expert guidance, the boy announced, "I've got it!" sounding surprised at his success. He looked up, beaming proudly, and promptly broke sterile technique as he shoved a shock of curly red hair out of his eyes.

"Good show," Earl said. "Now change your gloves!"

The orderly who had taken tails was draining the contents of the bladder through a tube to a transparent collecting bag marked for measuring output. A reassuring grin spread across his ebony face. "Your kidneys are working fine, Mr. Brady."

"Bloods drawn and gone for type and cross," Susanne said at Earl's ear, still waiting to pass her tube, "and GI's been called to scope him."

J.S. connected her needlework to one of the overhanging bags of blood. "Femoral line's in," she said, her tone breezily calm.

"Still the best hands in the business," Earl told her as he stepped to the counter and scribbled medication orders.

Susanne moved in with the tube.

One of her older colleagues, a speedy, gray-haired woman who wore colorful leg warmers and Reeboks, stepped up to help her. "Now you just swallow this down, Mr. Brady . . ."

Other voices reported.

". . . monitors on; patient wired . . ."

". . . BP and pulse holding . . ."

Earl relaxed a notch as he always did once a patient was lined and they were ready for any sudden nasty turns for the worse. He glanced up at the clock. "Wow! Congratulations, everyone. A hundred-and-fifteen-point-five seconds. My buy at the next party." He gave the dazed-looking Mr. Brady a reassuring pat on the arm. "You're invited, too, sir, except I'm afraid you'll be drinking milk shakes."

Once Susanne and he were out in the hallway, he asked, "Any other surprises to start the day?"

"None. You still got fifteen minutes until rounds. If you promise to be good, I'll give you my copy of the *New York Herald*, let you use our cappuccino machine, and not disturb you until eight."

"Susanne, I love you."

"Watch it, or I'll tell Janet."

"Hey, she knows I go gaga over anyone who offers me a cappuccino, a *Herald*, and the time to savor them."

Turning back toward triage, she said, "You just used up fifteen of your seconds."

Behind the closed door of his office—a spartan shoe box painted institutional green—he put his feet up on a hospital-issue gray metal desk, leaned back in the high-backed, maroon Naugahyde-covered chair that came with it, and savored the first sip of a cinnamon-tinged coffee. Some days it was great to be chief.

He felt at the top of his game. Fifty years old, lean in body and mind, he could withstand the physical rigors of emergency better than any of the Young Turks, and very few of the veterans could match him mentally. Susanne once told him her nurses had nicknamed him "The Thief" because of all the times he reached right up to the pearly gates and robbed Saint Peter of a soul already settled in for a grilling from the book of deeds. Even the departmental chaplains, she said, admitted that both God and the devil had to get up early if they wanted to beat Garnet to the punch.

He smiled at the recollection, having learned long ago not to take what people said about him too seriously. He knew his talent—the ability to read an unfolding ER scenario three steps ahead of trouble and jump-start his team accordingly. "Proactive" the more youthful members of his staff called it. "Goddamn teaching" was the term he used. Those who couldn't keep up, especially the administrators, had less-kind words. But they were the first to seek him out when a child, spouse, sibling, or parent was gravely ill, and a life was on the line.

He opened the paper. Page one gave the latest details about the interminable war on terror. Yet another Homeland Security alert took up most of page two. At the bottom were adds with pouty-looking boys modeling tuxedos for sale. Real men mustn't be a worthwhile consumer group anymore, he mused, savoring yet another sip of coffee. Then he read the lead story on page three.

> *Skeletal remains found fifteen days ago in Trout Lake, adjacent to the idyllic resort community of Hampton Junction,*

twenty miles north of Saratoga Springs, have been identified as those of a socially prominent fourth-year medical student who disappeared over twenty-seven years ago. Retrieval of the remains was a protracted affair requiring a special team of forensic divers to sift through mud at great depth in cold temperatures. Dental records and preliminary DNA results based on a lock of the victim's hair established that she was Kelly McShane Braden, twenty-nine years old at the time of her disappearance and the wife of Charles Braden IV, currently Chief of Cardiology at New York City Hospital.

According to Hampton Junction coroner, Dr. Mark Roper, Ms. Braden was the victim of foul play. "A fracture of her skull indicates she sustained a blow to the head prior to going in the water. Whether she died of head trauma or drowning is impossible to distinguish," he said yesterday, when results of his examination and testing were announced. Sheriff Dan Evans confirmed that heavy items found on and near the bones of her legs suggest her body was weighted and bound when disposed of in the deepest waters of the lake.

Her parents, Walter McShane, founder of the prestigious firm McShane Securities, and Samantha McShane, have demanded the police reopen the investigation of their daughter's case, but refuse to say anything further at this time. Ms. Braden's husband, Charles Braden IV, was unavailable for comment, but according to press reports at the time of the disappearance, claimed to have last seen his wife in the early evening of Wednesday, August 7, 1974, when she left his father's country estate near Hampton Junction to catch a train for New York. They'd taken a few extra days' holiday, and Ms. Braden habitually followed this schedule when she had early-morning classes the next day. Dr. Braden, whose office hours began in the afternoon, did not return to the city until late Thursday morning.

Ms. Braden's disappearance attracted a great deal of attention. Highly regarded by her instructors, and popular with her fellow students, she was at the top of her medical school class. Speculation at the time centered on a troubled marriage, which Dr. Braden vigorously denied, and a deliberate disappearance by Ms. Braden. The case yielded few leads. The strongest was provided by doormen at the couple's exclusive Park Avenue apartment building, who saw Ms. Braden get into a waiting cab with a man in the backseat on Wednesday evening. She returned the following morning, leaving several hours later with a suitcase, again by cab, but alone. She was never heard from again. The identity of the man who picked her up Wednesday night is unknown.

He lowered the paper, his stomach in free fall.

ER faded from his mind, and the usual noises outside his door—the beeping of monitors, the chatter, someone retching—became tinny and distant.

He took off his glasses and rubbed his eyes. He couldn't say for sure how long he sat there, his thoughts and emotions reeling.

A knock, and Susanne pushed open the door. "Sorry, Dr. Garnet, but we're starting—My God, are you all right? You look as if you've seen a ghost."

"I'm fine," he said, trying to give a reassuring smile. "It's just my stocks tanked again." He downed the dregs of coffee from his cup in a gulp, tucked the paper into his briefcase, and joined the assembly of residents and staff who were gathered around the chart rack listening to a resident summarize the cases. Those coming on duty looked as tired as the ones who were going off. The main differences between the two were the crisp white coats and pleasant body-wash scents of the newcomers compared to the wrinkled clothing and stale odors hanging about those who'd been working all night.

". . . presented with a squeezing chest pain radiating up the side of his neck. We gave him half an aspirin, stabilized him with oxygen, nitro, and IV morphine . . ."

"I need IV caffeine," whispered one of the medical students standing nearby.

"Sign me up," murmured another.

Earl barely heard any of it. The voices seemed to come at him through a hose. He thought of hair the color of sunlight turning scarlet, and felt his stomach lurch.

". . . the next patient is a man who claims his partner shoved the vibrator in too far . . ."

Had she been tortured, raped, died screaming?

He'd seen a lifetime of victims come through his ER, and needed no prompting to imagine how bad it could get. What if she hadn't been unconscious when her killer dumped her into the lake? She would have gone to the bottom in agony for air, knowing she was going to die, praying for it even.

He desperately tried to stop the images, but his mind poured them on, determined to scour his experience for detailed examples of what she could have been put through. It left him wanting to scream, to strangle someone, to hit back at whoever had so viciously hurt her. Yet he just stood quietly in the little crowd, his eyes brimming with tears, the ritual start to a day in ER unfolding around him as it had for over twenty years.

". . . the next patient presented with coffee-grounds vomitus and black tarry stool . . ."

So many people's stories over so many mornings, they extended back to his beginnings here, and farther, to the days of his residency, to medical school, and the time he loved Kelly.

But he could focus only on one story, his and Kelly's.

He had been the man in the taxi.

New York City

Dr. Melanie Collins, Chief of Internal Medicine at New York City Hospital, dropped the *Herald*, open at page three, onto the black marble surface of her kitchen counter.

Oh, my God! It didn't seem possible. Not now. Not after so long. Incredulous, she kept staring at the print.

Catching her breath, she gazed beyond the gleaming state-of-the-art appliances to the white birch floors running the length of her penthouse. The morning sun crept along the pale grain, enriching it. It would normally be her favorite moment of the day, the curtain going up on the chic, architectural masterpiece she'd created for herself—a space more fit for an upscale artist than a middle-aged physician. The light reached a long dining area with a mahogany table capable of seating twelve, a large round of white leather chairs and couches for relaxing, an entertainment center with a wide-screen television so thin she'd had it mounted on the wall amid an array of paintings—everything encircled by 180 degrees of full-length windows overlooking the Hudson River immediately to the west and downtown Manhattan to the northeast. Even the stretch of Japanese hand-painted screens that she'd had to place along the east windows glowed with a soft translucence that blended with the rest of the decor. This was her aerie, a hard-won prize for what she'd accomplished, the place where she found solace and comfort from the exhausting grind of the hospital. But the sense of inner calm it usually evoked failed to arrive. Instead, she felt a stirring of fear.

In the far corner, elevated on a shallow platform, was the four-poster where she routinely bedded men ten years her junior. She strode past it on her way to the bathroom and a large walk-in shower. Dropping her robe, she stepped in and turned on the spray full force. Underneath the hot needles of water, she splayed her fingers over her breasts and slowly ran her hands down her exercise-sculpted body. Yet her muscles remained tense. Was she herself now in danger? It had seemed best at the time to say nothing, especially since the police never found out where Kelly went after she took the cab. But if they ever did . . .

The thought sickened her. Because they would learn what she'd kept secret all these years, then come asking questions. Just the fact she hadn't told would look bad, perhaps be enough to make her a suspect—all because she had met with Kelly McShane on the day of her disappearance.

The University Club, Midtown Manhattan

"Shit!" Dr. Charles Braden IV threw down the paper, spilling his orange juice and knocking the glass to the floor. He signaled the waiter. "Pedro, I want more coffee, now."

Sitting across from him, Dr. Charles Braden III frowned. "Chaz, what's the matter?"

Chaz shoved the article at his father, then leaned back. The older man's handsome face remained as calm as if he were reading a weather report. Not even his posture gave any clue as to what the discovery of Kelly's remains could mean to the family, his lean physique still seemingly relaxed.

After skimming the article for a few seconds, he shot his son a withering look. "Now that's just perfect, Chaz. Yes, by all means, get mad. And where everyone can see, too."

"Shall I bring you a fresh cup, sir?" the slim, black-haired waiter asked, dropping a white napkin over the stain and cleaning away any splashed dishes. Pedro didn't see himself as a mere waiter. He was the protector of the propriety of the members he served. The greater the indiscretion, the more Pedro made sure his customers knew that they owed him big-time, but tantrums he handled with minimal fuss.

Chaz looked around at the other members who were finishing up their breakfasts. The paneled dining room was only half-full. Dim recessed lighting and lush plants strategically positioned in front of the dining alcoves guarded everyone's privacy almost as much as Pedro did. No one had so much as glanced his way.

But that would change.

Gossipmongers would soon be watching his every move.

Just like before.

And like before, they'd try to pin Kelly's murder on him, only then it was just her disappearance.

"I'd advise you to remain cool," his father continued, carefully placing the paper on the table. He leaned back, the thick bristles of his steely gray hair glistening silver under the light. "After all, we knew this was coming. They did let us know about finding her remains and about the forensic report. You've had time to prepare yourself." At seventy-four, the man could still sear his son's soul with that hard blue stare of his.

He couldn't go through it again, the police once more poring over every detail of Kelly's final days, probing, digging, questioning. He'd be right back in the nightmare, living in fear of a knock on the door, a phone call, a newscast. Chaz ran a hand over his thinning brown hair. "How can I stay cool?"

Charles Braden leaned forward and flashed the smile that made the world jump to his wishes. "By never forgetting that you're innocent. By remembering the police cleared you back then. By knowing I've already reminded a few key people in the NYPD of that fact. Trust me, they'll be looking for someone else."

"What about the media?" he asked.

"I can make a few calls to them as well. So stop looking so morose. As far as police and reporters go, I think you'll be pretty much left alone."

Long ago Chaz had tried to emulate his father's easy charm in getting people to do what he wanted, but he learned at an early age that he was lousy at it. He got better results by using raw power, and that only worked within the walls of the hospital. Even there he didn't have his father's facile ability to succeed as a doctor and reach the inner circles of power.

He was a drudge. Hard work and long hours had won him the position of Chief of Cardiology. The one category where he held his own was in physical presence. He, too, was tall and thin; people noticed when he walked into a room.

Pedro returned with an oversize cup filled with a particularly strong brew. Chaz thanked him, and doctored it with sugar only. To his disgust he saw his hand tremble slightly as he took a sip. "I won't be left alone if they find out I was the last one to talk with Kelly."

St. Paul's Hospital, Buffalo, New York.

Finally, the presentations were over. At this point Earl usually fired off a few pointed questions to drive home any teaching pearls. Today he felt more like firing off a machine gun. After a few uninspired attempts to come up with some zingers, he called it quits. His audience left, muttering in frustration, and a few of his staff gave him what's-the-matter-with-you looks.

All he could think of was, Who? Who had done this to Kelly? Some stranger? Her husband?

He tried to see patients, but the parade of faces and stories blurred into one another. As for his clinical responses, only the reflexes from twenty-four years' experience saw him through.

". . . Prilosec, Flagyl, and Biaxin ought to do the trick . . ."

". . . an ECG, blood gas, and nuclear scan of his lungs for starters . . ."

". . . albuterol by aerosol and IV steroids . . ."

He kept wondering if Chaz Braden had killed her after all. Yet why him, when he could have divorced her, ruined her burgeoning career, gotten back at her any number of ways? He continued to pummel himself with questions, sadness pulling him inside out one second, outrage filling him like a balloon the next.

Well practiced at putting on his "everything is fine" face for his patients and troops during the worst of cases, he could feel the tightly contracted muscles of his jaw and knew he looked drawn and tense. "What a lousy actor, you are," he muttered, disgusted with the pale imitation of his usual take-charge presence, knowing he shouldn't continue to work with his mind in such a tumult. "Can you cover for me?" he asked Dr. Michael Popovitch, his portly second-in-command, and one of his closest friends.

Michael looked up from a cut hand he was suturing and eyed Earl over a pair of bifocals. "Are you all right?" he asked.

"Of course. I've got some personal business to take care of."

"Go to it."

Earl walked quickly to his office, where he could steady himself in private. He flopped into the high-backed chair and ran his fingers through his gray hair. The steady *shush* of the air ducts in the tiled ceiling pressed in on him.

Away from the distractions of ER, he felt the initial numbing effect of the news subside as the slower, crawling emotions of grief took over. A tightness in his gut crept up to his chest, and sadness, no longer alternating with an urge to pistol-whip Kelly's killer, overwhelmed him. Its intensity surprised him; he'd not thought about Kelly for years. Perhaps the reaction felt so strong because he'd always told himself she was thriving somewhere, happy with a career, a man, maybe kids. That's how he'd imagined her when he first started to shut her out of his thoughts so that he could get on with his life and how she had remained until today, sealed up in rarely visited memories, but alive. Now her murder seemed fresh and recent—

A sharp knock interrupted his thoughts.

Susanne poked her head around the door. "Sorry, Dr. Garnet. We just got two ambulances from a three-car pileup on the ninety and another's on the way. Michael says he apologizes, but can you come?"

Michael wouldn't have had him called unless he was really needed. "I'll be right along."

Getting to his feet, he felt heavy, as if walking underwater. He heard a siren in the distance coming closer by the second, and his heart quickened. No matter how many years he'd had in the pit, that sound always got his adrenaline pumping. Rushing through the hallway toward triage, he tried to clear his mind for the work ahead, only to have more questions intrude.

Should he go to the police? Tell them everything? Or keep his mouth shut and hope they never found out? It had been such a long time. But if the police started searching for the man in the cab again . . .

An old fear swept through him, a dread of discovery he'd lived with since the day she disappeared. He couldn't say for sure when it finally faded away, sometime after he left New York at the end of his residency in 1978. Now it came back, a contagion roaring out of remission.

11:45 A.M.

"Telephone, Dr. Garnet," said a clerk in the nursing station, her eyes scanning his face. "Should I take a message?"

Her politeness disconcerted him. Everyone in the department had been treating him with kid gloves all morning. Obviously they all knew something was wrong. Normally that same clerk would stack up seven calls on hold, expecting him to take every one of them pronto, and he would have thrived on it.

He took the receiver from her. "Dr. Garnet speaking."

"Earl! It's Ronda. Did you read in the *Herald* that they found the body of that medical student you and my sister used to hang out with at NYCU, the one who disappeared?"

New York City University had been where he attended medical school.

He hesitated. "Yeah. I saw that this morning. A real shock."

"Must be. From what Melanie has told me about those times, I know the three of you were good friends."

"That we were."

"Better you be forewarned. The police will probably want to talk to everyone who knew her."

Exactly what he'd already figured, but hearing someone else say it made the squeeze he'd been feeling in his stomach cinch tighter. "Probably. I appreciate the heads-up. Did you reach Melanie?"

"I tried to call, but the hospital couldn't track her down. I left a message with her answering service. I'm going to be in Peds all day, so she'll be able to reach me."

"Well, thanks, Ronda."

The call gave him a new worry. Not about Ronda. They'd been friends for years, ever since Melanie told him to look up her kid sister when he moved to Buffalo to join the staff at St. Paul's. At the time Ronda had been starting her own specialty training in pediatrics. Now, twenty-four years later, she was married, had two kids, and was a veteran in her field. He and Janet had often enjoyed the company of Ronda and her husband during hospital functions. At the St. Paul's annual picnic, her kids played with Brendan.

No, the problem lay in who else Melanie Collins might have gossiped to about Kelly McShane and him being such "good friends." After all the new headlines, someone in their class, however oblivious of him and Kelly in 1978, might suddenly suspect the truth if unintentionally prompted by Melanie now. The police would be investigating murder this time, not a disappearance, and that was likely to make everyone they talked to turn amateur detective.

"Dr. Garnet, there's another call for you on line three. It's the police."

"What?" His voice sounded overly loud.

The clerk frowned at him. "They found the body of a teenage boy in a crack house on the east side. It's a DOA, but they want to know if we can make it official and do the paperwork. It's our district."

He felt the band around his stomach release a few notches. "Better we don't do a slough," he said. "I'll handle it myself."

Getting lost in an hour's worth of forms and someone else's heartbreak was just the diversion he needed.

"But I could tell them to bother another hospital—"

"I said I'd do it!"

The young woman's jaw dropped.

Immediately he regretted having snapped at her. "Sorry," he muttered, retreating into the hallway.

Keep hold of yourself, Garnet. Or when the police did come for him, his entire staff would say, "Well, he has been acting on edge lately."

Chapter 3

Running was a drug to Mark.
   Miss a day, he felt lousy.
Two, downright depressed.
Three, and he was convinced he had cancer.

He always followed the same route, turning left onto the road at the foot of his driveway, following it downhill a few miles toward town to loosen up, then going west on Route 4, a winding uphill grind that led farther into the mountains. How far he took it depended on the time he had and the caliber of tension he was trying to work off. Practicing medicine in a small town had different pressures than those of urban centers, but they were every bit as weighty.

This afternoon a heavy fog had settled into the valley. The tiny droplets it left on his face as he ran felt pleasantly cool, but it rendered the road, the forest, and anything else more than thirty feet away invisible, isolating him in a gray sphere of vague shapes. Yet as he passed through a corridor of towering maples and white birches, their foliage formed a canopy of iridescent orange and gold that floated above him like a gaily woven tapestry of silk. The effect became hallucinatory, and he inhaled deeply while he ran, as if to breathe in the color. The moist air filled his nostrils with the fresh smell of wet leaves, an aroma he found every bit as welcoming as the familiar scent of polished wood that greeted him whenever he entered the house he had grown up in.

Hampton Junction, Saratoga County, in the southern Adirondacks, was his home. An odd little town, its houses, businesses, and two churches stood scattered in a disorganized pattern as if the founders had thrown a handful of jacks into the hills, and wherever one landed, somebody built something. It continued to grow in an equally haphazard fashion. The official population of 2,985—the number according to the sign on the highway—hadn't changed since he was a kid. "No one ever seems to die in Hampton Junction without someone being born," went the joke among locals. In truth, nobody could keep track of the population anymore. With the surrounding countryside so full of chalets, the count for the whole area could swell to twenty thousand on a weekend, then shrink back to the core group on Monday.

He grew up here. His love of the outdoor life was one of the reasons he'd returned after med school. He avidly hiked, kayaked, or skied whenever possible, thriving on the endless sweep of mountain wilderness that surrounded him. The hills and peaks, having engraved themselves on his psyche, looked as right to his eye as their rocky surfaces felt to the palms of his hands when he climbed them. Thick deciduous forests in summer. Massive, blue-green conifers rich with growth the year round. The panoply broken only by tumbling mountain streams, surging rivers, and cold lakes. He found it a place of powerful beauty and awe-inspiring solace.

Yet these mountains weren't for everybody. Too much of them for too long at the wrong time, and a person with a troubled mind could end up so dwarfed by the vastness, so engulfed by the silence, and so hemmed in by the press of the forests that he panicked. That was the reason he'd forced Dan to take the diving course in Hawaii when they did three and a half years ago, just about six months after Dan's wife had left him. Heartbroken though not showing it, no kids, and working twenty-four/seven, but still, to Mark's eyes at least, a lost soul, Dan started to keep a wary eye on the surrounding hills. Mark knew he desperately needed the break. Sensory deprivation, isolation psychosis, fractured self-image—the terminology for it in textbooks was endless. "Bushed," the locals called it.

Mark took pride in never having had to wrestle this demon. His secret—conquer and reconquer the wilderness—put the curve of his Telemark turn or the imprint of his boots on it before it ever got to him. He also got out regularly, choosing medical conferences in places that allowed him to feast on theater, dive in warm blue water with limitless visibility, or climb above the tree line where nothing surrounded him but open space.

The pitch of the road steepened, and his legs started to burn. Normally he welcomed the challenge and usually increased his pace at this point, wanting to push himself to the maximum. Today he glanced at his watch and started back. He and Dan were to meet with a cold-case specialist from the NYPD in less than an hour. But with the ease of his descent, the melancholy that he'd been trying to work off returned.

As a boy he'd understood only that Kelly had left for her own unexplained reasons. The possibility of her being dead never once entered his mind. As a result he unquestioningly carried this version of events forward over the years, continuing to see her disappearance through the optimistic gaze of youth, determined to protect at least that piece of childhood from the harsher scrutiny of his adult eye.

Even now a particle of hope, a relic from his days with her—the part of life before his father died when it seemed easy to keep dark terrors at bay—insisted she couldn't have been murdered. But his clinical self, trained to stare at the worst possible truths and not flinch, knew differently.

Only in his memory did Kelly still gleefully win at Monopoly, stride through wildlife parks, and send sizzlers across strike zones.

Flashbacks of her crowded in . . . she arrived to baby-sit him wearing overalls . . . they made some fudge . . . he put chocolate freckles all over her face, and they tied her blond hair in two ponytails with red ribbon, like Daisy Mae's from his comic books. . . .

He started to sprint.

*   *   *

"Feels like I'm stepping on dog shit," the man who walked between him and Dan complained. His leather soles kept slipping on the wet mush of fallen leaves that coated the sidewalk. "Is it always so soggy up here?" His breath hung white in the mist, and his frizzy gray hair glistened from the moisture it picked up from the air.

"Pretty much, this time of year," Dan said. "We've already had a few dumps of snow, but the rain washed it away. Still, good shoes are a must."

Mark's own hiking boots had no such traction problems.

Their visitor, Detective William Everett, a cold-case specialist from the

NYPD, shivered and dug his hands deeper into the pockets of a light tan raincoat. Short in stature, his craggy face had the pasty gray complexion of a smoker, and he chewed gum about sixty times a second.

Reformed, Mark figured, recognizing a chiclet that the man had popped in his mouth as a common nicotine substitute. But he'd quit too late. A mewing wheeze accompanied every word he said, and his chest heaved from walking up the gentle incline.

"Must be nice when you can see everything, though," the detective added, peering into a fog so thick it made the houses along the road appear to be little more than looming gray cubes. "Or is this as good as it gets around here? Christ, you need a fuckin' foghorn just to take a hike."

A hike? Not with him along, or they'd end up carrying him. "You caught us on a bad day," Mark said, slowing his step so as not to set too fast a pace for their visitor. The man looked fifty going on seventy, and the loose semi-circles sagging from under his eyes suggested a lifetime of being tired.

"Still, even like this the air's a whole lot cleaner than in New York," Everett continued. As if to prove the point, he inhaled deeply, only his effort ended in a paroxysm of coughing that doubled him over. He spit on the pavement, then, wiping his mouth with a handkerchief, added, "So tell me about your town. This is the playground for the horsey set, isn't it?"

"Not really," Mark replied. "We're above the money belt."

"The what?"

"The wealth. It's more down around Saratoga."

"So the woman was dumped far away from where she lived?"

"Not too far. The Braden estate is only nine miles south."

"But you said the money—"

"Every town along the railroad took a flyer on being great someday," Dan cut in. "Saratoga Springs made it. Hampton Junction ended up a left-over water stop from the heyday of steam locomotives. Our roots are blue-collar, not blue-blood, but we're proud of it." He had a way of sounding defensive when dealing with outside officials, whatever their stripe. His speech would unwittingly elongate into a bit of a drawl, and, with his portly frame stuffed into a fleece-lined bomber jacket that strained at the zipper, he'd come off like a cross between Rod Steiger and a Rotary Club booster.

Mark figured the awkwardness stemmed from Dan being an outsider himself. As far as the locals saw such matters, a person could move to Hampton Junction, live and work in the place for twenty years, yet still not be "from here." Since Dan had arrived from Syracuse a mere decade ago, the townspeople considered him a newcomer, and, as he confided to anyone who would listen, it bugged the hell out of him.

"We tend to be more a lunch bucket crowd, our inhabitants mostly descended from train people," he continued, proprietary as any native son. "The crystal-and-silver bunch generally drew the line at building their big estates twenty miles south of this area. If it weren't for the fog, you'd see clapboard houses are the preferred style. As for all our vacationers and weekenders, they can't afford luxury addresses close to the horse race set either. You'll find them squirreled away in cottages and cabins all through the woods. Of course, there are exceptions, places where people have gone all out—"

"The Bradens were among those," Mark said, wanting to rein in the conversation closer to the business at hand.

"Really?" The New York detective briefly pondered the fact. "Now why would a family that powerful want to be away from their own kind and off by themselves?"

Mark shrugged.

"I don't know their reasons for sure," Dan said, "I suppose it's because they're what I'd call quiet money. They like to enjoy it with their friends, not show it off." Dan's voice had become normal again, the drawl gone and his manner casual, as if nothing had happened. But authority had been established and boundaries marked—Dan's way of trying to make himself appear an insider, at least to the eyes of a visitor.

"What about here?" Everett said, nodding to a massive shape that emerged from the gloom at the end of the street. "Is this more quiet money?"

"The quietest there is," said Dan. "Welcome to Blair's Funeral Home."

Even in the mist the structure appeared substantially bigger than anything they'd passed. Stepping through an elaborate wrought-iron gate guarding the entrance, they followed a well-raked path that meandered up a sloping lawn. What little foliage remained on the surrounding trees glowed a muted orange, like a bed of coals smothered in ash. As they drew closer the three-story mansion took on a warm yellow hue, and white railings of a long wraparound porch became easily visible. Capping the structure, a cupola with a black-shingled roof pointed upward like a witch's hat.

Mark grimaced at the thought of what awaited them inside.

Everett gave a soft whistle, "Christ, it's bigger than Gracie Mansion, where our mayor lives. Same paint job, though, except this one isn't peeling . . . his is. Death must pay good here."

Dan chuckled. "Not from us locals. We live forever. But the part-timers, the outsiders, after ruining their health with big-city stress and pollution, they all want plots where they spent their summers, sort of the ultimate vacation. Mr. Blair can hardly keep up."

They passed a gleaming Cadillac hearse parked at the head of a curved driveway. A haphazard cluster of lesser vehicles reached all the way out to the street. Mark had suggested they walk the block from Dan's office so as not to add a police car to the mix. He shipped most of the local dead here, and in exchange for the business got to keep his coroner cases in the refrigerator locker alongside the corpses slated to be embalmed. But, as old man Blair always reminded him, he had to keep his comings and goings out of sight and not disturb the viewings upstairs.

Mark led the way around to the back door, to which he had the key. They went down a wooden staircase and passed through a dimly lit hallway stacked with empty caskets. Some had sticker prices on them. There was a cloying sweetness in the air, offset by a hint of something sour.

Everett looked around and curled up his nose. "You do most of your autopsies in a mortuary? This place looks like it's owned by the Addams family."

"They let me use a slab in their refrigerator now and then. Autopsies we do at the hospital in Saratoga, or in Albany," Mark said.

With a second key he unlocked a large metal door at the end of the corridor and ushered them into a gleaming tiled room that was markedly colder than the temperature outdoors. A stainless-steel table with a drain at its center and a bucket underneath occupied the middle of the floor. Suspended from the ceiling was a large OR lamp, and around the walls stood big yellow vats connected by beige tubing to shiny silver probes that looked like giant needles. Glass jars containing various colored fluids lined the counters, and two metal cabinets filled with stainless-steel instruments were against the walls. The aroma of formaldehyde picked at the back of his nostrils like a swarm of ants. "Better breathe through your mouth, gentlemen," he warned, crossing over to what looked like a built-in filing cabinet with half a dozen giant drawers. He reached for the third handle down, and pulled out what was left of Kelly McShane.

Her bones had mostly come apart during the retrieval operation, and trying to lay them out in the correct anatomical order had taken Mark an entire weekend. He wasn't sure he got all the small phalanges of the fingers exactly right, and everything was still discolored brown. The forensics pathologist he'd talked to in New York had told him to do the best he could and not clean the specimen until their own cold-case specialist could view the remains. Consequently, the piecemeal skeleton and remaining strands of tissue had the appearance of something dug up from antiquity.

"Race you to the raft, Mark!"

A flash of golden skin parted the water, and the splash sparkled white in the sun. He plunged after her, laughing with delight as he frantically swam through her wake, then drew alongside, managing to touch the bobbing platform first.

Only now did he realize she had let him win.

"So what do you have?" Everett asked, quickly removing his overcoat and snapping on a pair of latex gloves he took from a box on the counter.

"First, what we didn't find. No jewelry, no buttons, no belt buckle, and not so much as a shred of clothing, some of which we figure should have survived in all that cold mud, so we assume she was stripped before going in the water . . ."

As he spoke, Mark envisioned her plunging through the murk, sleek and white as a taper, her strawberry blond hair streaming out behind her.

". . . nor were there any distinctive marks on the anchor and chain used to weight her down. What we do have are the remains you see before you, the obvious feature being the skull fracture." Mark retrieved a pen from his jacket pocket and used it to indicate a three-inch crack that cut across her right temple. Filled with debris, it stood out like a leech on the subtler corrugated markings where the various bony plates in the cranium joined together. "Whoever hit her knew exactly the spot," he continued. "The point of impact measured two finger widths above the zygomatic arch and a thumb width behind the frontal process of the zygomatic bone itself. That's directly over the middle meningeal artery." He picked up the skull, turned it over, and held it so the detective could look inside the cranial vault through the foramen magnum, the large opening through which the spine had been connected to the brain.

The interior emitted a whiff of rot.

Everett screwed up his nose and jerked his head away.

"See how there are bony splinters pressed inward," Mark continued, shoving the specimen back in front of his eyes. He'd be damned if he'd let this worn-out little man evade a single detail of what had been done to Kelly. The trick to getting the best out of cops was the same as with doctors—make them care. "They probably tore the vessel, setting off a massive hemorrhage. Pray to God she was still unconscious going in the water."

"Still?"

"Trauma that tears the meningeal artery causes a bleed between the lining of the brain and the skull. Sometimes victims stay unconscious until they die. Sometimes they wake up and are lucid for a while. There's a chance she was sent to the bottom awake and aware."

"My God," Dan said.

Even Everett looked taken aback. He rotated his neck as if it needed loosening up. "That's it?"

"There's nothing else to look at."

"So it's still a cold case." The detective pulled off his gloves.

"What do you mean?"

"I mean, I'd love to spend a couple of weeks up here and work the evidence with you. Hell, I'm in love with your town, even though I can't see it. It's everything New York's not, quiet, clean, and slow. Bet the fishing's great. Trouble is, you don't have any new evidence to work, and I got recent caseloads up the wazoo back home that do."

"But it's murder."

Everett's thin shoulders slumped, and he let out a rattling sigh. "It's a body, what's left of it, with a skull fracture. That anchor, chain, and padlock your retrieval team pulled up? We checked them out already. Virtually untraceable, they're so common. Otherwise, there's not a thing to point us where we haven't already been. NYPD investigated the hell out of her disappearance twenty-seven years ago, the same as if she'd been a murder case. Not only did every lead come up empty—especially anything having to do with our prime suspect back then, her husband—but the PIs hired by the girl's parents couldn't find anything either. Factor in all the clout old man Braden still has in New York City, no one's willing to put his son through a first-degree shit-ride again without a damn solid reason."

To this point, Mark had considered the detective's visit as simply the necessary first step in the NYPD resuming the hunt for Kelly's murderer. That they'd try to dump it never occurred to him. "That sucks!"

"You bet."

"And what would it take to reopen the case? I can't just let it go."

Everett shrugged and began pulling on his overcoat. "Well, say, you find a lead on the mystery man she met up with. We'd be on him in a New York minute."

"I find a lead?"

"You want more done, do it yourself, Doc. You and the sheriff here." He picked up his briefcase, snapped it open, and took out a pair of files, each the size of the Manhattan phone book. "I made copies of our records on the case, the basic stuff. Your body, your jurisdiction, guys. Sorry, but it's the best I can offer." He jammed the two tomes of paper into Mark's chest and walked out the door.

"Jesus, what an asshole," muttered Dan, and hurried after him.

Mark remained where he was, too astonished by the kiss-off to say anything. A slam echoed down the corridor, and once again he found himself alone with Kelly.

A half hour later he looked up from leafing through the material Everett had left, startled to see Dan standing at the door watching him. "Christ, I didn't hear you return."

"You were pretty engrossed in your reading. Find anything?"

"No. It'll take forever to go through this stuff." Mark slammed the files closed. "Can you believe that guy, laying the whole thing on us?"

Dan walked over and flipped one of the dossiers open again. Scanning the front page, he said, "Actually, it kind of makes sense."

"Excuse me?"

"You know what cracks cold cases?"

"What?"

He nudged the folder he'd been looking at back toward Mark. "One guy who can't get it out of his head. I'd say that's you, buddy."

5:00 P.M.
Geriatrics Wing,
New York City Hospital

Dr. Bessie McDonald didn't like seeing the sun go down. The gathering blackness reminded her too much of her own end of days, and her breathing got worse at night.

She felt depressed, stuck in her hospital room. At least the nurses had allowed her more than the usual personal effects to help make it easier. She had a dozen framed photographs—a black-and-white of Fred in his uniform, smiling before he went off to Korea to be slaughtered and leave her a widow; color snaps of her son, Fred Junior; portraits of her three young grandsons, all grinning at her with various front teeth missing. She'd also brought a set of figurines depicting a young woman doctor performing her daily functions: administering to a newborn baby, listening to an old man's chest, comforting a sick child. Though she never told anyone, the face on the porcelain statues was hers as a young woman, fired especially for her by a craftsman who had been her patient in the first years of her practice. She took nearly as much comfort looking at the figurines as at her family, not out of narcissism, but from pride at how she'd spent her life, from those early halcyon days up until the moment her own rendezvous with illness clipped her wings as a general practitioner.

She'd always been at risk of a stroke because of her crazy heart flying in and out of funny rhythms: a racing yet steady-as-a-jackhammer burst called PAT, or paroxysmal atrial tachycardia, when she was forty-three; then, in later years, atrial fibrillation, a chronic, wildly erratic tattoo. Whatever the beat, the muscle began to wear out, and eventually she slipped into congestive failure. Luckily, Melanie Collins saw her through it all. But she hadn't suffered her first embolic event until four years ago at age sixty-six, when a blood clot formed in the fluttering upper chamber, broke off, and flew into her brain. Initially paralyzed on the right side, she'd been left with just her speech affected, again thanks to the precise diagnostic skills of Melanie and the quick use of clot busters—thrombolytic enzymes that break down the blockage before damage is done. Therapy got her back to talking so that no one would notice; however, at times, she had trouble finding the word she wanted.

The lasting harm had been done to her work, the ordeal derailing her from the practice of medicine for nearly a year. Although she'd arranged for a temporary replacement, many of her patients worried that she would stroke out again despite her intention to return, and found new doctors. With each departure, the sense of purpose she fought so valiantly to regain shriveled a little more.

Then, just three months ago, while digging in her garden, her right side went numb. She tumbled to the ground, her arm and leg like deadwood for all the good they were to her. She lay there, her face pressed into the earth, dirt up her nose, and bugs crawling between her lips. A worm's-eye view of the world, she thought, wondering if it would be the last thing she ever saw.

She'd had no pain, and knew this was the same kind of stroke as before, a blockage, not a bleed. If she got help fast enough, maybe the clot-busting enzymes that rescued her before could help again. Yet second by second, her time nearly ran out. When a neighbor spotted her and called an ambulance, she knew the three-hour window for treatment would soon close.

Once she got to the hospital, there had been no Melanie on hand to speedily diagnose and treat her.

"Since she's already anticoagulated, it must be a bleed," one of the ER residents, a sleepy-eyed kid, had said to her nurses as he methodically checked her reflexes.

No! she'd wanted to scream as she pawed feebly at his arm trying to get his attention.

He'd ignored her, and added, "Besides, we don't know how long it's been since she stroked out."

Two hours, forty minutes, asshole! There's still time.

"Send her for a CAT scan?" one of the women had asked, recording her vitals.

"Of course," he said, and wandered out of the room.

No, don't leave. Talk to the radiologist yourself. Bump me to the head of the line!

Three hours too late they'd made the correct diagnosis.

Her speech returned, but the delay cost her partial use of her right arm and her ability to walk normally. It also turned her into an old woman overnight.

"Hi, Bessie." A pint-sized nurse with a GI haircut and a name tag that read NURSE TANYA WOZCEK pinned to her uniform bopped across to her bed. "All set for your meds?"

"As much as I'll ever be."

Everyone called her Bessie. It sprang from her insistence that she be registered as Mrs. Bessie McDonald, not Dr. McDonald, during her admissions. "Things go wrong when they know you're a physician," she'd repeatedly explained to the admitting office. "Doctors, nurses, techs—they all start doing what they wouldn't normally do, second-guessing themselves. Leads to mistakes."

But since the night of this most recent stroke, she'd had plenty of time to do some second-guessing herself. Had they known she was a doctor, would they have listened to what she was trying to tell them?

"Here, let me prop up your pillows," Tanya said.

Bessie grew short of breath if she didn't sleep partially upright. The result of heart failure. "Thank you, dear."

"And here are your pills." Tanya handed over a paper cup that had five tablets in it.

Bessie poured herself a glass of water from her pitcher, then downed the bunch of them in a swallow. She'd been on them for years: Digoxin to control her heart rate and increase its pump action; furosemide to keep water from accumulating in her lungs; rampril to relax her arterial tree and reduce the cardiac workload; warfarin, also known as rat poison, the anti-coagulant that had led the resident off track; and a baby aspirin, to thin the blood and prevent more clots. As easy as one, two, three, four, five. Except having to take pills at all bored her, and the treatment, like all regimens, wasn't perfect.

To control her angina, she had to take a spray of nitroglycerine under her tongue, in addition to wearing a patch of it on her skin. The latter could be worn anywhere, but most patients put it on their arm or chest. She stuck hers on her ass every morning just to be contrary, having precious few other ways to say, *I'm here and I'll do things my way.*

"Skin's skin," she told the residents whenever they objected.

"You go right ahead and put it where you want, girl," Tanya would say to her in private.

She liked Tanya. The woman always worked evenings, which led Bessie to try figure out what this nurse did during the days. She never talked about herself, and, of course, Bessie never pried. The fun lay in the guessing, not the answers. Bessie's active mind grated against the hours of idleness and pounced on any puzzle for entertainment.

"I see you've been reading about Kelly McShane," Tanya said, picking up a newspaper from the nightstand that lay open to the article. "The whole hospital's buzzing about it."

"I'll bet. How's Chaz Braden taking it?"

Tanya looked up from scanning the column. "Do you know him?"

"He was my cardiologist the first time I got admitted for my heart, about six months before his wife disappeared. Didn't like him."

The nurse's expression slipped into neutral, and she glanced nervously at the doorway. "Can I get you anything? How about some juice?" Obviously, she wasn't about to engage in a round of bad-mouthing the man, which, of course, was professionally correct.

But not fun.

Tanya leaned in close as if fluffing up the pillows a second time. "Our supervisor's warned us not to gossip about it, but I bet you want to tell me every word of what went on back then, don't you?" she whispered, dispatching propriety with a grin.

Nice girl, Bessie thought. "Of course I do."

"Well, it'll have to wait. You're not my only patient, you know." She gave a conspiratorial wink. "But maybe later, when I drop by with your needle."

6:00 P.M.
St. Paul's Hospital,
Buffalo, New York

Earl sat rereading the article for the tenth time when a quick rap on the door startled him.

Janet walked in. "Hi, love. Got a minute for me? It's been a hell of a day in the case room." She came up to him and pulled off her surgical cap, her short blond hair popping out from its confines like a golden star burst. She flipped the paper aside and pulled him to his feet, slipping her arms around him.

He felt his wife's slim body beneath her OR greens, but returned the hug woodenly.

"Hey! That's no way to treat a lady," she said, pushing back and smiling up at him. Tall as he was, his six-foot frame outranked hers by only a couple of inches. Whatever she saw in his expression, she immediately knew that he was upset as hell. "Earl, what's the matter?"

He sighed and handed her the article.

"Did you know her?" she said after skimming through it.

"She was in my class."

"My God! That's awful. I'm sorry. Were you friends?"

"She was in my study group. Along with Melanie Collins, Ronda Collins's older sister, and, of course, Jack MacGregor," he quickly added, giving her names he knew she'd recognize.

On hearing *Jack MacGregor*, Janet grimaced, and a pained expression crossed her face. MacGregor had died two years ago saving Earl's life.

"There were a few others with us whom you don't know," Earl continued, feeling uneasy.

She read a little more of the column. "How creepy. Did you have any idea she'd been murdered?"

"No."

"Even after she just disappeared without a trace?"

"We all thought she'd run away from her husband. It really wasn't a happy marriage."

"But no word from her, and you suspected nothing?"

"Of course we were worried. But you don't know the man we thought she was escaping from. She'd told most of us she was going to leave him, yet insisted we not try and trace where she went. She was afraid he'd track her down by following us if we tried to contact her, so we figured that was why she just cut off all ties. After the police found no evidence of foul play, as far as I was concerned, no news meant she'd gotten away, free and clear."

"Do you think he killed her?"

"Chaz? He was mean enough to. I met him during our cardiology rotation at NYCH and when Kelly had our group up to their country home. He could be a bit of a charmer on the outside, but always found a sneaky way to criticize her, hiding it in a joke. And he could sure throw back the martinis at her parties. His comments got more cutting as the day wore on. None of us liked the son of a bitch."

She put down the paper and studied him. "You sound angry."

"I am. She was a friend. We all felt protective of her, especially since the rest of the class had given her the cold shoulder from the get-go. Most figured her a dilettante who was just slumming, riding the Braden name. Then when she worked her butt off and cut it better than a lot of them, they resented her more."

"Sounds like she was a pretty remarkable lady."

"She wanted to do pediatrics, and would have been great at it. Whoever killed her snuffed out all that."

"But you went on thinking she'd run off, even when her parents insisted her husband had a hand in her disappearance?" Janet's blue gaze grew skeptical. "That doesn't sound like the poke-his-nose-where-it-doesn't-belong man I married. Didn't you wonder why she never so much as contacted them?"

"She seemed to have little to do with her mother and father. I never knew why and, believe it or not, since it wasn't any of my business, didn't ask. As I said, we all wanted to believe she'd successfully pulled off a vanishing act. It seems stupid now, but we convinced ourselves."

Janet studied him a few more seconds, put her hands around his face, and kissed him gently on the lips. "She was lucky to have you as her friend."

Some friend, he thought.

She turned for the door. "I've got to get back to the case room, but should be home in a couple of hours. Can you stop by the store and pick up some milk?"

"Sure."

"And tell Brendan I'll be there to tuck him in. Poor little tyke probably feels abandoned."

"How about I promise we'll sandwich him between us for his story tonight."

She laughed, said, "Love you," and was gone.

He hadn't lied outright to Janet, but what he'd left unsaid seemed tantamount to lying . . . big-time.

The ache in his gut spread through him—like a stain.

8:00 P.M.
Geriatrics Wing,
New York City Hospital

She had no idea how long she'd been dozing when a soft cough roused her. "Hi, Bessie."

She blinked a few times to bring her eyes into focus on the figure who was standing inside the room. "Melanie? Melanie Collins?"

"Yes. I just dropped by to say hello."

"My, I didn't hear you come in."

"Little wonder. You were snoring like a truck driver. How are you doing?"

"Well, I obviously could have used you when I came into ER three months ago."

"Oh, Bessie, I'm so sorry I wasn't there."

"Pull up a seat." She gestured to the little-used visitor's chair with her good arm.

Melanie obliged.

Soon they fell deep in conversation making small talk, but after a few minutes Bessie inexorably returned to her present plight. She found release in complaining about it to other doctors, knowing they would best understand the scope of the outrage that had been done to her. When her own patients had gone on and on about their various illnesses, reciting the relapses and symptoms far more than necessary for her to make the diagnosis, she thought it was because they had little else to talk about, their diseases having pervaded every aspect of their lives. Over the last few months she'd come to realize that they'd been venting, sharing their symptoms so they wouldn't feel so alone—a compulsion, she ruefully acknowledged, that she couldn't even stop in herself.

"So-called emergency doctors—they simply didn't get it the way you did."

"Well, I knew your history. And remember, you were already admitted for pneumonia, so there were no delays. Who knows what would have been the outcome if I hadn't had you on the floor and under my thumb when it happened? But since I did, the rest was easy—"

"Easy my ass, Melanie. Remember, you're talking to a physician here. Don't make excuses for their shoddy work by minimizing how great you were."

"Now, Bessie—"

"I know full well that the blood tests indicated I was properly anticoagulated and shouldn't have had another embolus. But unlike the bozos this last time, you were smart enough to treat the patient—"

" 'And not the test.' " Melanie gave an understanding shake of the head. "I know. I tell that to the residents all the time."

"I hope those young punks in ER have at least learned to listen, or pay attention to someone even when they can't talk."

"I'm sure they have."

"But look at me." She laboriously raised her right shoulder and upper limb. Her hand and fingers drooped off the forearm, curled into a lifeless claw. "God, I didn't think I'd end up like this."

"I know."

"And does anybody want to talk about it? Not on your life. They all think I'm going to sue."

"Are you?"

"Of course not. I'm a doctor. I won't go after my own. But I damn well want them to improve—be like you were in training."

"Bessie, you're making me blush—"

"In 'seventy-four you did nothing less than give me the second half of my life. The residents back then would have done me in, too, if you hadn't stopped them. I'd never have seen my grandchildren. So give credit where credit is due, I say."

"It was nothing."

"There you go again. Nothing? My heart racing. Unable to get my breath. And everybody shouting, grabbing at the ECG tracing. I remember everything like yesterday."

"Well, you know how it is in a precode when only residents are around."

"But you measured out the rhythm and saw it for what it was."

As part of developing the lore of her own sickness, Bessie had never stopped extolling to anyone who would listen how someone so young had maintained the presence of mind to pick out such a subtle distinction on a cardiogram in the midst of all that wild confusion. As she told and retold the story, she recalled seeing everything as if from the wrong end of a telescope, feeling desperate for air despite wearing an oxygen mask, and being about to pass out. The chief resident kept yelling for intravenous digoxin while others stuck her with IV needles and shouted a flurry of other orders:

"Furosemide!"

"Nitro!"

"Morphine!"

Like happy hour at a bar, she'd thought, watching the darkness close in on her.

A nurse had brought the syringe of digoxin up to the rubber injection port on a small intravenous bag.

Then that lone clear voice. "No! This is dig toxicity." And a dark-haired girl with a plain face had grabbed the needle away before it could be injected. "The rhythm strip shows atrial flutter with block," she added, speaking firmly and loudly enough to cut through the melee without resorting to panicky shouting like everyone else.

The rest of the team had immediately turned to give her their attention. "Look," she said, running the long strip of paper upon which the ECG had been printed through her fingers, handling it like a ticker tape and pointing out the salient features.

Yes, yes, yes, the doctor in Bessie McDonald had thought, her hearing intact enough to pick up sufficient snatches of the quick-fire explanation to know it was correct even as her vision narrowed to mere pinpoints of light.

Atrial flutter with block, a hallmark of digoxin toxicity, meant a far too rapid heartbeat where the upper chambers, the atria, pounded along at 300 a minute, and the lower chambers, the ventricles, contracted at exactly half that rate, 150 a minute. The trick? To recognize it from the other arrhythmias where the atria and ventricles raced ahead at the same speed and the drug of choice was more digoxin. Had the chief resident succeeded in giving an additional dose to Bessie, however, he would have entrenched the problem, rendering her myocardium twice as resistant to treatment, and she could have died. Pumping at that speed, the chambers weren't emptying properly, and her lungs were filling up with fluid. While the other drugs they'd ordered would help empty it out, the definitive step to solve the problem—slowing down her heart—had to be done by a synchronized countershock of electricity.

Melanie had come through for her on that count as well. Bessie felt the paddles lathering up her chest with lubricant, then "Pow!" A huge white light ripped up the inside of her skull. Yes! Despite the sensation of being kicked by a horse, the jolt of direct current, she knew, would stun the atria, render their conduction pathways refractory to the fast impulses, and allow her own natural pacemaker time to reassert itself. Within minutes she began to feel better, opened her eyes, and saw Melanie smiling at her.

"Quite a feat for a fourth-year student," Bessie said. "You know, up until that point, I got the impression nobody on staff appreciated your skills."

Melanie chuckled. "Hey, that's the job of teachers with medical students. Keep 'em tired and feeling stupid. Makes it easier to stuff them with knowledge. But to what do I owe this trip down memory lane?"

Bessie reached for the paper with her good arm. "This got me going," she said, tapping the article about Kelly McShane. "It all happened that same year. I remember her. She was so pretty and pleasant around patients. I thought then she'd make a great doctor. And if you recall, Chaz Braden had been my cardiologist. Come to think of it, he kept ignoring my complaints of being nauseated. That should have tipped him off my digoxin level was rising."

"You've got a pretty good memory for something so long ago."

"What do you expect? I nearly died. As for the time when Kelly McShane disappeared, I figure just about everyone remembers that, at least where they were."

"How do you mean?"

"Thursday, August 8, 1974. That was the night Nixon resigned. He gave a TV speech at nine P.M, announcing he'd be gone by noon the next day. I was glued to my TV at home. And in my office, Friday, the patients and I watched his departure from the White House. I'll bet you can tell me where you were, too."

Melanie frowned a few seconds, as if trying to recall her whereabouts, then shrugged. "Not really. I remember it happening, but not where I was. Must have been busy days on the floors. Say, the nurses told me you're going to your son's home to live." She got up and walked over to the family photos on the bureau, leaning over to get a better look at them.

Bessie immediately felt excited. The mere mention of what lay ahead brought her to life again. "That's right. Me on the Big Sur. Fred Junior and his wife have built their dream house, including a cottage for me, plus arranged for private nurses, all thanks to the dot-coms. The kid had the smarts to sell before they went bust, and I'm going out in style."

"Hey, I think you should take a doctor along with you." She delicately fingered the frames as she looked at the pictures one by one.

"Come along. That would be the dream team, having you in charge. You've always been there for me, when you've been there at all."

Melanie laughed and moved to inspect the figurines near the head of the bed. "Will you listen to yourself? You can't blame gibberish like that on the stroke."

"You know what I mean. You saved my life twice. Why not a third time? I'll bet there are lots of opportunities for someone like you in California."

"Be careful. I might take you up on it." She carefully picked up the piece depicting Bessie examining an old man. "This is beautiful. Is that you?"

"A long time ago—" She stopped short at the sight of Tanya standing at the door. How long the young nurse had been there she couldn't say. "Yes, Tanya?"

"I'm sorry to interrupt, Bessie, but it's time for your shot."

"Oh!" Melanie said, peeking at her watch, "Well, guess I better be off, then." She quickly replaced the porcelain figure.

Bessie flashed an annoyed look at Tanya for interrupting them. She'd been enjoying the company. "Oh, Melanie, please don't go."

"I really have to. Sorry it took me so long to stop by, yet better late than never, eh? Have a good sleep, and I'll try to see you before you leave."

Obviously their visit was over. Contemplating the striking woman Melanie had become in middle age, Bessie reached for her hand and took it in hers. "All the best."

"To you as well," Melanie said, returning the gesture with a warm squeeze.

Out of nowhere an insolent little question popped into Bessie's mind. How come such a good-looking woman had never married?

Once she'd left, Tanya walked over to a stand where a small, multidose bottle of heparin and packets of needles were kept.

Low molecular weight heparin was another anticoagulant, this one used in small injected doses to prevent blood clots from forming in the limbs of patients who were bedridden. She wouldn't normally have needed it, being on warfarin and the baby aspirin already, but having thrown two emboli from her heart so far, the doctors were taking no chances.

Which was fine with Bessie. No way did she intend to be waylaid again and miss the Big Sur, she thought, watching Tanya, who stood with her back turned as she drew up the injection. Her annoyance with the girl vanished. After all, she'd just been doing her job. "Don't worry, Tanya," she said with a chuckle, wanting to make amends for her nasty glance of a moment ago. "I won't faint if I catch sight of the needle."

The nurse laughed, but continued to shield the syringe from Bessie's view as any thoughtful nurse or doctor does when preparing a hypodermic for a patient. "I know, Bessie. It's force of habit. You'd probably do the same with me if the situation were reversed." She dropped the bottle in a plastic container for medical waste, pivoted around, and walked to the bedside. "Where do you want it?"

"Actually, in the mornings I've started giving them to myself."

"Oh?"

"Yep. In case they want to keep me on the stuff when I go to my son's. I don't want to be totally dependent. Just leave the syringe on my nightstand."

Tanya frowned. "You're sure?"

"Yep."

Tanya hesitated, the capped syringe in her hand, then shrugged. "Okay. You're the doctor," she said with a grin, and placed it on Bessie's side table along with an alcohol swab. "But I can't stay to talk. We're short-staffed again."

Time to sleep, Bessie decided.

She rolled over and reached for the syringe and swab. "Might as well be at the good old belly button," she muttered, whipping up her nightdress and exposing what looked like a horseshoe of pinpricks around her umbilicus. She wiped the skin with an alcohol swab, then managed to bunch up a roll of flesh using the limited movements of her right forearm. With a quick thrust, she sank the needle in to its hilt, and slowly pushed in the plunger.

Chapter 4

Mark brushed aside a cobweb and sent a nest of spiders scurrying for cover. From a wall of cardboard cartons, he pulled out the third box he'd been through that evening. He was in the basement of his house, the home where he grew up and now lived and worked, rummaging in the inactive files that his father, Dr. Cam Roper, had stored here for as long as he could recall. The voice of his mother complaining about it ran as clear as a recording through his head.

"Honestly, dear, you've got lots of space in that office of yours in the village. Why clutter us up with this junk? We could make a workshop down here."

"That's why I'm filling it up with this stuff," his dad had whispered to him, then winked. "To make sure I don't have to spend our Saturdays down here building stupid shelves."

Our Saturdays. Mark smiled at the resonance those words could still evoke.

That was before he'd lost them both.

First his mother. Pricked her finger on a needle, he'd been told. Then she fell sick and died in a matter of days. To a five-year-old boy it sounded like something out of a fairy tale, an evil spell cast by a wicked dwarf involving a spinning wheel. But no magic kiss brought her back. Later he'd learned the needle had been a syringe, and the evil had been meningococcus bacteria from a patient with meningitis. She'd infected herself while helping out at his father's office drawing blood samples.

Two years later his father died, killed in a freak explosion.

Aunt Margaret, his mother's older sister, already widowed at fifty-five and childless, had insisted on moving in and taking care of him. "For a while," the crusty old woman told him at first.

She'd stayed for good.

Even when he'd come back from medical school, she continued to live here. At the time he sensed she wasn't finished watching over him. Since they were each other's only family, he didn't mind.

Initially he'd set up his own office in town, finding one with a spacious apartment above it. But when Margaret died, he moved in here, practice and all. Just until he had time to dispose of the estate, he told himself. That was two years ago.

Outside the wind had come up, moaning and whistling against the wooden slat door that led to the yard. The beams above his head creaked and groaned as if the whole structure threatened to lift off the stone foundation, but it never had and, Mark guessed, never would. He easily ignored the sounds, having snuggled under blankets and fallen asleep to them throughout his life. Instead he concentrated on going through the *Mc*s.

"You have a dad who's a great doctor, you know," Kelly had said to him on many occasions, puffing him up with pride. "He saw me first when I was a little girl and was very sick. Now I'm healthy, but he's still the one I talk with. Lucky you to have him all the time."

Not for long.

The summer she disappeared, he lost his father in the autumn.

Funny about sound memories. Recalling a person's voice seemed far more vivid than conjuring up a face. It was as if the dead spoke to him.

He moved on to checking the *B*s.

Whenever Kelly came up from New York, she'd always made it a point to come over. As a little boy Mark assumed it was to play with him, especially since she had been his baby-sitter for most summers up until medical school kept her in the city. She always made such a big deal out of seeing him, scooping him up in her arms for a hug and a big smooch. He smiled, remembering how her skin smelled like cinnamon. She made him feel important, the first adult outside his mom and dad or aunt to do so, and he loved the way she fussed over him on account of she liked him, not simply because they were related.

But the truth was she'd also been there to see his dad. An hour became a slow, unendurably long torture whenever he had to wait outside the study, listening for the two of them to finish talking so she'd be all his again.

Kelly might have told his father about her troubles. And if he acted as her physician, even if only as a sounding board, he might have kept a file documenting whatever they discussed. If such a record existed, Mark figured he might find an adult's point of view as to what was going on in Kelly's life just prior to her death.

His own youthful recollections of that time came to him filtered through love. When his mother died, Kelly became so much more to him, even though she was in medical school by then, and her visits were less frequent. For a year he felt safe only when she hugged him, said everything would be all right, and softly sang to him. "Puff the Magic Dragon," "Yellow Submarine," "To Every Season"—no matter what the lyrics, her voice in his ear made them both invincible. Eventually his mother's death started to seem long ago, and at times he could again be a carefree kid in endless sunny days. She'd given his childhood a reprieve, resurrecting it before the world grew dark again.

He flicked over voluminous sets of labeled manila tabs before *Braden-McShane, Kelly* popped up. *Looks promising,* he thought. the folder being thicker than the rest. Pulling it out of the box, he carried it over to a workbench, snapped on a lightbulb that dangled from the ceiling, and opened the front cover.

The first page contained a faded clinical entry dated *July 13, 1951.*

His father's first year in practice. He began to read.

> *Kelly is six years old. Mother states she's had a long-standing stomach disorder that no doctors in New York have managed to help her with. Complaints, according to her mother, range from intermittent abdominal pain, nausea, loss of appetite, irregular bowel movements, and diarrhea alternating with constipation. The problem has been episodic since infancy. No history of fevers. No history of tarry stool or blood by rectum. No discoloration of urine, nor jaundiced skin or eyes. Recurrent nonspecific rashes. Repeated investigations, including X rays of her upper and lower intestinal tracts using barium, have been negative.*

Rest of Functional Inquiry: Negative.

Immunizations: Complete to date.

Surgical History: Appendectomy at age four, subsequently reported to be normal. Laparotomy at age five, for abdominal pain NYD, results negative.

Family history: No siblings. No history of allergies, diabetes, arthritis, nervous or psychiatric disorders in either mother's or father's family (according to the mother's account).

Social History: Father is founder and president of a brokerage company in New York. Mother active in some charities, but looks after Kelly herself. No nanny or nurse.

Kelly initially shy, but on careful questioning reports no abdominal symptoms of any kind today.

Physical Exam:

Appearance: Well-groomed. Blond hair, blue eyes, thin physique.

CVS: Normal heart sounds. BP 85/60; P 88

Chest: Clear

Abdomen: Non-tender, normal bowel sounds, no bruit, no masses, liver and spleen normal. Surgical scars RLQ and mid-line below the umbilicus consistent with history of appendectomy and laparotomy.

External genitalia: Normal

Limbs and extremities: Normal

Skin: No rashes at present.

EENT: Normal.

Head and Neck: Normal

Neurological Exam: Normal

Impression: Healthy young girl. Functional GI disorders and neurodermatitis, both secondary to stress.

Plan: Prescribed fun and sun. Good nutrition. Frank discussion with Mrs. McShane stressing the absence of any physical illness in her daughter. Follow up in one month to see how child is doing, or immediately if symptoms return (which isn't likely).

Mark started to flip the page when he saw written faintly in pencil off to one side the word *Mother?* He smiled. His father had obviously nailed the problem, diagnosing Kelly's symptoms as the result of a high-strung parent.

No further entries appeared on the other side of the paper. Clearly Kelly's mother hadn't brought her daughter back. Probably hadn't liked the "frank discussion."

He shivered. The dampness down here had already penetrated his bones, but now he felt a draft around his legs. He got up and walked over to the slat door that was taking the brunt of the wind. A flow of cool air from where the bottom had warped out of the frame ran across his feet. He grabbed an old coat and stuffed it into the opening.

Seated again, he came to a sheet not so faded, but nevertheless aged. It had brief entries running from July 1, 1970, to July 3, 1974. Each one was identical. Three words: Psychiatric support therapy. Mark let out a solitary quiet chuckle. He'd been right about Kelly discussing her issues with his father. But the man had done what he, Mark, did when the material was so sensitive the patient wanted it to be kept absolutely secret, even from people authorized to look at the record—simply recorded that the session took place, not what was said.

Discouraged, he went on to the third document, a sheet of flowered stationery folded in thirds.

Opening it, he read:

July, 14, 1974

Dear Doctor R,

The salutation made him smile. Kelly had always called his father Dr. R.

> *You were right. I was not being candid with you when we met two weeks ago. There is a reason I'm so happy, and you are the first and only person I can tell.*
>
> *I've met a man.*
>
> *A wonderful, caring man who loves me, and I love him.*
>
> *What a release to be cherished, respected, and liked. I feel as if all the other garbage has fallen away, and I'm free, with a new life ahead of me. Whether it will be with him or not, I don't know, but I'm full of hope. I haven't decided yet what to do about it all, and look forward to talking over possible strategies with you. But I am ecstatic!*
>
> *Regarding the other two matters, we must discuss those. Whatever I plan for myself, I can't leave and let them go unresolved.*

Can we have lunch at the Plaza on Saturday, the twenty-seventh? I can't bear to go to the estate on weekends anymore, and have pleaded hospital work as my excuse to stay in the city. Waiting to see you then.
Love,

Kelly

Mark's pulse leapt.

The *man* could be the mystery person in the cab. If his father had kept the appointment with her, she'd probably told him who it was.

He quickly pulled out and unfolded the next two sets of documents in the file, hoping to see a note or follow-up letter about their meeting.

No such luck. In his hands he held photocopies of some New York City Hospital M and M reports, or Death Rounds, the conference that reviews patient morbidity and mortality.

What the hell were these doing here? Scanning through them, he saw that they were accounts of two separate cases involving digitalis toxicity. The first patient had lived, the second had died, but there were no names listed, only chart numbers, standard practice to preserve anonymity in such investigations. One was dated January 1974, the other June of the same year. They must be misfiled, he concluded, laying them aside.

The final contents were old newspaper clippings lauding the Braden family's involvement in the community. A FAMILY AFFAIR read the headline of one. It praised the volunteer work of Mrs. Charles Braden and her daughter-in-law, Kelly McShane Braden, at a local home for unwed mothers called The Braden Foundation Clinic founded by Dr. Charles Braden III. LIKE FATHER LIKE SON ran the lead of another article featuring Chaz helping check out a newborn at another of Dad's projects, an upscale maternity center in Saratoga Springs.

Nothing of use, Mark decided. The Bradens were renowned for lending their name to high-profile charities, as well as feeding the family fortune through commercial medical ventures such as high-priced private clinics. In fact Charles had pioneered the concept of combining the intimacy of home delivery with the latest in obstetrical technology in freestanding facilities, then franchised it through a well-known hospital chain. Mark returned the clippings to the file, having no idea why his father had stuck them here.

Still, he had Kelly's letter. He'd contact Everett first thing in the morning and tell the detective he'd found proof that she had a lover. Chances were he might have been the mystery man in the taxi.

To which Everett would say, Who was he?

And he'd have to admit he didn't know.

At that point Everett would probably hang up on him.

Shit!

He had another thought. Why hadn't his father passed the letter on to the police? Obviously he kept it to himself even after she disappeared.

As Mark picked it up and read it again, it sank in just how abstract Kelly was to him. How different and tormented she must have been from his sunlit memories of her. He never caught so much as a hint of her unhappiness or that she needed to escape from it. Nor had he any specific recollection of her last days in Hampton Junction. He remembered only his father telling him that she'd had to leave without saying good-bye.

"Then I'll say hello when she's back," Mark had said, accustomed to her comings and goings to medical school. But as days turned to weeks with no sign of Kelly, those few words with his dad became the landmark that stuck, not whatever laughing encounter with her that had been his last. Unlikely his take on her with the eyes of a seven-year-old would help explain anything about those final weeks anyway. Hell, he still had trouble reconciling his version of the woman he had known with the grisly remains lying in the mortuary.

He continued to stare at the letter. It at least pinned down one event in the countdown to her murder. The day Kelly and his father planned to have lunch together, presuming they met, she had little more than a week to live.

He pictured them at the Plaza. Had she been as rapturous and exuberant as she sounded in her writing? Was his father happy for her? Did they order champagne? The image of them toasting her well-deserved joy, oblivious to death being so near, filled Mark with sadness. Dreams could be so puny, struggle, hope, and daring so futile. She was on the verge of achieving everything—being a doctor, finding a man who loved her, making a clean break with her past. It made her moment of celebration seem all the more cruel.

Then a chill that had nothing to do with the cold shimmied through him.

That meeting, if it took place, also marked what would be the final two months of his father's life.

10:00 P.M.
Buffalo, New York

"Can we do a cuddle sandwich now, Daddy?"

Earl looked up from his computer screen to see Brendan, dazed and tousled, totter through the study door. "What are you doing awake?"

"Isn't Mummy home yet?"

"I'm afraid not." He stood and picked the boy up. "But it's back to sleep for you."

"Why?"

"Because it's very late."

"I mean why isn't she home?"

The vagaries of labor had sabotaged yet another evening of all three of them being together, but try and explain that to a four-year-old. "I told you, sometimes babies don't want to come out on time," he said, placing him in bed and tucking in his covers.

"Can't she make them?"

"Sometimes, but not tonight."

"She could holler real loud at them, like she does for us when we're playing outside, and it's time to eat."

He grinned down at the budding obstetrical genius. "Mummy won't be home until long after you're asleep."

"I can stay awake."

"No, you can't."

"Look. My eyes are open wide." He scissored his lids apart with his fingers and grinned like some goofy space creature.

Earl slowly reached toward him with twitching fingers. "Not for long."

Brendan started to giggle. "Yes, for long."

"But Mr. Tickle's here."

His small hands flew out to grab Earl's. "No, not Mr. Tickle," he squealed, wriggling with delight in his bed. "Cuddle sandwich! Cuddle sandwich!"

"Time to sleep, little man."

"Tomorrow morning?"

"Hey, you're as relentless as your mother."

"What's 'rentless'?"

"Relentless. It means you never give up."

"Do I get a cuddle sandwich?"

"Okay. Tomorrow morning, you can crawl into bed between Mummy and me, but not until the sun comes up."

"Promise?"

"You bet. Now good night, and let's see who can give the strongest hug."

Brendan's arms flew around Earl's neck and squeezed for all their worth. The embrace had the restorative power of a resuscitation. "Night, Daddy," he said.

Earl gently held him a second longer, pronounced him the winner, and turned out the light.

A quarter of an hour later, alone in his own bed, except for Muffy sprawled on her back, he once again wrestled with what to tell Janet. There'd been small follow-up stories on the evening newscasts, and other New York papers posted updates on their web sites. The only new development was that the NYPD had turned the investigation over to the local authorities in the Adirondacks who had found the remains. Anyone with pertinent information on the case should contact Sheriff Dan Evans or Dr. Mark Roper, coroner. Earl recognized a slough when he saw it, having had his own share of unwanted work dumped on him.

At first he'd felt relief. Recalling the sleepy countryside surrounding Chaz Braden's estate, he couldn't imagine there being much of a police force there. Any attention to her murder would probably focus on local acquaintances of hers. It might even be directed at Chaz again, and this time subject his alibi for the day she disappeared to the rigors of small-town scrutiny. After all, weren't rural murders more apt to get solved than urban ones, what with everybody being into everybody else's business? It was their equivalent to live theater. Rather than draw the curtains and remain uninvolved, people noticed things, stored them up, and kept them at the ready for later tellings. As long as the case was out of the NYPD's hands, no one would be stirring up old memories in his former classmates, and he might be home free. So why say anything to Janet and worry her for nothing?

Because he felt as if he was betraying her by staying silent.

He rolled over and picked up the original, well-creased *New York Herald* article from his nightstand and studied it again. The name of the local coroner, Dr. Mark Roper, seemed vaguely familiar. Now why, he wondered, did it resonate?

Then he remembered.

Kelly had sometimes talked about a Dr. Roper. He was the man who encouraged her to go to medical school and whom she often visited, confiding her problems to him whenever she went up to Hampton Junction. He even counseled her to escape her marriage to Chaz.

Could this Mark Roper be the same man? Hell, if he was, he must be in his early seventies. And that would mean trouble if Kelly had told him everything. The guy could be making a beeline to find him right now, which would take about a day. Shit, he might already have contacted the Buffalo authorities and a cruiser could be on the way to pick him up.

Earl lay still. Feeling his heart start to race, he fought the compulsion to get up and peek through the bedroom window to make sure that a squad car wasn't pulling up to the front door.

But had she referred to that doctor as Mark? It didn't sound right. Yet a second physician called Roper in so small a place was unlikely.

He got out of bed and went to his study to check the directory of licensed physicians for New York State. He skimmed through all the Ropers, finding only one whose office address was Hampton Junction. Except it couldn't be Kelly's Dr. Roper. This man's license number indicated he'd been in practice only seven years.

The original Dr. Roper's son? he wondered. That could also be problematic if the father were alive and capable of discussing what he remembered about Kelly. The name Earl Garnet might still come up.

He undressed and returned to bed, hoping he could escape into sleep, but thoughts of Kelly persisted. He found himself drifting back to 1974.

*   *   *

It had been the time of Watergate, Nixon's ignominious slide toward the disgrace of his resignation, when the anatomy of the president's self-destruction, like the Vietnam War, was documented in wall-to-wall television coverage. His downfall seemed suited to the little screen, running daily as it did with the incremental revelations of a soap opera, something Earl and his classmates could tune in to after skipping weeks of episodes without feeling behind in the story. As medical students in their most clinical year yet, they had little time to pay it more attention. But they never missed *M*A*S*H*.

At the movies, portraits of evil topped the big box office hits. Robert De Niro emblazoned himself on everyone's memory in *Godfather, Part II*; but for making them cringe, nobody topped Roman Polanski when he sliced open Jack Nicholson's nose in *Chinatown*.

As for music, they couldn't get through a day on the wards without hearing the radio blast Paul Anka's "Having my Baby" or Barbra Streisand's "The Way We Were." In the OR surgeons cut and sewed to newcomer Elton John's big hit, "Bennie and the Jets."

But to Earl's gang, only one troubadour counted.

Thousands of tiny flames, each a point of light held aloft, filled the darkness.

Bob Dylan stepped forward on the stage.

Robbie Robertson stood to the right of him, lean as a silhouette hunched over a guitar, The Band at his back.

> *You say you love me,*
> *And you're thinkin' of me,*
> *But you know you could be wrong.*

He snarled the last word, loud and long.

The crowd roared the words with him.

"You sing that like you mean it," Jack MacGregor called to Kelly. Shadows played over his thin face, resculpting its hollows.

"You better believe I do," she yelled back. Her eyes danced in the flicker of the tiny fires.

Earl had rarely seen her look so radiant.

> *. . . you go your way*
> *and I go mine.*

It was at that moment she slipped her hand into his and simply held it, the darkness preventing anyone from seeing.

Melanie Collins leaned toward him from his other side. "Some study group," she said, then laughed.

"And we'll be payin' dearly for it, children," Tommy Leannis added from his end of the row, the musical lilt of his Irish sounding false. His constant fear of failure emanated off him like a bad smell and made him a fifth wheel. Yet he insisted on tagging along whenever they knocked off the books for a night, as if he was just as afraid to be alone with all the material they still had to learn.

"It's all right, Tommy," Kelly hollered back at him, never letting go of Earl's hand. "If an old woman like me can get through, what have you got to worry about? Top five, all of us," she predicted, sounding confident in the din.

> . . . *Then time will tell just who fell,*
> *And who's been left behind . . .*

Earl's senses had contracted solely to the feel of her fingers entwined in his. He kept his eyes on the stage, uncertain how to respond. He already knew he loved her, and before that night had wondered if she felt just as strongly about him. But he'd never dared to speak his feelings, frightened that the crystal clarity of such words would shred the fragile, amorphous limbo in which they remained close friends, able to speak intimately of everything else, without ever trespassing on her marriage. Yet this sudden overture—her fingers played over his like flames—invited him to risk that step, and the possibility exhilarated him. Feeling her start to withdraw, he immediately tightened his grip, and she gently squeezed back. He stole a look sideways and saw her staring straight ahead, apparently enraptured by the music. Then she smiled, slowly, as though savoring something delicious, and her hand clung hard to his.

After the concert all of them trooped toward the subway, arms linked and voices raised in loud renditions of what they'd just heard.

Jack, Melanie, and Tommy scooted across the intersection at Forty-second Street ahead of them. "I don't want to go home," Kelly whispered, as she and Earl waited at the red light.

"Where then?" said Earl, trembling inside, all the time wondering, *What about your husband?* But he was too intoxicated by her to put the brakes on.

"Offer to stay behind until I get a taxi," she whispered before they rushed to join their friends.

He nodded.

"Guys, I'm going to take a taxi tonight," she announced when they reached them. "It's too late for a woman alone."

"You three go ahead. I'll make sure she gets one," Earl said, certain they'd see through him. "No cabbie in his right mind would stop for a gang of rowdies like you."

"Well, I'm insulted," Jack quipped.

"Come, children. 'Tis back downtown where we belong," said Tommy, linking arms again with Melanie. Then all three of them disappeared down the entrance to the Forty-second Street station, their voices echoing back above ground until the noise of traffic swallowed up their off-key singing.

Earl felt acutely self-conscious. *What now?* he wondered, turning to look at Kelly.

She studied him a few seconds, then moved closer and took his hand. The wind played with her long hair, and strands of it brushed against his face.

"Earl, whatever happens between us, just remember that my marriage to Chaz is finished." Her voice sounded as steady and matter-of-fact as if she were giving a case history on one of their patients. "He's a brute, and I intend to leave him. That mess has nothing to do with you."

Her face upturned to his, the glitter of the streetlights captured in her eyes, the scent of her—all drew him in. He lowered his head and gently kissed her.

*   *   *

He awoke to find Janet leaning over him, her lips caressing his. "Hi, love," she said, glancing down to where the covers slipped below his waist. "You seem happy to see me."

Wednesday, November 7, 2:30 A.M.
Geriatric Wing,
New York City Hospital

Bessie woke up shivering.

God, had they turned the heat off?

She huddled deeper under her blankets, and realized her nightgown was soaked, her skin clammy.

What was going on? She'd never had night sweats before.

And they weren't welcome, usually being the portent of a serious problem. An infection, some inflammatory condition, even an occult carcinoma—her mind automatically scrolled through the list, until she put a stop to it. No point in getting ahead of herself. The proper thing to do would be to see if they kept recurring, then tell her doctors. A solitary sweat didn't necessarily mean much. But she should take her temperature. Whether she had a fever, and if so, how high, would be important to know. A big spike would shift the diagnosis toward an infectious cause; low grade, it could signify anything.

But she didn't feel feverish.

If anything, she was really freezing, as in cool to the touch, not hot the way someone feels when they have a fever with the flu or pneumonia.

And she was hungry. Her stomach seemed clamped in on itself because it was so empty. That was new. Since entering the hospital she'd practically no appetite at all.

She reached for her call button to summon her nurse and ask for a thermometer.

Then hesitated.

The night shift here were often a bitchy bunch. Most were floats, especially on geriatric floors where the mission was custodial, not nursing in the curative sense. Always understaffed, they rarely missed an opportunity to express what a burden the elderly were. Most requests for the simplest of items, like a bedpan or medication for pain, they met with rolled eyes and exaggerated sighs. They saved outright contempt for those who committed the ultimate crime of placing extra demands on them by being sick as well as old.

No, better she not invite the witches to her bedside. Leave everything until morning rather than risk trouble now. Not that she'd tolerate any rudeness from one of those shrews. She felt uncharacteristically aggressive tonight.

Curling into a ball, she drew the covers over her head, trying to conserve body heat.

It didn't help.

He skin continued to feel slimy. The pain behind her eyes grew worse.

She emerged and reached to where the call button was pinned to her bedding. Her hand shook as she gathered it into her palm and pressed.

"They better not mess with me tonight," she muttered, staring through the gloom at her closed door, waiting for one of them to arrive.

No response.

Bloody cows!

She pressed again.

The silence of her room became a rushing noise in her ears. The moon outside her window shone unusually bright. It hurt her eyes to look at it, yet the darkness closed in on her, immune to illumination.

She pushed the call button over and over.

It mustn't be working, she thought, tugging on the end that looped past the head of her bed to where it attached to the wall.

It came freely as she pulled, until the plug itself lay in her hand. Staring at it, she had to make a massive mental effort to realize it wasn't hooked up anymore. Her thoughts all at once shattered into fragments, and she couldn't thread them together.

"Help!" she screamed. "Help me!"

No response.

"Come and help me."

Still nothing.

That's right, she remembered, her mind working again. People shrieked and yelled all night on this ward, yet no one paid them any heed.

With great effort she kicked off her covers.

The shivering increased, and she could feel her limbs twitch in the cold. Somehow she managed to get them over the edge of the bed.

Now to sit up.

Her vision dimmed, and she became locked in the black confines of her own skull. Then tiny explosions of light, like stars scintillating in space, invaded the darkness. These stars grew taller and wider, becoming squares of white, each encroaching on the night and peeling it away in strips. The experience seemed vaguely familiar, but her mind couldn't piece her symptoms into a diagnosis. Neither could she see where to plug in the disconnected wire.

She pushed herself erect until she perched on the side of the mattress, her bare feet brushing against the floor, her thinking reduced to shreds of instinct until she felt only the impulse to launch herself forward and walk.

She levered herself off onto the cold tiles and took a step, flailing ahead with her arms like a blind person.

She took another step, and flailed some more, seeking something to lean on.

But she found nothing.

She tottered forward.

And slapped her palms against a wall.

Her thinking cleared enough to remember where the door should be and, feeling her way along, she lurched toward it. When her fingers found the handle she steadied herself, took a deep breath, and pulled it open. "Help me!" she cried, barely able to keep herself upright. "Help me! Help me! Help me!"

Her voice blended in with the howls and shrieks of the senile old crones on the ward, the ones whom a phenothiazine cocktail never seemed to knock out and whose pleas to go home reverberated ceaselessly up and down the halls.

She felt certain that their calls sounded louder tonight. How could she have ignored such cries before, the way the nurses did?

She tried again to make herself heard, yelling as she sank to the floor, half-in, half-out of her room. Her mind vacillated between lucid seconds of frantically attempting to figure out what could be happening to her and timelessly floating through a searing light that she still found familiar— something some patients had once described to her, yet she couldn't quite remember their disease.

The plaintive wailing grew in volume, closed in and swallowed her.

Chapter 5

"**D**r. Roper, you said my arthritic knees would be better by now. Look at them. They're the size of cauliflowers."

"What I said, Nell, was that the pills would make the pain better, not that they'd take away your arthritis."

"But the pain came back."

"Are you still taking those pills the way I told you?"

"The prescription ran out. I figured you only wanted me to take 'em for a month. That's all the time your father ever needed to get me better."

She'd also been a quarter century younger back then. Mark turned to wash his hands at the sink in his examining room, not wanting the feisty octogenarian to see his grin. Nell had been coming to him about her knees for seven years, ever since he'd reopened his father's practice, and she'd argued her way through each visit. The idea that a prescription must be refilled and the medication taken longer than a month had never taken root beneath her frizzy white hair. It had nothing to do with poor memory or a lack of confidence in him. She resisted growing old and the idea she could no longer shake off what ailed her. She still lived independently, her mountain cabin twenty miles north of town on an isolated road overlooking the Hudson River Valley. The only reason she'd recently agreed to let a local handyman cut the twelve cords of firewood she used every winter was that he had four kids to feed and obviously needed the money. But Nell herself wasn't isolated. Known for her prize-winning recipes at the fall fair—her peach cobbler had taken home the blue ribbon seven years running—her kitchen was a much-visited mecca for anyone caring to pick up her pearls of culinary wisdom. She also reigned as the unofficial queen of the town's gossip network, a function she dutifully filled by welcoming all visitors and spending hours on the phone. The acquired information made her one of the most sought-after guests for Sunday suppers, afternoon bridge parties, and socials at each of the town's two churches, neither clergyman willing to yield her soul to the other side, or go without her contribution of cobbler.

Slowly wiping his hands with a paper towel, Mark laboriously explained yet again that she must ask Timmy Madden, the pharmacist, to refill her prescription when she ran out.

Nell sighed, having endured his lecture while tugging her well-stretched pair of elastic stockings over varicose veins as thick as quarter-inch ropes. "And how are you doing, Doctor?" she said. "It must have been a shock, pulling the bones of Kelly McShane out of the mud. Who do you think killed her?"

Now he understood the real reason she'd bothered to come and see him. "I don't think anything, yet, Nell, and I couldn't tell you if I did."

"Oh, come on. Was it that rotten husband of hers?"

"Is that what everyone around here has decided? That Chaz Braden murdered her?"

"You betcha'!"

"Anybody got any proof?"

"He's mean and was known to get drunk on more than one Saturday night. It's a bad mix."

Street justice in rural America could be just as arbitrary as its urban counterpart. In the countryside, though, it tended to be unanimous. "And that's enough to make you sure it's him?"

"Yeah. Now tell me what you think."

Mark chuckled. "My lips are officially sealed, Nell. Besides, you and your friends have probably already snooped out everything there is to know."

She gave him a no-harm-in-trying shrug, then cocked her head and slipped him a sly jack-o'-lantern smile, missing tooth and all.

A reminder of another argument he'd lost—getting her to wear the partial plate a Sarasota dentist made her.

"You still seeing that pretty veterinarian from New York?" she asked.

Reason number two for the visit.

Nell had always been uncommonly interested in the women who'd occasionally visited him. From the very first day of his return she seemed to have elected herself the local record keeper of his private life. "We keep in touch, Nell," he said, helping her off the table.

Little wonder she chose now to get an update, especially if she and her friends really had exhausted all they could say about a twenty-seven-year-old murder. While Halloween and Thanksgiving provided lots of gossip—who was shooing away the kids, who intended to run the Christmas pageant, what couples were taking separate holidays—the weeks in between yielded few topics for discussion.

"Not much to interest a young woman around here these days, I guess. Only us old folks left," she continued, sitting down to put on her shoes—Nike air pumps that she'd sworn more than once did more for her arthritis than anything he'd ever given her.

"Nell, you're the youngest 'old folk' I know."

"Did you ever ask any of them pretty girls to marry you?"

"Nell!"

"I like your hair cut short like that. It's black as your mother's but gives your face the same lean good looks your father had. What with that hunky physique you've built up hiking and running all over the mountains, the girls should be falling down over you. The only problem is you're getting that same sadness in your eyes that he had."

"Jesus, Nell!"

"Oh, go on. Who's more fitting to talk frankly with you than me? I watched your mother change your diapers, bless her dear departed soul. And I used to baby-sit your father when I was a teenager."

"I know, Nell." As they chatted he helped her down a short hallway and into the center of what used to be his parents' living room but now served as his waiting area. It was packed as always, and she routinely saved a zinger or two for this audience, all of them nearly as old as she was, most of them women.

"Guess what's the trouble with your generation?" she asked.

"I got a feeling you're going to tell me," he said, resigned to his usual role as her straight man.

"None of you want to buy a cow because you get your milk for free."

He started to laugh, along with everyone else. "Nell, you're wicked."

"Maybe you should take me out."

"I couldn't handle you."

"Tell me, did that veterinarian woman cook?"

He felt his face grow warm. Banter with Nell in private was one thing. In public it could get embarrassing. "We ate out a lot when she was here," he said quickly, trying to end the conversation.

She flashed him that jack-o'-lantern smile again. "Well, you know what I always say?"

He rolled his eyes. "I'm afraid to ask."

"If she's no good in the kitchen, she won't be worth much in the bedroom."

The oldsters found this one even more uproarious.

"Oh Nell, how naughty," yelled one of his blue-haired regulars.

"But ain't it the truth?" she fired back.

The woman giggled. "I'll say."

A large lady gestured with her thumb to a distinguished, white-haired gentleman at her side.

"Fred here adores my pot roast."

He turned beet red and fiddled with his hearing aid.

Nell proceeded to lead the rest of the room in a free-for-all of off-color innuendos about food and sex. It grew so loud that Mark barely heard the phone ring. He didn't have a secretary. Hiring anybody locally had proved impossible. Whomever he picked, someone inevitably commented, "I don't want that person seeing what's in my file." Since he knew his patients the way only a country doctor could and the practice pretty well ran itself anyway, he'd kept it a one-man operation—except when it came to all the forms for Medicare and Medicaid. They drove him crazy. His aunt Margaret used to process them for him. Now a company from Saratoga did it. They charged him a hefty commission, but he figured it well worth the price, since he could use the extra hours to run or hike.

"Dr. Roper," he answered, blocking his other ear in order to hear over the brouhaha.

"Mark, it's Dan. Hey, sounds like you're in a tavern. The whole gang there, huh?"

"Yep. Everyone over seventy-five is here to party. That's my waiting room!"

He chuckled. "Well, I hate to be the pooper, but I've got Chaz Braden and his father, plus Kelly McShane's parents in my office, all of them squabbling over her remains."

"What?"

"It started last night with phone calls from their lawyers, just as soon as Everett made it official that everything is now in our hands."

Son of a bitch. "I'll be right over."

* * *

Dan's office was in a large, colonial building that dominated Main Street. Shabby wood siding toward the back made it look as if the contractor had run out of money. Once nicknamed the White House, the building hadn't been painted in years and was now a sooty gray. Inside, county officialdom was cut down to size. The courthouse, the jail, a records room, the fire hall, the police station—all were crammed into three floors and a basement. There was even a small coroner's office that Mark used only during inquests or for campaign headquarters on those occasions when someone challenged his reelection.

Floorboards creaking under his feet, he walked up to a door with a clear window that had SHERIFF written across it and peeked in at the people he'd be dealing with.

Dan slouched in his chair massaging his temples. An immaculately groomed, sophisticated-looking older woman sat across from him. She wore a well-tailored black suit and hat. Lord, Mark only saw hats like that in old movies these days. She held black leather gloves in her left hand and kept tight hold with her right on the gold clasp of a black snakeskin handbag in her lap. Behind her stood a compact man, also elderly, but his tanned complexion, though creased, had a youthful tautness that was at odds with his shock of white hair. Arms folded across his chest, his mouth grim, he seemed to be studying his shoes.

Kelly's parents, Mark assumed. He hadn't seen them since he was a small boy. They'd moved away shortly after their daughter's disappearance.

Charles Braden III was the only one who seemed to be at ease. Mark remembered him vividly from his days as a resident at NYCH when the man served as outgoing chairman of the Obstetrics Department prior to retirement. Still sleek, sporting the same wiry, brushed steel haircut, and dressed in a two-thousand-dollar suit, he leaned against the wall, hands in his pockets.

By contrast, his son Chaz looked anxious, though no less sartorially splendid. His wiry body was taut; dark circles underscored his eyes.

Mark took a breath, squared his shoulders, and walked in, adopting the swift stride he used to impose his authority while making rounds at Saratoga

General, another arena where money tried to outrank him. "Good afternoon, everyone."

They all looked up at him.

Before Mark had enough time to clear his throat, Mrs. McShane was on her feet, her handbag placed precisely on her chair, and standing before him. "Dr. Roper, I am Kelly's mother—"

"Samantha, my dear—" Her husband followed on her heels, reaching out, placing his hands supportively on her shoulders.

She wrenched away from his touch. "Please, Walter, let me have my say." She turned a beseeching face to Mark. "Do forgive me, but I simply must demand a little respect here as Kelly's mother." She had a tremor in her voice that reminded him of Katharine Hepburn's performances in her later movies like *On Golden Pond* or *A Lion in Winter*. "My darling girl meant everything to me and to learn that I was right all along, that she didn't run away from us, that someone viciously murdered her—well, I'm sure you understand how devastating, how traumatic this has been for me."

From behind, Mark heard one of the Bradens mutter, "Garbage!"

Samantha obviously had also heard. She drew herself up to her full height, but didn't turn around. "As I was saying, Doctor, it should be a parent's right to bury her only child, her beloved chi—"

"For heaven's sake, Samantha," Chaz said, stepping forward. "You and Kelly hadn't exchanged a single civil word in years before she—"

"That's quite enough!" Walter said. His arm shot protectively around his wife's shoulders. "And after all you put Kelly through during those years, how dare you say anything about us. The least you can do now is agree to let Samantha give her a proper, loving funeral."

"I have every right to bury my wife," Chaz shot back. "Every right. It was you two and Kelly who were estranged, but we, Kelly and I, were not. Let me repeat that. We weren't the ones estranged, and I insist—"

"You insist?" An incredulous look rearranged Samantha's beautifully made-up face. "All her friends said she wanted to leave you, and you know it. If Kelly estranged herself from anyone, it was you."

"I don't know any such thing!" Chaz said, alarmingly red in the face.

"And you drove her away from me," Samantha continued. "Every chance you had. You're the last one who's going to take her from me now by trying to turn the tables on me like this." Walter still steadied her as if she were a fragile piece of Baccarat.

This was fast growing out of control, Mark thought. He glanced at Dan, who shrugged, rolled his eyes, and raised his hands as if to say, "See what I've been trying to deal with?"

Then Charles Braden III moved into the middle of the fray. "Chaz, please, we know you adored Kelly and are distraught, but, as I've said before, have a care for a mother's feelings as well. Do sit down, Chaz." He squeezed his son's shoulder. "And let's all try to remember that Kelly would have been dreadfully upset by this wrangling."

Although Charles sounded reasonable, Mark thought, the guy was so smooth he reeked of hypocrisy. Time to take charge himself, and impose his own agenda. "Listen up, people," he said, moving to position himself behind Dan. "I'm afraid neither side will get any satisfaction today. Her remains are evidence still, and I'm not releasing them to either party." He knew that he couldn't get anything more out of the bones from a forensic point of view, yet instinctively balked at letting them go.

Everyone looked surprised.

"I thought you'd have done everything necessary by now," Chaz said, walking quickly around the end of Dan's desk to where he could stand toe-to-toe with Mark. He exuded anger, but also seemed edgy, his fingers continually opening and closing as if he were practicing his grip. "What are you playing at?"

Not exactly a presence to back down from, Mark thought. *In fact, why not probe a little. See how the man reacts to the prospect of his wife's death being looked at locally.* "You think I'm playing here, Chaz? This investigation is just beginning, and I'm bound to hold Kelly's remains for as long as I need to do a proper inquiry."

He got even more flushed. "You? But the NYPD told me as far as they were concerned it was a cold case. They're not working on it."

"They dumped it in Dan's and my laps."

"That was just for you to do their paperwork, for Christ's sake. Any fool could see that. Surely you're not going to drag this out?"

Mark caught the condescension, and an old enmity stirred. But he kept it in check.

Nevertheless, he saw Dan looking up at him apprehensively.

"Listen to me, Roper," Chaz said. "You may think you're some kind of big shot here, being coroner and all, but I can rally enough votes to fix that at the next election."

Mark's discipline in dealing with assholes nearly folded. He smiled, slowly, showing his teeth a few at a time. "Take your best shot."

"This is not fitting for Kelly," Braden Senior said. His tone had the quiet authority of someone who never raised his voice to get an order followed.

Mark had to admit Braden had spoken the truth. "I'll say it's not fitting." He kept his gaze on Chaz.

"There can't be much more you need to examine," Braden Senior continued. "Besides, both the McShanes and my son and I probably will lawyer you to death if you persist. Now I'm no judge, but in a court of law you'll be hard-pressed not to accord both families the closure of putting her in a grave."

Again, Mark knew he was right.

"So for our Kelly's sake, why not now?" Braden Senior pressed.

Mark looked over at him. "Can you people agree on arrangements so that Dan and I don't have to decide between you? Neither of us is a Solomon, you know."

He got no immediate response, except Chaz walked over to rejoin his father.

Mark forged on. "Mrs. McShane, you mentioned a funeral, right?"

She nodded slowly.

"What if you agreed to hold the funeral, which Chaz and his father may attend, and let the Bradens hold a memorial service a couple of weeks later, which you and your husband may attend?"

Samantha appeared to be taken aback, but to his right he could see that both the Bradens were smiling, albeit reluctantly.

"I think you are a Solomon after all, young man," Braden Senior said. "A real peacemaker. Well done."

Braden was complimenting him. Dan looked relieved, and the McShanes appeared to accept his compromise. Out of the corner of his eye he saw that even Chaz nodded slightly. Why, since he had put this potential fracas to rest, did he have such a bitter taste in his mouth?

4:00 P.M.

Mark started his run as usual, going down to the foot of his driveway and turning left. After this afternoon's business, he figured it would take at least an hour on the road to work off the tension.

The air was cool, the light gray, and leaden clouds promised snow. He'd worn gloves and a hooded track suit, but initially he still felt cold. He also carried a small flashlight in his pocket since it would be dark before he finished.

By the first hundred paces, he started to feel the flush of his endorphins. Within fifteen minutes, his runner's high kicked in like a shot of morphine, first vanquishing the pain of protesting muscles, then wiping the Bradens and McShanes off his radar. His world became the sound of his breathing, the thudding of his heart, and the soft slap of his running shoes on asphalt. When the first few flakes began to float down around him and fall on his cheeks, he even welcomed their sting against his skin as they melted, the sensation invigorating him. It was a mindless state, and he reveled in it.

Thirty minutes later, well along the uphill part of his trek, he trotted by a gated muddy road that led into a thickly forested property. Off to one side a rusted plaque pompously announced THE BRADEN FOUNDATION CLINIC.

At least they hadn't hung a scarlet *A* in front of the place.

He had passed this place a hundred times, never giving it a thought. But now, the crumpled clipping about the place that his father had kept popped to mind, and on a whim, he slowed, walked over to where a wire fence abutted against the post at the right of the entrance. Ignoring a faded NO TRESPASSING sign, he climbed to the other side. The rickety barrier swayed under him, suggesting the whole thing might soon collapse, maintenance obviously no longer a priority.

He started along the center hump between two little-used ruts, resuming the same jogging pace as before. The falling snow disappeared as soon as it hit the bare earth, and in the brittle undergrowth of wild grasses that lined a shallow ditch on either side it collected around the roots like frizzy bits of fluff before melting. The sight made him feel slightly forlorn, not an unusual emotion at this time of year; he preferred it when everything finally turned white and Christmassy. Lately, though, as the change of season drove away the summer crowd and emptied the countryside, instead of enjoying the drop in his workload, he sometimes felt left behind. The sensation, when it occurred, puzzled him. He had nowhere else he wanted to live or work. No matter. Whatever it was that disquieted him, he figured it couldn't be what he'd seen happen to Dan and others. He just wasn't the type to get bushed.

Deeper into the woods the russet foliage of ancient giant oaks intertwined to form a thatched arch high above his head and cast a further layer of shadow over the thickening dusk, forcing him to watch his step.

In the far distance he heard the "Boom! Boom! Boom!" of rifle shots.

"God, I hate hunting season," he said out loud. He'd not worn the prescribed orange vest or gaudy cap, so he began to whistle at full volume between breaths, figuring that making a lot of noise was his best protection against being mistaken for a deer. Every November he and Dan hauled out some poor Joe who had a stray bullet or crossbow arrow in him. He medevacked the living by helicopter to the nearest trauma center, usually Albany; but sometimes, when patient volume at local facilities made them too busy, he had to ride with the victim, fighting to keep him stable all the way to New York City and his old alma mater, NYCH. The dead they body-bagged and sent to Blair's.

He rounded a bend and stepped out of the shadows into a clearing the size of a baseball field. At its center stood the lifeless hulk of the building. Made of stone and four stories tall, it had the dimensions of a medium-sized apartment block and had most of its windows punched out. Not even falling snow in twilight could soften the dreariness.

He hadn't been here since sneaking in with friends when they were kids. They'd deemed it "haunted" back then and prowled the dark corridors as a rite of passage. Even a few of the broken panes were their doing. The rest had been target practice for the crowd that roamed the woods at this time each year.

Might as well take a look, he thought, not that he expected the reason for his father's interest in the place to jump out at him. But as coroner he'd learned the value of visiting a site. Every place had a feel to it, and sometimes the physical layout of a building spoke to him. It didn't necessarily give answers, but often begged specific questions—Who was here? And why? What were they doing? How did their presence relate to the death under investigation? And in forensics, like medicine, the first step in solving a problem was asking the right question.

He started across the open space, pushing through the bare branches of bushes and saplings that were waist high. These soon gave way to a field of spindly grass up to his knees. Dormant like everything else and beige in color, it appeared to have once been a lawn that had long since gone to seed. Several medium-sized trees dotted the area.

He mounted a half dozen stone steps and stood in front of a massive wooden door suitable for a cathedral. He gave the ornate handle a jerk. Locked solid, just as it always had been. *No matter,* he thought, walking over to the broken window he and his pals had used. Verifying that the frame was still free of glass bits, he hoisted himself up on the sill and crawled through.

A familiar musty smell of mold, dust, and dead mice filled his nostrils, sharp as memory. It was much darker in here, and he fished the flashlight from his pocket. Passing the beam around the room, he found his bearings as quickly as if he'd been here yesterday. He and his buddies hadn't known then the exact nature of what once went on inside, only that it used to be a kind of hospital where women without money came to have their babies. Eyeing the wooden counters and ceiling-high shelves that he'd scrambled up and over while playing tag, he now figured this must have been the reception area. He stepped through its only doorway, and the wooden floorboards creaked loudly, as they'd done two decades ago. Staring down the dark passageway that ran the length of the building, he felt a familiar, yet old anxiety reassert itself. Then it had been part of a game, titillatingly effervescent, the sort of thrill he experienced in a horror movie or at the summer carnival's House of Terror, not the foreboding he sensed now. His beam of light didn't help any, making the faded wood along the barren corridor only seem more ghostly.

He began to walk, having no idea what he was looking for, yet kept his mind open to impressions, allowing them to play loose and free through his head where, with luck, they would offer some brilliant insight into what he saw. At least that was how it was supposed to work.

On either side of him were small bare rooms, each about fifteen feet square, twenty of them in all. Bleak and dismal under his white probings, the curls of peeling paint on the walls and clumps of dust on the floors cast shadows that made everything look ragged. Sleeping quarters? The idea of being shut up in one of them, even when it would have been clean and less decrepit, gave him the creeps.

At the far end of the hallway, he came across a pair of large, tiled chambers situated opposite each other, many of the white ceramic squares cracked or missing altogether. In one a row of round black holes across the floor indicated where the toilets had stood; in the other a half dozen open stalls stripped clean of all nozzles and taps, even the drains, were all that was left of the communal showers. Scratching noises came from deep within the uncovered plumbing, and he pictured legions of rats waiting down there, ready to crawl out as soon as night fell.

He found a stairway and headed for the upper floors.

Mark imagined the culture of shame and censure that had driven all those women to this bleak, isolated place. The practice at the time would have been to whisk them away from their homes, out of sight of friends and neighbors as soon as they started to "show" in the second trimester.

Steeped in guilt, they'd then endure months of waiting in "homes" such as this. He could almost see them, heads cowed over swollen bellies as they shuffled to and from their rooms, made to feel they'd sinned by the sanctimonious silence of the staff. At least that's how it had been described to him by some of the veteran nurses during his obstetrical training. They'd wanted to impress on the residents how far society had come regarding single moms.

The second floor was a carbon copy of the first. The third and fourth the same. Looking out a window he got a bird's-eye view of the grounds. Through the falling snow and dying light, the stalks of grass now seemed black, resembling a wildly irregular bed of needles amidst an encroaching border of brush. He scanned the edge of the trees beyond, making sure that none of the shooters he'd heard earlier had taken a notion to come here and fire off a few more rounds to test their marksmanship.

Still alone, as far as he could tell.

Continuing to use his flashlight, he descended to the basement and strode through an area of sinks, counters, and wires dangling out of walls.

Must have been the kitchen.

Down another corridor he passed several big rooms, the functions of which he couldn't fathom. Through a particularly large metal door he entered the biggest room he'd seen so far, the walls covered in green tiles, a central drain in the floor, an abundance of plug outlets along the baseboards, and a solitary, heavy-duty electrical cord sheathed in metal dangling out of the ceiling. For an OR lamp, he thought. This had been the delivery room.

He played his light at where the examining table would have been, and found himself thinking of the ordeal the women must have suffered through at that spot. Their eyes bulging from the iron grip of contractions, they would be spread-legged under the white glare—like specimens. From the stories he'd heard, the pain might have been compounded without anyone with them to hold their hands, stroke their heads, murmur comforting words, or even say their names. Instead, they'd feel only the cold probe of steel instruments, hear nothing but their own cries and clipped orders to push, see little else but a ring of censorious eyes above a circle of surgical masks. At the final expulsion, would they strain to catch a glimpse of the child as the cord was cut, before the tiny infant, wrapped in a blanket, was whipped out of the room, never to be seen again?

His fists tightened.

But those were the norms back then. What had any of this to do with Kelly, and why had his father kept newspaper clippings about a place of such misery? He'd come no closer to answers to those questions. He hurried back up the stairs, playing his beam of light from side to side, making sure no wandering rats were anywhere near. He made his way to the front room, slithered out the window, and stood on the stone steps, taking in deep, long breaths of the cold night air. The snow came down more heavily than before, and in the dim illumination of twilight he could see the beginnings of a lacy white pattern between the stalks of grass. Once more he peered along the forest's edge, checking for hunters.

No one.

Walking quickly, he started toward the dark opening in the trees, where he would pick up the dirt road. He felt the cryptlike heaviness behind him, and despite himself kept taking quick glances over his shoulder. Only the black line of his own footprints disturbed the charcoal-shaded landscape.

Not paying proper attention to the ground in front of him, he'd gone less than a dozen steps when he stubbed the toe of his running shoe on a rock and tumbled forward. He sprawled onto what felt like a sheet of plywood that sagged under his weight. He quickly rolled off, got to his feet, and, using his light, looked more carefully at where he'd fallen. Sure enough, a four-by-eight rectangle, the standard size of a plywood sheet, lay outlined in a dusting of snow. "Jesus Christ," he muttered, remembering what would be under it.

The well.

They'd avoided it like the plague as kids. Avoided all wells. Every mother in Hampton Junction drummed the rule into her children from birth. Still, now and then a kid tumbled down an uncovered shaft, driving the point home with brutal clarity.

These wells had been dug deep, sometimes 150 feet to reach a stable water table, and the water was cold. A few children had actually survived the ordeal of falling in, hypothermia having kept them alive until they could be retrieved and resuscitated.

Mark lifted the board and saw a four-foot-diameter hole lined with mortared rock. These were the old kind, drilled and dug by hand a century ago and made to last. Cautiously leaning over, he probed the darkness with his flashlight. He saw water about forty feet down. It had been raining a lot, so the level was high. God knows how deep it was. He picked up the rock he'd tripped over and dropped it in. The splash echoed back up at him, and air bubbled to the surface for what seemed a long time.

Better tell Dan to have the Braden caretakers get it fixed before some child fell in. He wasn't sure if that would still be Charles Braden's responsibility.

The run through the forest seemed darker than before, and he used his light. The snow had started to penetrate even here, reaching the ground and creating a glistening carpet of white that sparkled in the beam. Overhead it accumulated along the tops of twigs and branches, making silver webs throughout the trees, as if giant spiders had been at work while he'd been inside.

He rounded the bend that had kept the grounds private from people peeping in at the gate. Feeling chilled, he pulled the hood of his jacket tighter and picked up his pace.

He still kept looking over his shoulder. The solitary line of his footprints ran back as far as he could see, and he thought of all the four-legged prey that would now leave distinct tracks as they fled the men with guns.

When he returned his attention to the path ahead, he saw two figures silhouetted against the gray opening at the end of the road.

He stopped.

They just stood there, absolutely still.

"Hey!" he cried out, shining his light in their direction. The beam barely reached them. He couldn't see their features by it, but it illuminated the area enough to make out the shape of the rifles they were carrying, the barrels vaguely pointed at him. "I'm Dr. Mark Roper, the coroner. You shouldn't still be out here after dark."

No reply.

Not that he expected them to jump when he spoke. His authority over hunters kicked in only after they shot one another. "There's no trespassing here," he added, remaining motionless. He didn't think for a moment they'd take a potshot at him, but being in front of anyone who might be liquored up and have their weapons off safety made him very cautious.

He heard them laugh, then saw them turn and walk back toward the highway.

Mark exhaled, his breath white on the frost. Only then did he realize he'd been holding it. He quickly ran the rest of the way to the road, feeling a sense of relief once he emerged from the murk of the forest to the lighter shades of darkness.

"Assholes!" he muttered, starting toward home. After thirty yards he spotted where their tracks led back into the forest. He ran by, trying not to look in that direction, but he could feel their eyes on the back of his neck all the way to the next bend.

* * *

"I'll go out there, but they'll be long gone," Dan said, sinking his fork into an extra wide wedge of apple pie.

Mark sipped his tea. "I figured you might find their truck or car at the side of the road somewhere and ticket the hell out of it."

They were in Hampton Junction's best eating establishment, its name, *The Four Aces,* scrawled in big purple neon letters across the front windows. Inside the lighting was as dim as in any New York City lounge. The room itself was long and narrow, a bar running the length of the back wall, the booths for eating lined across the front. It boasted the finest home cooking of any restaurant in the state, and most of the townspeople agreed, barring Nell, of course.

Dan and he were at their usual table in the corner, where they could talk privately and see anyone approaching in time to shut up before being overheard.

"I'll try my best, Mark. Did you have a good run, otherwise? You don't look as relaxed as usual."

"Not really. By the way, there's also a well on the property that needs a cover."

"Really? Shit. I'll have to contact old man Braden's caretakers. What did you go in there for anyway?"

"Last night I found clippings about the place in an old file my father had on Kelly."

Dan's fork stopped midway between his plate and mouth. "Oh?"

For the next five minutes the man didn't eat a bite as Mark summarized what he'd found, leaving out the specifics of the medical entries. "I'll make you copies of the articles and the letter. As for Dad's clinical notes, there's nothing much there anyway." They'd worked enough cases together to develop a routine. Medical records remained confidential and off-limits to the sheriff. But Mark had no hesitation signaling when they weren't relevant anyway.

Dan went back to his eating. "Shit! You've been busy."

"Except we're not much further ahead. The letter just confirms that she had a lover. It isn't enough to get Everett back on the case."

Dan chased down the last few crumbs of crust on his plate. "Probably not."

Mark sat staring out the window, saying nothing.

"Hey. Are you sure you're all right?" Dan asked, after downing the remains of his coffee in one swallow.

"Of course. Why?"

"You got that look in your eye."

"What look?"

"Like you're about to take another trip."

"What the hell are you talking about?"

"You've taken a lot of trips this year. Let's see, there was London, San Moritz, Cancún, Hawaii, South Beach in Florida—"

"Those were conferences."

Dan grinned. "Yeah, right. As if you suddenly forgot so much medicine you need twice as many refresher courses?"

"Have you got a point to make?"

"I do. This comes from one who has been there. Don't let yourself get bushed. You remind me of myself after Marion left."

On the drive home Mark turned the radio up loud, hoping a dose of music would blast his brain free of the day's dregs. As if the Bradens and the McShanes weren't enough, the last thing he needed was a little homespun advice. He knew Dan meant well, but the guy's butting into his private life irritated him. The trouble was Dan had no one to care about, nothing coming of the attempts he'd made to start dating again. Being a forty-year-old cop in a town most people considered as exciting as Mayberry, he'd only been able to muster a few summer romances with women who'd come here to vacation. Predictably, they left in the fall.

Not much different from his own ladies, he had to admit, and cranked up the volume even more as the strains of a familiar song filled his Jeep.

> *. . . When the night*
> *has come,*
> *And the land*
> *is dark,*
> *And the moon*
> *is the only light*
> *we'll see . . .*

Flashing along tendrils of mist, his high beams picked up a truck parked over on the shoulder of the road. Nearby a huddle of men, most of them still carrying their rifles, were lined up taking a piss. One of them toasted him with a silver hip flask as he passed.

> *. . . No I won't be afraid,*
> *Oh I won't be afraid,*
> *Just as long as you stand, stand by me.*
> *So darlin' darlin' stand by me . . .*

He belted out the chorus as loud as he could.

Chapter 6

Feeling gloomy and foolish, Mark was back at the bar picking up his second glass of white wine. He was gloomy because of the event itself— a memorial service for a woman who'd died twenty-seven years ago. The tributes by high school, college, and medical school classmates had seemed thin and hollow to him. No one captured Kelly's real warmth and sense of mischief. Rather, they'd remembered her as some kind of hard-working, self-sacrificing tin saint. And Samantha McShane. The woman made a complete ass of herself, droning endlessly how she suffered over the loss of her beloved daughter. Her lengthy, self-aggrandizing remarks made him sick. By contrast, Chaz's tribute to his wife came across as sur-prisingly dignified and tender.

He sauntered to the far corner of the impressive mahogany-paneled room, took a healthy swig of wine, and looked over the small crowd. Oh, yeah, he felt foolish all right. How in heaven's name had he convinced himself that he was going to find leads by talking to the people who came to this service?

A prick named Tommy Leannis, a plastic surgeon who'd been a resident with Kelly, had blown him off, seeming afraid that the Bradens wouldn't approve of his talking with the coroner. Another med school friend of Kelly's, Melanie Collins, made him feel uneasy with her not-so-subtle sexual come-on. She was at least fifteen, maybe twenty years older than he, and a good-looking old gal, but her assertiveness was a turnoff. She helped in one thing she told him, though. She'd said that "a person could hide everything but two conditions—being drunk and being in love"—and that Kelly definitely had been in love at the time she'd disappeared. In love . . . the man in the taxi. Damn, he had to find that guy.

Braden Senior had been smarmy as ever when they'd exchanged a few words, and Chaz seemed even more nervous than he had been in Dan's office. Mark got nowhere fast with either of them. Time to toss back the rest of his wine and leave, he decided, when he spotted a tall, slim man with a very attractive blond woman on his arm, one of the few couples he hadn't yet approached. He put down his glass, went over, and introduced himself.

"Ah, Dr. Roper, the coroner on the case," Earl said. "I'm Dr. Garnet, but call me Earl. This is my wife, Dr. Janet Graceton."

They all shook hands

"So tell us," Earl continued, "what's your connection to Kelly, other than having had the investigation dumped in your lap?"

The comment took Mark by surprise. "How did you know it was a dump? You're not connected with NYPD are you?"

Earl laughed. "No, I'm in ER at St. Paul's Hospital in Buffalo, though some of my staff probably think of me as a cop."

"And I deliver babies," added Janet, her smile bright. "We're definitely not with the police."

"But bureaucracy's bureaucracy," Earl continued, "and I've had a lifetime of stuff shuffled my way. As soon as I saw the article in the *Herald*, I figured they were sloughing the whole thing onto you."

"I'll say they did. Though I would have done whatever was necessary anyway, to bring Kelly justice. She was a very special lady."

"You knew her?" Earl asked.

"Only as a kid."

"Really. What do you remember of her?"

"Like I told everyone here, I remember the important stuff for a seven-year-old boy. She could ride a bike like the wind, had a jackknife dive to die for, and when it came to cannonballs, no one on the dock was safe."

Earl laughed again, even though his eyes remained sad. Mark found him more sincere than those who'd gushed over Kelly at the service. He immediately liked Earl Garnet.

"What else?" Earl asked.

And Mark had figured he'd be the one asking the questions. "Well, I guess what I recall most was how much fun she was. She always made me feel great."

"She sometimes mentioned a Dr. Roper. Was he your father?"

"Yes."

"She spoke very highly of him. Said he was the one who gave her enough confidence to apply to med school."

"I know she sure liked talking with him. They'd spend hours together in his study. He actually was her doctor for a while. I found his old file on her in our basement."

"It must be especially sad for him, knowing someone murdered his protégée."

"At least he was spared that. He died nearly a couple of months after she disappeared."

"Oh. I'm sorry. I didn't know."

"It was all such a long time ago."

"Yet her disappearance must have been painful for him and for you. Did he ever talk about it?"

Boy, this guy likes to probe, Mark thought, also realizing that he didn't mind. Earl seemed genuinely interested. He could tell by his eyes. They never wavered from him. "Actually, I didn't know she had vanished. My father told me only that she'd gone away, and I had no idea I'd lost her until much later. As a result I haven't any traumatic last-time-I-saw-Kelly stuff to cloud my memories of her." He found himself smiling. "So all of them are pretty happy. My favorite even now is of us spending hours on the dock, swimming and joking together. She especially liked watching the clouds and making crazy interpretations out of the shapes."

Earl's face suddenly grew animated. "Ah, yes, Kelly and her cloud game. It was fun—"

"You played it with her?"

"Yes—" He seemed to stop himself, his expression growing serious again. "It must be hard for you, investigating who killed her, yet having been so close." Oddly, he sounded guarded now.

Shit, surely this man wasn't going to suddenly bottle up the way Leannis did. Then he noticed how still Janet Graceton had gotten and the sideways look of astonishment she gave her husband.

The moment hung there, the seconds elongated.

He didn't figure it out.

It simply popped into his head.

Intuition, insight, instinct—whatever, he just knew. This guy had loved Kelly. He must have been the one!

As he cast about for what to say next, a dark shape moving across the other side of the room drifted into his field of vision. He turned to see Samantha McShane glide toward Chaz Braden, a half-finished drink in her hand.

"Murderer," she said, her voice low, yet the guttural sounds traveled throughout the room.

Chaz froze, his own drink halfway to his lips.

"You killed her! I know you did. I've known it for twenty-seven years." Samantha's anger brimmed into tears, a few of which coursed down her cheeks, leaving faint tracks in her makeup.

Chaz went white.

Walter came running up and tried to take her by the elbow. "Samantha, for the love of God!"

She shoved her husband's hand away and looked at him, her stare fierce, her tears stopping as quickly as they'd come. "This man murdered our Kelly, I know he did. And he has to be brought to justice. He has to!"

As Samantha verged on the edge of hysterics, Mark realized just how unsteady, even volatile her emotions were.

While everyone nearby remained too shocked to move, her husband managed to slip an arm around her shoulders, whisper into her ear, and begin to walk her to the exit.

Suddenly Braden Senior was at his son's side.

"Unfortunate dear," he said loud enough for all to hear. "Overwrought, understandably." Once Walter McShane had led his wife out of earshot, Charles turned to the rest of the group, and added, "It's tragic, but the woman's sadly unstable. Of course she's distraught, but has always been far too emotionally charged and changeable. Bad for Kelly, bad for the marriage. Sorry for the disruption, but I'm sure I can count on your understanding."

The sheer unflappability of the man took Mark's breath away, until he noticed Braden's right fist was clenched so tightly that the knuckles were white.

Chaz eyed the remnants of his drink and placed it untouched back on the bar. The color still hadn't returned to his face. But when he saw Mark looking at him, he responded with an angry glare.

The embarrassed silence slowly dissolved as people resumed their conversations in small groups.

Mark turned to resume his own conversation with Earl and Janet, but saw them headed for the door.

On impulse he followed at a discreet distance, not at all sure what he would do.

*   *   *

"So tell me about Kelly," Janet said, settling back in her chair.

Earl paused with his fork halfway to his mouth.

He and Janet sat across from each other at a table by one of the big windows in the main dining room of the Plaza Hotel. It offered a view of Central Park across Fifty-ninth Street, but he'd barely noticed. He also found the food tasteless—most of his dinner remained on his plate—and Janet was uncharacteristically quiet. Despite sensing his act about Kelly grow rapidly transparent, like a con artist hooked on his own lie, he continued the sham. "What everybody said about her gave a pretty good picture." His breezy tone sounded false to his own ear.

Janet's glacial blue eyes held steady on him. Finally, she reached across the table, touched his hand, and interlaced her fingers with his. "It's time you told me what's up here."

He felt sheepish. "It's ridiculous. I don't know why I didn't tell you right out—didn't want to worry you was the main reason. I'd hoped the story would go away. The NYPD obviously weren't interested, and after a few days of holding my breath, nobody from Hampton Junction came knocking on my door either. But now, by keeping quiet, I've made such a big thing out of something that happened so long ago—"

She raised the fingers of her free hand to his lips and silenced him. "Earl, what's the deal? Were you two lovers?"

He sat there, feeling caught, his quiet serving as an admission of . . . of what? Not guilt. He felt more regret and sadness than shame. "How did you know?"

She shook her head, obviously incredulous that he had to ask. "I could understand it being a shock—all these years you believed she'd escaped, and now you find out she had been murdered. But your needing me to be with you at the funeral, your being in a daze for the last week, then your letting slip about Kelly's cloud game—"

"I'm sorry—"

A waiter arrived to clear away their plates, and Earl welcomed the hiatus in his apology, then had no idea what to add when he left.

"She was married," Janet said after a few seconds, almost to herself.

"I know, but as I told you before, there were problems, big ones."

She shook her head and gave him a smile as if he were an errant medical student. "And you got involved with a woman old enough to know better. What'd she say? 'Mister, my husband doesn't understand me'?"

"It wasn't like that. In fact she hardly ever talked about her husband's problems."

"Then how was it? My God, Earl, I mean I knew I wasn't the first in your life, and you weren't my first, but I sure never messed with married men. Considered them tainted meat."

Earl winced at Janet's characteristic candor. Yet she didn't seem to be upset so much as pensive. "What can I say, Janet? Over the first few years of med school Kelly and I spent a lot of time talking together. She told me the trouble she was in, and I was young and stupid. I guess I got caught up in rescue fantasies."

"You guess?"

Nothing, not even a lifetime of medical experience, had ever enabled Earl to unravel the mysterious power Janet possessed to make him explain himself. He knew only that once she got him started, he found it hard to stop.

"Okay, so I was an idiot. But I don't regret trying to help her. As Chaz became increasingly abusive and controlling. I honestly thought she and I were good for each other, that we'd get her out of her mess, then see about us. Besides, you weren't anywhere in sight to 'save me from myself,' as you so often put it, for about another fifteen years."

"Hey!" she said softly. "Of course you tried to help her. You're a compassionate, caring man. It's one of the many things I love in you."

"I mean, it's not like I've been nursing a flame for her all these years."

"I know."

"Hell, I haven't even thought about her in two decades."

She sat back again. "And that confuses you—how it still can hurt, as if you lost her all over again?"

Like a surgeon probing for physical signs, she'd put her finger exactly on his pain. "Yeah," he admitted. "Since I read about her body being found, I'm all tangled up in feelings from when I was twenty-four. Even though I'm not that young guy anymore, I can't cut myself loose. Weird, eh?"

"Not so weird."

"No? It is for me."

She grabbed his hand again and gave it a squeeze. "Do you want to talk about it?"

"It wouldn't help any. What to do now is the important question."

"How do you mean?"

"The newspaper article I showed you? I'm the mystery man in the cab."

As did most surgeons, Janet had nerves of steel, and even the nastiest surprises couldn't catch her off guard. Yet her pupils pulsed wide. "That was you?"

"Yeah, and maybe the cops haven't taken up the chase just yet, but that Dr. Mark Roper will be trying to pin a face on him."

"Oh, my God."

"So do I go to him or the NYPD and make a clean breast of things before they get to me? As nice as Roper was, he made me nervous."

Though they'd been talking barely above a murmur, she leaned forward close enough to whisper. "And confess you were having an affair with her? That's nuts!"

"It'll be worse if I say nothing and Roper or his sheriff find me out on their own. At the very least they could charge me with obstruction of justice, now that it's officially a murder case."

"And how the hell will you explain not coming forward for twenty-seven years?"

"I had a lot of reasons, some pretty complicated, but I could make them understand."

"Try me first. I'm a lot more sympathetic."

"Okay. For starters, from the very beginning she made me promise never to reveal our affair."

"Jesus, Earl, give me a break!"

"Hear me out. At first I thought she wanted to avoid a scandal. Adultery is no small thing, and back then it was a very big deal. But, no, that wasn't it. She told me later that she really didn't give a damn what people thought, that she worried about Chaz and how he'd react if he ever found out. The possibility of losing her obsessed him, which fueled the abuse, to the point she figured not only did she have to make a clean break—disappear, change her name, and start over—but he must never know about our affair because it might enrage him even more."

"She wouldn't even trust you enough to tell you where she was headed?"

"Refused, but the issue wasn't a lack of trust."

"What then?"

"I told you it was complicated."

" 'Screwy' is the word I'd use, Earl."

"Okay, okay! She wouldn't tell me because she insisted she wasn't going to ruin my life with all her baggage."

"Her baggage?"

"Will you just listen? She knew she'd already jumped into Chaz's arms to escape her parents. As a result, she didn't entirely trust her feelings about me, wasn't sure whether she loved me or was just using me to escape again. She promised to contact me if she ever figured it out and the time was right."

"When the time was right? You've got to be kidding."

"There were other issues, too. Ones that even I hadn't thought of until she warned me."

"Such as?"

"Such as how powerful the Braden family was at the hospital and NYCU. If Chaz ever did find out about me and Kelly, not only would he go after her, she was certain he'd get 'Daddy' to pull enough strings that I'd never graduate from medical school. So she remained adamant I do nothing to risk that happening, such as trying to follow her, and refused to tell me where she'd be in case I might come anyway."

Janet mulled that over a few seconds. "But after no word from her at all, you didn't get suspicious something had happened?"

"Of course! I was frantic. I even took my month's vacation and went searching for her, despite the promise I made. But just like the police said, there were no leads."

"Didn't you ever think then she might have been killed, that her husband had gotten to her after all?"

"At the time I couldn't think of anything else. Whenever I saw Chaz Braden in the hospital, I could barely keep myself from grabbing him by the throat and demanding to know what he did with Kelly."

"Yet you still didn't go to the police."

He felt his cheeks start to burn again at the thought of how he'd floundered around like a complete wimp—so detestably opposite to the man he'd become. "No, I didn't. I made a decision to keep quiet and save my ass."

Janet's eyebrows quirked.

"I'm not proud of it," he continued, "but logically, I couldn't see any point in doing otherwise. The police already suspected Chaz, and were investigating him big-time. Me, Jack, Melanie, and Tommy Leannis—we'd all told the cops everything we knew about her relationship to him, how possessive he could be, and verbally abusive. If I had confessed our affair, it would have taken their attention off him, maybe even shifted it to me, disgraced Kelly, and probably tanked my chances at NYCH. So I kept my mouth shut."

"But when the police didn't make a case against Chaz—"

"I again considered taking matters into my own hands. I even began to follow the creep, waiting for a chance to get him alone."

"My God, Earl—"

"Don't worry. I came to my senses before anything happened. What I saw, the way he ran around, red-faced, pestering everyone in my class, even me, to find out if we knew where she'd gone, I began to think maybe he hadn't done anything to her and couldn't find her either, that she had just run away after all, gotten rid of her ghosts, and didn't see me as part of her life anymore. It took a long time, but eventually I accepted it . . ."

As he talked, he realized just how immature his desire to rescue Kelly had been. Yet he let himself be so stupidly vulnerable back then, enamored by a notion as old as Galahad, Lancelot, and Robin Hood—saving damsels in distress. Talk about naive. What's more, the belief that he'd pulled it off—helped her get away clean from Chaz and freed her from her own ghosts—it was simply the way he needed to see things, the better to sustain himself while he got over her.

Had he learned from his folly? In a way. After all, he went into a career in ER, where he could rescue people from their worst physical catastrophes, after which they'd be whipped out of his department to face their personal demons in the care of others. It was a disconnect that suited him just fine to this day.

He reached for her hand. "I would have helped her differently now. I guess that's part of what's got me so tangled up—knowing I might've made a difference if I hadn't been so clueless."

"You still don't believe Chaz killed her?"

He sighed deeply, as if to exhale his doubts. "I must have been wrong about him, too. His looking for her was probably a cynical act he put on to throw us off. It obviously worked."

She slouched in her seat. Anyone looking at her would have thought she was studying the chandeliers and frowning in disapproval.

"So do I go to the police?" he said after what felt like minutes.

She looked directly into his eyes. "Jesus Christ, Earl, you expect the cops to believe a story like this? Let's see. They couldn't pin anything on

Chaz in 1974. Now they find the body, and you pop up with your tale of being the mystery man, of having been her secret lover, and, what I predict will be their personal favorite, you didn't tell anyone because you've been maintaining a noble silence all these years. They'll fall down laughing, then have a field day twisting it all around so you look guilty as hell. As for what the press would do to you, don't even think about it."

"What's the alternative?"

"Talk to a lawyer."

* * *

He lay wrapped in layer after layer of sleep, the kind that enveloped him only after he and Janet made love.

Yet a ringing drilled into his head.

He felt Janet's leg draped over his, and opened his eyes, expecting to find himself in his own bed.

Instead, ornate swirls on the ceiling of their hotel suite spun like pinwheels in the ever-changing, neon glow from outside the window. He glanced at his watch and saw it was only 10:00 P.M.

After dinner they'd no sooner gone upstairs and closed the door to their room than Janet pulled him to her. "I want us to forget everything, at least for now," she whispered, her lips at his ear.

His own desire had swelled to meet hers, displacing all anxiety, and he lost himself in her arms, for a while.

"Dr. Garnet here," he said, fumbling the receiver to his ear.

"Dr. Garnet, it's Mark Roper calling. I hope it's not too late to disturb you, but I wanted to catch you before you left town. I think you'd be interested in seeing my father's old medical file on Kelly."

"What?"

"It contains a letter describing a man she met, someone she loved."

Garnet felt his heart quicken. "Really."

"I suspect he's the one she got into the taxi with the night before she disappeared."

Earl felt a chasm open at his feet. Into it fell Janet, Brendan, his life. "I see."

"Do you? Shall we have breakfast together to discuss it?"

* * *

A dozen floors below, Mark hung up and stared at the ceiling. Garnet's agreement to meet with him vanquished any doubts he had about him being Kelly's lover. Not bad for a part-time coroner from the sticks. Twelve hours in New York and already he'd uncovered the secret that had stumped the NYPD for twenty-seven years.

He'd followed Garnet and his wife back to their hotel, then booked a room for himself, dumping his plan to return home that night. After reviewing all his files on Kelly, he went down to the hotel's business center, where he spent time on the Internet planning what he would do.

Having successfully completed the next step, hooking Garnet into a tête-à-tête, he felt like celebrating.

Grabbing the phone, he called a number he knew by heart.

"Dr. Caterril speaking," said the woman who answered.

"Hi, Mandy. It's me."

"Mark?"

"The one and only. And how's the most beautiful veterinarian in all of Manhattan?"

"I'm fine, but where are you calling from?" She sounded put out rather than excited.

"The Plaza. I was down here on a coroner's case, but unexpectedly had to stay the night and wondered if we could get together."

Her silence gave him a sinking feeling.

"Well, I would have loved to," she said after a few seconds, "but I can't tonight."

He heard a male voice in the background. Mandy lived alone.

"Of course," he said, immediately casting around for a way to say goodbye without embarrassing either of them. "I just took a chance, never expecting even to find you in on a Saturday night. Stupid of me not to have called before and set something up."

She laughed. "I won't argue with that, Mark."

"Well, next time lots of warning."

"Yes, I'd like that. Perhaps we could have lunch."

Ouch! He'd been demoted. From lover to former boyfriend status, all in an instant, suitable for get-togethers in public places, a greeting kiss on the cheek, but the rest of her body arched safely away from him. "Take care, Mandy."

"You too."

Definitely taken down a few rungs. Well, what did he expect? He hadn't exactly broken her door down with return visits or rung her phone off the hook after her last weekend at Hampton Junction. To be honest, he hadn't bothered because he knew there was no point. Mandy Caterril would never be happy away from her poodle practice in Manhattan. Just like Shauna, the uptown physiotherapist, before her, or Cindy, the TriBeCa theater director, before them.

East Side, West Side, all around the town. The tune popped into his head. Wonderful, beautiful, fun women from every part of the greatest city on earth, and not a hope in hell any one of them could cope with being the mate of a country doctor. As far as they were concerned, he'd made a mistake choosing to practice where he had.

Shit! Enough with the gloomy woulda, shoulda, coulda crap. He didn't feel like just rolling over and going to sleep either. He grabbed the *New York Magazine* by his bed and flipped through the theater section. But it was long past curtain time, both on and off Broadway. Ought to kick himself in the ass for not having planned ahead and at least given himself a show.

Then he had an idea.

A crazy idea, but one that would be exactly the no-strings-attached, one-night-only encounter he felt in the mood for.

"Could you connect me with the home of Dr. Melanie Collins, please," he said, having contacted an operator at New York City Hospital. "It's Dr. Mark Roper."

"The Chief of Internal Medicine?"

He hadn't known that about her. "Is there another Melanie Collins?"

"I'll see if she'll take your call," said the man on the other end. He didn't sound very hopeful.

"Dr. Roper," Melanie said, when he was plugged through to her. "This is a surprise."

"It is for me, too. I had to stay over unexpectedly. If you have time, I wondered if we could continue our conversation about Kelly?"

She gave a throaty chuckle that made more than his hopes rise. "Sure, if you like. But I just ordered some Chinese food. Say, why don't you come on over here and share it with me—they always send too much—and I'll open a bottle of wine."

It was so blatant a response to his overture, despite its being exactly what he had in mind, he went briefly dumbstruck. What was his problem? Seconds ago he'd wanted her to say yes. Now he balked. Why? He certainly had no hang-ups about women who took the initiative, in fact, quite enjoyed them. The age difference? No, he'd been there, too. Yet from the place in his stomach that turned when he encountered a bad taste or a foul smell, he once again felt a slight revulsion. This wasn't right for him. "Oh, thank you, that's really generous, but I've got an early meeting, which is why I'm staying over. I was hoping we could talk on the phone."

"I see." Her tone of voice had cooled to about minus twenty. "Of course. What did you want to know?"

Chapter 7

The wind buffeted Mark as he jogged across Fifth Avenue toward the side entrance of the Plaza, but he didn't feel cold. His run up to the reservoir and back had left him hot and sweaty. A funnel of gold leaves spiraled to the ground and swirled around his feet. Looking over his shoulder to the east, a streak of dawn bright as a polished steel blade hurt his eyes. He hurried inside and, when he got to his room, showered for a long time. Needles of steaming hot water pelted his skull as he lost himself in the din. Then he turned the cold on full.

An hour later he was ready, his head buzzing from the cups of black coffee he'd downed thanks to room service. Carrying his briefcase, he arrived at the Palm Court early only to find Earl already seated at a table reading the Sunday *Herald* while sipping a cup of coffee. Earl looked rested, clear-eyed, and calm—everything Mark wasn't.

He'd been on the Internet until two-thirty, having gone back to learn more about Earl in preparation for their meeting. The man was impressive. Stellar in the field of emergency medicine. A long string of journal publications bearing his name. And a nose for rooting out trouble. More than once he'd made national headlines for his part in exposing deadly malfeasance in the health care field, often at great personal risk. Definitely not the sort to bend under pressure, cow before danger, or compromise to save his own skin. But he might do the right thing on behalf of Kelly.

"Morning," Earl said, appraising him with the thousand-yard stare Mark would expect from someone who'd survived over twenty years in the pit and thrived on it. Gone was any hint of the sadness he'd seen at Kelly's wake. This was a guy on full alert.

Mark slid into the chair opposite. "Morning."

This early on a Sunday the ornate, gold-and-cream room was nearly empty. Waiters in green-striped vests descended on them, handing them menus, filling their water glasses, offering coffee, juice, croissants, jams, and butter, then suggesting a selection of entrées to start.

"I'm fine," Earl said

Mark ordered tea.

The staff retreated, disappointment etched on their faces.

Before Mark could say a word of his carefully prepared intro that he hoped would ease the tension, Earl spoke. "If you're here as a cop, Mark, get on with it, and I don't talk to you without a lawyer present." His voice was calm, his manner pleasant, but his gaze rock hard.

Shit! "Please, Dr. Garnet. I'd prefer we keep this informal, off the record, and that you simply tell me your take on what I found in my father's files."

Earl studied him, eye to eye, but said nothing.

Mark opened the briefcase, retrieved a copy of Kelly's letter from a manila folder, and placed it in front of him. "To begin with, here's what she wrote about you."

Earl regarded it skeptically.

"Just take a look. If you don't feel comfortable talking about any of it, I go my way and do what I have to do. You do the same. But I think we can avoid that."

He didn't make a move.

"Dr. Garnet, I figure there are two possibilities here. Either you're the good man that letter and your record say you are, or you've been a brilliant fraud, and should be made to answer to the police about your affair with Kelly and what part it played in her disappearance. Me, I'm betting on the first."

Earl picked up the sheet of paper and began to read intently, the tension draining from his face. Within moments, he was trying to fight back tears.

*　　*　　*

Her words on paper sounded as clearly in Earl's head as if she spoke them in his ear. From the secret place his memories of her had hidden themselves over half a lifetime ago came a rush of forgotten sensations—the musical sound of her voice, her scent, the electric feel of her fingers on his flesh. And his agony after her disappearance.

> *I've met a man.*
> *A wonderful, caring man who loves me, and I love him.*
> *What a release it is to be cherished, respected, and liked. I feel as if all the other garbage has fallen away, and I'm free, with a new life ahead of me. Whether it will be with him or not, I don't know, but I'm full of hope. I haven't decided yet what to do about it all, and look forward to talking over possible strategies with you. But I am ecstatic!*

In a scar so hardened with time that he barely knew it was there, something gave. It felt as real to him as if withered bands of connective tissue no longer able to hold their burden had split open, and a release he'd never expected to find spread through him. Decades after the doubts stopped mattering, he finally learned she'd loved him.

Logically he knew that after all these years he shouldn't have been affected so deeply. Not until he brought his hand to his mouth in a reflex of disbelief and felt his tears did he realize he'd involuntarily begun to cry. "Excuse me," he said, hastily dabbing his eyes with his napkin. "This took me by surprise."

"I understand."

In Mark's quiet voice Earl recognized the same nonjudgmental tone he'd often used himself to encourage a distraught patient to talk. Damned effective. He found himself wanting to explain his reaction, especially to someone who'd known Kelly. That Mark was also the son of Cam Roper, the man in whom she'd confided, made it seem even more like speaking directly to a link with her. "I thought she just ran out, on me, on medicine, everything. That I loved her more than she loved me. That she simply wanted to disappear . . ." He wiped his eyes again. "Sorry. The human heart can be a sneaky organ."

"We both lost a lot that summer."

Earl tabled the napkin. "Yes, you said she was like a sister to you."

Mark seemed about to say something, but instead reached into his briefcase and placed a file on the table. "This contains photocopies of everything in my father's chart on Kelly." He flipped open the cover. "What do you make of that?"

Earl glanced down at the page and found himself looking at a record of Kelly's visit to Cam Roper as a little girl. Soon hard clinical logic displaced the emotional quicksand of the last few minutes—ER had trained him to make that kind of quick change with personal feelings—and he studied it with his full concentration. Reaching the end, he flipped the paper over. "No follow-up?"

"Apparently not."

He needed only a few seconds to piece together his initial opinion. "I'd suspect the symptoms were functional, possibly stress-related, just as your father did. I'd also agree with his insinuation in the margin that the mother played a big part in the problem. Clearly she ran from doctor to doctor, probably needing excessive reassurances that her daughter was okay. Except . . ." He trailed off, interrupted by the memory of Kelly arching against him, making love with the lights off. Always with the lights off because of the scars. But he could feel them—a bad job by whoever had closed the wounds, both of them being as rough and wide as a small rope. On their first night together when he asked about it, she grew embarrassed. "I had problems when I was a kid. It's over now. Please, don't talk about them. They're so ugly." But of course he'd eventually seen them, catching glimpses in the ambient light through the window and once by a full moon, when she fell asleep lying on her back with the covers half off. They looked like sterling ridges on a silver tray.

"Except what?" Mark asked.

"Those scars bothered her, even into adulthood. I'd say they were left by a surgeon who could have used some practice."

He flipped ahead, seeing entries indicating Cam Roper had provided Kelly with support therapy over several years, from 1970 until 1974. "Obviously these sessions involved other kinds of scars. Invisible ones. God knows Chaz gave her enough cause for grief, and Samantha wasn't exactly a mother of the year."

Mark nodded.

"What are these doing here?" Earl asked, finding what he immediately recognized from their format as reports from NYCH Death Rounds.

"I don't know. I didn't look at them too closely—figured they must have been misfiled."

Earl riffled through them. After years of auditing his own department, he could read the chart of a resuscitation and run it like a movie in his head. He just didn't glean information; he could place himself in the middle of the action and sense whether the team had worked together with grace or in utter discord. Most telling was the order sheet. The time entries indicated what drugs they gave in what sequence and revealed not only whether they'd done the right things, but if they'd been fast enough doing them. In minutes he had both cases pegged and more. "Now we're getting somewhere, Mark."

"Really?"

"Oh, yes." He spread the papers out between them. "First the cases themselves. Both received the right treatment in a timely enough way, but the woman was a close call. Initially, whoever ran the arrest almost fell into the trap of ordering more digoxin. See where the order's been written, then canceled?" He pointed at the appropriate line. "One person figured out what was really going on in the nick of time. After that, everything went like a charm."

"Okay, but that hasn't got anything to do with Kelly—"

"Not so. Look at this signature on one of the orders."

Mark peered at the paper. "I can't make it out."

"Not surprising, given how we all scrawl our names." said Earl. Doctors' signatures were always indecipherable. That's why residents and physicians had to enter their training or license numbers after anything they wrote in a chart. "But some of these stand out to me because we were in a study group together all through med school. I'd recognize them as surely as if I'd gone through a yearbook of old class photos." He picked up the photocopy of Kelly's letter, folded it to the bottom third where she'd signed *Kelly*, and shoved it beside the order sheet. "Recognize the handwriting?"

Mark grabbed both papers and held them up together. "My God, it's her signature!"

"She was there, Mark." He pushed the order sheet for the man who'd died toward him. "And at this patient's resuscitation as well. Her name appears several places."

"My God." Mark looked up from studying the papers. "But you said they managed this guy fine from the get-go, besides the fact he died."

"Right. His was the more typical, straightforward presentation of digoxin toxicity, the usual slow heart rate that, when a patient's on the medication, immediately makes us all think of the right diagnosis. So everybody was on the ball with him."

"So why would my father keep a copy of either case in her file?"

"Look at the staffman's initials on both order sheets."

State regulations demanded that all orders by trainees must be counter-signed by their supervising physicians. Most scribbled only their initials and license number.

Mark once more peered at the entries. "C. B.—Chaz Braden?"

"We can check his license number to be sure, but I'd say that's the reason these files were with your father."

"Because they were Chaz's cases?"

Earl leaned back and took a sip of what by now was cold coffee. "Because Kelly feared Chaz," he said.

Mark stopped midway reaching for his teacup. "Pardon?"

Earl leaned forward. "Think about her preparing to run from a man who might come after her. Maybe she brought his M and M cases to your dad and asked him to check them out, hoping to find if hubby had screwed up, trying to get something that would have given her leverage over him. She might have figured on using it to keep him at bay, making it easier for her to leave." He picked her letter up from the table and pointed to where she'd written:

> *Regarding the other two matters, we must discuss those. What-*
> *ever I plan for myself, I can't leave and let them go unresolved.*

"She could be referring to something her husband did wrong with these two cases."

"But you just said, apart from a close call, they were free from screwups."

"That brings us back to your original question—why your father would bother to hang on to them. He must have still thought something seemed wrong. After all, even a case review can miss mistakes."

"Not often."

"They would if the doctor in question was an amoral son of a bitch intent on covering them up and had successfully falsified the records. Maybe Kelly and your father wanted to subject Chaz's work to a bit more scrutiny."

Earl knew he'd made spectacular leaps in logic to entertain such an extraordinary set of conclusions. He also knew they'd have to go through the original files in their entirety to ever prove what he'd just suggested. Even then, supposing his hunches were correct, they still might not find anything incriminating if Braden had covered his tracks well enough. But this was the first sign that evidence against Chaz might exist after all—evidence that would show he'd made lethal mistakes, then tried to hide them, and that Kelly found out, perhaps confronted him—he grabbed the order sheet from Mark, his excitement growing.

"I think I can make out a few other names from my class. Two of them, Tommy Leannis and Melanie Collins, attended the memorial service. And check this out. According to her signature here, Melanie seems to be the one who counteracted the order for digoxin and saved the day. With the license numbers of the people I don't recognize, I could track them down for questioning as well. Maybe a few of them will tell me whether they remember anything screwy about working with Braden on cases involving digoxin. Most of us recall errors by our former professors, though we wouldn't dare talk about it much at the time." As he spoke, a sense of exhilaration swept through him. After nearly two weeks of holding his breath, helpless to do anything—the worst kind of agony for someone whose every instinct in a crisis is to act—he had something concrete to pursue.

"Wait a minute," said Mark. "I'm the one to follow up on that. You and Kelly weren't as discreet as you think."

"What do you mean?"

"I mean the last thing you need is for one of your former classmates to put two and two together the way I did and nail you as the mystery man. Somebody is liable to do exactly that if you show undue interest in solving Kelly's murder. I can just hear Chaz Braden suggesting the idea that his wife had realized she'd made a mistake having an affair, but you killed her when she tried to break it off. The NYPD would be back in the case and on your ass in a flash."

"And I'll say the mistake she made was to tell Braden she intended to leave him, and he killed her for it."

"Terrific. The cops will throw you both in jail—"

"Mark, I'm doing it, and that's that. The only hope I have of ever getting free of this mess before it destroys my whole fucking life is to catch the real killer, presumably Chaz Braden. The people we need to talk with at NYCH—classmates, nurses, and doctors—they're all of the era when I did my training there. Chances are they'll still consider me one of them and will open up, despite pressure from the Bradens on everyone to keep their mouths shut. Even the ones who think they don't have any information, if I can get them reminiscing, might spill something useful." He turned back to Kelly's file. Nothing but a bunch of newspaper clippings remained. "Now what the hell are these?" he said, picking them up.

Unaccustomed to being opposed or explaining his actions once he'd made up his mind, he considered the issue of who would do what closed. The sooner Mark realized that asking Earl Garnet to stay hands off and lay low was tantamount to telling him not to breathe, the better the two of them would work together.

"Articles about the good works of the Braden bunch," Mark said in a quiet voice, the argumentative tone from seconds ago vanished.

Obviously a fast learner.

Earl skimmed through them as best he could, the faded cuttings not having reproduced well in the photocopier. They seemed unremarkable. "Mean anything to you?" he asked.

Mark shook his head. "Nothing, other than my father saw fit to keep them."

Earl laid them aside. "That's it?"

Mark didn't answer immediately. He still seemed subdued by their little dustup.

Get over it, Earl thought, watching him take another sip of tea.

"Not quite," he said, putting down his cup. "I want to know if Kelly ever talked to you about her relationship with her mother."

"No. She was estranged from her parents, but never seemed to want to talk about it. Why?"

"Twice now Charles Braden has given the impression that he thinks Samantha had a pretty sick relationship with Kelly. At first I thought he was just being manipulative, subtly blowing smoke, trying to take the heat off his son by making us go after her, but seeing the woman's behavior this afternoon, maybe she does bear looking at."

An image of scars the size of ropes popped back into Earl's mind. "After Kelly's disappearance, what did your father say?"

"As I told you after the memorial service, only that she'd gone away."

"Did you ever overhear him suggest Samantha might have harmed her?"

"No."

"What about later, when there was no word from her? Any show of worry from him that maybe something had happened to her, and she didn't run off after all? In other words, was he less blind than the rest of us?"

"There was no later, not for him. As I said before, after Kelly's service, he died that September."

Earl immediately regretted being so curt with the Q&A. "I'm so sorry, Mark."

The younger man's muscular physique seemed to shrink in on itself. "Yeah. I missed him a lot."

Earl instinctively sensed it was his turn to encourage talk. But not by asking questions. Simply by listening.

Mark took another sip of tea. "My mother died two years earlier, meningitis—an accidental stick with a needle from an infected patient— so after his death, my aunt Margaret moved in to raise me." He paused and smiled. "Crotchety, rough as sandpaper on the outside, but someone real special where it counted. I sure knew I was loved . . ."

As Mark talked about his childhood, he noticeably skirted how his father had died, and Earl didn't ask. Losing both parents so close together had to have scarred the boy. Yet here he was, apparently tough-minded, certainly personable, and, Earl suspected, a dedicated doctor. He'd have to be, choosing to work solo in such an isolated place that held so many devastating memories for him. Or maybe keeping to himself was the legacy of what he'd been through.

". . . I didn't take over my father's practice so much as resurrect it. Aunt Margaret, like my mother, had also been a nurse, so when he died, she advertised for a new doctor to come in and replace him. It never happened. His patients ended up going all the way into Saratoga Springs. But as my residency neared the finish, just about everybody in the community besieged me to pick up where he left off." Mark leaned back in his chair and studied the bottom of his cup, momentarily lost in his own thoughts.

"And why did you?" Years of eliciting painful histories from reluctant patients also taught when a nonthreatening prompt or two would keep a person talking.

"Drawn to it, or maybe *lured* is the word. The shrinks would say I was probably looking for the dad I lost by trying to be like him. And for happiness. I had it there, until everything changed."

"Did Aunt Margaret have anything to do with it?"

"I know what you're thinking. That she encouraged me to follow in Dad's footsteps. In fact, she did just the opposite. To her dying breath she made me promise to get out of Hampton Junction. 'Anybody living in hills by choice wants to keep the world out,' she used to say. 'Go and doctor people where they want to let the world in, and you'll be happier.' "

"Was she right?"

He shrugged, still cradling the empty cup. "Depends on what day you ask me. I get to do more in the boonies than I ever would in Manhattan. That makes me strong clinically, and I love that. But I do crave my trips out. It's conferences, ski trips, diving, and theater, whenever I can swing it."

Earl smiled. Mark's openness, even about what must be painful for him, suggested someone rock solid despite his childhood trauma. It also probably meant he didn't get much of a chance to talk about himself. He'd have to be lonely up there, intellectually as well as emotionally, with no colleagues to rub elbows with day to day. "I bet you'd put a lot of us city docs to shame," he said.

"I hold my own. And I do get to teach. Residents often come to me from NYCH for their rural rotation. In fact, one's due in another week or so. That part I love. But sometimes, lately, while I can look straight up at the stars to the end of the universe, the trees and hills close in from the sides so heavily it's like nothing else exists."

Earl never wanted to feel that trapped.

**Later that same Sunday,
11:55 A.M.**

Amtrak's Empire for Albany rolled out of Penn Station and up the shores of the Hudson, first stop Yonkers. Mark managed to find a window seat on the side overlooking the river. As the train wound along its edge, he watched the mighty waterway rush in the opposite direction toward the ocean. He always found release in the transition from the press of New York and trackside buildings to the gentle sweep of bulrushes, distant trees, and faraway hills. He felt it even when the season drew the landscape in bleak, prewinter blacks and browns, and the low sky, laden with snow, ran north like an empty gray highway. The ability to see farther here coupled with the sense of relief of no longer having so many people crowded around inevitably allowed him to breathe easier and think more privately, maybe even more clearly.

The sway of the car rocked him to the edge of sleep, and his mind's eye wandered along images of Samantha and Chaz at odds over Kelly, Melanie Collins eulogizing Kelly, Earl crying over Kelly's letter. How differently he'd begun to see Kelly these last few weeks. A woman who had ducked confrontation with her estranged parents and never resolved the problems that alienated her from them. A woman who ran rather than worked things out—even running from Earl. Someone who sought her sense of self and security through others—the Bradens, Earl, his own father. Even, in a way, through medicine. She must have been driven, succeeding at med school the way she did. No, Kelly was neither the flawless saint who had been put on a pedestal at the service nor the victim who had so enthralled Earl. Instead, he began to construct the picture of a very troubled woman who escaped from one problem directly into another.

The car lurched, startling him from his twilight reverie.

He focused instead on what he and Earl had decided. It was to be a simple division of labor. Earl would do the legwork in New York, despite the risk of singling himself out as a suspect. What a hardnose he'd been about that. Little wonder the guy had such a record for finding trouble. And did he treat everyone as if they were his intern and he'd be in charge? Shit, that had grated. Even so, he liked the man.

For Mark's part, he would use his position as coroner to request the hospital to identify the two patients whose mortality and morbidity reports they'd examined. He'd first try persuasion, falling back on his old ties with NYCH. He'd made a lot of friends there during med school and his residency, some as influential as the Bradens. If that failed, he'd resort to official channels and exert his power of subpoena. Problem was, the process would begin in county court, wind its way through judges in Albany, and probably get him a response from Manhattan by next Easter. Better he get results with honey than have to try vinegar.

He also intended to chip away at Chaz Braden's alibis in Hampton Junction during the week of Kelly's disappearance. The town had its share of people like Nell, with sharp eyes and long memories. One of them might have noticed Chaz when he was supposed to have been in New York.

Earl had suggested it might be useful to stir up local memories, very circumspectly of course, regarding Samantha McShane around that time. Circumspectly indeed . . . with all the nosing around he was going to do under the watchful eyes of Nell and her network.

Not that he'd have trouble getting people to tell him things. One of the burdens of a small-town practice was knowing the secrets of an entire community: the lies, the concealed failures, the hidden disappointments, the masked betrayals, the deeply buried hatreds—all eventually told to him, as surely as the threads of a web led to its center. These days people seemed to feel more comfortable confessing to a physician than to a minister, priest, or rabbi. He figured it had to do with a doctor's obligation to be nonjudgmental.

The train slowed, and the stop for Poughkeepsie, a gray brick station blackened with grime, eventually slid into view. As he watched the people get off, his cellular rang.

"Hey, where are you?" he heard Dan say as soon as he pressed the TALK button. "I expected you back last night."

"You sound like a wife."

"No, just a mother hen."

"Something came up in New York. I'll tell you all about it when I get home. Should be there by three-thirty."

"Would her name be Mandy, by any chance?"

"No, Mother! And if you've nothing better to do than carry on like Nell—"

"Hey, I've been busy. After you showed me all the press clippings your daddy kept on the maternity center and the home for unwed mothers, I got to thinking."

"Yeah?"

"I wondered if he'd had a similar interest as coroner, so I spent this morning going through all the crates of records we got stored in the White House beneath the jail. Sure enough, he saved a couple of boxes of stuff in there about those two places. Considered it important enough to mark Do Not Discard on the side, and nobody did. Looks like death certificates and birth records."

Mark felt his heart quicken. Death certificates from the home for unwed mothers would have come to him routinely because the place fell under his jurisdiction. But the birth records, and anything at all from the maternity center, he would have had to send for specifically.

"Now I can't make head nor tail of them," Dan continued, "but I figure you might be able to tell what he was after."

"I'll swing by the White House and pick them up on my way home."

"There's more. I spent all yesterday looking through the copy of the NYPD file you left me. Their investigation back in 'seventy-four was pretty complete. They even pulled Kelly's phone records from her Manhattan apartment. That's where I found something else interesting."

Dan had to get a life, he thought. This twenty-four/seven stuff might be good for law and order in Hampton Junction, but not for his mental health.

"She made three long-distance calls the morning of her disappearance. The first was to the Braden estate. One of the maids told the police she remembered Kelly asking for Dr. Braden. The maid told her he wasn't in and that Chaz had already left for New York.

"Kelly placed her next call to the home for unwed mothers. No one there remembered it. Maybe she didn't identify herself, the police figured, and was still trying to reach Chaz. He occasionally dropped in at either place on his way to the train and did consults on newborns with heart murmurs. Except that morning he went directly to the station, by his own account. The police checked. The time lapse between the time he and the house staff said he left and how long he had to catch the morning express to Manhattan allowed no detours. So if she did call looking for him, she would have been told he wasn't there either. At least that's what the police report figured."

"Okay."

"Kelly made a third call, this one to the maternity center, presumably still looking for Chaz. Again, no one remembered her phoning, but the police once more didn't make anything of that."

"Where's this going, Dan?"

"That last call cost her four-fifty. The two previous ones less than a dollar. I didn't think anything of the difference at first. Hell, a long-distance minute on hold would have eaten up a buck easy those days, before the breakup of AT&T. But I took a closer look at the record, and found she spent ten minutes on the line. She might have reached him there."

"You mean Chaz Braden lied about going straight to the station?"

"Not only that. If he stopped by the clinic, he would have had to have left the house earlier than he said to make the train at all."

"And the household staff and people at the clinic went along with the lie?"

"Probably because they'd no choice but to protect their boss's son or lose their jobs."

It didn't make any sense. "Why would Chaz risk so many people being able to expose him?"

"The key lie would be his insistence that he hadn't spoken with her since she left the estate bound for New York the day before."

"Any theory about why he wouldn't want the police to know something so mundane?"

"You tell me. But if she talked to him, at last we'd have a chink in that prick's story."

2:30 P.M.
LaGuardia Airport,
New York City

"Hope you don't have stinky feet," Earl said to Janet, watching the security officers make a lineup of passengers take off their shoes. The roar of a departing plane blistered the air, making him raise his voice.

"Smart-ass!" She stepped in close to him, took his face between her hands, and gave him a long soft kiss on the lips. "You be careful," she whispered in his ear.

"I love you, and give Brendan a hug for me."

"You bet. And you call to give me an update every night."

He grinned at her. "Sure."

"It's not funny, Earl. You make your poking around too obvious, and I'll end up reading your name in the *Herald. Mystery Lover Found.*"

"Come on."

"Come on, yourself. Chaz Braden looked like a big vulture, hanging around at the memorial, eavesdropping on everyone. He'd love to find out whom she met in that taxi and shift suspicion from himself. And from the angry expression on his face whenever he glanced in your direction, I'd be afraid he already suspects that you were having an affair with his wife."

"If you asked me, he looked pissed off at all Kelly's old friends. He probably thinks it could be any of them. Otherwise, he would have served me up to the cops by now."

"My, aren't you reassuring?"

He grinned down at her, tightening his embrace. "You look beautiful."

"What I am is frustrated. There are leads Mark Roper should be following that have nothing to do with her old friends and needn't put you in danger."

"Like what?"

"I've been thinking about Kelly, and there's a piece missing. The first thing a woman in her predicament would do is arrange a divorce. Back then, God knows where she'd have had to go. Reno, maybe? Mexico? The Dominican Republic? Did you try that angle when you looked for her?"

"No, I never thought of it."

"A man wouldn't. You tell that Mark Roper he should see if she got that far. It might help him piece together her movements before she died. He has to do that, at least, if he hopes to find new evidence to prove hubby or mommy or whoever killed her."

"I'll tell Mark."

The boarding call for her plane came over the PA.

"Good-bye, love," she said, giving him a second kiss even softer than the first. "And don't forget. Call me every night, be careful of Chaz Braden, and talk to Mark about what I said."

He pressed her to him, savoring how slight and yielding she felt beneath her coat. "Yes! Now go."

She stepped into the inspection area, slipped off her shoes, and stood with her arms wide, ready to be electronically frisked. On the outside she looked remarkably calm. But he knew otherwise. Whenever she felt really scared, she started giving him instructions.

4:00 P.M.
Hampton Junction

Mark knew someone had been in his house the minute he stepped in the door.

Little things were out of place.

The separation between coats and jackets in the front hall closet had changed. A week ago he'd moved the summer ones to the back and the winter gear to the front, so the positions of those items remained fresh in his mind.

Someone also appeared to have gone though the pockets, the material of a few being pulled almost inside out.

In the former living room, where he'd set up his waiting area, the phone and clock on an end table weren't in their usual positions. He kept the face of the latter at an angle so everyone could see the time from any chair in the room, the phone placed off to one side so as not to obstruct the view. Instead they were placed one in front of the other.

Growing increasingly alarmed, he rushed into his office, which had once been the dining room.

All his computer equipment remained in place. The usual stack of unopened mail alongside a pile of unsent billings and recent test results that needed to be put in their proper files—he was weeks behind in his paperwork—were where he'd left them. Turning to the steel cabinets in which he kept patient records, he found them locked. No marks on the metal casings suggested an attempt to force them open.

Thank God, he thought, looking around the room, unable to see anything missing. The adjacent examining room also seemed undisturbed. *The drug cabinet,* he thought, and ran to the back room, where he'd installed a medium-sized safe to store a supply of narcotics—codeine, percodan, and morphine—along with other controlled medications such as tranquilizers.

He found it intact.

Nor had there been any obvious attempt to tamper with it.

So what could an intruder have been after if it wasn't computer equipment or drugs?

A third possibility crept to mind as insidiously as a chill. What if anything of interest was still here because the thief hadn't finished robbing him?

He went very still.

The house itself didn't creak tonight since the wind was light. He heard nothing else.

Had the person escaped?

Either the kitchen's back door or the basement door could have been forced? Or one of the ground-floor windows could have been broken.

He pulled out his cellular and called Dan. He'd just left him at the White House, having already picked up the boxes of birth records.

"Someone's been in my house," he whispered as soon as the sheriff answered.

"Mark?"

"Yeah."

"Jesus, is anything missing?"

"Not that I can tell in my office or living room. I haven't checked the rest."

"Why are you whispering—Jesus Christ! Is the person still there?"

"I don't know."

"I'm on my way. Get out of there, Mark! Wait in your Jeep with the doors locked. Better still, drive to a neighbor's." He hung up.

Good idea.

Except it would take Dan at least ten minutes to get here. That might let whoever it was get away, free to try again.

Tiptoeing back into his examining room, he looked around for a weapon. He kept hammers and axes in the basement. All he could think of to defend himself with was his largest syringe and needle.

So armed, he crept out of his office and silently made his way to the kitchen. Peeking through the swing door, he saw nothing.

He stepped through.

Nobody.

He made his way to the stairs and started up to the second floor, trying not to recall old black-and-white movies where the killer lurked in the dark at the top of the landing. He raised his needle, holding it out in front of him at arm's length.

No one jumped him.

One by one he checked the bedrooms.

Empty.

That left one other possibility.

At the same time he heard the distant wail of Dan's siren.

He quickly descended to the first floor, ran back into the kitchen, and threw open the door to the basement. Figuring Dan would be here any moment, he went on the offensive.

Flipping up the switch, he flooded the darkness below with light, and yelled, "Okay, you! The cops are at the door, and I'm armed. Identify yourself now!"

The only sound was Dan's siren getting closer.

"Do you hear that? Now give up and come out."

Still no response.

Emboldened, he started down into the single big room. Within seconds he'd checked out the few nooks and crannies where someone could hide.

Not a soul.

Beginning to wonder if he'd been mistaken about an intruder, he turned to go back upstairs.

And saw the coat he'd laid across the bottom of the basement door over a week ago.

It lay pushed to one side, the way it would have been if someone had come in, and, it being dark, not realized it was there. He walked over and tried the door. It was locked, but the mechanism had to be a half century old and could have been easily picked, then locked again on the way out.

He stood there wondering what his uninvited visitor might have wanted and found himself staring at a wall of boxes—his father's old files.

Oh, shit, he thought, quickly crossing over to check. They appeared just as he'd left them, but with a queasy feeling he pulled open the one containing the original records on Kelly. Chaz Braden could have over-heard his conversation with Earl Garnet at the reception about having found old files on her. Had he thought it might contain something incrimi-nating and tried to steal it?

Almost to his surprise he located the folder exactly where he'd left it. He flipped through the contents to verify nothing had been taken. The record of Kelly's first visit as a little girl—check; Kelly's letter—check; notations of psychological counseling—check; two dig toxicity case reviews—check; newspaper articles—check. Nothing missing.

Crazy idea anyway, he chided himself. It would have been too obvious a move, even for a klutz like Chaz.

He was returning the folder to its slot when he thought, *Wait a minute.* He'd kept the contents in the same chronological order he'd found them. Done it out of habit. Doctors always kept the contents in each section of a file, from clinical notes through consults and special entries to test results, in the sequence they were received. It made it easier to review and follow a case that way. His father would have done things the same. It was no ac-cident Kelly's letter had followed after the entries for psychological coun-seling, because that would have been the order his father received it. And after photocopying the file Mark had put it back in that same place. Yet just now he'd found it in front of the entries for psychological counseling.

Someone had definitely gone through Kelly's file.

Chapter 8

Dan sipped at his coffee. "You're sure nothing's missing?"

"Nothing." Mark downed his tea in a gulp and refilled the cup from a blue pot big enough for ten. Seated at the kitchen table, he grew impatient with Dan. "He checked to see what information I had on her."

"But I can't just accuse Chaz Braden of looking at your files because you think one piece of paper was out of order."

"I know it was out of order, Dan. I'm meticulous about not mixing up the pages of a medical file. Of course Chaz did it. Who else would care?"

"I don't know. But if someone busted in here, he did the neatest job of breaking and entering I've ever seen."

"He came in here. That coat on the basement floor didn't move itself."

"But the locks haven't a mark on them. No forced windows. Not so much as a missing pane of glass. If you weren't obsessive about your papers, we'd have never suspected anyone was here. I doubt Chaz Braden has those kinds of skills."

Mark's stomach muscles tightened. "Maybe he hired somebody. Besides, anyone could have picked that basement lock."

"It would take a real expert not to leave at least a scratch or two. And how would Chaz even know you had Kelly's old medical file?"

"He must have overheard me telling Earl Garnet."

Dan sighed and took another sip from the mug with the caption SLOWLY APPROACHING FORTY written on the side. Mark always reserved it for his visits. "If you made better coffee," he said, pulling a sour face and pushing out of his chair, "I'd stick around. As it stands, I figure the ghost who broke in here is long gone. But I do suggest you get a better lock on the basement door."

He thanked Dan for coming and saw him to the door. As for his assertion the intruder was long gone, that could be, but Mark dug out his old baseball bat from the basement and put it in the front closet, just in case.

He laid out the contents of Kelly's file on his kitchen table sheet by sheet, like a deck of cards in a game of solitaire. Then he went over and over them. He still couldn't see any patterns or sequences by which he could connect one to the other.

Only guesses.

Such as the reason his father saw Kelly for therapy. The logical assumption—she'd been working through her problems with Chaz, or maybe even her unresolved issues with her parents. But why five years? Most support therapy interventions went on for twelve months, sometimes twenty-four, unlike psychoanalysis, in which the progress got measured in decades.

Or how *the other two matters* she'd mentioned in her letter—*I can't leave and let them go unresolved*—might tie in with the discrepancies in her phone bill. Suppose she actually reached Chaz at the maternity center and threatened to go public about the M and M cases if he didn't let her go. That call could have been what got her killed. It would certainly be a conversation Chaz would not want revealed. If that were the case, however, wouldn't it have been simpler for him just to admit she'd contacted him, then make up some benign story about what was said? He shouldn't have had to risk an elaborate lie and claim he never even spoke with her. No, there had to be some other explanation.

But empty theorizing wouldn't get him anywhere. He needed some way to check out his hunches.

He shifted his gaze to the morbidity-mortality reports that seemed to be so in order and looked at where Melanie Collins's signature appeared.

Last night over the phone she'd gone on at length about Chaz. A lot of what she said was, "Kelly told me he berated her night and day . . . Kelly said his rages frightened her . . . Kelly felt repulsed when he wanted sex." Maybe Kelly also confided how Chaz mismanaged his patients. Or perhaps Melanie had seen for herself.

But would Earl mind if he called her, after being so explicit about dealing with his former classmates himself? Surely not. That was for people like Tommy Leannis, who clammed up to outsiders.

He dialed her number and got a busy signal.

Try again later.

In the meantime he went back out to the Jeep and carted in the boxes that Dan had discovered in the White House. Now why the hell had his father collected all these? he wondered, first unpacking what amounted to stacks of birth records from the home and laying them out in piles on the floor. At least they were already in chronological order, spanning the years from 1955 to 1975. He made a quick estimate of the total by counting out one hundred of the documents, then using the height of them as a measure. Approximately thirty-two hundred women delivered their babies over the twenty-year period, a good two-thirds of them in the first decade of operation. Each record had a six-digit number, same as a hospital chart, but carried no identifying information about the mother other than her age and area code. The personal data, he figured, must have been kept separate for confidentiality reasons. Flipping through them, he saw that most of the women had been young, some lived in upstate New York, but the majority came from New York City. The specifics as to the infants—sex, physical status at birth, the presence of any congenital defects—was standard. The death certificates—he'd thumbed through only twenty-one of those for the home—were in keeping with the number of babies he would have expected to die, given the perinatal mortality rate of seven per thousand that prevailed at the time. The papers also indicated that a great majority of the infants became wards of the state in public orphanages, yet in a separate pile, the records showed that the home arranged private adoptions for 180 of the babies. The bottom line—everything seemed in impeccable order.

Next he laid out the birth records for the maternity center in Saratoga Springs. There'd be no site to visit there. Dan had stuck in a note saying the building had been torn down in the 1980s, replaced by a health spa.

The height of this pile reflected nearly double the number of births at the maternity center as compared to the home, six thousand by his estimate. But the place had approximately the same number of infant deaths, only twenty to be exact. Money and good prenatal care halved the going rate for mortalities.

He spent the next few hours meticulously studying the documents but still couldn't find anything wrong. Another time, perhaps, when he wasn't so tired, and he began to gather up the papers, wondering if for now he shouldn't lock everything in the White House for safekeeping. But having had virtually no sleep for thirty-six hours, he settled on putting the records in his drug safe instead.

His gut started to burn like an overused muscle, the result of too much tea, no supper, and a whole lot of frustration. He made himself a sandwich and poured a glass of milk.

This time when he called Melanie, she answered on the first ring.

"Hello?"

She sounded tired.

"Hi."

"Mark! Are you still in New York?"

"No, I've retreated back to the woods."

"Ahhh—that's a waste."

"I know." He laughed.

"I'd like to see you," she replied.

"Next time I'm in town."

"Mark, I could use some country air." It sounded like an order.

Whoops! "Great. Let's arrange it sometime. But after hunting season's over. It's like a remake of *Deliverance* around here right now." What were white lies for but to let everyone back out of embarrassing corners with feelings intact?

She gave her throaty chuckle. "How about a couple of weeks from now?" she persisted.

Oh, brother. On second thought, why not just have her come? Like nuts to the squirrels, it would give Nell and company enough to chew on the whole damn winter. "Melanie, I have to ask you something. Do you mind if we talk business a sec?"

"Shoot!" Her voice had snapped to attention.

"I've been going over old records related to Kelly's death, specifically my father's old medical chart on her. In it I found photocopies of M and M reports on two cases of dig toxicity in 1974, the year of her disappearance. Her name was on the order sheets, as well as yours. And get this, the staff person initialing the orders was hubby Chaz."

"Really?"

"Yeah. I don't know what to make of them or why they'd be there. I wondered if maybe Kelly asked my father to review the cases because she thought there was wrongdoing somewhere."

"On the part of whom?" She sounded astonished.

"Her husband. I thought perhaps she'd been looking for something to hold over his head in order to keep him at bay, as part of her plan to leave him."

Silence reigned for a few seconds. "I see. I suppose that makes sense."

"What I wanted to know, Melanie, was if you can recall anything suspect about Chaz Braden's clinical work that year. In particular, do you re-member any issues around his management of patients on digoxin?"

"Not generally. Do you know the patient names?"

"Not yet. I only have chart numbers."

She chuckled yet again, the tone a pitch higher this time. "Sorry. You'll pardon me if I don't recall all the cases I wrote orders on. Will you be looking up the original charts?"

"No, Earl Garnet's getting those—" He could have kicked himself. Blurting out to the likes of Melanie Collins that Earl was helping him—what an asshole move. More than anyone, with her intuition about Kelly being in love, she could nail Earl as the man. God, he sucked like an ama-teur at this sleuthing stuff. "I needed someone who'd been in her class to question her contemporaries," he quickly added. "Had to twist his arm, yet he finally agreed."

"But Mark, I could have helped you."

Yikes. "Oh, I knew you would, Melanie. The thing is, since I'm basi-cally questioning if Chaz's competency was an issue back then, the in-quiry could get nasty, and I thought it better to ask someone well beyond the long arm of the Bradens." Amazing how quickly he could come up with a credible lie when he had to.

"Chaz isn't the brilliant man his father is," Melanie said, after a long si-lence. "But he makes up for it by being fastidious. Drives people nuts, the way he always double-checks and micromanages things, yet by putting in long hours does get things done. A real workaholic. So let's just say he wouldn't be chief without 'Daddy' pulling the strings. But out and out negligence? No way. Not even 'Daddy' could cover that up these days."

"What about in 'seventy-four?"

"I don't know. Maybe. Those days he was only a few years out of a cardiac residency and up-to-date in his training, so he appeared to do pretty well. As son of the big man, he certainly got the benefit of any doubts over his clinical abilities. I don't think anyone in the hospital besides his father and friends of Kelly knew about his weekend drinking then. We only learned of it through her and what we saw for ourselves at parties up there. The truth is, most people at NYCH didn't even realize what a bastard he was until much later."

"So there could have been more chance of an error by him going unde-tected in 'seventy-four?"

"It's worth a thought, isn't it? Certainly no one would have been keep-ing a suspicious eye on him. Listen, Mark, I have to go. Rounds start at seven, and Monday's always a monster for consults in the ER. When you know the names of those patients, give me a call. And I'm penciling in a visit with you for two weeks from now."

He thanked her and said good night. The first thing that came to mind after hanging up had nothing to do with the case.

If he kept picking the Melanies of the world, he told himself, he might turn into another Collins—a middle-aged physician coming on to horny, lonely thirtysomethings for sex and company. The thought gave him the creeps. Yet if someone as successful and good-looking as she could end up that way . . .

He eyed his desk. Paperwork and unopened mail, never something he attended to promptly in the best of times, had piled up more than usual since Kelly's body had been found. And he had his own monster day tomorrow, the weeks before the snow flew always being a busy period, his elderly patients needing flu shots and final checkups before they tucked themselves in for the winter. Tucking in . . . exactly what he needed to do for himself. He was beat. He detoured by the closet, then took himself and his trusty bat to bed.

Monday, November 19, 8:30 A.M.
New York City

The rhythmic electricity in the streets of Manhattan never changed for Earl. Even in old thirties movies Fred Astaire could be dancing along Times Square, and in the background there would be the purring motors, strident horns, thousands of teeming footsteps and bobbing heads, all syncopated to the buzz of chattering voices and leaving little doubt where Busby Berkeley or Gershwin got their inspiration. These days, he figured, those same rhythms spawned the beat to hip-hop, but the sound remained the same, and it washed over him as he walked down Second Avenue toward New York City Hospital.

Standing in the building's shadow, waiting for the red to change at the intersection of Thirty-third, he closed his eyes. The familiar cacophony carried him back in time, to the point he imagined he would open his eyes again to find Kelly, Melanie, Tommy, and Jack at his side, impatiently waiting at that same stoplight, fretting about morning rounds.

He blinked and was alone. The two who were dearest to him in those days were dead—Jack, his closest friend, who'd sacrificed his life for him, and Kelly. Tommy had parlayed his B-student vexations into the stuff of a grade-A whine-ass, and Melanie, always a coquette, had apparently become the female counterpart to a roué.

The light changed, and he started across, huddled in his raincoat as wind and drizzle gusted up Thirty-third from the East River.

The cement-and-glass structure where he'd been forged into a doctor loomed over him, its upper stories lost in fog. For an instant it reclaimed the hold it used to exert on his nerve, jacking up his heartbeat and giving the acid in his stomach a stir before it just as quickly became simply another hospital, no different from the hundreds he'd visited in various official capacities throughout his long career.

Still, when the sliding doors opened to receive him, and hospital smells assaulted his nose, he felt caught in the crosscurrents of then and now.

Security was as meticulous as in his own St. Paul's, the officers checking photo ID, scanning him down for metal, even having him remove his shoes. "No stinky feet," he murmured, smiling to himself and missing Janet after his night alone in the hotel.

His grin must have made him look suspicious because a frowning guard gave him another extrathorough once-over with his wand before sending him through. But they did have his visitor's badge waiting. Mark had obviously been on the job as far as greasing the administrative wheels.

He set out for medical records, pushing through the rush of white-coated students, interns, and residents, all scurrying after the flapping white coats of their appointed staff person and engaged in the constant banter of questions and answers that had been the method of choice for teaching medicine since the days of Socrates.

"What's the differential of a solitary swollen red joint?" demanded an elegant gray-haired woman leading her pack into the outpatient's department.

"Traumatic, inflammatory, septic," a blond young man with the shortest clinical jacket in the group snapped back at her.

"Very good. Now what's the most likely diagnosis in the inflammatory category?"

"Which joint?" demanded a woman with red hair pulled back in a ponytail.

The staff woman's eyes arched in a show of approval. "Good question. The case we're about to see involves a knee."

"Gout," the redhead said without hesitation.

The group disappeared through a swinging door.

Earl passed a treatment room off ER where another youthful trainee, this one masked and gloved, frowned mightily as he wielded a suture and hemostat over a child's lacerated cheek. Pulling the knotted thread tight, he reached for scissors on a sterile tray, fumbled them, and they fell to the floor. Glancing around, he quickly retrieved them and brought them back into his sterile field.

It's not my turf, Earl tried to tell himself, then thought, *What the bloody hell!* "Excuse me," he said, sticking his head in the door before contaminated steel touched flesh. "Get a new set and change your gloves!"

The young man went crimson behind the white mask, even his ears turning scarlet. "Yes, sir!" he said.

Earl watched him comply, then added, "You pull that again in this lifetime, I'll personally bounce you from the program." Without waiting for a reply, he turned back into the corridor, but not so quickly that he missed the who-was-that-mean-ass frown appear on the would-be doctor's brow.

Memory led him the rest of the way through the labyrinth of elevators, stairwells, and hallways to the lower levels where, in the bottom layer, like a sediment of secrets, a low-ceilinged subbasement the size of a city block held a half century's worth of clinical files.

"A tomb," Kelly had once called it, striking a dramatic pose, "where the fates of a million souls are stored."

The place gave him the creeps. There had been perks, however, to their working down here on chart audits, usually at night and often alone. Earl smiled, recalling how they had sometimes put the maze created by rows and rows of shelves loaded with charts to good use, quietly engaging in a few secrets of their own.

A plump, gray-haired receptionist greeted him at the front desk. "Ah yes, Dr. Garnet, Dr. Roper had us prepare what you have clearance to review." Bifocals dangled from around her neck on a gold chain and a pin depicting Snoopy holding a paw to his mouth, the bubble caption reading SHHH!, decorated her collar. "Here is the woman's chart; it's still active. As you'll see, she's had a ton of visits over the years, and is now a patient in our geriatric wing. Been here three months. Unfortunately, you won't be able to talk with her. She had another stroke thirteen days ago."

"A stroke?"

"Bessie McDonald's her name. Tragically she's in a coma. We got permission from her family for you to look at her charts, provided you promise to inform them what it's all about, especially if you find anything. I've attached her son's phone number to the front cover. He lives in California."

A coma. Terrific! "Certainly I'll notify them—"

"When I called, both he and his wife were overcome with curiosity about why you'd be interested in her case."

"Well, thank you for your trouble—"

"Oh, no trouble at all. When our CEO tells me to do what I can in helping out a coroner, I don't spare any effort." She popped her glasses onto the tip of her nose, looked at him over the top of the frames, and gave him a knowing wink. "Especially when it has to do with a twenty-seven-year-old murder case."

Jesus, so much for keeping his purpose here confidential. "Look, I don't know who you heard that from—"

"Oh, come now, Dr. Garnet, I can put two and two together. Dr. Roper's the coroner investigating Kelly McShane's death, and the attending physician for the specific admission you wanted to check was Dr. Chaz Braden. What else could it be about, though I can't imagine what the link might be . . ." She trailed off, clearly hoping he'd fill her in on the details.

"You don't tell that to anyone else, understand?" Earl said instead, astounded someone so chatty could be chief guardian in an area bound by law to be a hub of confidentiality.

Her eyes opened wide with astonishment. "That's the last thing you need to worry about." She spoke with the you-can-trust-me sincerity of someone who actually believed her own lies. "Now as for the deceased man, his chart is in the microfilm library. It's at the far end of the main hall—"

"I know. I did my training here and can find it okay."

She grinned at him. "Of course. But you don't remember me, do you?" She held out her hand. "Lena Downie. I was a clerk back then. Now I run the joint." She gestured behind her where the administrative offices were. One of the doors had her name on it "You were one of the bright lights around here. And you've done well. I've read in the papers about your exploits."

Earl felt his cheeks grow warm as he took her plump fingers in his palm and gently gave them a shake. "Thank you. But I'm sorry I don't recall—"

"Don't think anything of it. I was a skinny young woman back then. I'm a grandma now. So what's the connection between these cases and Kelly's murder?"

"Dr. Roper asked me to help out on a matter, and I'm not at liberty to discuss it." Polite words, but his tone said, "None of your business!"

"I remember Dr. Roper, too," she said, her armor not even dented by his reproach, "though he was here much more recently. A fine young physi-cian. I also met his father once. He was a real gentleman as well."

"Really," Earl said, wondering what it would take to shut her up. He picked up the chart, all four volumes of it, each three inches thick—*War and Peace* looked slim by comparison—and carried them to a nearby desk.

"Yes. It was around the time you were a student here. I remember be-cause I'd only been on the job a few months and got in trouble because I gave him a couple of charts to look at. He'd showed me his identification, and I thought it sufficient, his being a doctor and a coroner, without real-izing he wasn't on staff here. I nearly got fired over it. He was super though. Took all the blame—said that he hadn't thought to go through channels and should have known better. Saved my skin, I tell you."

Earl came to a standstill. "You remember what year that was?"

"Of course. Summer of nineteen seventy-four, when I first started. That was also the time when Kelly Braden disappeared. Was Dr. Roper Senior investigating that case, too?"

"Too?"

"Boy, that was some story back then, with all the speculation going on about what had happened to her, pointing fingers at Dr. Chaz Braden. I be-gan to think this hospital was like Peyton Place. Wouldn't have worked anywhere else. So come on, tell me. What have these two charts to do with Kelly?"

God, there was no stopping her. He figured any chance of keeping a low profile among anyone else within earshot had just died as well. But there might be an upside to this woman's appetite for other people's business. "You've got quite a memory, Lena."

"People think working in records must be the dullest thing. Hey!" She gestured to the rest of the building stacked above them and leaned toward him. "Everything of importance that happens in this Casablanca comes through my domain." She'd finally lowered her voice.

He took a look around. As far as he could see they were alone. At least he'd caught a break in that regard. But the stacks ran deep, and any num-ber of people could be back in there. "I bet you don't miss much either," he whispered, still not willing to risk being overheard and hoping she'd take the cue.

She gave him a wink. "You got that right." She'd dropped to a register suitable for a conspiracy.

"Maybe you could help me."

She grinned. "Maybe."

"I know it was a lot of years ago, but do you remember when exactly Dr. Roper's father came here looking for the charts he was after that summer?"

Her smile lit up the entire basement. Obviously she enjoyed the intrigue. "How could I forget when it almost cost me my job? Toward the end of August, about two weeks after Kelly disappeared." A look of astonishment swept over her face. "My gosh, had he discovered something?"

Earl ignored the question. "Any way you could find out what charts you gave him?"

Her expression faded, and she sadly shook her head. "Sorry. I never really looked at them."

That would have been a bit of a long shot, he admitted. Nevertheless, the rest of story intrigued him.

He began to repeat his insistence that she not mention what they'd talked about to anyone when she squinted into the air as if trying to make out something not readily visible. "Wait a minute," she said. "I do recall an interesting detail about those files. Never would never have remembered it if you hadn't got me thinking. He asked for the charts the same way young Dr. Roper did this morning. Didn't have the names, only the numbers. And something else similar. I remember having to fish one of them out of the DECEASED section back then, exactly like now." She tapped her temple and gave him a knowing wink. "One alive. One already dead. Makes you wonder if I haven't just given you those same two files, doesn't it?"

He found a table off in a corner, opened the first volume, and began to read. The jumble of pipes running overhead groaned and clanked, exactly the way they had a quarter century ago, and the air ducts filled his ears with a rushing noise, making them seem plugged with water. He shivered, feeling as cut off and claustrophobic as when he'd been a student.

A particularly forlorn moan raced through the plumbing and traveled the length of the room.

Like an angry spirit, Earl thought.

That same day, 3:50 P.M.
Twenty Miles North of
Hampton Junction

"A woman having to give up her baby, now that's a misery of the worst kind," Nell said, grimacing as if she'd just tasted something sour. The lines ringing her face deepened into a map of disgust. "All those girls up there, shamed into hiding, simply because they fell in love with the wrong man at the wrong time."

"Did you know anybody who worked there?" Mark asked.

"Nobody who's still alive. The heyday of the place was in the fifties, before the pill. You'd be surprised at the number of women who had to find so-called homes like that, or worse, deal with some butcher in a back room with a pair of knitting needles. Thank God the kids in the sixties freed sex from the prudes."

He knew from experience that to get anything from Nell, he had to first let her ramble about whatever was on her mind—her way of downloading mentally to make room for whatever he had on his mind. As she talked, he idly gazed around the interior of her living room. The log walls were aged a deep brown, but she'd kept them polished to a rich luster with wood oils. Small windows, a necessity to keep out the cold in the era before thermal glass, prevented what little afternoon light remained from making its way inside. Yet the place wasn't gloomy. A fire in the stone hearth at their feet provided its own special illumination, and oil lamps—tall, elegant, and bright enough to read by—filled the house with a golden glow. Not that the cabin didn't have electricity. Her son put in recessed lighting along with baseboard heaters decades ago, yet she favored the softness of flame.

To his left a partially drawn curtain hung over the entrance to an adjacent room, where a brass bed covered with a handmade quilt—any antique dealer would kill for it—filled most of the space. Photos of her children and grandchildren adorned the walls. She'd positioned them so they kept watch on her while she slept. Off to one side a small extension housed a modest bathroom with an old-fashioned steel tub.

At his right a doorway opened into an equally tiny kitchen dominated by a magnificent woodstove. On it she'd prepared meals for her two children during the years she raised them alone, her husband having been killed in the Battle of the Bulge during the final months of World War II.

Even now she preferred its steady heat for baking to the gas range that her daughter had had installed so she needn't haul wood anymore.

That someone so old should live in such isolation appalled a lot of people in town, including the county social worker. Yet her son and daughter, each living on an opposite corner of the country, never pressured Nell to put herself in a home, and Mark supported the decision. He also certified her fit to drive the Subaru station wagon parked outside, provided she passed a road test in Saratoga each year. Geriatric wards, he thought. However much they dressed them up with balloons, sing-alongs, and bingo, they were death row, and definitely not for her. One day somebody would find her lying where she fell, and he'd make a final house call. Better that than sentencing her to die a day at time. It was the kind of judgment call that kept physicians second-guessing themselves, and every snowstorm he worried about her falling or lying helpless somewhere, unable to use the panic button she wore around her neck.

". . . back then, if you loved the wrong man at the wrong time, you were treated worse than a murderer." She ended with a cackle that might have split stone.

"When I phoned to invite myself for a chat today, Nell, you said you could tell me secrets about that home for unwed mothers."

"Supposing I did. Maybe I just said that to lure you here because I like your visits. Have some more tea." Before he could decline, she'd refilled his cup to the brim with tea she'd made from leaves, not a bag. "And a scone," she added, waving a platter of them fresh out of the oven under his nose. "Remember what I said about being good in the kitchen?"

He grinned, and took one. "Umm . . . that's scrumptious." He was swallowing as he spoke. "You must have been something in the bedroom, Nell," he added, figuring he could indulge her raunchy sense of humor for once.

She smiled, and for a second there flashed as youthful a sparkle as he'd ever seen in her eyes. "My husband and I were very much in love, Mark," she said in all earnestness. "Like your mom and dad. They had that special thing, too." She sat erect, proud, like a queen on a throne, secure where she'd reigned supreme as a mother and wife.

Any doubts Mark had about letting her stay here until the end of her days vanished in that instant, at least until the next big snowstorm.

An easy silence fell between them. He took it as permission to get on with his questions. "So tell me, Nell, did you ever hear anybody who worked in the home hint at shady stuff going on?"

"You mean illegal? No, not that I can think of."

"Then what secrets did you mean?"

"The local love nests, who did it with whom, and which ones ended up with a love child. But I'm not telling you any names. Oh, I know some of the other dried-up old biddies around town might like talking about that stuff, having nothing better to do for sex. Not me. There's no pleasure to be had in raking over that kind of heartache."

"You knew local women who had babies there?"

She paused before answering. "I knew of a few."

"Did you ever talk to any of them about it? How they were treated? What it was like?"

She grimaced. "Yeah, I talked to one. Talked to her a lot. She . . . she was a friend of mine."

"And what did your friend say?"

"What do you think she said? It broke her heart. She felt sad and cried all the time. Was miserable."

"Can you tell me any specifics? What she told you they put her through?"

Nell fixed her gaze on the fire and took a sip of tea.

Mark had learned long ago that unlike most small-town gossips who gave as good as they got when it came to passing on juicy tidbits, she preferred to hoard her information and force others to coax it out of her, thereby increasing the value of her revelations. But the look of distaste on her face told him her reluctance to talk now was sincere. For a moment he feared she might not tell him anything at all. "Look, I don't need to know her name. Just what she said about how the place operated."

Nell hadn't appeared to hear him. Just when he'd resigned himself to not learning anything helpful, she said, "The worst moment was when they whipped the baby away without letting her see it. She didn't even know if it was a boy or girl."

Mark said nothing, hoping she'd continue.

"Afterward she spent most of her time in her room. They gave a woman a couple of weeks to recuperate back then. She could have gone outside to walk, but could hear the babies crying through the open windows in the nursery. They kept them on a separate floor, away from the mothers, of course, but they didn't ship them off to the orphanage or hand them over to adoptive parents right away. 'To let them stabilize,' one of the nurses told her when she asked why. Knowing she might be listening to her own child proved too much. The crying noises began to sound like screams.

Even in her own room the sound came through, but there she could at least bury her head in a pillow to keep from hearing it . . ."

Nell's words reinvoked the slimy cold sensation he'd felt while standing in the desolate remains of that delivery room. It was all legal, though, charitable even, according to the times, and Nell probably wasn't going to tell him anything that would explain his father's interest in the home. Nevertheless, he settled back, sipped his tea, and continued to listen, just in case.

". . . even little things she found to be a humiliation, such as how her file was red, and all the other women's were green, to tag her as a local. Someone told her, 'It's for your own protection, so we can keep your records in a special lockup, away from the prying eyes of any staff who live nearby and might know you.' I suppose the idea made sense, but it just added to her feeling she had something to be ashamed about."

Mark shook his head at the sorrow of it all, then changed the topic to what he hoped would be more fertile ground, asking her questions about the week of Kelly's disappearance, specifically if Nell had seen or heard anything of Chaz Braden being around when he normally should have been in New York. "Remember, it was the Monday we didn't have Richard Nixon to kick around anymore," he reminded her, knowing she was a staunch Democrat.

Nothing.

He inquired about Samantha McShane and if anyone had seen her in the vicinity around that time.

Nell gave an indignant snort. "The woman hardly ever came into Hampton Junction. Like she was too good for us. The few occasions she did, when Kelly was little, I mostly saw her in Tim Madden's drugstore buying medicine while going on about how sick her child was. One day word got around that she tried that act with your father, and he set her straight. Kelly seemed to be more visible after that set-to, riding her bike into town and playing with local kids as she got older. But once Kelly grew up, left home, and married Chaz Braden, her parents weren't down here much, and eventually they sold the place. Probably because the Bradens virtually blackballed them from the social circuit. I used to play cards with a number of housekeepers who worked for that set, and they told me anyone who wanted a Braden at their party didn't dare invite Samantha or Walter McShane. From what I heard she became pretty much a recluse in her New York place as well. But why are you asking about her? You think she had something to do with the murder?"

"Now don't you start that story, Nell."

And so it went. Nothing she told him even hinted at a lead.

As it grew darker outside, snow flew horizontally against a double row of little squared panes that overlooked the Hudson Valley. He got up and peered outside. In the growing darkness snow clouds seemed to be building up over the mountains to the east, yet he could still see the river below, gray as a snake as it coiled through the hills. Despite the smallness and age of the cabin, it looked as solid as a well-made ship, and the wind driving the flakes couldn't disturb the quiet coziness within. He returned to his chair, accepted another cup of tea, and their talk moved on to the coming of winter.

"There were some funny things, though, come to think of it," she said after a pause in the conversation.

"Funny things?"

"About that home. You'd think with all the charitable spirit behind it, they'd have done more to make the place a little bit nicer."

"How could they, with a forbidding building like that to start with?"

"They had enough land to make it like a park in there, or at least put in a garden. I remember Ginny Strang, God bless her dear departed soul, telling me she suggested as much when she worked in the place. The women would have liked tending it for something to do, she figured. As it was, they only had a half-finished lawn to walk on and pretty much nothing to occupy them. Well, the idea was turned down flat."

All part of their punishment, he thought, more ghosts from the cryptlike rooms rising to stir his anger. "Obviously, you should have been running the place, Nell."

"I would have been glad to. But that's another thing. The way they hired people. Very few locals. And they never took anyone full-time."

"Oh?"

"I don't know why. Lots were willing to work from here, nurses trained in the war, but they only gave people two or three shifts a week, and mostly picked outsiders over us from Hampton Junction." She sniffed as if freshly offended. "I guess once again we weren't good enough."

"Now, Nell, it could be just as they did with your friend—their wanting to ensure the privacy of the mothers," he said, trying to mollify her. "With different staff all the time, and none of them likely to have any social contacts beyond the place of work, the patients would probably feel more anonymous."

She puckered her face at what he said and continued to look miffed.

"Come on, don't get upset over nothing," he pressed. Maybe he couldn't "cure" her knee, but he at least should be able to get her out of a snit. "I know it backfired for her, but given the censorious climate of those days, it makes a sick kind of sense. It's certainly the opposite of how we hire today, bending over backward to keep the same people around so the patients get to know who's taking care of them."

"Then how come it was identical to what happened at that fancy-schmancy maternity center the Bradens ran in Saratoga? No need for women to feel ashamed there."

"How do you mean?"

"They hired a few former nurses from Hampton Junction to work there as well, but none of them could get a full-time job at that place either." She finished with her scrawny head as erect as an eagle's and a *so-there* glare.

*   *   *

Snow made the dusk luminous. Even with four-wheel drive, whenever he topped thirty miles an hour the Jeep started to fishtail toward the ditch, and he had to wrestle the wheel against the pull of the slush. The road out to Nell's place was so infrequently traveled it was the last priority for the plows.

He rummaged through his CD holder and soon he crawled along to the breathy voice of Diana Krall singing "The Look of Love." The car heater quickly warmed the interior of the Jeep to the point he could open his jacket, and the wipers beat a steady rhythm against the storm. With his headlights switched low to reduce their glare against the flakes, he easily distinguished the swell of the road from the steep drop of its shoulders on either side. Better straddle the middle, he decided, having the highway all to himself and not wanting to skid anywhere near the edge.

He continued to feel disappointed that, pleasant as his visit with Nell had been, she'd told him nothing new about Kelly's murder or why his father might have been interested in either the maternity center or the home. Somehow, after his initial good luck with Kelly's old file and spotting Earl Garnet's role in her life, he'd assumed he was on a roll, that he'd continue to round up leads at the same speed.

Now he felt at a dead end, the next step as obscure and dark as the woods on either side of him.

He hoped Earl had fared better today. He patted his cellular phone in the breast pocket of his shirt, wishing he knew Earl's number, which lay safely buried in the wallet he was sitting on and would be hell to get out. No matter. He'd be home soon. The traction felt more secure now that he hogged the center of the highway, and he gently eased his speed up to forty miles an hour.

Settling back, he watched the sweep of flakes across his windshield as Krall drifted into another song. She seemed to be whispering it into his ear.

"... I get along without you very well ..."

A loud *thwack* sounded on his right, something stung the side of his face, and the glass immediately in front of him shattered into a silvery web of cracks around a small black hole.

"Jesus!" He jumped in fright against the restraints of his seat belt and inadvertently floored the accelerator. The Jeep lurched ahead, immediately swiveling to the left. He instinctively jammed on the brakes, and felt the staccato pump of the antilock system, but too late. In the snow-spotted blaze of his headlights, he glimpsed the edge of the road as it flew under him and the hood of his car nose-dived down a ten-foot embankment toward a ravine of open water lined with rocks. Amidst a deafening *bam* of impact and crunch of crumpling metal, he flew forward against the chest strap of his seat belt only to be pounded backward by the airbag exploding out of the steering wheel.

He felt he'd been hit by a giant boxing glove and struggled to breathe. After a few seconds that felt like minutes, he managed to suck in a breath.

He sat in total silence except for the howling of the wind and the occasional ping from the remains of his motor as it cooled down. Though the engine had cut out, the dash lights remained on. He brought his hand up to his stinging cheek and felt it covered with tiny sharp fragments. He looked over to the passenger door, and instantly a searing pain shot through the corner of his eye. "Shit!" he screamed, covering it with his palm, but not before he saw a pattern of splintered glass around a central hole identical to the one in front.

He'd been shot at! One of those fucking drunk hunters had taken a shot at him.

The burning in his eye grew worse, but fury overruled pain. He snapped open his safety belt, and after a couple heaves with his shoulder against the door, managed to push it open and crawl out. "You fucking asshole!" he hollered at the woods on the other side of the road where the shot had come from. "I could have been killed!"

A steady rush of wind through the trees, and the soft hiss of flakes striking the ground amplified the silence.

"You son of a bitch, come and help me. I've got glass in my eye."

No answer.

Christ, would the shooter just run away? "Help me, dammit!"

Nothing.

Son of a bitch.

Still cupping his injured eye, he squinted with the left at the damaged Jeep.

The right high beam, still shining bright, faced straight down into a shallow stream of water that he only then realized he was standing in. The ambient light showed him the front wheel on his side of the vehicle had become part of the doorframe. And he could smell gasoline, a lot of it. Pushing off from where he'd been leaning on the hood, he turned and started to climb back up toward the highway. But his boot slipped on a rock, and he pitched forward into the water, landing on his hands and knees. "Goddamn it," he yelled, the pain in his eye trebling to the point he hardly noticed the burning cold up to his wrists and thighs. He quickly got to his feet and jammed his fingers under his arms, where they continued to burn. Some water ran down his legs into his boots, soaking the lower half of his trousers, but the all-important feet and toes stayed mostly dry.

"You've got to help me!" he hollered one more time, knowing the gutless creep had probably run off, saving his own skin rather than facing up to his brainless act. He didn't need his help anyway, he thought, reaching in his shirt pocket for his cell phone.

It was gone.

Oh God, he thought, looking down where he stood. By the reflected glow of the headlight, he saw the end of it sticking a half inch out of the water. It had fallen out when he fell.

He snatched it up and flipped it open.

Dead.

He heard a soft *whump* behind him, and a sudden orange glow came from beneath the Jeep.

Ignoring the pain in his eye, he started to run along the streambed. If it blew, he'd get a backful of steel.

He cut right, and started scrambling up rocks coated in snow. He reached the road and, crouched low, made a beeline for the far side, slipping as he ran.

The Jeep exploded just as he reached the far ditch. He threw himself facedown on the snow-covered dirt and heard bits of metal fly over his head. Peeking through his fingers with his good eye, he saw the entire forest light up in the glow, the trees and glittering ground between cast in flickering gold.

That's when he saw him.

In a growth of young birch a man stood watching, as casually as if at a bonfire, his eyes fixed on the burning car, gun held at the ready across his chest. The peak of a camouflaged hunting cap hid his face.

Mark's insides crawled toward his throat.

What kind of creep would deliberately shoot someone off the road, then hang around watching?

A very dangerous one.

The initial burst of light subsided, throwing the interior of the woods into darkness.

Mark riveted his gaze in the direction where he'd seen the man. Could the guy be waiting to take another shot, the initial one intended to hit him after all? He'd obviously ignored the shouts for help.

No, don't go overboard here. The man's hanging around didn't necessarily mean he intended to fire again or meant to seriously injure him in the first place. The guy could be watching to make sure he got out okay. Probably he hadn't even expected the car would blow up, and was now shitting bricks, not knowing whether his "prank" had ended up killing someone.

Not that he, Mark Roper, was about to put the asshole's mind to rest by standing up to show he'd gotten safely away.

Metal groaned as it twisted in the heat, lightbulbs blew apart with loud popping noises, and a sickening perfume of burning paint, melting plastic, and rubber filled the air.

But try as he might, Mark couldn't ignore the darker possibilities running through his head. Icy rivulets of melted snow dripped down his back, and his eye throbbed more fiercely. The man could be a certified crazy. Having taken a potshot and done this much damage, he might decide to finish off his prey.

Or an even worse scenario: This was no random act, and Mark had been deliberately ambushed.

After all, in Chaz Braden he had an enemy with reason to want him out of the way. But how could that asshole or anyone else have known to lie in wait for him on this road at this time? No one followed him on the way out to Nell's. There hadn't been another car on the road.

He continued to stare into the forest. Had the man with the gun seen him run to this hiding spot?

Maybe not. He'd bent low and dashed to the shadows of the ditch before the blast illuminated the place he'd crossed.

But the guy would only have to check around the remains of his Jeep to find boot prints in the snow. What if the idiot took a notion to follow him?

Time to get farther away.

He ran along the ditch. After a hundred yards, repeated spills into a creek that meandered under the snow had him soaking wet. As he put more distance between him and where the man had been in the woods, the wind cut through his clothing, making him shiver. He'd soon be in big trouble with hypothermia if he stayed out in this for very long.

Yet the nearest house was Nell's, ten miles back, and the first houses at the outskirts of town lay ten miles ahead.

Normally an easy run, he might not make either because of the cold.

His own home was less than three miles away, on the other side of a range of hills to his right. The distance wasn't any big deal—a forty-minute walk in the city, plus he was in good shape—and the forest would provide cover, both from a pursuer and the wind. But it was across rough country, a trek difficult enough during the day, let alone at night.

He peered up over the edge of the highway.

Not a headlight in either direction. He could easily freeze to death waiting for someone to come along.

He looked over toward the fiery wreckage again. The glowing orb of light encasing it created the impression of a macabre Christmas ornament suspended in the darkness. At the edge of the sphere he saw movement, and the silhouette of the hunter strode across the road.

The man stood a few moments facing the fire, his back to Mark. He was as tall as Chaz Braden, but bulkier. Yet winter clothing under the camouflage clothing could produce that effect. Still cradling the gun, he reached into his outfit, pulled out a hip flask, and took a long drink.

Enough trying to second-guess a creep, especially one who was all boozed up.

Mark turned and, staying low, ran to the woods. A few yards into the trees he found it considerably darker, but could still see the pale surface of the snow on the ground and the trunks of the trees ahead of him. Holding his hands out to ward off any low branches, he pushed deeper, balancing speed with stealth. His only hope would be to get as much of a lead as possible before his attacker found his trail.

Glancing back over his shoulder and through the trees, Mark saw the man's silhouetted form circle the car, then kneel where tracks would have been. The figure reached into his pocket, and, seconds later, a tiny beam of light shot out from his hand toward the ground.

Mark pressed ahead all the faster.

The floor of the forest sloped steeply upward, and his breathing quickly became labored. The trees overhead were old, big enough to have blocked the sun for the last hundred years, so there was little new undergrowth to ensnare him. But the rocks and wet leaves beneath the snow made traction difficult, and with each step forward he seemed to slide halfway back. Every now and then a branch caught him across the face, and the pain in his injured eye seared as hot as if a live coal were stuck in it.

But up he went, able to use the left eye by squinting the injured one closed. Having adapted to the dark, he could see enough to grab low-hanging branches and pull himself along whenever his feet started to skid.

Taking another glance backward, he saw the man with the rifle following his thin cone of light across the highway toward Mark's first hiding place.

He kept going up, figuring he was now a hundred and twenty yards from the road and had probably climbed a hundred feet of elevation.

Two ridges lay ahead, each about five hundred feet high with a shallow valley between them, some of it open ground. But if he could reach the first ridge well ahead of the hunter, he could widen his lead going down the far slope, possibly even get out of rifle range. That might discourage his pursuer from following him.

His right eye, tearing profusely, clamped itself so tightly shut in reflex to the pain that he could barely keep his left one open. He had to use the fingers of his left hand to pry the lids apart. Even then he couldn't manage more than a squint and found his field of vision cut in half.

He tried again to glance behind him. The man, little more than a dark shape in the open snow at the highway's edge, stood directly below him now and looked right up to where he climbed.

He can't see me, Mark thought, keeping his panic in check.

His tracker shouldered the rifle and started after him, once more following the thin beam of light, presumably playing it over his footprints.

Mark estimated he had a hundred-and-fifty-yard lead. Not much of an advantage over a bullet. He redoubled his efforts. Everything depended on how far down the other side of the ridge he could get before the gunman reached the peak and drew a bead on him.

His breathing grew more ragged, and his boots kept slipping, sapping energy from his legs until his calves burned. But at least he wasn't cold. The exertion made him warm, so much so that as sweat began to cling to his shirt, he hardly noticed his wet pants. Now and then he scooped a handful of slush into his mouth and gulped it down between gasps of breath. The coolness actually felt good. But as soon as he stopped to rest, his damp clothes would accelerate heat loss and quicken the onset of hypothermia.

But as much as the trees blocked the wind down here, high overhead it roared through the branches, obliterating any noises the man below made. *That better work both ways,* he thought. Whenever one of the low limbs he grabbed as a handhold snapped off with a *crack*, he imagined it could be heard for a mile. He tried not to think of the man stopping, unshouldering his rifle, and aiming at the sound. He took yet another furtive look. Mark could no longer see him, not even the thin beam of light. But he could see his own trail, leading to him like a tracer bullet.

Up he went, his legs and arms aching from the effort. He could only hope the man behind him had as much trouble.

As the slope became steeper, more slippery, he had to reach directly in front of him to grab rocks and roots buried in the ground so as to propel himself upward. He mustn't slip now, or he'd slide a lot more than a few steps, possibly all the way to the feet of his pursuer. He tested each handhold before actually gripping it, his exposed fingers aching with wet and cold, and kicked at every toehold to secure an extra half inch of footing.

He must be near the top, he told himself. The wind sounded louder. And some of what he crawled over became bare rock. In spots it became even too steep to hold an accumulation of snow, and he crawled over bare rock, part of a granite spine that ran the length of the crest. That meant no tracks. Mark felt a sudden burst of elation. If the top was just as bare, he could not only get ahead of the son of a bitch, but run along the ridge before starting down, then lose him altogether.

He hoisted himself over a ledge and stood on a shelf of stone in a full blast of icy cold. He'd made it. He also instantly started to freeze. His damp clothes flattened against his skin, and the chill cut through him as if he had nothing on. The worst were his fingers, which immediately cramped and curled into claws. But the stony ground beneath his feet, though coated with ice, had been blown clean of snow just as he'd hoped.

He quickly looked around, making sure his would-be assassin hadn't somehow beaten him by taking a different route. To the right and left he saw only naked rock disappearing into the gloom. On the horizon in front of him, the wind was rolling back the cloud, exposing a dazzling strip of stars and a full moon low in the sky. He must get to the safety of the woods before it got any higher. Once it lit up the snowscape below, he'd be like a mouse running from a hawk in the clearings.

Huddled low and keeping his feet wide apart so as not to slip, he thrust his hands under his arms and scurried along the top of the ridge. After about a hundred yards he jumped down onto a bushy shallow ledge on the far side. He saw a gradual, snow-covered slope fifteen feet beneath him. Once there he would be a dozen strides from the trees. He'd need to smooth over any prints he left, then count on the wind to do the rest. With a bit of luck, the man behind him might have already lost the trail and not be able to spot it again.

He moved to ease himself over the rocky edge and lower himself to the ground when a movement in the darkness below, another fifty yards farther to his left, caught his eye.

He stood absolutely still.

Staring down into the shadows, he saw nothing more and thought he must have imagined it.

Until a shape darker than the woods crept toward him and quickly became a human form.

But it couldn't be.

He had such a head start on the man. How could he be here already?

Choices raced through his mind. Should he scramble back down the other side? Stay crouched on the ledge? Maybe he hadn't been seen yet. Or any second there'd be a bullet. He drew his breath, determined not to scream and beg.

The figure crossed about ten yards below him. Mark could easily see the dark outline of a rifle barrel held upward toward the sky. But the man's head seemed turned toward the forest, cocked to one side as if he listened for something down there. Not once did he glance up where Mark lay crouched.

Was it the same person who'd first shot at him? Had he found a less steep way up after all? Or was it someone else? His build looked slimmer, though in the dark Mark couldn't be sure. An accomplice of the man who'd pursued him, perhaps, lying in wait, knowing his partner would chase the prey up to him?

Whoever it was remained focused on the forest below, looking down the hill, away from the ridge.

Some accomplice.

Mark breathed as softly as he could. The cold continued to rip through him, and he started to shiver. He clamped his jaws closed to keep his teeth from chattering.

The man beneath him continued to listen and stare into the woods, the white vapor of his breath whipping into the night.

If he turned, they'd be looking right at each other. Mark quietly curled into a ball and crept back against the bushes, burying his head in his arms to mask the white traces of his own breath in the frost. With his good eye he squinted along the ridge to see if the man he'd thought was on his heels had arrived.

No one.

Was the man not thirty feet from him the gunman?

No, Mark finally decided. From all the years he'd hiked and played around these hills he knew for certain there was no shortcut.

So who was this guy?

Just another hunter out poaching who had nothing to do with his pursuer?

Or is it me he's listening for?

His shivering grew worse. His fingers ached. His eye throbbed.

He glanced once more along the ridge.

It was fully bathed in moonlight now.

There, against the sky, appeared the shape of a man climbing into view, a rifle on his back. An instant later he knelt and probed the ground around his feet with a penlight.

Chapter 9

Earl huddled against the wind at the Thirty-third Street entrance, cupping the mouthpiece of his cellular with his hand. Horizontal needles of rain stung against his skin. Everyone else rushing by seemed to have an umbrella. He eyed a kid who had been selling them out of a garbage bag and signaled him to bring one over, all the while continuing his conversation with Janet. "I came up empty. The only significant thing is that Cam Roper, Mark's father, might have looked at those same charts just after Kelly went missing. Except he probably didn't find anything either, or he would have done something about it. I can't reach Mark to tell him. His phone doesn't seem to be working."

"It's still pretty bizarre, those records attracting his interest," Janet said.

"If I'm right about Kelly trying to find evidence of malpractice to use as leverage against Chaz, then maybe Cam Roper had followed up on those suspicions, or at least started to before he passed away." He fished five bucks out of his pocket, and gave it to the pint-sized merchant, who cut the gloom with a grin as bright as polished ivory. Popping open what looked as flimsy as a bat wing and was undoubtedly stolen goods, Earl instantly felt better, but had to speak up as the rain drummed on the black material, creating the din of a thousand impatient fingers. "Cam could have thought she'd confronted Chaz with some grievous error he'd made that would ruin his career, and he'd killed her for it. Except Roper Senior likely came to the same conclusion as the M and M reports. 'Unexpected but unavoidable digoxin toxicity with no obvious cause.' "

Janet said nothing.

In the roar of the storm he thought the connection was gone. "Janet?"

"I'm here."

"So what's got your tongue."

"I hesitate to say it, but there's another possible scenario."

A wave of static interrupted them. "Go on," he said, when it cleared.

"Somebody could have tried to murder those patients by secretly injecting extra doses of the drug."

"That's pretty far-fetched."

"But not impossible. It's occurred in hospitals before."

"But no one ever raised the possibility of foul play here. Certainly it was never mentioned in the charts."

"That doesn't necessarily mean it didn't happen."

He exhaled the way only a former smoker can—long, slow, and from the bottom of his lungs. "Being unable to talk with either of them means I may never know."

"What about family?"

"I talked with the woman's son this afternoon, but he never brought up anything of that sort. I can call him back and ask him outright if she ever mentioned having any enemies or suspicions of someone trying to harm her, but I think he would have mentioned it if she had. As for the man who died, he'd no next of kin, so there isn't a hope of finding out more there."

She fell silent again.

"It isn't entirely a dead end," he continued. "I've arranged to meet with the floor staff involved in her care. Maybe they can tell me if she ever mentioned anyone who might hurt her. And it turns out Melanie Collins continued to see the woman as a patient from time to time over the years, so maybe she'll be able to fill me in on something I'm missing." He'd already left several messages on her service, asking her to call, but she hadn't gotten back to him yet.

This time Janet let out a sigh, minor-league compared to his own. "Good luck, love. Oh, by the way, I looked up divorce law on the Internet, and as far as I can see, she'd have gone offshore."

Once Janet got an idea, she was relentless. "That may be, but the police found no record of any plane or boat tickets in her name."

"That doesn't mean she didn't intend to go there. Maybe her killer stopped her before she could make the move. All I know is, find a woman's divorce lawyer, and you find someone who knows a lot about the woman."

                        *   *   *

Mark huddled in the bushes, trying to blend with the scrubby growth.

The man on the ridge looked up from his study of the ground and seemed to stare right at him. Then he looked in the other direction, and finally rose to his feet. If he'd seen Mark or the hunter below, he showed no sign, turning away and peering into the night.

The hunter must have been outside his line of sight, Mark thought. Otherwise, if they were together, why hadn't he called to him? Even if they weren't, he would still have reacted, possibly even mistaken him for Mark and taken a shot at him.

Instead the man walked off in the opposite direction, playing his light over the snow on either side of the spiny path.

Mark exhaled in momentary relief.

Looking down he saw that the hunter hadn't budged, his dark form still visible, his breath coming out in well-spaced puffs. By counting the interval, Mark estimated that whoever he was, he'd controlled his respirations down to ten a minute, which took rock-solid nerve.

As Mark watched, the man slowly leveled the gun barrel as if he were about to shoot something farther down the slope. Again he seemed to be listening.

Mark heard nothing but the rush of the wind.

From within the darkness of the woods leapt a great amorphous shadow in what initially appeared to be a singular movement. Immediately it flew into pieces, the parts darting through the trees at the forest edge, each zigzagging around the trunks like formless gray spirits.

Three shots rang out, but, like smoke, the creatures had vanished.

Except for one.

Its antlered head twisted round, and it spiraled to its knees, staggered up on its legs, then pitched forward again. It writhed in the snow, kicking and thrashing its neck side to side as if to shake off what had felled it. Black stains pooled on the snow, and the writhing eventually slowed. It raised its head once more, as if straining to see the moon through the treetops, its mouth open and gasping. Then it collapsed, its mighty struggle giving over to lesser quiverings.

The hunter walked over and put a final bullet into the buck's head.

Mark spun around in time to see the first man standing stock-still in the distance, staring toward the sound of the shot. He then scurried over the edge of the ridge and ran back down the way he'd come.

7:00 P.M.

Mark hated all-terrain vehicles. Gas-powered models were carbon-monoxide-spewing noise polluters. Battery-operated versions, though quieter, tipped, killed, and paralyzed just as many victims as their noisier cousins. But among hunters, especially the middle-of-the-night kind, they were the transportation of choice this time of year, before the snow got too deep.

Perched on the back of a red, four-wheel-drive minitractor, he said nothing of this to his grizzled driver as they bounced over the nonwooded sections of the valley. Rather he expressed profound gratitude for the ride home, especially given that the old guy had had to make a choice whether to haul Mark or the deer out first.

Mark had won, and got a shot of the man's whiskey to boot.

He occasionally had to grab his host's shoulders to keep from falling off. Under a blue-checked hunting jacket he felt muscles hard as tangled ropes despite a face etched with so many wrinkles they were like rings of a tree and gave an age near eighty. That made him from an era in which men took down deer to put food on the family table, not for sport.

When they pulled up to the back fence of Mark's property, his driver didn't give a name, and Mark didn't ask. But the handshake between them felt firm, also from another time, when it would have been only natural for a man to help a stranger.

Mark watched him ride off to fetch his kill. The wind had chased away the storm, and the moon was at its zenith now, its light filling the country-side like clear blue water. Soon his rescuer was but a soundless dot churning a path back up the far slope.

Marked climbed the rickety log fence and headed over the field toward his house. The snow was barely six inches deep, and he had no trouble walking. All he could think off was a hot shower, clean clothes, and something to eat. Then he'd call Dan, and have him get his ass over to Chaz Braden's place to ask some pointed questions—

His thoughts came to an abrupt halt.

The lights were on in his house.

And against the upstairs curtains he saw the shadow of someone walking about, moving from room to room.

Too incredulous to move, his brain clicked into action.

Braden!

That ambush and chase had been nothing more than a diversion, intended to keep him out of the way so the son of a bitch could search his house again.

"Well no goddamn way," he muttered, sprinting for the back door.

He reached it in less than a minute, and, finding his key, let himself in as noiselessly as he could.

Sure enough, he could hear the floorboards above his head creaking as the intruder continued to walk back and forth.

He crept out of the kitchen, through the hallway to the stairs, pausing to pick up the baseball bat he'd put back in the front closet. He glanced outside, and to his amazement, saw a dark station wagon parked in his driveway. *Bloody nerve,* he thought, and, holding his weapon at the ready, crept up the steps.

The creaking seemed to be coming from behind the closed door to his guest bedroom.

Get ready to be welcomed, visitor, he said to himself, reaching the landing and weighing the heft of his weapon. He wanted it to be Chaz. Wanted to terrify the creep, confront him about the shooting, about Kelly, make him blurt out a confession or two.

He crossed the final few feet and, holding the bat in his right hand, slowly turned the brass knob with his left. He took a few slow breaths, preparing himself for battle.

"Freeze, you asshole!" he roared, flinging the door open and leaping into the room, the bat cocked over his shoulder.

A young woman with long black hair whom he'd never seen before clutched a bathrobe around her and let out a bloodcurdling yell the whole county would hear.

Before he could react, she pivoted on one leg and came at his head with a karate kick.

* * *

His skull hurt.

And his neck.

"I'm lucky I didn't kill him," a woman said.

"I'd say he's the lucky one," a man who sounded familiar replied. "Where'd you learn to kick like that?"

"At a karate school in Paris."

He must have fallen asleep on his couch with no pillow—that would explain the pain—and left the TV on.

"Could you have fractured one of his vertebrae?" the man asked.

He knew that voice. Must be an actor he'd seen before.

"Not without breaking my foot. It feels fine."

The woman's voice he didn't recognize at all.

"Well, I'm glad of that, for both of you."

Wait a minute. That wasn't an actor. It was Dan. What would he be doing on a television show?

Before he could open his eyes, someone pried his right lid up, beamed a white light directly into his pupil, and peered at him through the opposite side of an ophthalmoscope. "Stop it." He moaned, and tried to move away from the glare, still feeling he had a hot coal buried in there. But a burning sheet of pain snapped up the back of his head and stopped him.

Then he remembered what had happened.

"Something has abraded your cornea, Dr. Roper," the woman said from somewhere beyond the glare, "and I don't think it was my toenails—wait a minute. Sheriff Evans, can you hand me my medical bag?" She removed the ophthalmoscope, leaving him momentarily blinded, but he could hear her rummaging around for something.

"What the hell's going on?" he mumbled, unable to make his mouth move properly.

"Hold my light, please, Sheriff," she ordered, and brought a tiny pair of forceps into view.

"Now wait a second—"

"Don't move, Doctor."

Before he could reply the white glare of the scope floodlit his eyeball again, and her fingers pulled the lids even farther apart.

He winced at a slight stinging sensation, then it was over.

"There," she said, suddenly releasing her grip and allowing him to retreat back into darkness.

The hot coal sensation had vanished. He still felt a slight burning, but found it tolerable.

She studied the tip of the tiny forceps in her hand. "You had a piece of glass stuck superficially in the conjunctival membrane. Luckily it wasn't embedded in the cornea and came out easy enough. Here, press gently with this," and she placed a gauze pad over the eye.

"Who are you?"

"Lucy O'Connor. I'm so sorry, but when you leapt into the room like that, I acted on reflex."

He tried to get up, but another spasm shot up from between his shoulders to the top of his scalp and changed his mind. As he flopped back down, the hard surface made him realize that he was still on the floor. "Lucy who?" he asked between gritted teeth as his neck muscles uncoiled.

"Lucy O'Connor, your family medicine resident for the next three months. I wrote you that I'd be arriving a day early."

"Oh, my God. That's this week?"

She ripped strips of tape off a roll and began to apply them across the gauze to hold it in place. "Of course I don't know if you'll still have me. I really am sorry, but you looked like a wild man, all dirty and wielding a baseball bat. Frankly, I thought you were going to kill me."

Mark forced his good eye open and encountered the same tumbling black hair and white complexion he'd first seen on entering the room. "Weren't you supposed to be someone named Paul?"

A frown overshadowed the deep brown eyes hovering inches from his own. "He and I switched at the last minute," she said. "You didn't know?"

He shook his head. Bad move. New spasms raced each other to the base of his skull. Wincing, he added, "And I thought he, I mean you, weren't due until next Tuesday."

"You're sure you didn't get a notice? The hospital moved everything up so I'd be back by mid-February to cover the floors when a lot of residents take a winter vacation." As she talked, her hands continued to work with the tape. "The program director told me he wrote you about the changes weeks ago."

His cluttered desktop leapt to mind. "Oh, God." He groaned. "I haven't opened my mail for the last—"

"You can let go now," she interrupted, and deftly finished anchoring the improvised eye patch with a final strip of adhesive. Her fingers were firm as they worked, yet her touch was light. "There. That should hold until we find you a proper one."

"I really am the one to blame, Dr. O'Connor—"

"Please, everyone calls me Lucy."

"Of course. But how did you get in here?"

"I'm the guilty party on that one," Dan said, hovering over her shoulder.

Returning her equipment to a worn black doctor's bag, she smiled up at him.

It was a dazzler—what his father used to call a real string of pearls.

"Yes. Dan's been most kind to me. When I couldn't find anyone here, I asked around town where you might be and got sent to your office at the White House. Luckily, Dan had been working late, and after I told him who I was, he figured you wouldn't want me waiting in the cold."

Mark saw a flush of pink in the sheriff's plump face.

"I dug up your spare keys and brought her back out here." He gave a little shrug that seemed to say it was the least he could have done. "I knew you'd want me to." Then he started to chuckle. "I sure didn't expect this, though. Luckily I left her my cell number, and she called me after she coldcocked you. When I got here, she was standing over you with the bat." He turned to Lucy, laughing even harder. "You should have seen your face when I told you who he was."

She grinned back at him. "At first I thought you were kidding. Then when I realized you were serious, I felt I'd die."

"Well, if he'd jumped out at me looking the way he did, I'd have shot him."

They both had a good laugh over that prospect. Mark just held his head and gritted his teeth.

"But what happened to you?" Dan asked him. "You look as if you've been through hell."

"You're not going to believe this, but—"

"Before you two start chatting," Lucy interrupted, "I need to examine Dr. Roper further." Her fingers slipped behind his neck and applied gentle pressure to the tip of his seventh cervical vertebra. "Any tenderness there?"

"No. But I really have to apologize—"

"How about there?" she cut in, her fingers slipping up a notch.

"No. You see, someone broke in here last night, and I thought you were him—"

"And there?" Her touch found vertebra number five.

"Fine. I'm sure they're all fine."

"For the moment, I'm the doctor, Doctor." She gave his fourth cervical vertebra the once-over. "Is there pain here?"

Pretty damn sure of herself for a resident, he thought. He found her exam uncommonly thorough. He also found himself wondering about her age. She looked older, leaner than the usual crop he got up here. Male or female, they all seemed barely out of their baby fat these days. She also had a hint of sadness in her eyes that the usual polished faces lacked.

Once she pronounced that he could safely stand up, he cautiously rolled on his side and managed to push himself to a half-sitting position without setting off the muscles in his neck again. With her on one arm and Dan on the other, he got all the way to his feet. He had a headache, but nothing else. "I'm glad you went easy on me," he said, hoping to relax the worried look on his two helpers' faces.

Lucy's frown deepened. "Part of my reflex. If I hadn't held back, you would have been dead."

From the matter-of-fact way she said it, he thought she must be kidding. But her expression remained all business. In fact, she appeared downright calm for someone who'd just clobbered her teacher-to-be. He liked that, figuring she didn't rattle easily. And now that he was upright, he also realized how petite she seemed, her head coming up only to his shoulders. Of course her being in bare feet and still clothed in an oversize bathrobe helped make her look tiny. But there had been no mistaking the strength he felt in her hands and arms as she supported him. "Now let's see if you can walk on your own," she said, very much in charge.

He made it to the doorway, no trouble. "How long was I out?" he asked, pivoting around to make the return trip. The general rule was that anyone who remained unconscious more than twenty minutes after a blow to the head warranted special observation for subsequent damage, including a CT to rule out a fracture or bleed.

"Don't worry. I'd say five minutes, tops. No need for a CT. But I'll wake you on and off tonight, just to be sure."

This woman knew her stuff. "Thanks, but I don't think that'll be necessary—oh, shit."

"What?" the two said in unison. Alarm creased their faces as they rushed to his side.

"Whoa! I'm fine. I just realized I hadn't made arrangements for where you were to stay yet. Normally male residents stay with me, but the women I billet with a local family—"

"Dr. Roper!" Lucy's concerned look vanished with a laugh, and her eyes lit up like sun-kissed earth. "For a young-looking guy, you're certainly old-fashioned. I've been living in coed quarters for the last seven years, plus I grew up with four brothers, so if it's okay with you, I'll be fine right here."

Mark felt at a loss for words. "Of course, if you like, you're most welcome . . ." He trailed off at the sight of Dan rolling his eyes toward the ceiling and smirking at him.

"Great," Lucy said, looking around the room. "I loved the feel of this place the minute I stepped inside. There's a real sense of home in these old wooden houses. Reminded me of where I grew up outside Montreal."

"Oh, you're Canadian?" Mark said, all the while thinking he might not be old-fashioned, but Hampton Junction sure was. Nell would bust an artery spreading the word about this one. Dan, still behind Lucy's line of sight, didn't help matters any, shaking with laughter, his face red from trying not to make a sound.

"Originally," she replied, "but I've been so many places, especially in the last seven years, I don't know what I am anymore. Maybe a citizen of the world? Say, I checked out your kitchen. You obviously don't eat in much, but there's the makings for tea. I'd prescribe a cup for all of us. You two go downstairs and get it ready while I change."

Obediently following her orders, Mark led the way. He used the opportunity to inform Dan of his ordeal.

"Jesus!" Dan responded, after hearing the story. "You could have been killed. And not just by that yahoo. Those poachers get so tanked up they're liable to fire off a shot if a leaf rustles. You tearing up the ridge must have sounded like a whole herd of deer."

"I don't think it takes much guesswork to finger who it was—"

"Now, Mark—"

"My question is, what are you going to do about it?"

"One thing I'm not going to do is go into the Braden estate leveling accusations against Chaz without a shred of evidence."

"Shred? Who the hell else would want me out of the way? Admit it. Or are you too afraid of them?"

Dan bristled, and his face went livid. "You've no cause to say that."

"Then what's the problem?"

"No problem! I'm always careful not to go off half-cocked with unsubstantiated allegations." His tone of voice had turned icy. "But I learned long ago to be very cautious about taking on some people more than others."

The hurt in his baggy eyes bothered Mark. But he wasn't in the mood to pamper bruised feelings or allow reelection worries to sidetrack going after Chaz. " 'Unsubstantiated allegations!' You saw how the guy went toe-to-toe with me in your office."

"Any witnesses tonight?"

"Well, no."

"Can you identify this figure you saw in the woods?"

"Of course not. He was too far away. With his hood plus cap—"

"So it could have been any drunk taking a potshot—"

"But he came after me."

"Did you see him then? Maybe he realized he'd crossed the line, wanted to make sure you weren't hurt?"

"Jesus, Dan, can you hear yourself?"

"It's what Braden would say, or at least the army of lawyers he'll hire would. What do you expect? I repeat, there'll be no accusations against the likes of that family with nothing but your word against his. At least not by me!" Dan's voice held rock steady despite the anger in it.

"Okay, so what are you going to do?"

"I'll get two men out there tonight and make sure what's left of your Jeep stays a secure crime scene. We'll also take a look at the tracks you and he left, but just along the highway. I still have to consider the possibility it isn't Chaz Braden we're after, and won't risk anyone else's life by asking them to go into the woods after an armed drunken maniac who's bored with deer and wants a crack at two-legged prey—"

"You're not telling me you really believe this could be anyone but Chaz—"

"I'm telling you it's my job to take into account every possible scenario just as you do when making a differential diagnosis as a doctor. What's more, if you were thinking clearly, you wouldn't want me to act rashly about Chaz Braden. I don't know what it is between you and him, but you're not exactly rational about the guy."

"What do you mean?"

"You're always on the edge of losing it around him. I thought *you* were nearly going to go at him in my office."

Mark said nothing, but felt his own face grow warm. He fought off the urge to tell him he was full of shit.

"We nail him, it's got to be done by the book, understand? It's not fear that makes me more careful around the likes of him. It's a fact of life you need a better case against Braden-type money. Otherwise, those lawyers will have Chaz free in a heartbeat, even if we do get evidence he's the one. That's American justice, bucko, so get used to it. Cool your jets, Mark, and let me do my job. You got no cause to think I won't. And in the meantime, I suggest you take care of your own hangups about that family. They're clouding your judgment."

The burn in Mark's face increased. "I just want a crack at him, to tell the son of a bitch that I know it was him. That ought to make him think twice before any other anonymous 'hunters' take a shot at me."

"Will you listen to *yourself*? I've never seen you so readily jump to conclusions on a case before."

His cheeks felt on fire. He didn't often have disagreements with Dan, but when he did, the man could be a frustrating, stubborn opponent, especially when what he said had the sting of truth. He had to admit, the Bradens brought out the worst in him. He couldn't just pin it on their preoccupation with the business and political side of medicine, though that did grate. But similarly inclined doctors elsewhere didn't skewer his professional objectivity and make him run around "half-cocked." No, this ran deeper. Just being around them got him on edge, yet he couldn't quite put his finger on it. Nevertheless, he'd have to rein in those feelings if he was going to do his job as coroner. "Sorry, Dan. You're right. I was out of line."

The man's broad face relaxed a little, but the pained darkness in his gaze remained. "Hey, we all have our peccadilloes—"

"Wow, you two look serious," interrupted Lucy, sweeping into the kitchen dressed in jeans and a white shirt untucked at the waist. "Hope you've at least put the kettle on." Before they could answer, she opened one of the cupboards and came up with a canister of tea leaves that Mark didn't even know was there. In seconds she had them steeping, then continued to poke through the cupboards.

Fifteen minutes later they were refilling their cups and sitting down to a late supper of omelettes that she had whipped up from remnants of food she'd found in his refrigerator. "Only a month past the *best before* date," she said of the ingredients, eating with the quick efficiency most doctors learn from having to grab a meal between calls. "And whatever kind of cheese you once had, it's turned to a Roquefort look-alike. But I think we'll live."

"Mark keeps the take-out food industry going in this town," Dan teased. "Even has his own table at The Four Aces."

"Four Aces? Sounds like fun."

"It's Hampton Junction's combination bar, home-cooking restaurant, and dance hall," he added, giving Mark a wink. "I'm sure your host here will be glad to to show you around."

Lucy flashed that brilliant smile again. "That'd be fine. But my being here is bound to generate enough rumors as it is, so I'll tell you right now, and everyone else in town, I'm strictly an aboveboard kind of woman. So you can assure folks their doctor will be safe with me. Besides, I'm engaged. My fiancé lives in New York."

Dan blushed, his forkful of eggs halfway into his mouth. "I'm sorry, I didn't mean to insinuate—"

"No offense," Lucy said, waving off his apology and never missing a bite.

It didn't make any difference to Mark. He'd no more think of dating a resident than his sister, if he had one.

That same evening
The Braden Country Home,
South of Hampton Junction

"What did I do to warrant such a moron of a son!"

Chaz Braden felt his head spin. The scotch he'd been nursing all afternoon had hit him hard as soon as he came in from the cold to the warmth of the house. Outside he'd kept himself just nicely topped off. "I only meant to scare the son of a bitch," he said, trying not to sway in front of his father, loathing himself for feeling so beholden to him.

"Beware a father of spectacular ability," Kelly had once told him in their early days together. "They never let you fail, always stepping in to take over, and that leaves you weak."

He'd scoffed at the warning, having always relished growing up in privilege and figuring he deserved an edge in life.

He caught a glance of his hangdog face in a nearby gilded mirror. It reminded him of putty, and he immediately looked away. Yet he continued to stand there, fifty-five years old and pathetic as a fucking teenager being chewed out for screwing up again.

"You idiot. A bonehead play like that is so obvious. Who else will he think did it but you?"

It took all his concentration to come up with a reply. "Roper didn't see me. And I had no car to spot. One of your men dropped me off—told him I just wanted to take a crack at the deer that hang around the ridge out there. On my way back to the highway afterward, I called him on my cellular to pick me up again, but closer to town. That way I made sure he didn't see Roper's wrecked Jeep." Despite his best effort, he slurred his words.

"You'll have left boot prints, tire tracks—"

"The woods are full of hunters with boots, and by morning the plows should have cleared the road—"

"It was stupid—"

"I know! But do you have any idea what I'm going through? The whispers at the hospital again. The other doctors shunning me again. Patients transferring out of my practice again. Secretaries and nurses afraid to be alone in a room with me. So to hell with you and your sanctimonious crap about what I should and shouldn't do. Why shouldn't I send the little fuck scurrying down the other side of the ridge with bullets at his heels?" The room pitched to one side, and he sat down on the nearest sofa. *Christ, I shouldn't have drunk so much,* he thought, gripping his head between his hands and trying to stay the terrible swirling in his brain. In a few seconds it steadied. Without looking up, he could feel his father looming over him and sensed the man's disgust. A wave of defeat swept through him as tangible as the effect of the alcohol. And as familiar. He'd mostly given up the latter, but had been succumbing to the former for years. "I'm sorry," he muttered, defiance draining out of him. There was no point in fighting the man. Never had been, never would be. Nor of fighting to be free of Kelly. In the world's eyes he'd always be her killer.

Between his fingers he could see the spacious room where he'd once believed he could be happy with her. Everything was decorated in beige, cream, and gold—the chairs, sofas, tables, lamps, even the walls and chandeliers—befitting a gilded lifestyle. Except it only reminded him of stale marzipan—ornate on the outside, hard and crumbly within.

His father sat down beside him. "Why, Chaz?" His tone of voice was surprisingly quiet, almost tender.

Good question. It had all been an impulse born of booze, lack of sleep, and being powerless to regain control over his life. "I'd gone off the wagon, had a few drinks, and listened in on the tap your men put on his phone. I heard Roper call that old busybody Nell and invite himself out there to ask her a bunch of questions about us. I lost it. It's bad enough at work, but now, with him stirring up shit here . . ." He couldn't explain the rage inside him. It was as if for that one moment Mark Roper had seemed responsible for all the innuendo, all the accusations of the last few weeks, and the temptation of taking a shot at the bastard, making it look like a hunter's stray bullet, proved too hard to resist. Then seeing him take off into the bush, tail between his legs, it felt so damn good to have the upper hand, he couldn't help but go after him. "*Pow! Pow! Pow!* All the way home. It would have been fantastic, having him in my sights, driving him like a scared rabbit. And I would have, too, if that other hunter hadn't been there."

"Thank God he was," his father said, rolling his eyes at the ceiling. He stood up from the couch and, running a hand through his steely hair, started to pace. "Chaz, once you take over the family affairs after I'm gone, you'll run things your own way, with the help of your mother if she's still here. But there's one practice of mine I advise you to adopt."

Chaz groaned inwardly and sank back into the sofa, sending the contents of his skull into yet another death spiral. He couldn't endure one of his father's when-I-kick-the-bucket talks just now. And he couldn't stand to hear him nonchalantly mention "mother," the woman who had exiled herself to a permanent around-the-world cruise years ago rather than risk losing her share of the many family business interests in a messy divorce.

"Did you ever wonder why I only choose security people who are ex-military?"

"Because they're trained to kill bad guys with a flick of their eyelashes?"

"Besides the obvious."

Chaz said nothing, knowing his immediate role was to shut up and learn.

His father stopped by the fireplace, picked up a poker, and used it to stoke a bed of coals beneath a smoking log. "I find men whose particular skills were in special operations, the kind that involve entering premises by stealth and obtaining information with no one the wiser that they've even been there. That's how we can keep abreast of potential problems like Dr. Mark Roper—with subtlety and finesse, not bullets and car crashes. Am I understood?"

Chaz just nodded, and sent the looping in his head to new levels.

"Did anyone see you come in just now?"

"I don't think so."

"Good. Now the first thing we do is get you back to New York. My chauffeur will drive you there tonight. No stops, and you come into your apartment through the garage so as to avoid the doorman. Tomorrow you make a big deal about having had the flu and returning to the city. My driver will say whatever we tell him, so we'll fudge the time you left. Make it earlier, and he'll attest you were well past Albany at the time in question."

He nodded again.

"Before you go, have a look at these photos. Tell me what you think." He threw a stack of large prints on the coffee table between them.

Chaz, still cradling his head with one hand, focused on the first image. He found himself looking at a medical record for Kelly dated July 1951. "How'd you get these?"

"Subtlety and finesse, remember?"

Chaz rubbed his eyes and strained to read the writing in the photo. "So she had cramps as a kid," he said when he finished, "and her mother interfered then as she does now. What good does it do us to have this?"

"Keep going."

He looked at the next set of pictures. Again he wasn't impressed. "Cam Roper spent years talking with her. We knew that. He's the bastard who put ideas of medical school in her head."

"Oh, I think our Kelly had a mind of her own." He reached over and handed the next photo to Chaz personally.

Chaz started when he recognized her familiar handwriting. The sight of it catapulted him back to the early years when she wrote him every few days about their plans, the wedding, the life they'd have together, and a bittersweet ache for squandered chances gripped his stomach. But as he read further, a fury as consuming and fresh as if he'd intercepted the letter the day it was written enveloped his chest and squeezed. "That bitch. That betraying, lying bitch . . ." Speechless with anger, he rose to his feet and let the photo fall from his hand. He'd loved her, wasted his life over her, his whole goddamned life, and it just kept getting worse.

His father walked behind him and gave his shoulders a squeeze, then started to massage them with his surgeon's fingers, strong and penetrating. It felt good. "Easy, son. I know seeing this must hurt. But surely you had your suspicions."

The roiling in Chaz's stomach grew worse.

"The good news is it may finally be your way to get clear of her."

"Nothing will ever do that, not after all this time."

"It will if we can give the police her lover."

The effects of whiskey and exhaustion left him slow to react. "You mean give the letter to the police?"

His father broke off the massage, exasperated. "Of course not. How the hell would I explain where we got it? No, we first find out who this man was, then hand him over. They get a new suspect, and you're in the clear."

His brain emerged from its misery. *My, God!* he thought, seeing the glimmer of a way out.

"Don't you have any idea who it might have been?" his father asked.

Chaz felt an old resentment rekindle itself—no, the right word was jealousy. Jealousy over anyone she had befriended and seemed to have fun with. Not that he suspected an affair back then. He hated how her moving close to others meant she drew away from him. But now he could find the bastard who'd been screwing her and stick him with her murder. The idea lit a fire in him.

So which one had cuckolded him?

A guy in her class? Or one of the residents two years ahead of her. Hell, it might even have been a colleague of his, sharing consults with him during the day and banging her at night.

Someone outside the hospital?

Someone not even a doctor?

He ground his frustration between a fist and a palm. "We'll never figure it out!"

"If we keep track of Mark Roper's conversations we will."

"I don't understand."

"He knows about this letter," his father said, walking over and retrieving the copy from the floor. "That means he'll be looking for the man as well. We listen in, and sooner or later he may end up talking to or about the guy. Then either he turns him in, or we do it for him."

Chaz's hopes stirred again. "That sounds as if it just might work."

"I also want you to see the rest of these." His father handed him the remainder of the photos from the file.

"What are M and M reports doing here?"

"I thought you'd tell me. Aren't those your initials signing off the resident and student orders?"

Chaz had to hold the snaps just right to see the writing. "Yeah, but what have they got to do with Kelly?"

"Could they have been what your darling Kelly was trying to hold over your head so you wouldn't go looking for her?"

"But it concluded here nothing was wrong. During my entire career I don't recall ever being faulted for using digoxin incorrectly."

"What exactly did she say to you the night she disappeared? Can you remember?"

Remember? How could he ever forget?

She had ambushed him as he left his Park Avenue office around five that Thursday afternoon. It was hot the way only New York could get in August, when the city sealed itself in its own bubble of dirt, exhaust, and exhaled CO_2 from eight million people.

Kelly's white dress had seemed to float on the humid air as she walked out from under the awning of the next door coffee shop. He had no idea how long she'd been waiting there. The only warning of the extent to which she was about to shake his world was the ferocity of the expression on her face.

"I'm leaving you, Chaz," she said, stopping while still five feet away, her arms folded across her breasts. "Tonight."

"What?" The people pushing by on either side of them blurred, the traffic noises sounded hollow and distant. He stepped toward her, his hands ready to grab her arms.

"Don't come any closer or I'll scream!"

The sibilant command stopped him cold. He hated public scenes. No doubt that was why she had staked out his office and caught him in a crowd. Seething, he remained where he stood, aware again of the people jostling his shoulders and wondering if they heard her. "Damn it, Kelly." He spoke through clenched teeth. "What do you think you're doing?"

"Leaving you. And don't try to follow me, or I'll ruin your career—put a stain on your record that'll never come out."

"What are you talking about?" His cheeks burning, he took another step.

"I warn you," she said in an overly loud voice. People turned to look at her. Some gave him funny glances. But no one stopped.

Except Chaz.

"Daddy's little progeny headed to be Chief of Cardiology," she said, her voice taunting and still far too loud for his liking.

"Well, forget about it," she went on. "One patient dead, one near dead, both on your watch. I can make you equally responsible, or not."

"What patients?" He could barely keep from lunging at her, as enraged at her slipping from his control as at what she said. But occasional passersby still seemed to be paying attention, especially to her.

"Think I'd tell you now, so you could make records disappear? Just know there's a viper in your nest, and you missed it."

"What are you talking about?"

"Stay away from me," she said, louder than ever, "and I'll clean it out so there's no reflection on you. Come after me, and your dream of being top dog at NYCH or anywhere else that counts is over."

"Kelly, for God's sake—"

Kelly gave him a look of triumphant defiance, turned on her heel, and ran to a cab parked a few car lengths away. Before he could think to race after her, she jumped inside, and the driver pulled away.

"Chaz?" His father's voice pulled him back to the present.

He found himself staring at his own clenched fists. He'd never told the police of the encounter. And gave only the sketchiest details to his father. He'd been too humiliated to say more.

"Chaz, I asked if you could recall exactly what Kelly said to you that last time you saw her. Didn't she threaten you in some way?"

Before answering, he took a slow deep breath and forced his hands to relax. "Yes. But what she said to me, word for word, was 'One patient dead, one near dead, both on your watch.' "

"So these two cases could be exactly what she was talking about?"

"I suppose so."

He began to collect the photos. "Do you remember these two people?"

"Are you kidding? I'd have to see their full charts."

"Of course." He thought a few seconds. "But better you not ask for them. I'll stay here tomorrow to greet our guests, then early Wednesday morning take the train to New York. I'll slip into medical records and discreetly pull the dossiers myself, unofficially of course, and find out what you might be up against without tipping off Roper or anyone else that we know about them."

A familiar fatigue engulfed Chaz as his father's preemptive strike to take charge did its usual work and drained whatever reservoir of strength he might have called upon to fend for himself. As if that part of him ever had a chance to exist. It lay withered and shrunken, the way any organ would end up after a lifetime of disuse.

. . . Beware a father of spectacular ability . . . They never let you fail, always stepping in to take over . . .

Her words taunted him from the grave.

Tuesday, November 20, 6:00 A.M.
Bacteriology Laboratory,
New York City Hospital

Donna Johnson, third-year medical student and part-time lab technician, was sound asleep on the staff-lounge couch when a noise out in the lab wakened her.

What the hell? No one should be there.

She stayed curled up in the darkness, her black skin an advantage for once. If anybody found out she sneaked in here to sleep, it'd be, hello pink slip, good-bye job.

The soft whir of a computer fan started up, a musical chord sounded as one of the countertop units was brought on-line, and a ghostly blue glow seeped through the wraparound windows separating this room from the rest of the bacteriology department.

Definitely somebody there. Thank God whoever it was hadn't turned on the overhead lights. The place where she lay remained in deep shadow.

Unable to see her watch, she'd no idea of the time. Without moving off the couch, she strained to see the wall clock out in the lab proper, keeping her head below the level of the sill.

She had trouble making out the numbers, and only then realized her glasses had slipped off as she slept. Hopelessly myopic without them, she felt around in the dark. No luck. They must have fallen down between the cushions. She again squinted toward the clock face, and figured it must be near six, the hands seeming to make a near-vertical line.

Shit. Let's hope this early bird will be quick. The day shift would be showing up in an hour. And she had to pee something awful. She lay back on the couch and tried to ignore her bladder. That just made the urge stronger. She raised her head enough to see over the sill, praying the person would be gone.

She could make out the back of someone in a white coat hunched over a computer while writing on a piece of paper.

Hardly anybody had cause to do emergency cultures or gram stains in the middle of the night. ER prepared their own slides to look at under the microscope, and on the floors, except for life-threatening infections such as meningitis or septic shock, most samples could wait until morning to be processed.

So who the hell was keeping her from going to pee?

The individual clicked off the computer, plunging the lab back into total darkness, but the thin beam of what must have been a penlight snapped on. The user walked it toward the far corner of the lab, passing between columns of fluorescent digital readouts and rows of black microscopes barely visible in the ambient light. He, or she, paused by a rack of unused petri dishes—round shallow containers lined with bouillon agar used to grow bacteria cultures—and slipped one of them into the pocket of the white coat, then continued to where the incubators glinted in the dim illumination.

A click, and one of the counter lights came to life. The black silhouette pulled on a pair of latex gloves from a nearby box, reached into the hood, and began to retrieve stack after stack of petri dishes, laying them out on the counter so that the identifying labels would have been visible, then returning them to the incubator. After five interminable minutes—Donna was crossing her legs and gritting her teeth—the person laid a specific dish aside, carefully lifted off the glass lid, located a supply of culture tubes on the lab bench, and, using the sterile Q-tip from one, scooped up a good-sized chunk of agar. Retrieving the unused container pocketed earlier, the figure then ran the swab over its surface, presumably plating out whatever organism had been harvested. Returning the original sample to its place in the incubator, the silhouette then extracted a Ziploc bag from another pocket, sealed the newly plated dish in it, snapped off the gloves, dumped them into a wastebasket, and turned off the counter light. Once more the thin beam of the penlight cut through the darkness, moving toward the door. The snap of the lock opening sounded loud in the absolute silence, and the white-coated visitor, momentarily framed in the faint light from the hallway, was gone.

Pretty fuckin' furtive, thought Donna, intrigued enough by what she'd just seen to forget the urgency of her previous problem.

She had her own small light to get around, a tiny red bulb on her key chain, and used it to make her way to the computer where the visitor had been working. Entering the access code, she clicked up the most recently viewed page.

Whoever it was had been after the preliminary culture results of specimens currently being incubated in the lab. Scrolling down the screen she saw:

Neisseria gonorrhea.
Streptococcus pneumoniae.
Staphylococcus aureus.

From her studies, Donna knew they were nasty bugs, but nothing out of the ordinary for a hospital.

Campylobacter jejuni.

A commonplace pathogen ingested from undercooked beef or chicken that could cause enteritis, or the runs. Easily treated with ciprofloxacin.

Salmonella.
Shigella.

More serious causes for the runs. Quick to act, would have victims shitting blood, but again, readily treated.

Escherichia coli 0157:H7.

Oh, oh. This one was trouble.

Her memory spit out the pathogenesis. As few as ten organisms could cause an infection. The symptoms were puking and pouring out bloody diarrhea within forty-eight hours. But it was the toxins released by these particular bacteria that could really hit the victim. Ten percent of the time they produced a nightmare condition called hemolytic uremic syndrome by attaching themselves to receptor sites on the inside surface of a patient's blood vessels. This would cause red cells to rupture, platelets to fall, bleeding to increase, kidneys to fail, and the brain to seize. Once it got that far, the victim had a 50 percent chance of ending up on dialysis and at least a 5 percent chance of winding up on a slab in the morgue. For *Escherichia coli 0157:H7* was the organism responsible for what the media called *Toxic Hamburger Disease*, but it could also be transmitted in water.

At least, that was what she remembered reading in her books.

Troubled, she went over to check out the incubator. Everything seemed in order. But other than going through each culture to see which had had a scoop removed, there was no way of knowing which dish had been sampled, or why, or even if there was anything amiss in what had been done. Perhaps it was only a graduate student doing research who needed a specimen of a particular organism for some project.

One thing was certain, she wasn't going to say anything. Otherwise, she'd have to explain why she'd been in here.

Her beeper went off, and she jumped, the high-pitched signal splitting through the quiet like a burglar alarm. The tiny message plate indicated the telephone number for ER. They'd need bloods drawn and analyzed or urines spun and looked at under a microscope.

But first, she had to find a bathroom. And her glasses.

Chapter 10

The aroma of a geriatric ward in the morning always got to Earl. It wasn't just the hint of human waste mingled with the smells of coffee, eggs, bacon, or other offerings on the breakfast menu—he encountered those every day in ER. It was the staleness of the air. It seemed as locked in as the patients, and had both a sour and soapy-sweet odor that hung heavy, a pungent reminder of failing flesh.

As he made his way toward the reception desk through the flow of orderlies, nurses, and elderly patients, a young woman of medium height dressed in a jogging outfit stepped up to him and eyed his identity badge. "Ah, Dr. Garnet. I've been expecting you."

Her shaved haircut made him wonder if she'd either had chemo, treated herself for lice, or done a recent stint in the Marines. Her ID read NURSE TANYA WOZCEK.

"Hi," he said, shaking her hand. "Are you one of the people taking care of Bessie McDonald?" From her civies he figured she was off duty.

"Yes, I'm also the only staff person willing to talk with you. Want a coffee?"

"What?"

"Do you want a coffee?"

"No, I mean *yes*, I do. But what's this about there being no one else—"

"First, I suggest you see Bessie and speak with the resident who was on duty the night she became comatose. He's with her now." Without giving him a chance to reply, she led the way down the hallway, navigating between the shuffling men and women in housecoats, most inching along with the aid of walkers. "You and I can speak afterward," she added, glancing back at him over her shoulder.

"But what about the other nurses—"

"Everyone knows you're investigating something in connection with Kelly McShane's murder and that it involves Chaz Braden. They aren't willing to speak out and risk his reprisals."

Caught off guard, Earl reflexively went on the offensive. "Who told you such nonsense?" Damn that talkative Lena Downie. She must have spilled the beans after all. So much for keeping his interest in the case on the quiet side. But maybe he could still bluff it out. "That kind of rumor is far from helpful—"

"Come off it. We figured it out as soon as the request to see Bessie's charts for 1974 came through. Since Chaz Braden was her doctor at the time, and the coroner who made the application for the files is the one investigating the killing—it wasn't hard. What we can't put together is the tie-in between Kelly's death and Bessie."

"Oh?" It was all he could think of to say.

She punched in a code on an electronic lock and let them into a small kitchen. Within minutes he had a styrofoam cup filled to the brim with steaming black sludge—what his residents would have called a real stomach-stripper. Not even a triple milk and double sugar helped tame it any. He took a sip to be polite, trying hard not to wince.

"I want you to know Bessie was fine when I went off duty that night," she said, pouring a coffee for herself.

"Okay," he said, indicating with a shrug she should elaborate as they continued down the corridor.

"It doesn't strike you as odd? The newspaper article confirms that Kelly's remains are found, and within twenty-four hours, Bessie is in a coma."

"Now wait a minute. Surely you're not insinuating—"

"I don't like coincidences!" She ran a hand over the stubble on her scalp. "Especially convenient ones."

Earl didn't like coincidences either. Most doctors didn't. But he'd also an ingrained aversion to melodrama. "If you're suggesting what I think, isn't it a little over the top?" He'd lowered his voice, passing a couple of nurses who seemed to have stopped what they were doing and grown very quiet. "Could we perhaps have this conversation where it's a little more private?"

Tanya's drawn face relaxed into a smile. "Of course. Sorry." She turned her attention to the gray, loose-skinned inhabitants who wandered the place like ghosts, greeting them by their first names as she made her way along the corridor.

An old lady, drooped over in a wheelchair and mumbling to herself, lifted her head and responded, "Morning, Tanya." A food-spattered hospital gown lay draped over her like a drop cloth.

An elderly man wearing oversize trousers held up by red suspenders leaned against the wall, his hands resting on the head of his cane. He gazed blankly at her, clearly not recognizing who she was, or perhaps it was the sound of his own name he found perplexing.

All along the hallway wrinkled features brightened into wispy, almost hopeful smiles, as if the sound of someone calling them had penetrated the gray limbo where they lived and ignited the flicker of a shared dream. At last someone they knew had come here and would take them home, back to where they could remember.

Heartbreaking as this was to witness, Earl liked Tanya's tenderness toward her patients. She could engage the remnants of whoever they once were with a warm hello or bestow a moment of dignity on them simply by addressing them with respect. Too many doctors and nurses burned out in what the cynical called "exit medicine."

"As to what I'm suggesting," she whispered, once they reached a section that was free of her coworkers, "I know it sounds off the wall, but I'm just so upset. She was my patient for the last three months, and I really grew to like her. We don't get many who can actually make it out of here, and she had a chance to end her days in style, compared to the dead ends that await these other lonely souls. Around here, that's like a little miracle, and I got caught up in it." She turned and stared him right in the eye, her intensity startling him. "So let's just say I want to make sure you consider all the possibilities before you conclude what happened to her."

Strange woman. Intense, even a touch paranoid perhaps, but sincere. Maybe she thought she'd missed a subtle clinical sign or dismissed something Bessie McDonald had said that might have warned of another stroke being imminent. Sometimes grasping at impossible scenarios was easier than admitting a mistake, especially a near-lethal one. "You're positive

Mrs. McDonald was okay? The harbingers of throwing off emboli can be very subtle, as I'm sure you know—a little shadow on the visual field, transient numbness or weakness in a limb—"

"She would have told me. She was a physician, a GP."

The news took Earl by surprise. "Nothing on her chart indicated she was a doctor."

"She wouldn't allow it, nor us calling her doctor."

"But why?" Any patients he'd ever had who were physicians usually trumpeted the fact to everyone and anyone who came near them, as if it was a Visa or MasterCard for special treatment.

" 'Makes people nervous, and that's why things always go wrong when an MD is the patient,' she used to say."

Earl shook his head. He felt the same way, but had never prevented his profession from being stated in a medical file.

"She was so set on getting to her son's," Tanya continued, "she never would have ignored any warning symptoms."

Earl nevertheless resisted joining her flight of fancy. "There also might not have been any warning symptoms."

"I know."

"And she had a lot of risk factors. Another stroke isn't improbable."

"I know that, too."

"So why the suspicions?"

She quickly glanced around. A few steps away a woman stood with a blank, dark-eyed stare on her face and her gray hair in wild disarray.

But no staff were in sight.

"Because I think Chaz Braden is a slimeball who's capable of anything," Tanya said, and continued down the corridor.

Earl hurried after her. "Care to elaborate?"

"Not really. If I get caught bad-mouthing the bastard, I'll be out on my ass."

"Then will you answer some specific questions by 'yes' or 'no'?"

"Depends on the question."

"Did Mrs. McDonald indicate she knew anything about Kelly McShane's death?"

"No."

"Did she insinuate anything incriminating about Chaz Braden?"

"No."

"Did she ever express having any fear of him?"

"No."

"Did she indicate to you she had anything at all to tell about her admission under Chaz Braden in 'seventy-four?"

Tanya spun about to face him again. "Yes. She said she didn't like the man, and wanted to talk about it, but I was too busy at the time. And I repeat, when I left her that last night she was fine."

Sounded as if Tanya did feel a tad guilty. "So you didn't listen to an old lady go on about a former doctor she'd disliked twenty-seven years ago—not exactly a cardinal sin."

"If I had taken the time—"

"She still would have had her stroke. I don't see why you're so quick to suspect foul play."

Her shoulders rose, a sign that he had irritated her. She stopped at a closed door and gestured that he should enter. "See Bessie McDonald for yourself, Dr. Garnet," she said through clenched teeth. "Then let's talk about what you think happened."

They walked in on an elderly woman laid out still as a corpse in a hospital gown. An orange tube stuck out of her mouth from which intermittent gurgling noises came as her chest rose and fell. An IV tube ran from a clear bag of fluid into her left arm. A transparent catheter protruded from between her legs and carried urine to a bag strapped on the railing at the side of the bed. A multiscreened monitor flashed continuous readings of her vitals.

At a glance Earl took in that she was breathing on her own, had been receiving sufficient hydration to keep her kidneys functioning, possessed a normal heart rate, rhythm, and blood pressure, and, according to the information relayed from a clip on her finger, just about perfect oxygen levels in her blood.

So why wasn't she sitting up and waving at him?

A young man in a white coat looked over from where he'd been methodically tapping at her knees with a reflex hammer. He had bushy red hair, and his name tag read DR. P. ROY. When Tanya made the introductions, he practically clicked his heels.

Earl got down to business. "So what happened?"

"The night staff found her unresponsive on the floor at the entrance to her room around 4:00 A.M.," Dr. P. Roy began. "They immediately called me."

"She was seizing when you found her?"

"No, but there was a lot of blood in her mouth and tooth marks on her lips and tongue. Grand mal was obvious."

"Vitals?"

"As you see now."

"Did you do the DONT?"

"The what, sir?"

"The DONT. Dextrose, oxygen, narcan, and thiamine." He was stating an anagram he always used to teach residents the basic ER approach to coma, listing the first variables to be thought of whenever a patient presented with an altered level of consciousness. An IV bolus of dextrose, or sugar, would have corrected hypoglycemia. A measure of her O_2 saturation would have signaled any respiratory causes for the coma, and the administration of oxygen possibly turned them around. Narcan would be the antidote to reverse a narcotic overdose, and thiamine administration treated a deficiency of the vitamin that sometimes caused persistent confusional states in malnourished individuals, such as alcoholics.

Dr. P. Roy flushed. "Well, no, not exactly, sir. I did make sure her airway and O_2 were okay. But it seemed pretty obvious she'd had another stroke and seized."

"Really? Any focal signs in your neurological exam, now or then?" Earl referred to the abnormalities of sensation, movement, and reflexes that would have occurred in the specific region of her body controlled by whatever part of the brain a recent embolus might have injured.

"No, at least not any new ones that I could tell. She did have some minor abnormal reflexes from her previous event."

"Shouldn't there have been at least a change in those, if you attributed her seizure to another massive embolus? And it would have to have been massive to leave her comatose, wouldn't it?"

"Well, yes—"

"Did you do bloods at all that morning?"

His face brightened. "Of course. They were all normal, including her sugar."

"Was that sample drawn before or after you gave her an IV?"

Roy grew red in the face again. "After."

"How long?"

He swallowed. "About an hour later."

"An hour?"

"I ordered they be taken stat, but, well, on this ward, especially at night, we aren't given much of a priority by the lab—"

"Could you excuse us a minute, nurse?"

Tanya nodded, then slipped out the door.

Earl closed it behind her. "You should have insisted they make it a priority, Dr. Roy." He had no patience for that kind of passivity in his own department, and always taught his residents to stand up to it.

"Why—"

"Had she signed a do not resuscitate order?"

"No, but I figured—"

"Figured you were her last stop before she got to God, and she deserved your best shot at bringing her around."

"But—"

"What was in the IV?"

"Two-thirds, one-third," he answered, referring to a common intravenous mixture of sodium chloride and glucose.

"So even if she was hypoglycemic when she'd seized, you'd expect a normal level of glucose afterward, since you had been infusing her with it."

Roy flushed some more. "Yes, I guess, except why would this patient be hypoglycemic in the first place? She didn't have a history of diabetes, let alone diabetic medications."

"Ever hear of a medication error?"

Roy went an even deeper shade of red.

"The point is," Earl continued, "at the time of finding someone comatose, you can't presume anything about how the person got that way, especially since they can't tell you what happened. So you 'do the DONT' as we say, running through all the possibilities beginning with checking her serum glucose. And if you haven't got a dextrose stick handy, you still can figure that a single rapid bolus of concentrated IV glucose never hurt anyone, even a diabetic." Untreated, nerve cells die by the millions for every second hypoglycemia is allowed to persist, and the patient is at risk to seize, choke to death, or lose enough brain tissue to end up a living vegetable. Every first-year medical student knows this, so Earl saw no need to point it out to Roy. "It's good you at least gave her some sugar," he continued, "but it was too slow and too little, as far as being any therapeutic benefit to her. All you accomplished was to wipe out any evidence that her level had been low in the first place." Any medical student would also know that if Dr. P. Roy had acted properly, Bessie McDonald might not be in her current state. No point to rubbing it in. This guy looked sunburned enough already, and no one could ever prove it. But that's what he would have trouble living with, once he digested all the facts. He'd never be able to disprove it either.

"Hey, I did do an O_2 sat, and it was fine just as it is now, and if she mistakenly got a narcotic overdose, her respirations would have been suppressed," he said, beginning to sound more annoyed than defensive. "As

for thiamine, she sure as hell hadn't been malnourished or gone on a recent bender . . ."

Earl ignored whatever lame excuses the kid offered up—chances were
good he wouldn't screw up his next coma case—and refocused on what
bothered him most about Bessie McDonald—her lack of focal signs.
"What's her level of consciousness today?" he asked, referring to a scor-
ing system by which a patient's response to verbal and painful stimuli was
measured.

Roy looked taken aback, having built up a good head of indignation
trying to justify himself and implying that an outsider who wasn't on staff
had no business berating him anyway. "Lousy," he said after a few seconds, his face sullen. "She's a three, exactly like the night we found her."

A dead body would earn as much, just for being there.

"You ordered a CT scan?"

"What was the point? I thought I knew the diagnosis—a massive stroke—
plus the lady was gorked."

"Has your differential expanded any, after our discussion?"

He sighed heavily. Deflated, he seemed a shirt size smaller and an inch
shorter, as did most kiddie-docs foolish enough to attempt a head-butt
with a veteran rather than admit a mistake. "A CT will be done later today,
sir," he said, his unconditional capitulation made evident by the sudden
disappearance of the word "but" from his vocabulary. "And an EEG."

The former would visualize the extent of damage from a recent blood
clot, if that was the cause. The latter, an electrical encephalogram, would
pick up any remaining spark of electrical activity in the cortex of her
brain, the stuff of walking and talking.

Earl asked Tanya to come back in the room. "You said she was found on
the floor by the door?"

"Yes. We think she knew something wasn't right and was trying to get
help."

"She didn't use the call button?"

"They found it unplugged."

"I think she must have pulled it out by accident when she reached for
it," Roy added.

Tanya's brow arched, but she said nothing.

Earl followed her back toward the nursing station. "Anybody see Chaz
Braden around here that night?"

She immediately slowed. "So you agree with me, that it's possible he
did this to her?" she whispered, once they were side by side.

"I agree only that it doesn't look like a stroke, nothing more. For God's sake, don't go spouting crazy ideas."

She gave him a "yeah, right" look.

"So did somebody see him?"

"No. I already checked. But that doesn't mean he wasn't on the floor. Coverage is minimal that shift, and he could easily have sneaked in."

"Care to tell me now why you're so down on him?"

"Why? My reasons have nothing to do with Bessie."

"I want to know the extent of your beef with the man, and if that might cloud your judgment toward him."

She walked a few steps farther without saying anything, then slowed her pace until they were walking alongside each other. "I worked in cardiac ICU before being transferred here. He's a slimeball. Put his hands on me one night. I complained, and got transferred for my trouble. Not that I mind it here. I like old people. But my training is in critical care."

He eyed the procession of elderly men and women tottering back and forth along the corridor and wondered how he'd feel if someone pulled him out of ER to plunk him down in their midst. "Quite a culture shock," he said.

"But don't think I'm fingering him just because I want to get even with the guy. I really liked Bessie. If someone did mess with her, all I'm after is to damn well make sure nobody just shuffles what happened here under the rug. They're a little laissez-faire about relapses and death around this floor for my liking."

Earl again sympathized. Geriatrics was a discipline of settling, becoming resigned to death; in critical care, however, as in ER, they defied it.

"There's another person to whom she might have confided. Dr. Collins visited her that night."

"Melanie?"

"Just a social call. Bessie wasn't admitted under her this time. But she thought the world of Dr. Collins. Told me more than once how that woman's fast action staved off her first stroke. She blamed her current doctors for not doing the same."

"Why do you think she'd tell Melanie anything about Chaz?"

"Bessie had been in a mood to talk about him, and I don't think she intended to be flattering. Since I didn't have time to listen, maybe she bent Dr. Collins's ear."

Earl thanked her and took the elevator down to the ground floor where he slipped outside the Thirty-third Street entrance, determined to contact

Melanie. In the harsh glare of winter sunlight, he joined the other cell phone users who restlessly circled and turned like pigeons flocked at the pedestal of a statue, their murmurings rising above the noisy morning traffic.

He had to settle on leaving her yet another message. Why wasn't she answering her calls?

An attempt to reach Mark yielded the same out-of-order recording he'd gotten last night.

"The whole planet's gone wireless, and I can't talk to a soul," he muttered, waiting for an operator to get him the man's home number.

This time he got through.

"Roper."

"Mark, it's Earl Garnet. I've got news."

"I hope it's better than mine. But you first."

Earl told him all about Bessie McDonald, including the possibility that a few weeks after Kelly's disappearance his father might have pulled her chart along with that of the man who'd died of digoxin toxicity. As he talked, he heard an annoying series of *clicks* on the line. *Probably the result of a poor connection,* he thought, ignoring them.

10:30 A.M.
Hampton Junction

Mark could tell a lot about a medical resident's skill after observing the person handle a single patient.

Watching Lucy O'Connor, he waited until a half dozen of his regulars had passed through her hands before he admitted she practiced medicine as well as he'd first thought, she was that good. Most trainees managed a small number of people while he saw to the bulk of the visits, the entire process made much longer by his need to review and sometimes revise what they did. So far Lucy had seen all the morning appointments by herself, doing it as efficiently and thoroughly as he normally would. On checking her work, he found himself discussing cases with her on the level of a colleague, and she referred to recent journal articles with ease. What impressed him most was how, while drawing on an academic knowledge base that he considered awesome, she kept her therapeutic decisions practical and her recommendations for referrals or tests tailored to what they had available in the sticks.

And the local vote was unanimous.

"I like her!"

"She's wonderful."

"Not like those other 'kids' they usually send you."

So he sat at his desk with time on his hands while Lucy worked the examining room. Besides using the opportunity to arrange for a loaner Jeep with his insurance company and make a stab at the piles of unopened mail, he kept trying to make sense of everything Earl had told him.

That his father had gone after those same two charts didn't surprise him. After all, it was evident from Kelly's file he'd had an interest in them. What that interest had been, he still hadn't a clue.

The coincidence of Bessie McDonald slipping into a coma the night after Kelly's body was identified—that left him incredulous. He couldn't help but speculate how someone could have arranged for her to convulse herself into the far side of oblivion. As ideas popped into his head, he grabbed a pencil and started to jot a few down.

Strychnine?

Convulsions were a hallmark of its lethal effects. Not only would it be detected on testing but also would leave a telltale rictus grin on the victim's face. Not much of a choice if the "relapse" were to be taken as natural.

What about something that caused seizures but wasn't normally thought of as a poison? There were a lot of medications with convulsions as a side effect that wouldn't initially be thought of as an agent to test for, as long as no one suspected unnatural causes. Lidocaine, the antiarrhythmic and local anesthetic, for instance, could cause prolonged seizures if given intravenously in large enough doses. But it or other drugs wouldn't be so likely to escape notice in a forensic investigation. After all, a suspicious toxicologist could think up just as many agents as any poisoner when it came to screening for the pharmacology of deliberately induced status epilepticus. Would Chaz, for instance, have been reckless enough to assume no one would consider the woman's coma to be the result of foul play?

Maybe . . . or maybe not.

Mark grabbed his copy of *Harrison's Principles of Internal Medicine* off his bookshelf and opened it to the section on seizures. Finding a table listing their causes, he considered other possibilities.

Trauma—too obvious.

Alcohol—too messy.

Recreational drugs—too obvious and messy.

Metabolic disturbances: Hypocalcemia; hypomagnesemia; hyponatremia—now here was something.

Some of these could be induced by medication, but persist after the offending pills were discontinued.

Take severe hyponatremia, a low sodium level in the blood, as an example. It could be brought on in susceptible individuals by certain diuretics, even at normal dose levels.

But that couldn't be the case here. It would have taken days, maybe weeks to make it happen, not twenty-four hours. Unless Chaz, or someone, hadn't waited for the police to confirm Kelly's identity before making his move against Bessie. After all, he knew what the result would be, and it made sense to act ahead of time—no, that didn't work either. The blood tests they'd done on Bessie the morning they found her would have revealed the drop in sodium.

Of course, there was the possibility of induced hypoglycemia. A shot of short-acting insulin could start a nondiabetic's blood sugar heading downward in less than an hour, the maximum effect occurring within five to six hours. Since the nurses hadn't been able to pin down the precise time of the seizure, the insulin could have been wearing off after they found her, and the intravenous dextrose she received would have masked any lingering effects. As for the time sequence, she would have had to receive the injection before midnight. Chaz could easily have concocted a reason to be in the hospital at that hour, though he'd have been taking a chance slipping into her room himself. So maybe he'd arranged for someone else to do his dirty work—He threw down his pencil and crumpled up his notes. *Listen to me,* he thought. Last night's attack had him so chomping at the bit to nail Chaz, he was becoming obsessed with the man, dreaming up ludicrously wild scenarios about him.

For the hundredth time he eyed the phone, willing Dan to call with word on what he'd found at the wreck and whether he'd talked with Braden. Phoning the sheriff himself wasn't exactly an option, having already bugged him so many times Dan had told him to back off.

He returned to opening his mail, trying to keep his mind off it all.

A few envelopes down the pile he found the letter from the Dean's Office with Lucy O'Connor's records and an accompanying letter explaining the change of schedule. Skimming through her résumé, he read she had completed medical school at McGill in Montreal, but had applied to the

NYCH family medicine program after seven years in the field with a group called *Médecins du Globe.*

Wow, Mark thought, immediately recognizing the name. Those people were the Marines of medicine. Working out of Paris, the organization was known worldwide and had received the Nobel Peace Prize for going into areas of conflict all over the planet to treat civilian casualties. Anybody involved with them worked under the most grueling of situations. Not only would the job have been mentally devastating—a lot of volunteers returned with post-traumatic stress disorders—but physicians sometimes died, killed either by bullets or the diseases they were treating—cholera, dengue, Lhasa fever, and a host of other infectious horrors he'd read about but never faced firsthand.

No wonder she knew her stuff . . . and karate.

What also struck him was how quickly she'd been accepted into the two-year program at NYCH. She'd only approached them in June of the previous year, less than three weeks before the usual July 1 start of any residency. Her introductory letter stated she'd completed her current tour of duty with *Médecins du Globe* earlier than expected and inquired if they had any vacancies. The last-minute request for a position came with a half dozen glowing recommendations from her current colleagues and former professors at McGill. NYCH had immediately snapped her up.

Obviously they had an opening, he thought, knowing many posts went unfilled these days since HMOs were making the healing profession less attractive than an MBA. But she also must have impressed the admissions board as much as she was in the process of wowing him. They wouldn't take just anybody.

He was about to put the papers away when he spotted the correspondence regarding her rural rotation. It was dated November 6, two weeks ago exactly, requesting the program director to allow her to switch her slot so as to do her rural training period as soon as possible. To facilitate the change, she'd even foregone her own vacation. Her manning the wards at the time the hospital would be most short of house staff was her offer, not the insistence of the director.

I'm flattered, he thought. He proceeded to file everything where he'd be able to find it again when her three months were up and it was time to fill in the evaluation forms. But from the looks of her, he could have filled them out now. It would be *A+* right across the board.

He tried to get through another few letters, but once more his thoughts turned to Bessie McDonald and ways of inducing a coma.

Within minutes he was arguing with the head nurse of the geriatric wing at NYCH, insisting they check their short-acting insulin supplies to see if any were missing.

11:00 A.M.
Medical Records,
New York City Hospital

"Dr. Garnet," Lena Downie whispered at his shoulder, "it's the call you've been expecting from Dr. Collins."

Finally! he thought, following in Lena's wake as she led him to a phone behind the front counter. She had the rolling gait of a female John Wayne.

"Melanie?"

"Earl! Sorry I didn't get back to you earlier, but I've been up to my ass in crocodiles with budget meetings last night and rounds this morning—"

"Hey, don't apologize. I've been there many times."

"What can I do for you?"

"Bessie McDonald, a former patient of yours, is the woman whose M and M report was in Kelly's file. Mark said he spoke to you about it Sunday night, but didn't have the name yet."

"Bessie? Well, my, God. That's a weird coincidence. I knew she'd had a relapse two weeks ago. The nurses on her floor notified my office that she was found comatose one morning at 4:00 A.M. I'd even dropped in for a long overdue visit the day before, and she was fine—well, you know how these things go. I just assumed she must have thrown another embolus. But it was her chart Mark asked about? This is really strange. Do they know what happened to her?"

"The CT shows no infarcts, so it's probably metabolic, but—"

The sight of Lena hovering nearby interrupted him. "I need to talk with you in private," he said instead.

"Sure. I've got rounds until five. How about we meet at my apartment? I can make us a pitcher of the best martinis you ever had, and we can discuss whatever you want with no interruptions."

"Sounds good."

She gave him the directions.

Back at his desk, he returned to what he'd been doing since morning—
reexamining Bessie's old records from 1974 to the present. The reason?
Tanya Wozcek had gotten him thinking the worst. Yet he'd gone over
everything a second time and still couldn't find a single entry that suggested an error in her management back then. At least not the kind that
gets written down.

So he'd gone searching through the rest of her old charts, checking subsequent admissions to see if she had any tendency to develop any transient
metabolic states that might have spiked her digoxin level, yet been missed in
'seventy-four because they came and went: things like renal failure from dehydration; side effects of other medications; interactions with those drugs—
he looked for them all.

The result? Nothing.

That left only two other possibilities: the sort of accident that occurs in
the syringe, a nurse drawing up too much digoxin—or what Janet had suggested, a deliberate overdose. Given that the same woman now lay in a
coma, also unexplained, tilted him toward the latter.

However, the records here only went up to the admission under Melanie
four years ago, the one Tanya had mentioned. The more recent entries
would be in her active chart on the floor. Should he go back upstairs and
poke through them too? He glanced at his watch and saw it was nearly
1:00 P.M. He might as well, to be complete. After all, he had the rest of
the afternoon before Melanie got off duty. He could also try to reach
the people whose resident numbers were on the old M and M reports,
if the teaching office could track them down for him. Who knew what
bizarre piece of information one of them might remember that would prove
useful?

Before closing the chart, he took a final glance through the clinical
notes Melanie had written at the time of the first embolus, refreshing his
memory about what had been done so he could more easily pick up the
threads of the patient's story when he got to the floor.

Precise, to the point, and clear, they documented why she had thought
McDonald's symptoms were the result of a clot, not a bleed, and warranted immediate thrombolitic therapy. Earl was impressed. The symptoms and signs distinguishing one from the other were subtle. In his
own ER he'd seen seasoned neurologists dither over similar cases, then not
insist as authoritatively as they should have for an immediate CT, thereby
wasting precious minutes. Not Melanie. "Eyeball to needle time" as the

residents called it, or the duration from when they first saw the patient to the infusion of a clot buster, had taken three-quarters of an hour, which meant she hadn't squandered a second in making her own diagnosis and getting radiology to prove it. "Well done, Melanie," he said under his breath.

As he walked out the door, Lena gave him a frosty good-bye, making it clear she hadn't appreciated his denying her a chance to eavesdrop.

Chapter 11

"I read your transcript today," Mark said to Lucy, as they shared a late lunch of soup and salad at his kitchen table. "No wonder you handled yourself so well with my patients."

She chuckled, with her mouth full of lettuce. "My past was no secret, if you'd read your mail lately. That's quite a pile on your desk."

"It's a bad habit of mine, avoiding mail. All I seem to get is forms, bills, and professional questionnaires. I hate paper-maze stuff."

"Join the paperless society and use e-mail."

"I did. That gave me even more junk to deal with, so I canceled it."

"I'm surprised. You being way out here yet not wired—"

"Oh, I'm on the net and have necessary passwords that let me access labs and X-ray departments to get test results." He knew he sounded defensive, but he didn't want this sophisticated, world-traveled lady to think he was a hick.

"It's just that I never met anybody in America who doesn't have e-mail," she said.

He grinned and held out his arm. "Want to touch me to see if I'm real?"

She laughed, skewering what looked like half a head of Romaine with her fork and toasting him with it.

"Tell me about where you were stationed with *Médecins du Globe*," he said, figuring he'd mangled the pronunciation.

Her smile vanished. "I'm afraid it was the grand misery tour, from Papua New Guinea tribal wars to refugee camps in Somalia, Rwanda, Bosnia, and Albania."

There was hardness in her voice that told him she didn't want to talk about it. "I can only imagine what you've seen," he said, after casting about for something to say. It sounded lame.

She remained quiet for a few seconds, then asked, "You were never tempted to join? Obviously you have a taste for challenge, working out here."

"No, never tempted."

"Why? Most of the time we're not getting shot at, if that's what you mean. Much of the work is a lot like this morning. Sick people come in, tell you what's the matter, and you treat them. Except we deal out of tents and the backs of trucks."

He noticed how she talked about the work as if it were ongoing for her. As for her making it sound routine, "Yeah, right," he said. "You guys are awesome. It sure explains how you seemed so comfortable handling my patients. This practice must seem like child's play compared to what you're used to."

The corners of her mouth twitched upward like a pair of mischievous quotation marks. "Well, we did have distractions in the field that you don't, like local warlords to keep happy, and creepy crawlies in our sleeping bags, which I can definitely say I do not miss."

"Don't sell the Adirondacks short in the creepy crawlies department."

"What do you mean?"

"When I was in medical school I did a rotation through an ER in Lake Placid. A hiker came in with puncture marks on his leg claiming a rattler bit him."

"I thought there weren't any poisonous snakes in upstate New York."

"That's exactly what they told the hiker in ER. Wouldn't give him antivenom."

"So what did he do?"

Mark's grin widened. "Went back to the trail where the damn thing attacked him, found it, and killed it with a tire iron. He returned to the hospital and threw it on the desk of the triage nurse. He got the shot."

Lucy started to laugh. "No!"

"Saw it with my own eyes. It was even in the journals. Apparently the rattler escaped from a reptile zoo nearby. Taught me to always believe the patient." He glanced at his watch and pushed away from the table. "We've got to get moving. House calls."

*   *   *

Lucy followed Mark's directions along an unplowed back road. A brilliant sky provided the perfect blue to contrast with the fresh snow, the sun cast a glitter over everything, and the mountainous contours in the distance seductively beckoned him to ski their curves.

"You know what I love about the first winter storm?" Lucy said as she navigated the coiling road much faster than Mark would have liked.

"What?" He began to keep a wary eye on the ditch, as if that would protect them any.

"Overnight it smooths away all the boundaries, curbs, sidewalks, roads—the things that tell us where to go or what lines to stay between—and makes a place seem all so open, as if for once we can go any which way we want and ignore the rules."

"Really." Pressed against the passenger door as she slithered through yet another turn, he wondered if she meant it literally. "How come you dropped out from all the excitement of *Médecins du Globe* to take a residency in family medicine?" Perhaps if he got her talking, she'd slow down.

"There are only so many nights a person can sleep on the ground worried about bullets and bugs. I was due to come home."

"Where's that now?"

"New York. I can't get enough of the city."

Like all the other women he knew. "So how did you like McGill?"

"Ah, Montréal," she said, leaving out the *t* and pronouncing the city's name the French way. The ease with which she slipped into the accent suggested a facility with the language rather than affectation. "Wonderful."

"I take it you speak French?"

They weaved through an *S* that should have qualified them for the Grand Prix circuit, and a smile created tiny creases around her eyes.

He had to admit she was a superb driver.

"Raised with it," she said. "My mother was French."

"But O'Connor is Irish."

"That's Dad. He worked for a petrochemical company when he met Mom during a posting in Montréal. Fire meeting fire, those two. For my brothers and me, it was like living between two opera stars—passion personified."

"You grew up in Montreal?"

"First years of my life only. Dad led us all over the world, including the Middle East. I guess that's where I inherited my wanderlust. But enough about me. Tell me your story, Dr. Mark Roper, starting with what the hell happened to you last night. I presume it's got something to do with why you don't have wheels today."

Should he confide the events of the last few weeks to her? Part of the curriculum he promised residents included exposure to the world of a country coroner, so why not? After all, it would be no different than trusting her with medically confidential material in his files. "You read about the body of Chaz Braden's wife being found near here?"

"Who at NYCH hasn't? I also saw your name in the paper, and Dan's too, come to think of it, in connection with the investigation." Her eyes widened. "Does that case have to do with last night?"

"I'm afraid so." He began to relate the events that had unfolded since he and Dan discovered the remains at the bottom of Trout Lake. As the story progressed and he recounted his childhood impressions of Kelly, Lucy's expression grew somber. When he described what he'd found in his father's medical files, quoting parts of the letter by memory, she shook her head.

"That ill-starred woman," she said. "To sound so happy—yet be on the brink of her death. Do you have any idea who the man was?"

"No," he answered, a little too quickly, and moved on to describe how Chaz Braden had been a suspect at the time of the disappearance, then cleared by the police. He also filled her in on the file Everett had given him. He left out a lot, too, said nothing about Chaz's or anyone else's behavior at the funeral, and, when recounting the previous night's shooting, made no mention of who he suspected had been the man with the rifle. After all, she was a resident in the hospital where Braden worked. Whatever he thought of the creep, he had no right to share his suspicions. They could blight any future teacher-resident relationship she might be obliged to have with Chaz as part of her program.

When he'd finished, she gaped at him in amazement. "You think he killed her, then tried to kill you because you're onto him?"

"I'm not saying that."

"But you feel it was him, don't you?"

So much for pulling off the persona of being an unbiased investigator. He'd have to be more careful to distance himself from whatever he said about the case to her, but she felt so much more a colleague than a protégé. Still, he held to propriety. "No comment, Dr. O'Connor, and you don't talk about this conversation with your friends back in New York, understand?"

"Of course not." She sounded annoyed with him for even thinking such a thing.

"Sorry, but this is a murder investigation, and I want it done by the book, so nobody can scream 'foul.' "

"I understand entirely." Her tone said the opposite.

God, he hated when women did that, got all frosty and reasonable, while making it clear they thought he was full of crap.

They drove a few miles without saying anything, the easy ambiance they'd first established replaced by awkward silence.

Why should he feel so bad? It wasn't as if he'd overreacted.

A few more miles went by.

Okay, maybe he overreacted a little bit. She must have felt he was putting her in her place, or something silly like that.

But he definitely didn't have anything to apologize for.

Not a damn thing.

Nothing.

"Sorry, Lucy, for speaking so sharply. After last night, this case has me on edge."

"Oh, don't apologize. You're absolutely within your rights, protecting the integrity of an inquiry."

Like hell she thought that. "No, I apologize."

It still didn't feel right between them. The only way to make amends was to go on taking her into his confidence. "Now let me tell you the rest of what you need to know, then I'd like to hear your ideas." He continued the story, describing the morbidity-mortality reports in Kelly's file, the fact that someone had broken into his house after the funeral, apparently to go through them, and what happened to Bessie McDonald two weeks ago. "I've recruited one of Kelly's former classmates to go over the woman's files. Her coma seemed a little too convenient for my liking."

Lucy continued to drive without speaking, but obviously lost in thought. The chill had vanished and Mark started to relax, finding her speed didn't bother him as much. It wasn't reckless, and he'd often driven faster. He just resisted relinquishing control to someone else behind the wheel.

"I really would like to work on this with you while I'm here," she said after a few minutes, "if you'll accept my help."

"No question of it. Your rotation is meant to let you experience all aspects of being a rural physician, and this business is part of my job."

She glanced over at him. "Solving Kelly McShane's murder has to mean a lot more to you than just being part of your job. From the way you described knowing her, she must have been very important to you as a child."

The velvet quiet of her voice surprised him more than what she'd said. "Yes. She certainly was special."

"Your telling about her, what she'd been like, really got to me. I couldn't help thinking . . ."

"She reminded you of yourself, maybe? Young, ambitious, ready to take on the world?" He'd said it without thinking, and no sooner were the words out of his mouth, he felt presumptuous at finishing a thought for her.

Lucy flushed. "I was thinking how close we were in age. She was just three years younger than me when it happened."

A few minutes later they pulled into an unplowed driveway beside single-story bungalow not much bigger than a single-car garage. White smoke drifted out a rusted stovepipe protruding through a tar paper roof. The wood siding had once been painted lime green, but not recently. What few flecks of color remained appeared about to blow off, and the surface beneath had weathered to a nice gray.

"Who are we seeing here?" Lucy asked, getting out of the car.

"Mary Thomson and her sister Betty. Mary's got terminal breast CA, but refuses hospitalization." He grabbed his black bag from the backseat and trudged through an unbroken half foot of snow toward the front entrance. "With Betty's help, I'm keeping Mary at home as long as I can." He rapped sharply on a new-looking white door with a large windowpane covered by a curtain on the inside. "Betty, it's Dr. Roper."

Introductions having been made, he and Lucy entered the bedroom. He removed the dressings from under Mary Thomson's right arm and exposed a glistening black cavity the diameter of a walnut where the tumor had eaten through the skin of her axilla. Thousands of tiny, scarlet metastases extended to the middle of her chest, rendering it red as a boiled lobster, and from biceps to wrist her arm was swollen the size of a thigh. Where her breast had been, the tissue lay stretched and scarred, some of it cratered like a lunar surface. Everywhere he touched felt hard as wood, and a cloying aroma of decay hovered over it all.

"Now you don't be shy, dear," Mary said to Lucy, flashing an overly white smile of false teeth that seemed too big for her gray, gaunt face.

"Take a good look, and ask me anything you like." Lying flat for the examination, she had been sitting propped up against a bank of pillows to greet them when they arrived. Just the simple act of getting upright, he knew, exhausted her, but it remained her way of welcoming visitors to her home, and she always made the effort. "Arm swelled up like that after radiation to the nodes under my arm," she continued. "Blocked the lymph ducts. At least that's how Dr. Mark here explained it to me."

Lucy smiled down at her and slipped on a pair of latex gloves. "How's your pain?" she said, with the same softness Mark had heard in the car. She gently slid her hand over Mary's inflamed skin, carefully palpating every inch of the way.

Cuts right to the heart of the matter, Mark thought. With cancer, pain management mattered most, and too many doctors sucked at it.

Mary looked over to him. "Can I tell her, Doc?"

He adjusted an IV line attached to Mary's left arm. At the other end of it stood a small, square machine winking fluorescent green numbers at them. An electrical wire connected it to a button by her hand, completing the circle. "Go ahead," he said. "We can trust her."

"Dr. Mark and I are breaking the law," she whispered, giving a conspiratorial grin. "Every time I push this," she added, pointing to the button.

"Mary's the best teacher you'll find when it comes to home care and using morphine on demand," he said. "It's not so much illegal as controversial outside a hospital, and the law's a little gray on the matter. Of course, we keep mum about it, so as not to become a test case."

"But I'm no junkie. Don't use much more now than I did when Dr. Mark first got this contraption for me."

"What you are, Mary, is a very brave woman," Lucy said.

Mary gave a faint laugh. "My sister Betty out there, she's the brave one, putting up with me like this. Not many let their kin pass on at home these days."

"Mary, I noticed there were no tracks in the snow today," Mark said. "Didn't one of the social workers pass by? I specifically told them to see if you and Betty needed anything every morning."

"Oh, I said not to bother, since you'd be here. They got far more needy folks than us to worry about."

After they'd had Betty's tea and were back outside, climbing into her car, Lucy asked, "How long?"

"A month, maybe more. I doubt she'll last till the end of your rotation."

As they picked up speed on the highway, Lucy's cellular started to ring in her purse, which she'd propped on the console between their seats. One hand on the wheel, she fumbled for it, managing to spill the contents at his feet.

"Merde!" he heard her mutter as he retrieved the phone from amongst the debris. Dan's number flashed beside the caller identification icon.

"I found your cellular," the sheriff announced as soon as Mark answered. "One of my men stepped on it under the snow."

"Terrific. You got any more useful information?"

"The shot came from behind on the passenger side, then out your front window, just as you thought. We'll never find the bullet."

"Shit!"

"It gets worse. After I left your place last night I swung around to the office to pick up my camera and flash. Went out to the wreck to try and get shots of boot impressions in the snow, but the wind had already blown them in."

"Hey, I told you you shouldn't—"

"I made some phone calls, and here's the interesting part. The staff at the Braden estate insist Chaz is in New York."

"But that's the sort of crap they would say."

"I also called his office in New York, and was told he's home with the flu."

"Again, figures."

"I then call him at home and am told Dr. Chaz Braden is so sick he's in bed."

"Wall-to-wall alibis."

"But she'll see if he'll take the phone."

"Oh?"

"On the line he comes, and, sounding gravelly voiced, tells me the same story. I said I was sorry to bother him. He said it was no trouble. I told him we'd had a problem yesterday evening with drunken hunters taking potshots at passing vehicles and described what happened to you. He replied, 'That's terrible,' then asked why I was calling him. 'Just wanted to check if you were having similar problems near your place,' I answered. He explained that since he had been ill and left for New York sometime after three in the afternoon, he couldn't say what happened around his place last night. I thanked him, and we hung up."

"So what's so interesting? It's exactly what I'd expect from the son of a bitch."

"Oh yeah? That mean-mouthed bastard hasn't been so cordial to me since the first day he came round after I took office. Even then he made it clear that he saw me as small-time, that he was big-city, and that meant I should stay out of his way. Yet here I am calling his big-city self to check on his whereabouts, and he's polite as can be. What's a country boy to think?"

Mark perked up. "He's worried."

"Yeah. And coming from a guy who normally scoffs in my face, that's almost as good as an admission he pulled the trigger."

"So you've tossed out the drunken hunter idea."

"Let's say I moved it to the back burner. But I can't arrest Chaz for suddenly being courteous to me. We still don't have any evidence he took a shot at you."

Discouraged, Mark hung up at the end of the call and started to salvage the contents of Lucy's purse from the car floor. The slush from his boots had left everything soggy. A packet of photos had spilled out, and fanned at his feet like a deck of cards.

"I'm afraid these may be ruined," he said, picking them up and separating them out in the hope they'd dry. He couldn't help seeing they were all of her in a group hug with four young men. Everyone had broad smiles, and seemed to be from the four corners of the earth. One had Asian features, another Polynesian, the third appeared to be North American Indian, and the fourth, brown-skinned, could have been from anywhere on the planet. Behind them stood a white wall with a red tile roof.

Could one of them be her fiancé? "I'll spread these out on the backseat. You might be able to save them."

"Thanks. We rarely see each other these days. I don't know when there'll be another chance for all of us to be in a picture together."

He twisted around and began to place the shots side by side. When he'd finished and she still hadn't elaborated on who they were, he arranged the pictures a second time.

"So how do you like our little United Nations?"

"Are they your colleagues from *Médecins du Globe*?" Mark asked.

She laughed. "No! Those are my brothers."

"Your brothers?"

Her smile widened, and she seemed to enjoy his confusion. "Yeah. We're all adopted."

He looked back at the pictures. And at her. "That's really, cool," he said.

"Mom couldn't have kids, but came from a big family and wanted the same, so she and Dad picked us up wherever he was stationed."

"Amazing," said Mark, reaching back and carefully picking up one of the photos. "So tell me who's who."

5:15 P.M.
Battery Park Towers,
New York City

Earl sank back in a deep, white leather chair, slowly rotating the tapered stem of his martini glass, and looked around him. "This is quite the place, Melanie."

"I like it." She occupied a matching sofa across from him, her legs curled beneath a black dress that set her off in stark contrast to the upholstery. Behind her, along the windows facing east, ran a row of attractive oriental silk screens blocking the view. "The residents tell me some tall son of a bitch wearing a visitor's pass is stalking our hallowed halls and kicking butt whenever he finds a slacker."

"I wouldn't put it that way."

"Why not? You never could let anything slide, Earl. I doubt that part of you has changed." She raised her glass to him in a toast.

Not in the mood for reminiscing about their impressions of one another, he simply shrugged and toasted her back. "Tell me about Bessie McDonald," he said, without pausing to take a sip. "Did she say anything about Chaz Braden that night you visited her two weeks ago?"

Melanie frowned at him. "And still the same old stickler for getting down to business, I see." She took the time to drink deeply from her tapered glass, the contents a blue concoction she'd made up before he arrived—crushed ice with curaçao, orange vodka, and white rum according to the bottles still on the counter. She waited for him to join her.

He didn't.

"You don't like martinis? I can get you something else." She started to get up.

"No, Melanie, this is fine. Just tell me if Bessie said anything about Chaz Braden."

She settled back on the sofa. "Well, actually she did. You see, just that morning she'd read in the paper about Kelly's body being found, and that got her talking about her admission back in 'seventy-four.'"

He felt a surge of excitement and leaned forward. "Go on."

But after listening to Melanie describe her conversation with her former patient, he fell back in his chair, deflated. It told him nothing new.

"Bessie was my first big case, Earl," Melanie continued, her voice earnest. "If there's a moment when I can say I became a doctor, when all the theory suddenly became clear-cut action, it was the night we resuscitated her. Apart from that, I don't recall much about her admission. But to this day I've had a special place in my heart for late bloomers. You know the kind of residents I mean. Nondescript performers one day, then in comes the patient with a problem that they nail before anyone else, and it sets off a spark."

Earl remembered Melanie coming out of herself in her fourth year, but not that her emergence centered around any specific case. Yet he'd certainly seen exactly what she described happen with his own residents. Reliving this personal epiphany of hers, however, didn't offer a clue as to what secret Chaz Braden might have been trying to cover up. And Melanie, along with everyone else at the hospital, seemed unable to explain why Bessie now lay in a coma. "Some transient event" had been the best the neurologists came up with after looking at the tests Dr. Roy arranged.

He glanced to his left. Through the west windows he could see the black water of the Hudson where it splayed out to combine with the East River, then continued to flow toward the ocean. He felt the pull of the current on his mood. Even his calls that afternoon to former classmates who'd worked on the digoxin toxicity cases had yielded nothing but exclamations of surprise at his contacting them and no useful recollections about Chaz's or anyone else's competence with the medication. There were a few other people yet to reach, but he doubted they'd be any more helpful.

He raised his glass and took a long sip of Melanie's creation—a blue lady she'd called it. Not bad, for a martini. He usually found them bitter. This had a refreshing, fruity taste.

"Did you have any part to play in the second case, the man who died?" he asked. "I saw your name on the order sheet there as well."

The makings of a grin played at the corners of her mouth. "Could be. You see, after my triumph with Bessie, I was the floor's authority on dig for a while, so likely I stuck my nose into that resuscitation as well, if I was around. But I'd have to look at the chart."

"Would you mind? And could you take a look at Bessie's old file as well?

Those notes might jog your memory about something that's not written down."

"Sure." She leaned forward to take his half-empty glass, got up, and walked with it toward a stunning kitchen area that he knew Janet would die for. Except it looked so polished, he doubted Melanie did any cooking in it.

"That's a bit of a long shot, isn't it?" Melanie said, opening a refrigerator the size of his minivan and pouring him a refill from a small pitcher of the cocktail that she'd left chilling in the freezer.

"It's still worth pursuing, given what little we have. Keep this under your hat, but unofficially Mark Roper thinks Chaz Braden somehow got Bessie to slip into a coma so she couldn't talk about what happened back then."

She started, looked up from refilling his glass, and the blue slush brimmed over the rim onto her hand. "Now there's one hell of a big leap," she said, reaching for a cloth to clean up the spill. "Has he any proof?"

"Just his gut."

She returned with the drink. "How does he think Chaz could have precipitated a coma?" She stood over him, still holding his glass and wiping its stem.

"First of all it would have to be a drug that couldn't be traced. He figures a shot of short-acting insulin could have done the trick. Think about it. The onset of profound hypoglycemia would occur in a matter of hours after Chaz gave her the injection. A protracted insulin coma would in itself destroy a pack of neurons. Throw in prolonged convulsions and an extended obstruction of her airway, both of which he could have reasonably anticipated since he may have made sure she couldn't summon help—they found her call button unplugged—Bessie wouldn't have much left between the ears. In other words, she'd be exactly the way she is now."

"I see." Melanie continued polishing the outside of the glass. "You haven't told me what you think."

"Two cases of unexplained digoxin toxicity under Chaz Braden twenty-seven years ago, the year Kelly died, and the survivor now lies in an unexplained coma that occurred less than twenty-four hours after forensic experts identified Kelly's body. That's a lot of mystery illnesses clustered around a common set of events. Yeah, I'm beginning to go along with the idea there's a connection."

Her caressing action with the cloth slowed to a stop. "But do you believe Chaz is responsible for it all?"

"The man's such an ass, part of me wants to say, 'Who else could it be?' "

"And the rest of you?"

He shrugged. "It bothers me the police investigated the hell out of him for Kelly's murder, yet couldn't nail him. So let's just say that while he's still number one in my book, and I think what happened to Bessie McDonald is somehow linked to Kelly's death, I'm also keeping an open mind as to the possibility of other suspects." He was thinking of Samantha McShane.

Melanie remained perfectly motionless.

He felt a crick in his neck from looking up at her.

"What about making a case against Chaz regarding Bessie?" she asked after a few seconds.

"Maybe we'll luck out and someone will remember seeing him on the floor that night. If so, we could connect the dots for the police and point them to him. Then he'd at least have some explaining to do."

"That army of lawyers his daddy keeps will say otherwise."

"There's another potential charge that would make everyone, including those lawyers, look at him in a different light. Someone took a shot at Mark early last night—"

"A shot?"

"Yeah, with a hunting rifle. He skidded into a ditch, and Mark thinks it was Chaz's work as well. Put a chink like that in his armor—it's reckless endangerment at the very least, if not attempted murder—Daddy won't be able to protect him. Maybe then we can tie him to Bessie, and ultimately Kelly."

"It all sounds flimsy."

"I know."

"And if you can't finger him for taking a shot at Mark?"

"We're screwed, all the way back to square one. We'd have to get him another way, or go after someone new."

She studied him for a few seconds, then seemed to realize she still held his drink. "Oh, how rude of me," she said, and placed it in front of him. Reentering the kitchen, she stopped at the sink and began to wash her hands, allowing the water to run down her forearms and off her elbows.

Out of habit from scrubbing up, Earl thought. When distracted, he sometimes did the same.

"If you like, I can order some food, and we can reminisce the night away," she called over her shoulder, actually sounding festive.

Jesus, he thought, starting to feel uncomfortable. *Is she coming on to me?* "I'm sorry, Melanie, but I only have time for the drink," he said, attempting to extricate himself as painlessly as possible from any overture she'd just made. "I've a ton of e-mails waiting from my department, and will be hours dealing with them. You know how it is, everyone getting the urge to make decisions when the chief's away, and then no end of sandbox spats."

She reached for a towel. "You're sure? There's some terrific gourmet French I could have here in twenty minutes."

"Sorry. But this hit the spot." He picked up the drink, toasted her with it, and took three healthy swallows, enough to make her think he at least appreciated her bartending efforts. Nasty-tasting concoction.

Then he stood.

She walked over and took his hand. "You always were a stubborn man, Earl." She leaned forward and kissed his cheek. When he returned the gesture, she leaned in, her breasts brushing up against him.

She hasn't changed a bit, he thought. *Still making passes at any half-decent-looking guy.*

Outside her building, walking toward the pedestrian overpass that crossed the southern tip of West Street, he figured he'd handled the visit smoothly enough. She hadn't even asked whom he suspected of being Kelly's lover. Always a lousy liar, he'd been apprehensive about putting on a show of ignorance.

He looked up behind him and saw her backlit like a tiny mannequin in her penthouse window. To the east, piercing as a phantom pain midst the glitter of lower Manhattan, loomed the area she'd screened off—the void where the Twin Towers once stood.

5:45 P.M.
Hampton Junction

Mark had shown Lucy a full menu of how the human body could fester and fail.

At Zackery Abrams's she'd seen how pressure sores on a forty-year-old paraplegic could crack the skin along a thigh and open it to the bone. IVs, dressing changes, antibiotics, and painkillers simply held the fort. Skin grafts should have been next, but Zak wouldn't leave his four-year-old daughter, Christina, in the care of a foster home. "Her mother was killed in the same crash that cost me the use of my legs," he explained to Lucy, his wan face hardened against the sort of wound that no treatment could cure.

In Christina Halprin's home the sixty-two-year-old woman explained how her heart was so feeble she could go into acute failure, her lungs filling with fluid, just from making love with Mel, her husband. Rejected as a transplant candidate, and already on every known cardiac medication, she insisted Mark prescribe enough diuretics in order that she could take an extra dose now and then, enough to see her through a special evening with Mel. "So far so good," she told Lucy, her voice lowered and a soft flush spreading across her cheeks. "Think about it, honey. It's the one moment when my damned body still feels wonderful. You always read about men going in the saddle. Why not me?"

Lucy got them back out on the highway, and they drove in silence for a while.

"It's not bullets or bugs you'd be afraid of," she said out of the blue after they'd gone a few miles.

"What do you mean?"

"Before, when we were talking about *Médecins du Globe*, it's the having to settle you couldn't stand, isn't it? You couldn't settle for what we do out there, could you?"

"Something like that."

"I mean, the care you give these people in the middle of nowhere is awesome. And sophisticated. I bet it would kill you to stand by and let a single one of them die a day sooner or suffer a minute longer than they had to for want of medications or equipment."

"Hey, I'm not some kind of keep-'em-breathing-at-all-costs nut."

"No, I didn't mean that. It's just what you do here compared to what we did in the field. Christ, sometimes it was so primitive we were limited to providing little more than food, water, and simple hygiene."

He said nothing, yet brought his breathing close to a halt, as if her words were about to cut close to a vital organ. The image of his father, a blackened form, the eyes still alive, crept out of the nightmare where he kept it buried. He immediately shoved it away.

"I mean, you really go all out, won't—no, make that *can't* settle for less."

Again he said nothing, wishing she'd take the hint that he didn't want to talk about it.

"I meant it as a compliment," she added, his silence obviously making her uneasy.

"Look, if they're comfortable and want to stay home, and I can swing it, why not? All it takes is I make a nuisance of myself at Saratoga General, borrowing stuff, so don't make too big a deal of it. Besides, I haven't many cases like these, and the local medical profession isn't comfortable about the ones I do. 'Roper's specials,' the doctors in town call them. But they go along because they'd rather lend me what I need than have my Medicaid and Medicare bunch take beds away from their upscale, private-insurance crowd." He hoped now she'd let it go.

"Well, I for one think it's cool, and a hell of a lot more useful than having to watch someone die for want of 'stuff' as you call it. They haunt you forever, every lost one."

He stared straight ahead.

She had him pegged, all right, and that left him uncomfortable. She must have heard what had happened to read him so well. He wasn't used to feeling so exposed, yet he forced himself to meet her gaze.

The hint of sadness that he'd caught a glimpse of in her eyes last night had returned in force, and her face sagged into a bleak look of defeat. She'd been describing her own scars, not his.

"You're right," he said, relaxing a little. "When it comes to human misery, I'm a retail kind of guy, good at handling it case by case. But wholesale slaughter . . ." He shuddered, television images of sick, starving babies and children flooding into his head.

"It takes courage to know your limits, Mark." Her voice became soft. "Believe me, I didn't know mine when I went overseas. Waded in naive as a schoolgirl, then had no choice but to cope."

Apart from his giving her the occasional direction, they didn't talk for a long time. It wasn't an uncomfortable silence. She simply seemed as lost in her own thoughts as he in his.

He found himself wondering about her fiancé. She hadn't mentioned him, despite being so open about her family, brothers, work—almost everything under the sun. Obviously she intended to keep that part of her life private.

They pulled into a parking lot in front of a sleek glass-and-steel, tan building made up of three- and four-story modules, each floor wrapped in black-tinted windows. A modest plaque on the snow-covered grounds near the front entrance read NUCLEUS LABORATORIES.

"The place looks like a cubist's limousine," Lucy said. Even at this late hour there were few parking spaces. She pulled into one close to the front door. "What's a fancy operation like this doing out here?" She reached into a small cooler lodged on the floor of the backseat and retrieved from it the brown paper bag containing a half dozen blood samples they'd drawn from patients over the course of the day. Holding it up between them, she added, "Obviously you don't keep them in business."

He grinned, took it from her, and got out of the car. The cold tingled the top of his ears. "Some conglomerate built it about five years ago," he said, leading the way up a wide set of freshly shoveled stone steps. He gestured to the dark line of thick forest on the perimeter of the property. "Liked the cheap real estate and low taxes, I guess. They mostly do work for insurance companies that underwrite employee health plans for a slew of head offices in New York City. The volume's huge, and they ship a refrigerator truck worth of samples up here every night of the week. The lab provides state-of-the-art service that does everything from routine bloods to genetic workups for research groups. Even Saratoga General and hospitals in Albany contract out their more exotic testing to them. I'm told that all these things taken together bring in more than enough to pay the heating bills."

"No offense, but why do they bother with you?"

He winked at her over his shoulder. "Because I know the manager. Come on and see science fiction in the sticks."

They approached a sliding glass panel that opened automatically and admitted them to a marbled reception area befitting any Park Avenue address. The click of their shoes on the floor echoed like castanets.

"Hi, Doc," said a spindly, white-haired security guard seated behind a polished curved console with a dozen video screens. He pressed a button that unlocked one of the six mahogany doors behind him with a loud click.

They passed through into a long, white corridor.

Minutes later they shook hands with Victor Feldt, a broad-faced, big-bellied man with a walrus mustache and a complexion that easily flushed. His cheeks glowed as he greeted Lucy. "Welcome to our lab, Dr. O'Connor. May I show you around?"

"Oh, I don't want to be any trouble—"

"You don't take the tour, you'll hurt his feelings," Mark interrupted. "Victor lives for the chance to show off his pride and joy to visitors, especially ones in the business."

Victor turned a shade more crimson. "Now that's not true, Mark. I just thought she'd be interested."

"And I am, Mr. Feldt. Lead on. This facility looks amazing."

His cheeks got so red, Mark wondered if he shouldn't take the man's blood pressure. He'd been treating his hypertension for years, but Victor kept going off the pills whenever he got a new boyfriend because they affected his sex life. Not that that happened often, Victor being one of the few gay men in Hampton Junction.

Let him have his fun talking shop with Lucy, Mark decided. The blood pressure could wait.

He followed along behind, having received the tour several times during the facility's first years of operation. Impressive as the layout was—room after room of spinning centrifuges, automated conveyers feeding trays of sample wells into multitask analyzers, chorus lines of pipettes dunking into specimens and sucking them up fifty at a time, then reams of tiny tubing carrying the fluids to more machines that would perform another fifty tests on each of them—it still accomplished nothing more than the basic job of any hospital lab. Break the human body down to a measure of its red cells, white counts, and biochemical ingredients—sodium, potassium, proteins, albumin, and so on. Except this outfit scaled itself to process ten times the load of any single health care institution.

Mark watched Victor animatedly explain the details of the operation to an extent that went far beyond what Lucy could possibly want to know, a mark of his loneliness for intellectual company as much as his enthusiasm for his work. He'd arrived from New York when the lab opened, but gravitated away from Saratoga, unable to afford a place among the rich and famous, yet wary of the homophobia of Hampton Junction. So he'd settled on the no-man's-land between the two, a pretty but isolated cabin by a lake not far from here, where his lifestyle wouldn't raise eyebrows. When he wasn't involved with anyone he substituted the Internet for companionship, and owned one of the most awesome computer setups Mark had ever seen in a private home. Victor approached Mark to be his doctor after several bad experiences with a few general practitioners in Saratoga. "Nothing overt, just that they were old farts and not at ease with handing the potential health problems of someone who's gay," he'd explained. "On the other hand, I hear nothing scares you."

They neared Victor's pièce de résistance, the section where they did the DNA analyses. Located in an area behind glass windows that could only be accessed through an airlock, some of the machinery looked similar to the other equipment they'd seen, but many pieces were right out of *Star Trek*, and workers inside wore protective clothing.

"Just like in making CDs, we keep a dust-free environment to reduce the risk of contaminating specimens," Victor explained. "We have a dozen PCR machines, and three dozen electrophoresis units . . ."

As Victor expounded on the technology of breaking down DNA and separating out specific genes for identification, Mark noticed a change since he'd last been corralled into a tour. There were far more people working in this unit than he remembered, and now it was after hours. "Business must be good as far as the DNA department goes," he said jokingly, as they returned to the front entrance.

"Booming," replied Victor in complete earnestness. "We're even testing for genes that don't have a confirmed link to diseases yet, but may be a potential risk."

"Who wants that information?" Lucy asked.

He shrugged. "The New York corporations that have contracts with us. Seems particularly to be the new wave in executive health plans. And, of course, research labs. But we figure the real up-and-coming market will be aging baby boomers who want to know if they've got the gene that killed Mom or Dad. Screening for the mutations linked to breast and ovarian cancer, colon cancer, Alzheimer's—you name it. Real cutting-edge stuff . . ."

Mark cringed as Victor talked. Unfortunately, his prediction had already begun to materialize. Recently a chain of stores better known for selling soaps and shampoos began to market an expensive screening test to detect genetic defects linked to breast and ovarian cancer, placing the devices on display alongside bath oils and bubble beads. And last month his patients started to bring in magazines normally associated with tips for beautiful homes and fine gardens that now carried ads urging readers to get genetically tuned in to what they should eat and drink by screening for disorders affected by diet. The trouble was, not everyone who has a genetic defect will go on to develop the disease they are at risk for, and at this stage of the game, no one could pick the winners from the losers. Rampant commercialization of the technology would lead to widespread, fruitless, and potentially harmful anxiety, while places like Nucleus Laboratories made a pile of money telling healthy Americans that they were sick. He and Victor had already had heated debates over the issue. But this was Victor's moment in the sun with Lucy, so Mark held his peace.

As she drove the car out of the driveway, Lucy asked, "Is Victor a friend?"

"Actually, he's a patient."

"Really? I took you for friends. But around you it's hard to tell the difference."

"How do you mean?"

"You have a really nice way with patients. A lot of the people who were in your office today consider you both friend and physician."

"And how do you know that?"

"They told me so. It was neat to hear."

"Sometimes it makes the job harder."

"You mean staying objective—"

"That's difficult enough. What I'm talking about makes being friends impossible."

"Oh?"

"People tell me almost everything that's personal and private, as they do most doctors. But in a place like Hampton Junction, I end up knowing both who's got the secrets and who the secrets are kept from."

"What?"

"Just the other day I was sitting in my office with a woman who sees me regularly for stress and a nervous stomach. The reason for her problems— she's afraid her husband is running around on her. We were interrupted by a phone call from a woman whom I'm treating for depression because the man she loves, that very same husband, won't leave his wife. They don't teach you how to manage that kind of situation in New York."

She gave an appreciative whistle. "Does it happen a lot?"

"Often enough. You'll probably go through a variation of it while you're here. After all, you're a fresh audience, so people will definitely let you in on the seamier sides of life in Hampton Junction."

She glanced sideways at him.

"Relax," he added. "It won't be that bad."

She smiled, but drove without saying anything. A few minutes later, she asked, "Show me Kelly's house?"

"Her old family home? It's long gone. Her parents sold off and moved back to New York after she disappeared."

"No. I meant where she lived with Chaz Braden."

"Sure. It's not far from here."

She followed his instructions, heading in the direction of Saratoga

Springs. After a few miles the thick forest gave way to a floodlit, rolling, snow-covered lawn surrounded by white fences adjacent to a lake. Ablaze with light and well back from the road stood a layered house with several wings emanating from a peaked center, the whole structure wrapped in a veranda. As a young boy passing by with his parents, it had always reminded him of a gilded bird trying to take flight. "Here it is. Rural chic of the pretend horsy set. Paddock style on the front yard, but nary a nag in sight."

She said nothing, but slowed as they passed the large wrought-iron gate that guarded the entrance. In the parking lot at the end of a quarter-mile driveway, a dozen limousines glittered like a nest of black beetles.

"That's odd," Mark said. "Old man Braden must be up for Thanksgiving this year. He usually doesn't show until Christmas."

"He's brought a lot of friends."

"When here, he's always having parties. Not that I'm on his guest list. Was, when I was a kid. My father used to get invited. I think that was Kelly's doing. I learned much later from my aunt that Mom hated going and thought the rest of them acted superior to Dad. But after my mother died, he and I continued to attend, 'for Kelly's sake' I heard him say more than once. Crazy, their looking down on him. Dad was more doctor than both Bradens put together."

When they got back to Mark's house, a shiny red Jeep almost identical to his own stood parked in the driveway. The keys and a note from his insurance company advising him that it was only a loaner until they settled his claim had been dropped through the mail slot in his front door. *Ride 'em cowboy,* he thought, pocketing the keys.

"Could I take a look at your father's file on Kelly?" Lucy asked after supper.

"Sure." He got it out for her.

Having leafed through the contents at the kitchen table, she came to the newspaper clippings on the Braden's charitable works. "What are these doing here?"

"I've no idea. My father kept them there. He also collected a pile of statistics on those two places, but for the life of me I can't figure out what he was after."

"Could I see them as well?"

Two hours later, papers spread out in front of her, on chairs, even over the countertops, she continued to pore over the data that had defeated him.

"Any luck?" he asked, standing in the doorway watching her.

"Oh?" she started, obviously surprised by his voice. "No, I mean I can't see anything glaringly wrong."

"Well, I'm heading up to bed. It'll be a big day tomorrow, everybody calling in to get tuned up for Thanksgiving."

"I'm going to work a while longer."

"Good night."

"Good night, Mark."

Chapter 12

"We only agreed to see you after checking your credentials, Dr. Garnet. I must admit, it appears you've had a very distinguished career," Samantha McShane said. "Surprisingly so."

For a guy working in Buffalo, Earl added, the unspoken qualification having practically leapt off her pinched lips. She sat on a round-backed, antique chair of a kind he'd seen in photos of Queen Victoria. Looking over the ornately furnished room, he figured Samantha must have gotten the rest of the old girl's movables as well. Walter McShane stood behind her, scowling, as still as a stuffed ornament. Clearly it was Samantha's idea that Earl be tolerated here at all.

"So what can we do to help you prove who murdered our Kelly?" she asked.

"Mark Roper has already let me look over copies of the police records, so I don't need anything there. I'm interested instead in what you learned from the private detectives you hired. Is there any chance we could look through their reports, maybe even talk to one of them? Do you know if they're still alive?"

Samantha looked up at Walter.

"I'll see what I can do," he muttered.

"Perhaps you could forward whatever you come up with to Dr. Roper. I don't plan to be in New York much longer—"

"No!" Samantha said, sitting even more bolt upright than Earl would have thought possible. "That man has his own agenda in all this."

Walter left his perch and wandered over to to a large bay window overlooking Central Park West and gazed out at the green space beyond, his jaw a study in tension.

Earl focused on Samantha. "Why would you say that, Mrs. McShane? Dr. Mark Roper has demonstrated an ironclad objectivity in pursuing what happened to Kelly—"

"Tell him, Walter," Samantha said, swinging around to confront her husband's back.

"I don't think it's anybody's business, Samantha." He spoke without looking at her.

"I want him to know, Walter."

He simply shrugged.

She returned her gaze to Earl. "A mother feels these things so much more acutely, Dr. Garnet. I'm sure you understand this, as a medical man. The loss of a child is the worst possible pain . . ." Her eyes watered over, and tears careened down wrinkled cheeks that seemed parched as washed-out gullies. Pulling out a hanky from the sleeve of her dress, she dabbed at her face, all the time slipping glances over at Walter as if checking whether he was watching.

He wasn't.

The waterworks stopped. "Would you like to see Kelly's room?"

Now the man pivoted to face her. "Really, Samantha—"

"If he wishes to see it, Walter, he can."

"Yes, I would like to, Mrs. McShane." Earl tried not to sound too eager, but the caustic exchange between the couple was not only unpleasant, it put a damper on what Samantha could say. If he maneuvered her out of Walter's earshot, she might let something useful slip.

"Come, Dr. Garnet" She got to her feet, then led him along a dingy hallway to a closed door. Opening it, she stepped inside.

Earl followed, and had to stifle a gasp.

Brightly lit and painted yellow, it still resembled a little girl's room. Stuffed animals lined the bookshelves. A frilly gold-colored duvet covered the bed. Porcelain figurines of soulful-eyed children, kittens, and puppies filled a corner display case. But what most took Earl's breath away were the photographs of Kelly and her mother. None of the images were unusual in themselves, but hung all together they overwhelmed him.

To his right were pictures of a much younger Samantha holding her infant daughter, rows and rows of them. They progressed through the usual moments that parents capture—Kelly as a baby sucking a bottle, sitting with a hand of support at her back, eating with a spoon, toddling between Samantha's legs. Then came Kelly the little girl—walking without support, running with a ball, posing in a party dress, diving off a dock, riding a tricycle. In these she wore the same goofy, self-conscious grin he'd sometimes seen in Brendan when he got in front of a camera. In others she seemed more sullen. The shots evolved into Kelly riding a two-wheeler, swinging a tennis racket, standing on skis, and participating in the innumerable other activities of an older girl. In these photos she wore a frown more frequently, as if she preferred not having her picture taken at all.

He stepped closer and noticed other details. In an inordinate number of them where Samantha appeared, the woman stood front and center, beaming a smile that commanded the viewer to pay attention in a way that thrust Kelly into the background.

And in shot after shot, Kelly seemed to be eyeing her mother, not showing fear necessarily, but a sadness in her gaze and with her mouth taut with strain. In some, she even appeared to be leaning away from her.

Prophetic, he thought.

"You can see we were very close," Samantha said from behind.

He couldn't believe she could be so oblivious to how Kelly's expressions in the later pictures said the opposite.

"Inseparable, in fact," she continued. "It's hard to tell from these, but she was a very sick child."

"Really?"

"Yes. I hadn't any idea what to do with her. She was forever complaining of stomachaches and bowel problems. I took her to no end of doctors, but no one ever figured out what was wrong. And Walter couldn't be there to help, his being away on business all the time. Not that I blame him for leaving her illness all on my shoulders. He had to take care of his firm, so I soldiered on alone, a full-time mother, of course. There was no paying strangers to take care of Kelly in this home, the way women do all the time with their children today."

He swallowed so as not to show how repugnant he found her performance. "What sort of illnesses did Kelly have?"

"As I said, no one ever diagnosed her. The best attempt came from an
old general surgeon in Saratoga who agreed to operate on her, twice. But
even he couldn't diagnose what was wrong. Do you have any idea what
kind of ordeal that can be for a parent?"

Oh, brother, he thought, scars the size of ropes flashing to mind. Making as if he were still studying the gallery, he asked. "What about Dr. Cam
Roper? He saw Kelly once. Didn't he say she was fine? At least that's what
his files indicate."

"That quack? He was the worst of them all. Made the most terrible allegation that a mother should ever have to hear. He's the reason I won't deal
with Mark Roper. Like father, like son, I always say."

He continued to peer at the stills, not wanting to risk charging in too directly. "Oh? What did Cam Roper say?"

"Why, he practically accused me of being the cause of Kelly's troubles.
Claimed I was making her sick—"

"That's enough, Samantha!" Walter said, standing at the doorway.

"Oh, Walter." She spoke his name as if uttering a groan of long-endured
pain. "I want Dr. Garnet to know how much that man hurt me, so he'll
understand what I've been through—"

"It's none of Dr. Garnet's business! Don't you realize he'll do the same
with what you tell him." He looked directly at Earl, his elderly face chis-
eled with anger. "It's disgusting, what so-called physicians get away with
saying, all in the cause of making a diagnosis. Well, I nearly sued then
rather than let anyone besmirch us. Lucky for him I backed off, but I won't
let you or anyone else stain our reputation now—"

"And I won't bottle up my agony, Walter, no matter what you say . . ."

Their accusations and innuendoes flew between them, filling the air
with acid rancor.

As he watched and listened, Earl's thoughts on the couple congealed
into specific clinical labels: narcissism, ego, denial—traits common in
everyone, but here they presented themselves in pathological proportions,
while under them all loomed a terrible diagnosis, just as Walter said.

10:45 A.M.
New York City Hospital

Tommy Leannis eased himself into a floral-patterned settee opposite Melanie Collins. She sat at a small glass table, pouring coffee from a sterling silver pot into delicate porcelain cups with matching saucers—not the freebie mugs sporting drug company logos that he and the other doctors in his clinic used. He glanced around the plush office, eyeing the thick mauve carpet, the oversize mahogany desk, and the matching wall-to-wall bookcase behind it. "You're sittin' at the top o' the world here, aren't you, Melanie?" he said, cheerily hiding the bitterness he felt at her good fortune. His own career had been a never-ending, sweaty scramble just to end up a mediocre plastic surgeon, competent enough to avoid getting sued, but no star. He'd never shaken off the insecurity that plagued him in medical school, and he incessantly second-guessed himself, going through life with constantly clammy palms. Melanie didn't have one damn bit more talent at medicine than he. How the hell did she manage to pull all this off?

"Sugar, Tommy?"

"One would be perfect, and just a drop of cream. I'm trying to keep my lean-and-hungry look."

She smiled, handed him his cup, then settled back in her chair. "I asked you here as an old pal to help me with a problem."

"Oh?" Old pal, his ass. What did she want? The woman hadn't once invited him here since she took over as Chief of Internal Medicine five years ago. He sipped the coffee; it was delicious, of course.

"It's about Earl Garnet. I've been beside myself, and maybe it's nothing, but the strangest thing happened last night."

"What's that?"

"Well, we were talking about Kelly—he's helping Mark Roper investigate her death—and I'd told Mark at the memorial service that Kelly was in love with someone at the time of her disappearance—"

"You did? My God, Melanie, if Chaz Braden hears you said that, he'll blow a fuse."

"I know, Tommy, but even he had to suspect. She was practically glowing before she disappeared."

"Well I never noticed." Neither did he want her to engage him in any talk of that sort. Maybe she felt immune to Chaz, because of her position, but he sure as hell didn't.

"Here's what's strange, Tommy. I figure Mark briefed Earl about what I said. Yet Earl never once asked who I thought her lover was."

"So?"

She hesitated, as if reluctant to speak.

He didn't say anything to encourage her, taking another sip of his coffee instead.

"So do you think it might possibly have been Earl?"

He nearly choked. "Goody Two-shoes Garnet? You've got to be joking."

"They spent a lot of time together, and were always talking—"

"I know, but he was so straitlaced." You ought to know, he nearly added, remembering that Melanie had made several obvious plays for Earl and gotten nowhere.

"I thought so, too, but maybe we were wrong. I mean, what do you think? Could it be that he didn't ask about Kelly's lover because . . ." She looked questionably at Tommy.

"It was him all along?" He digested the notion a few seconds, rubbing the palm of his hand through the bristly top of his hair, then chuckled, finding the idea not so crazy once he thought about it a bit. Chaz could be such a mean son of a bitch, why wouldn't Kelly have tried to sneak around on him? Tommy rather liked the possibility that she and Garnet had been fucking each other with no one the wiser. People who misbehaved, broke the rules, and didn't get found out always pleased him, especially ones who were so outwardly on the up-and-up. It gave sneakiness a touch of class. Maybe he, too, could slip through the cracks and beat the odds—a loser's lullaby, he knew, yet seductive enough to make him believe even a guy like him might take a chance and come up a winner.

"Tommy?"

She snapped him out of his reverie. "Sorry. The thought of them doing it, under our noses so to speak, took me a bit by surprise."

"Do you think I'm right?"

"Maybe."

"I was hoping you'd tell me that I was crazy."

He flashed a grin and toasted her with his cup. "Then my verdict, dear Melanie, is you're crazy."

"What do you think I should do?"

He ignored the question, too busy wondering if there might be a way to use this information to benefit himself.

11:20 A.M.
Central Park, New York City

Earl hurried along the Central Park side of Fifth Avenue. A north wind sent fallen leaves flying in front of him and whipped up the flaps of his coat in bullying gusts. Cellular in his hand, he punched the redial button for Mark's number. Still busy.

He walked a few blocks more, punched redial again, and got Mark's answering machine. "Mark, it's Earl. I just got out of the McShanes' apartment. Nothing like a home visit to get at the truth in a family. Call me back as soon as you can. I think I figured out what your father really meant in his notes about Kelly. I need you to tell me if you think I'm crazy."

He shoved the phone back in his pocket and increased his pace, as much to work off his excitement as to combat the damp and cold insinuating itself through his clothing.

Minutes later he felt the receiver vibrate. He had it to his ear halfway through the second ring. "Mark?"

"Yeah. What's up?"

"Get out your father's files and take another look at that medical report of Kelly's first visit. You know how certain symptoms and signs sometimes fit together to remind us, as doctors, of certain syndromes."

"Of course."

"I want you to read it over with a question in mind. If you saw that little girl in an ER today, what might you at least think of?"

"Why? I thought we already agreed that the problem was functional."

"Just humor me."

"Okay. Hang on a sec."

It seemed forever before he picked up again.

"I've got it in front of me."

"Give me the differential you went through to rule out organic causes for her complaints."

"That's easy. I first thought of chronic disorders such as inflammatory bowel disease or malabsorption syndromes. But my father said that she'd no history of fever, and her blood tests were repeatedly normal. Presumably that meant they showed no history of anemia, elevated sed rates, or protein deficiencies. Without those changes, I wouldn't even consider the diagnoses."

"What else?"

"You mean really bizarre stuff?"

"Yes."

"I don't know. If she continued to have complaints, and actually lost more weight or started to have night sweats, I might get more aggressive and want to rule out childhood malignancies, leukemia, lymphoma, that sort of thing. But it obviously wasn't any of those. Kelly lived to be a healthy adult."

"All the GI complaints. A history of multiple doctor visits, a surgeon persuaded to operate on a normal appendix and do a laparotomy. Batteries of normal blood tests and negative X rays. And the only concrete sign is her being slightly underweight? Add in the mother being a drama queen who even now uses Kelly's death to make herself the center of attention, and what does all that suggest? Would you still think the visit to your father involved nothing more than a neurotic, overprotective mother seeking excessive reassurances that her daughter was okay? Or would you think of a disorder that wasn't even officially recognized until about thirty years after your father saw them?"

"Oh, my God! You mean Munchausen by proxy?"

"I'm not willing to go that far. But there are disturbing similarities."

Munchausen by proxy syndrome was among the darkest of mental illnesses. Named after a German baron in the eighteenth century who'd been notorious for constructing elaborate lies to scam money from unsuspecting victims, it designated a disorder far more fiendish than any con for money. Parents, usually mothers, would deliberately inflict illnesses on their children. The techniques varied, from rubbing the skin raw to simulate mysterious rashes, through feeding them purgatives and laxatives to create bizarre GI symptoms, to smothering. An offender would then present her child to unsuspecting doctors as a medical mystery, and play the role of an untiring, long-suffering parent who sacrificed all to care for her child, reaping the subsequent attention bound to be lavished on her.

The literature related how a few carried off the ruse so well they'd been awarded Mother of the Year citations before being found out. The worst of them ended up killing their offspring outright, casting themselves in the part of the ultimate victim—a grieving mother—guaranteeing showers of sympathy. Earl's worst nightmare throughout a lifetime of practice, as it was for all physicians, had been that he would miss diagnosing one of these helpless children because a cunning parent outsmarted his clinical skills. Current estimates suggested 30 percent of the victims eventually perished, but the number could be much higher. Mortality statistics were hard to come by because some of the cases that ended in murder were misdiagnosed as crib deaths, and the children who managed to outgrow the clutches of their secret abusers as they became too old to fool might never be diagnosed.

Mark took a few seconds to reply. "You figure Samantha was . . . Jesus Christ, her own mother was deliberately making Kelly ill—"

"Whoa, Mark! Quit jumping to conclusions. No, I don't think it was as full-blown as that. At least there's no evidence of Samantha having gone as far as actually physically injuring Kelly. But there's one feature of that syndrome that does remind me of Samantha—the concerned mother carting her daughter from doctor to doctor, all the time insisting the child is ill, and, if her manner then was what it is now, playing the part of a self-sacrificing woman to the hilt."

"I never would have imagined anything like this."

"Neither did I, the first time you showed the file to me. But seeing Samantha today on her own turf . . ." He quickly related the highlights of his visit. ". . . the narcissism, the sense that only her grief counts, her forever playing to an audience, the fact she's even made a shrine to Kelly—it all fit together with a big clunk."

Mark let out his breath in a long, mournful whistle.

"Even if Samantha wasn't physically harming Kelly, and her particular game doesn't have its own fancy diagnosis," Earl continued, "years of telling her that she was sick, suffering from a mysterious, terrible ailment that the doctors could neither diagnose nor make better, would be devastating psychologically. She'd be left with problems of anxiety, self-esteem, image, trust—a host of difficulties . . ." That he could coolly paint such a troubled clinical picture of a woman he once loved brought him up short. "Well, you get the idea."

"No wonder my father had to give her four years' worth of psychological support therapy." Mark's voice sounded distant, as if he were thinking aloud.

Earl said nothing, thinking what a wounded soul she'd been, and he hadn't realized it.

"A wretched childhood like that," Mark continued, "and I never had a clue."

"How could you, being just a boy? Hell, she never even mentioned a word of it to me." *Yet I should have known,* he said to himself. "But from what her parents said today, or rather, what Samantha wanted to tell me but Walter made her clam up about, I think your father had confronted Samantha head-on about what was happening."

"What do you mean?"

"You know how we often don't write really legally sensitive stuff in our charts?"

"Of course."

"He hadn't put it in writing, but the way Samantha wailed to me about what terrible things he'd said to her, and how Walter went on about having nearly sued him over it, but then backed off, I figure your dad ultimately twigged to what really might have been going on—that's probably when he wrote *Mother?* in the margin—and did a follow-up visit with good old Mom and Dad where he made some pretty strong insinuations about the harm Samantha had been doing. Maybe he even threatened to report her if he ever got a whiff of any more visits to doctors over 'mysterious illnesses.' Judging from the fact that there were no more surgical scars from dubious operations, the ultimatum seemed to have worked."

"Son of a bitch."

"And here's something else. Read the letter Kelly wrote to your father again, especially the part that says, *Regarding the other two matters, we must discuss those. Whatever I plan for myself, I can't leave and let them go unresolved.*" Earl quoted it from memory. "One of the matters she intended to resolve might have been what her mother had done to her. That possibility gives credence to Braden Senior's insinuations about Samantha."

"That she might have killed Kelly?"

"We have to look at the possibility. Suppose on the day she intended to run off and start a new life, she finally confronted her mother. Samantha could have erupted in anger, shoved Kelly or struck her. The woman's fuse is short. Very short. You've seen it. I saw it this morning. What if she accidentally killed Kelly?"

Mark said nothing.

"Hello?"

"Yeah, I'm here. It's a thought, but something about it just doesn't sit right."

"What?"

"I don't know. Something."

"Something. That's all you can say?"

"Let me think about it."

"Okay, okay." They exchanged a few more suggestions about how to proceed. When he got off the call, Earl felt impatient. He wanted to go home, return to the present, his present—Janet, Brendan, and ER—not poke around in a quarter-century-old muck of other people's mistakes. It was all so dreary, and what difference did it really make? Kelly was so long gone.

The whole mess also reminded him how easily a life of promise and love could go wrong, perhaps the result of a single mistake or bad choice. Too often, innocence or guilt played no part. Some, like Kelly, flamed out. Others, like Chaz or the McShanes, let themselves sink inexorably into ruin.

No, he couldn't pull out just yet and leave loose ends that one day might not only ensnare him but devastate Brendan and Janet as well.

He shivered. Christ it was cold. Either that, or he was coming down with something.

11:35 A.M.
Medical Records,
New York City Hospital

"Could I speak with you a moment, Lena?"

Lena Downie looked up from the log she'd been reviewing at one of the workstations and saw Dr. Melanie Collins standing at the counter. "Why, of course." She walked over, holding out her hand in greeting. "What can I do for you?"

"Actually, we need to speak in private."

"Oh!" She glanced over to where the frosted glass door with her name and title stood closed. "My own office is in use right now." She leaned closer. "A confidential audit," she whispered. "But we'll use my secretary's. She'll be delighted to take a coffee break."

Within a minute they were seated across a cluttered desk from each other. Lena glanced at the adjoining entrance to her own domain, making sure it was shut tight, thereby ensuring both rooms were completely soundproof. "Now what can I do for you?"

"This is a sensitive matter, but I know you're used to dealing with confidences."

"Of course."

"It has to do with Kelly McShane's murder."

Alarm flickered through Lena, and she reflexively glanced toward her own office.

"You're one of the best informed people in the hospital," Melanie said, "and probably no one knows as many of the secrets in this place as you do—"

"Now really, Dr. Collins," she interrupted, feeling most uncomfortable.

"But you are. And I've been deeply troubled by something these last few days that I hoped you'd help me with."

Lena's curiosity won out over discretion. "Oh?" she said, reclining in her secretary's chair. Its spring-loaded back and coaster wheels caught her by surprise, nearly tipping her over.

"It has to do with Dr. Earl Garnet," Collins went on. "He probably was already down here, helping Mark Roper out with his investigation."

Lena simply nodded.

"Well, I'm convinced Kelly had a lover—you know how we women can intuit that kind of thing—and I told Mark Roper as much, figuring he had to know as investigating coroner, if he is to have any hope of figuring out who killed Kelly."

Lena's gaze once more flicked toward the adjoining door. Even with soundproofing it was definitely not the time for this conversation. "Uh, Dr. Collins, you're talking about things way beyond my purview—"

"Oh, I know it is, Lena, but please hear me out. I'm asking because of your instincts as a woman."

"Well, I'm very flattered, but—"

"Here's my point. Dr. Garnet's talked with me several times about Kelly. You know we were all friends back then?"

"Of course, but—"

"Yet he never once asked who I thought Kelly's lover had been, although I'm sure Mark told him that I thought she was having an affair."

"Really? You mean—" She immediately stopped herself. "Dr. Collins, this is not a conversation I feel comfortable with at the moment," she said instead, standing to end their meeting. "Perhaps at a later time."

Melanie seemed astounded. "But I thought you would be able to help me decide what to do. I've racked my brains wondering if I should go to the police or not. I mean, do you think Kelly's lover could have been Dr. Garnet? Did you ever hear anything to that effect?"

Lena would normally have jumped at the chance to be the confidante of someone with such a juicy secret. She'd have savored poring over the story, dissecting it piece by piece, adding whatever salacious bits of corroboration she might be able to pull from her memories of Kelly McShane and Earl Garnet. Yet having *him* right next door, soundproofing or not, made her extremely nervous. "I'm sorry, Dr. Collins, but really, I've nothing to say either way. I have no knowledge of an affair between those two, and whether you act on your suspicions is a matter between you and your conscience."

Melanie gave her an are-you-feeling-all-right look. "Of course," she said, clearly puzzled by Lena's refusal to discuss the matter. Getting to her feet, she shook Lena's hand. "And I appreciate your having seen me." With a parting smile, she left.

Lena let out a long sigh and, staring at her office, wondered whether she should say anything. He couldn't have overheard what they'd said; of that she had no doubt. She herself never heard her secretary on the phone. And what to tell him? Anything she came up with would only embarrass him. No, better she let him hear this piece of gossip from someone else. As for her own demeanor, should Dr. Collins's visit ever come to his notice, she'd acted impeccably. He couldn't fault her on that.

An hour later Charles Braden Senior asked Lena to join him in her own office. "Thank you, Lena," he said when they were seated, returning Bessie McDonald's charts to her. He'd been reviewing them since his arrival around ten that morning. "I'll want to look at the microfilmed case now, then I'll be catching an afternoon train back to the country. Chaz is ill, and I've got guests up for Thanksgiving."

"I'll help you get the microfilm set up, if you'd like."

"That would be lovely. I'm all thumbs with those things."

"Shall we go? I'll get the key."

By one-thirty he was back at her door. "One more thing, Lena. Before you leave today, I'd like these charts collected and left in your office so that I can come in over the holidays to have a look at them." He handed her a folded paper.

She opened it and read:

All the Morbidity/Mortality reviews of patients under Melanie Collins's care for the last twenty-five years.

Lena gaped at the note, astonished.

"Is there a problem?" Braden asked.

"No, sir. Not at all. Except there could be a hundred, maybe two hundred charts involved here."

"That's right. And again, I appreciate your discretion about this. Gossip is such a terrible thing."

She knew an order to keep her mouth shut when she heard one.

Chapter 13

Later that same afternoon,
Wednesday, November, 21,
2:15 P.M.
The Plaza Hotel

Earl slammed back in the leather seat as Tommy accelerated away from the snarled traffic of Madison Avenue and headed east on Sixty-second Street. He caught the green at Park, only to hit the brakes for a red at Lexington. "I know what you're thinking, Earl. Kind of a waste, my driving a Jag in New York. All that power, and I only get to make like it's a drag strip a block at a time."

"Uh-huh," Earl said. He wasn't one to get carsick, but neither did he appreciate having his stomach sloshed against his spine, then slung forward against the lap strap of his seat belt. "If you don't want me to upchuck on your calfskin interiors or polished mahogany dash, you better slow down." He tried looking at the horizon, but had to settle on a restricted view of the elevated FDR Drive and a glimpse of the East River beyond. It didn't help much. And the brilliance of the sky, a bleached polar blue, made his eyes hurt.

Tommy looked at him askance. "You're, kidding right?"

"Uh-huh."

He looked relieved. "But don't you just love the sound of that motor?"

Insecure Tommy, still needing everyone's approval. Earl swallowed hard to keep his lunch down.

The last thing he wanted was to go beer drinking with Leannis. It wasn't just the prospect of listening to the man's bravado and usual litany of worries that deterred him. After having worked the phones for the past few hours talking to more of the former students, interns, and residents who were involved with the digoxin toxicity cases, yet finding zilch, he'd nearly run out of reasons to remain in New York at all. Maybe he should go up to Hampton Junction and help out with the legwork. Unfortunately, the locals there probably wouldn't talk any more frankly to an outsider than the physicians here would have opened up to Mark.

The idea of squeezing out of this whole grungy mess for a few days to spend Thanksgiving with Janet and Brendan instantly became irresistible. He'd try to get a reservation as soon as he got free of Tommy, then tell Mark he could be back in a heartbeat, if needed.

He wouldn't even have had to be stuck with Tommy if he'd been quick enough when the call came through.

"Hey, Earl. Can I buy you a beer?" Leannis had said as soon as Earl picked up the phone.

He'd sounded pretty happy for the prince of worry. "Tommy?"

"Yeah, I know an Irish joint that's about a five-minute drive from those pretentious digs you're in. I'll pick you up outside the hotel."

"Hey, no! I'm waiting for a callback—"

He'd already hung up.

Tommy had never once initiated the two of them going out for a beer together their whole time in med school. Nor had he looked up Earl since then. The guy was after something. Stuck at an unseemly long traffic light, Earl decided he might as well make him get to the point.

"So what did you want to talk about?"

"I figure I needed to warn you."

"About what."

Another sprint start sent them roaring toward Second Avenue. "A strange conversation I had with Melanie this morning. She got me in her office, all worried about you and Kelly."

Something that had nothing to do with Tommy's driving tightened in Earl's gut.

"Oh?"

"Yeah. Apparently you two had a conversation last night. She found it suspicious that you never asked who she thought Kelly's lover was."

Earl's every instinct went on alert. "Kelly's lover?" He tried to sound curious, but not overly so.

Tommy gave him a sideways look as he rocketed through the next intersection. "Hey, Earl, come on. Don't play dumb. Melanie said she already told that snoop Roper that Kelly had the look of a woman in love. Naturally, she found it strange you never asked about it, since Roper must have made it part of the investigation you're helping him with. So now she's thinking maybe the lover was you."

Shit! Earl felt a cold sweat percolate on his back. He could kick himself for having made such an obvious omission. The only response he could think of was to act incredulous. "What? You're kidding me."

"Nope, and I figured you ought to know she's already making noises about reporting you."

"Oh, my God, that's ridiculous. I didn't ask what she knew about Kelly's love life because I figured Melanie would have told me anything of importance without me having to dig for it."

"Hey, buddy, you don't have to convince me. One way or the other, my lips are sealed. As I said, I figured forewarned is forearmed."

Earl's mind raced. Every emotion he could come up with that seemed appropriate for a guy wrongfully accused—astonishment, indignation, disbelief—he threw into his performance. "I'm calling her right now, and putting an end to this nonsense. Why, if a rumor like that got started . . ." He trailed off, digging out his cell phone, checking for her number in its memory, and punching ENTER. Let Tommy believe him, he prayed. And for Christ's sake, let Melanie believe him.

"Hey! She'll know I told you," Tommy protested.

"I can't just let her think—" Her answering machine interrupted, ordering him to leave a message at the sound of the beep. "Melanie, it's Earl. We got to talk. There's been a terrible misunderstanding, and I might have given you a very wrong impression. Please call me as soon as possible. It's urgent."

Tommy lurched the car left onto York Avenue.

Earl's stomach seemed to keep on going toward the river. "Jesus, Tommy, do you have to beat every car at every light—"

"Don't you be tellin' Melanie I warned you. But if you explain to her like you did to me—it sounded pretty good, that part how you thought she'd tell you anything important about Kelly's love life without your asking—she just might buy it."

Damn, Tommy doesn't believe me either. "Look, there's nothing to buy, Tommy. Kelly and I were just friends."

"Well, then, all's the more the pity, because our dear Kelly deserved a good man to love her before she died."

Earl snapped another sideways glance at the well-coiffed man, to see if he was being serious.

His lips were pressed into a thin red line.

"She had it rough all right," Earl said, the only admission he felt ready to make.

When they hit Tommy's watering hole, the patrons greeted him by name and the staff gave them attentive service. Earl nursed a nice Irish red ale and made small talk, all the time willing Melanie to call. His drink, cool and pleasant to the taste, seemed to rile his stomach and set it churning again. Nerves, he thought.

3:30 P.M.
Hampton Junction

"They fired you?"

Victor Feldt nodded, face crimson and lips trembling under his magnificent mustache. He sat on the edge of the chair across the desk from Mark, his huge frame hunched over, his beefy hands clasped together and working each other with the steadiness of a beating heart.

"But that's outrageous!" Mark got out of his usual chair and took the one beside Victor. "Why?" he asked.

Victor shook his head, pulled his mouth into a grimace, and swallowed a few times. His eyes glistened.

Mark let him compose himself.

"The reason they gave was that I showed unauthorized people around the lab," he said eventually.

"What?"

The big man shook his head again. "I've taken visitors on tours since day one. 'Good PR,' my director always said. To pull this now, I don't get it."

"But they can't do that. We'll get you a lawyer, sue them for unlawful dismissal—"

"It's no good. The rules are clear. They just never enforced them before."

"So why now? Who'd you show the place to that got them so upset?"

"Do you really want to know?"

"Of course."

"Try you and Lucy O'Connor."

He couldn't have heard right. "Pardon?"

But Victor grimaced, held his palms skyward, and gave a huge shrug.

"You're not serious."

"I'm afraid I am."

"Jesus Christ!"

"That's what my director said. He's as flabbergasted as I am."

"There's got to be some mistake."

"Oh, there's no mistake. They stipulated my alleged violation of lab security occurred between the hours of six and seven last night."

"Wait a minute. Let me go to your boss. I'll explain to him—"

"Won't do any good. My own boss was apologetic as hell. The order to can me came from the head office in New York."

"But how did anyone there even know about our visit?"

"That's what I can't figure out. I mean, security's extra tight these days. But this doesn't figure. It's overkill."

"Did the people in New York know you were showing two doctors through the lab?"

"I don't know. But my director did. When he got the order, he looked at the surveillance tapes and saw it was you, then figured the woman was one of your students. He even called New York on my behalf, arguing that you were the local GP and no more a security threat than he was. They weren't interested, and told him that unauthorized personnel were unauthorized personnel."

"But orders from New York to fire you because you showed me around. Why would somebody in the head office of a high-powered lab be so skittish?"

"Beats me."

Still dismayed, Mark began to think the worst. "Who owns Nucleus Laboratories?"

"A numbered company. You know how it works these days—nameless corporations within corporations."

"Could you find out who's at the top?"

"With all I know about their records? Give me a day. But what good will it do?"

"Just get me a name. I might be wrong, but this may have more to do with me than you. If that's the case, and I can prove it, we could get your job back."

Victor frowned "What do you mean?"

"Sorry, I can't tell you any more right now. But do this for me, and if a hunch I have plays out, chances are Nucleus Laboratories won't be causing either of us any more trouble."

"Us?"

"Yeah! Us. Hey, without you managing the place, how am I going to get my blood tests done?"

Victor studied him a few seconds, then the apprehension in his expression dissipated. "It's a deal, Doc. And thanks."

"As I said, you've done me and everyone in my practice a big favor for years. It's I who thanks you."

For a few seconds the rest of the man's flushed expression gave way to a hint of a smile, but couldn't quite deliver all of it. "Just don't tell anyone I'm doing it for you," he said, getting to his feet and shaking Mark's hand. "Not anyone. They find out I'm hacking into their business files, I'll be blackballed from working in the industry ever again—"

A knock on the door interrupted him, and Lucy poked her head in. "Oh, hi, Victor, I thought I heard your voice. Wondered if you wanted to drop over for dinner later."

"Oh, I couldn't—"

"Come on. I've had a fresh vegetable soup on a low heat all day that's a stew by now, so join us."

Victor looked at Mark as if for permission to cross the line that separates patients from doctors.

"Absolutely, Victor," Mark said, unable to think of any better medicine for the man than good company and a fine meal. "Please come."

"Why, thank you."

"Shall we say seven?" she asked.

"Yes, seven would be perfect."

Mark saw the hint of a smile beneath the mustache.

"Lucy, you gave that guy exactly what the doctor ordered," he told her, after Victor had left.

"What?"

"I'll explain later."

Mark and Lucy finished early with the afternoon's patients and took a short run together.

"You're in as good shape as I am," he said to her, as they started the uphill portion of his route.

She sprinted ahead and grinned at him over her shoulder. "The question is, are you in as good shape as me?"

Afterward they shared a pot of tea in his kitchen.

She sat curled up in a large rocking chair, holding her cup with both hands. "You could be right," she said, having listened to him explain his theory why Victor might have been fired.

Behind her the large cast-iron woodstove that had been the centerpiece of the room in both his mother's and aunt Margaret's day crackled with burning maple. It filled the room with a warmth that was far cozier than the baseboard heaters could provide, but Mark had hardly ever bothered to fire it up. Lucy, however, as soon as she learned it was functional, had sent him out to retrieve an armload of logs off the woodpile while she chopped up some kindling.

The sounds transported Mark back to a time when his home was a happy place, but the memories also carried the dull aching reminder of parents and childhood prematurely lost. Which was why he'd shunned stove fires in the past.

Yet this evening was different. Lucy's company mollified his usual discomfort with remembrance. How pleasant it felt at the end of the day to have someone with whom he could discuss the little victories. And the problems.

"Obviously I'm making someone nervous," Mark said, "Nucleus Laboratories must be a business interest connected to Chaz Braden. Why else would our visit bring down such a heavy-handed response?"

She scrunched up her face into a show of skepticism, making her look as if she were staring into a harsh light. "But how could your investigation of a murder twenty-seven years ago have any connection with a lab built in 1996?"

He shrugged, unable to give her an answer. "I just feel it in my bones. Chaz's name will be among the business interests running the place, I'm sure of it. What the tie-in might be to Kelly, I'll have to figure that out later."

"What if you're wrong, and there is no evidence that Chaz is involved? Or even if his name does appear somewhere in the hierarchy of the place, it doesn't prove anything is wrong. Lots of doctors have business interests in private labs."

"Then Victor's getting fired would be one big coincidence. Don't tell me you believe that."

"No, not really. I'm saying there may be another reason."

"Such as?" he asked, waiting for her to continue. Then he figured he knew what she must be going to say. Earlier he'd told her of Earl's astonishing revelation about Samantha and Walter McShane. "Okay, I have to admit, if the McShanes turned out to own a piece of Nucleus Laboratories—and they do have extensive business interests, if the *Wall Street Journal*'s to be believed— it might be her we're after. But why our visit would make either of them fire Victor is even more unimaginable than it is for Chaz. Besides, there's something that doesn't fit about the idea of Samantha killing Kelly. There should have been a different dynamic involved."

"How do you mean?"

"It didn't sit right when Dr. Garnet suggested it, and now I remember why." Earl's testiness when Mark hadn't embraced the idea outright also didn't sit well, but he kept that irritation to himself. Someday soon, however, he intended to point out that as coroner on the case, he outranked chiefs of ER from Buffalo. "During my psychiatry rotation at NYCH, we saw court tapes of women on trial for killing their children in what were believed to be Munchausen by proxy syndromes. Now Samantha didn't really fit that profile, but as Earl said, the dynamic of her playing a noble, self-sacrificing victim was similar. Well, here's something else she might be kindred in. Each one of those women had accepted her sentence with eerie equanimity, all the while protesting her innocence, as if her incarceration were simply another hardship to endure as part of being a long-suffering mother. If we're right about Samantha, she could have reacted that way, too, might even have reveled in standing accused by her daughter. It would have given her a chance at an ultimate performance, in court, before the cameras, playing the victim role of a lifetime—mother unjustly charged of terrible wrongdoings by the very child she'd so self-sacrificingly nursed through one mysterious illness after another. It's unlikely that she would have given up such an opportunity, let alone killed to avoid it."

Lucy took a sip of tea and stared across the top of her mug, appearing to digest what he'd said. After a few seconds she looked over at him. "Interesting, but did you ever think it might not be your investigation of Kelly's murder that's got whoever runs that lab so upset, but something else?"

That surprised him. "Something else?" Her open expression and glittering brown eyes were so lovely and vulnerable, he found them distracting. "Okay, what am I missing?"

She swallowed, seeming uncertain whether to speak, and curled her legs more tightly under her.

"Lucy?"

Her gaze drifted off him and wandered the room. "Something I've been mulling over, but didn't want to tell you until I could be sure what it meant. I can't even say now how it fits in with either Kelly or the lab." She again fell silent.

For the two days he'd known her, this self-assured young woman hadn't betrayed the slightest trace of indecision in her work. Yet here she was, hesitant to speak up. "Go on," he said, his curiosity growing about what could fluster her so.

"Well, it's personal, so bear with me—"

Mark's home phone began to ring, interrupting her.

He took the call on a wall-mounted extension near the back door of the kitchen. "Roper."

"Mark, this is Charles Braden calling."

He felt as if a bomb had exploded in his ear. "Ah, yes, Dr. Braden."

Lucy's eyes widened into a you've-got-to-be-kidding-me look.

He gestured her to join him in listening. "What can I do for you, sir?"

She huddled at his side, their ears sharing the receiver

"Well, you can not call me 'sir' for starters. Makes me feel ancient."

"Of course, sir—Dr. Braden."

"Call me Charles. I'd like that. Gives me the illusion of being closer to your generation than my own." He finished with a jovial chuckle.

"Give me a break," Lucy muttered, her eyes shooting skyward in disbelief.

Mark nudged her to keep quiet. "So what can I do for you, Charles?"

"You know how word travels fast in our little community. I hear you've got a very attractive houseguest staying with you. Why not drop around for drinks tomorrow night, and bring her along. This sad business with Kelly has reminded me how out of touch we've grown. Your father was a regular guest in our home."

Lucy rolled her eyes again.

"Yes, sir, I mean, Charles. Those were certainly memorable parts of my boyhood." He had to avoid looking at Lucy for fear he'd burst out laughing. "I'd love to drop over."

"Excellent. Shall we say around five?"

"Perfect."

They hung up, and Mark whistled.

"Talk about being invited into the lion's den," Lucy said, walking out of the kitchen.

"Where are you going?"

"Into Saratoga, to buy a dress."

"Do you want me to go with you?"

She turned back, her mouth cocked in a sly grin. "There are some things, my dear Mark, that a woman does alone." Pulling on her coat and shouldering her purse, she disappeared out the front door.

Mark stood looking after her. Whatever Lucy had been on the verge of saying before the phone call, she obviously thought it could wait.

Thursday, November 22, 3:30 A.M.
The Plaza Hotel, New York City

At first Earl wasn't sure what woke him.

Then the pain cut across his abdomen and doubled him in two.

"Jesus Christ!" He moaned, writhing in a ball.

His insides had been churning all evening. Once in bed, he'd tossed for a few more hours trying to fall asleep.

No way this could be from stress.

The cramps came in waves, hitting him like body blows. They were so closely spaced together that the pain from one hadn't released its grip before the next struck.

He got off the bed and tried to make it to the bathroom, but fell to the floor.

Again and again and again the spasms struck, leaving him drenched in cold sweat and biting his lips to keep from screaming.

He'd had his share of "tourista," especially during conferences to faraway places, but never experienced anything like this. Must have picked it up at one of the fast-food joints he'd been eating at these last few days. The most likely cause would be *Campylobacter* from undercooked chicken or beef, he reasoned during a few seconds pause in his symptoms. If he could just buy some Cipro—damn! It was Thanksgiving, and most pharmacies would be closed. No matter. He'd get Melanie to get him some from the hospital, providing he could reach her. Then maybe he could still make the trip home, though the idea of being stuck on the can for the whole flight—"Oh, my God!" he muttered, a new onslaught sending him rolling on the floor again.

This time it felt as if someone were twist-tying his intestines and dragging them through hot coals.

By 5:00 A.M. he relented and called 911, requesting they take him to ER at New York City Hospital.

The ambulance attendants tried strapping him down to the stretcher for the trip. He ended up breaking free and taking the ride coiled in a ball on the floor of the vehicle, threatening lawsuits, decertification, and free vasectomies with a dull scalpel on any man who touched him.

In ER his ordeal got worse.

"We can't give you anything for pain until the surgical resident examines your abdomen," said a young trainee in a short white coat who had to be the most junior student on the ER food chain. Christ, peach fuzz covered his cheeks.

"I'm Earl Garnet, Chief of Emergency Medicine at St. Paul's Hospital in Buffalo. Get me your staff person, or give me Demerol, damm it! And for your future edification, a surgical abdomen doesn't present as cramps."

The boy looked unimpressed. "Does this hurt?" he asked, palpating deep into his lower right side, then abruptly lifting off.

Nurses started IVs.

A clerk wrote down his mother's maiden name.

Someone took custody of his wallet; someone else drained a dozen tubes of blood from his arm.

"You haven't got a fever, and your pressure's fine," a nurse reassured him.

The surgical resident came, prodded his stomach a few times, then went off to consult with his staffman.

Still no one gave him Demerol.

"Not before the surgeon himself sees you." It became a reoccurring chorus.

"And where's the surgeon?"

"In the OR."

Where else?

He flagged another passing nurse, easily catching her attention as they'd parked him in the middle of a busy main corridor. Sporting tousled brown hair and covered in freckles, she could have been the kid sister of the lowly resident who checked him in, until she turned and he saw the triple silver rings piercing her eyebrow. He thought of J.C. in his own department, and felt oddly reassured. "I want to speak with the doctor in charge," he demanded for the second time since his arrival.

"He's managing victims from a bus accident," she called without breaking stride.

"Then phone Melanie Collins."

This got her to pause. "The Chief of Internal Medicine? I don't think so."

The fiery vengeance in his stomach shot to a new level, and he let out a loud groan, curling into a ball again. "Call her, please!" he managed to gasp between clenched teeth a few seconds later, his skin once more soaked with perspiration. "I'm a friend. Say that I need her help now!"

Whether his appearance, his use of "please," or his claim of being a personal acquaintance to an important doctor convinced her, he couldn't tell. She nevertheless walked to the nearest phone and made a call. She spoke a few words into the receiver, then stopped, a dumbfounded expression slowly spreading across her face like a connect-the-dot drawing.

"Dr. Collins will be right in," she told him with newfound respect.

"Thank you," he said, and forced a grin that must have made him resemble the grim reaper.

Twenty minutes later Melanie arrived at his bedside flanked by peach-fuzz and the ring-wraith. An additional bevy of students, interns, and residents formed a semicircle around them.

"Earl, I'm so sorry," she said, patting his shoulder.

"Me too. I didn't mean to haul you in here—"

"Don't think anything of it." She gave a thousand-watt smile and turned to her following. "Now, gang, let's give our distinguished guest a show of how to do it right. What's the presentation here?"

"Abdominal pain, crampy, generalized, and acute onset," peach-fuzz called out.

"Any vomiting or diarrhea?"

"No, ma'am."

"Vitals?"

"No fever, normal BP, but pulse is 120."

"Yours would be fast too, if you had the kind of pain that I know it would take to bring this man into ER. Any abdominal findings on exam?"

"Abdomen's soft, no rebound, no masses, no bruit, but increased bowel sounds."

"Urine?"

"Normal."

"Rectal?"

"Negative."

"You checked for occult blood?"

"None."

"So what's your thinking?"

"Well, first off I'd consider this to be pain from a hollow organ rather than a solid structure, given its colicky nature—"

"I don't want to reread the entire text on abdominal pain, so let's bypass the general stuff and pinpoint the most likely possibilities. Yes it's colicky, and originates from something hollow. But the lack of nausea and there being no focal, right-upper-quadrant tenderness means we don't even have to think gallbladder, and with a normal urine, it isn't renal. Any history of hypertension, Earl?"

He shook his head no, wishing she hadn't chosen him to grandstand on. But he was imminently grateful to her for coming in and getting things going, and if he had to endure a few minutes of being a teaching specimen, so be it. Besides, it wasn't entirely a waste. The latest rage in teaching hospitals was for the teachers to take a turn on the other side of the white coat. He'd let the residents know he'd had his, thank you very much, when he got back to Buffalo.

"So, his lack of risk factors, along with the absence of a pulsatile mass, means an aortic aneurysm is unlikely," she continued. "The patient being male, what's left that's hollow?"

"GI!" responded a bearded man at the back.

"Sold!" Earl said, figuring it was time to wrap up the bidding on his diagnosis.

But Melanie hadn't finished putting on her show. "Right. And since there's no vomiting, we can assume the problem doesn't lie in the upper gastrointestinal tract, which leaves us with?"

"Lower," her audience said in unison.

Get on with it, Earl nearly told her, his innards clamping down on themselves again.

"Now I know this thought process sounds oversimplistic, but it's what should have zipped through your heads in the first few seconds you saw this patient, and everyone's focus ought to have been on the lower GI for a nonsurgical problem from the get-go. Okay, what's the differential? But this time start with the most probable. Don't bother me with stuff about tumors, obstruction, ischemia, or chronic things like inflammatory bowel disease. And for God's sake don't begin with rare genetic disorders like porphyria. I hate having to look up those damn metabolic pathways."

A collective chuckle came from the group.

"Enteritis, colitis, or both," one of the young men said.

"Very good. The probable cause?"

"Viral or bacterial contamination from food," he replied.

"Which bacteria?"

"*Campylobacter jejuni*, salmonella, shigella."

"Treatment?"

"Hydration, electrolyte management, particularly potassium replacement, Cipro, and painkillers!" He spoke with the certainty of someone on a roll.

Yes! Earl wanted to yell out. You can replace peach-fuzz as my doctor.

"Not so fast," Melanie said. "Is there any danger in giving ciprofloxacin at this point?"

Oh, Melanie, he wanted to shout, surely old Earl Garnet didn't have to be treated by the book. Come on, give the Cipro. As physician to physician. Cut corners.

The bearded resident seemed at a loss for words.

"Any reason to wait for stool culture results before treating?" Melanie prompted.

The man stroked his chin as if contemplating a chess move, then shrugged.

Melanie searched the crowd for any other takers. There were none. "Okay, here's the teaching nugget of this case. The severity of Dr. Garnet's pain plus an apparent delay in the onset of the inevitable diarrhea makes me think this might be an organism other than the more common ones you listed. With them, the diarrhea usually follows closely on the heels of the pain. But with some of the enterohemorrhagic *E. coli*, where toxins are the culprit, they need time to work, and there can be the sort of delay we see here. In other words, the agent infecting Dr. Garnet may be none other than *E. coli 0157:H7*, which can not only cause a hemorrhagic colitis, but in 10 percent of cases, introduce toxins which attack the kidneys to produce a hemolytic uremic syndrome. The latest evidence suggests antibiotics may actually increase the risk of complications, so we hold the Cipro."

There wasn't a round of applause, but the appreciative nods as her audience dispersed and returned to their various duties were as good a stamp of approval as a teacher could get for first-rate bedside teaching. Earl had to admit he'd not heard of the subtle nuance she was making, but it made sense, and her zeroing in on it impressed him,

"Hope you didn't mind me putting you through that," she said, while checking the IV bag flowing into his arm—normal saline with an added dose of potassium—"but I wanted to set them straight after the inexcusable delay they put you through."

Be gracious, he told himself. "Hey, our residents are the same until we whip them into shape. You've nothing to apologize for, and thank you again for getting out of bed." And since he had her attention: "Melanie, I've also been trying to call you to clear up a misunderstanding—"

"Now you just stay quiet, and I'll have you comfortable in minutes." She pulled a syringe out of her lab pocket, stuck it in the side portal of his IV line, and began to push in the plunger. "No allergies I take it?"

"None. What are you giving me. Demerol?"

"You, my friend, get the big *M.*"

"Morphine?"

She nodded.

But morphine, powerful analgesic that it was, doctors seldom used for acute abdominal pain in ER. It could obtund consciousness to the point of suppressing respiration and cause serious drops in blood pressure. Neither of which was a good thing where issues such as staying awake enough to keep breathing or avoiding aspiration of vomit or fighting a low blood pressure from dehydration were concerned. Of course there were exceptional cases, but he didn't want to be one of them. "Listen, Melanie, I'm not that bad. Don't give me special treatment—Whoa!"

The potent opiate affected him immediately, taking away not only his abdominal spasms but every ache and pain he had, physical or emotional. He felt his brain slip into a warm puddle, where it floated without a care in the world.

"I'll make sure the nurses keep you well topped off," said a voice from the other side of the universe.

Must be God talking. Sounded like his kind of woman, one who knew her business.

Chapter 14

Mark stood on the back porch, sipping a cup of coffee that had come from the bottom of the pot. Along the horizon, a gray, hump-backed line of clouds strained toward the east, dragging their shaggy tendrils over the hills. The cold wet aroma of snow hung in the air.

He'd spent the morning in his office reading his mail and answering a seemingly endless stream of calls from patients. Most were trivial problems easily answered.

Between calls he'd puzzled over why Charles Braden had invited Lucy and him to his home. And stared at the ceiling to the sound of creaky floorboards as Lucy prowled around her room. What was up with her? When she got back from shopping last night, she'd prepared dinner and welcomed Victor with open arms. Then she'd kept them entertained throughout the meal with stories of warlords, strange animals, and field hospital hijinks. Afterward, Victor sat down at the piano and led them through the highlights of great Broadway shows. They belted out the tunes they knew and danced to the ones they didn't.

Victor had left in high spirits, yet as soon as he was out the door, she'd said she was exhausted and gone directly to bed.

This morning he'd wakened to the sounds of her in the kitchen and the smell of fresh coffee, but when he came down to join her for breakfast she retreated back upstairs, taking her cup with her, apologizing profusely that she had a ton of correspondence to answer and job applications to send out. "After all, by next July, I plan to be a working woman again."

Why was she avoiding him? From the creaking of the floorboards, she'd seemed to be doing more pacing than writing.

The phone rang for the umpteenth time, bringing him back inside.

"My knees are bothering me again."

Nell! Mark repressed a sigh, having no patience for their usual merry-go-round today. "When do you want to come in?" he said, trying not to sound too weary.

"Can't. They're too swollen. I need one of them house calls. And you bring that young new doctor I hear you've been traipsing all over the county with. Maybe she can help me."

Despite himself, he started to laugh. "Nell, you old fraud."

"Who are you callin' old?"

He leaned back in his chair and chuckled again, feeling better for it.

"Are you still interested in that maternity center Braden used to run in Saratoga?" she asked.

Mark leaned forward again. "Yes."

"Name's Diane Whigston Lawler. Her place is just off Route 9 toward the town. She was a local girl, good family, married one of them big shots from New York. Shortly after her first child, he divorced her for some model-actress. Bastard had the better lawyers and took the kid plus everything that wasn't nailed down. Her own family went bankrupt during one of those big savings and loans busts in the eighties. Lives kinda' poor now."

She gave him the exact address and telephone number. He recognized the street name, and figured the words "kinda poor" might be an understatement. The place was a trailer park.

"And I've been asking around like you wanted," she continued. "Seeing if anybody noticed Chaz Braden doing anything weird just before Kelly went missing."

"Any luck?"

"Also checked if Samantha McShane was around the area."

He shot upright. "Damn it, Nell, I told you don't do anything of the kind. In fact I gave you specific instructions not to go setting off rumors—"

"No luck with either. But I did come up with a few other tidbits and a name you might find interesting."

"Who?"

"Be here at seven tomorrow night, and I'll tell you over dinner."

"Nell—"

"Don't forget to bring your lady friend. Do you think she'd mind helping out in the kitchen? I can see if she's up to scratch."

"Nell, you stop that kitchen nonsense and tell me right now—"

He was talking to a dial tone.

He punched in her number.

Busy signal.

He asked the operator to interrupt, claiming it was a medical emergency.

The phone was off the hook. He sighed and glanced down at the scrap of paper where he'd jotted the number she'd given him. He dialed it, figuring anything would be more productive than trying to get Nell to behave.

A woman answered.

"Diane Whigston Lawler?" Nell hadn't said if she still used her married name.

"It's just Diane Whigston now."

Her voice was melodious, but deep and a touch husky, the way a smoker's can get. It also sounded big, and he imagined he was talking to a large woman. "Ms. Whigston, my name is Mark Roper. I'm a physician in Hampton Junction. I got your name from Nell—"

"Ah, of course. She told me you might be calling. I understand you're interested in the maternity center Dr. Braden used to run."

"Yes. I wonder if I could meet you and ask some questions about the place."

"Sure, but I don't understand. It's been twenty-nine years since my son Ronald was born there, and it's long been closed."

Diane Whigston must be the only acquaintance of Nell's who didn't know about his investigating Kelly's murder. Otherwise, she'd have guessed right away why he wanted to talk to her. For some reason Nell must not have told her. "Yes, it was a very long time ago, Ms. Whigston. You see, I'm looking into a twenty-seven-year-old murder, that of Kelly McShane. You probably read about the discovery of her body a few weeks ago—"

"So that's why you wanted to talk about the maternity center? You're after the Bradens! Well, if Nell had told me that, I never would have agreed to talk with you." The deep tones had suddenly turned shrill.

"No, Ms. Whigston, please, I'm not after anyone, just trying to gather as much information—"

"Dr. Charles Braden saved my little Ronnie's life, period. I've got nothing but praise and admiration for the man."

"I understand—"

"Ronnie wouldn't breathe when he came out, and that man went rushing out of the delivery room with him, giving mouth-to-mouth as he ran, and drove him to the hospital himself. Didn't even wait for an ambulance. One week later I first got to hold my baby when he personally transported my child back to me and placed him in my arms, just before I went home. I'll never forget that day, or my gratitude to Dr. Braden. So I won't be saying anything against him, ever."

"Ms. Whigston, please—"

"And Ronnie wasn't the only one he did that for. I've since met other mothers who say the same thing. And the nurses, they called him the miracle man when it came to saving kids. One told me he even kept an incubator in his car for just such emergencies. You won't find many former patients or staff willing to bad-mouth him."

"If you'll just let me explain—"

He found himself once more talking to a dial tone.

Now he understood why Nell hadn't told her who he was. Jesus, she could have warned him Diane Whigston was so prickly. Approached properly, the woman might have at least been willing to discuss the routine of the place.

He dialed Nell's number again. Maybe she could make things right with her friend, and he'd get another chance.

She picked up this time.

"Nell—"

And hung up.

He thought he really hadn't time for this when his phone rang again.

"Nell?"

"No, it's me," said Victor Feldt. "I wanted to say how much I enjoyed last night."

"Victor! Sorry, I just got cut off—I mean hung up on—"

"Old Nell giving you the gears again? I'll bet it's about Lucy. She want to meet her, check her out?"

"No—"

The big man gave a low, knowing chuckle.

It reminded Mark why he hated living in a goldfish bowl. "What can I do for you, Victor?"

"I haven't made much progress in tracking down who owns Nucleus, but what I found is some pretty weird stuff."

"Weird?"

"Yeah. The information is buried in a labyrinth of registered owner-ships. The amount of subterfuge here is really fishy. I'm staying on this. It's too strange."

"Any idea how long it will take?"

"Give me until tomorrow. I also thought of something else we should check out. What if the sudden tightening of security has to do with a request from one of the lab's clients? Maybe it's somebody at their end who's suddenly gone paranoid. Were that the case, would it help you to find out why?"

"What do you mean?"

"I've been talking to a few of my contacts at the companies that deal with us, telling them what happened, saying good-bye—you know, that kind of thing—and a few have said they're not surprised."

"Not surprised you got fired?"

"Not surprised that someone in their organization might be hypersensitive over an outsider seeing medical data about their staff."

"Well, they should be. Information like that is supposed to be confidential."

"What I'm talking about is above and beyond those usual types of concern."

"How do you mean?"

"There are huge shakeups going on in a host of companies, thousands of high executives being laid off. It shows up in the health plans, their policies not being renewed."

"So? Layoffs are happening all over the country. It's because of the economy."

"Not when they immediately turn around and rehire thousands more new staff. There's an equal number of new policies on replacements for the people they fired."

Obviously Victor was off on some wild-goose chase, probably as a way to avoid dwelling on his own firing. "And how would all that make some-one freak at my visit to the lab?" Mark asked, attempting to nudge him back to the reality of their current problem.

"I don't know. But if it were the case, would you want me to find out more about it?" he continued, sounding as eager for approval as a fawning puppy. "Tomorrow, when everybody is back to work from the holiday, I can call some additional contacts and try to get specifics on what's up, if anything, that might have spooked one of these organizations. If you like, I could even reach a few other people at home today, where they might feel freer to talk."

"Why not?" Mark said, thinking the whole thing was light-years removed from any connection to Kelly's murder or Chaz Braden, but even following up leads doomed to go nowhere could be the best thing for Victor right now. Despite his obvious capacity to enjoy good company and be the life of a party, he was so very solitary out here.

"And while I was going through all those records, I found a handful of doctors in New York who had a small account with us much like the one I arranged for you."

"I don't follow."

"You know, puny bits of business from a few private office patients— they stand out amongst our usual giant-sized contracts. What's really unusual, the master record of all test results ordered by this group isn't stored here. The system's flagged to forward them to another terminal, presumably back in New York. The point is, someone high up made the arrangements. That's head office territory—not like out here, where a guy like me has a certain amount of leeway to pull off what you and I had going, at least, until yesterday. I was thinking you could phone some of these doctors and ask, physician to physician, who they'd made their special deal with in order to set themselves up that way. It might get us closer to the actual owner of the place."

Not likely, Mark thought as he took down the names. He recognized some of them—a surgeon, a few internists, a gynecologist, and three very prominent family physicians who had taught him at NYCH during his residency. These were top drawer people. Yes, they would have professional ties with Chaz through the hospital, but he couldn't imagine why they'd need to make a private arrangement with an out-of-the-way facility. Their use of Nucleus Laboratories, even if it turned out Chaz owned the place, would likely be for mundane reasons, probably having to do with the patients' insurance companies insisting they use a specific testing center. "That's a fabulous idea, Victor," he said, continuing to hide his skepticism that any of it would pan out. "I'll try and contact them tomorrow. Thank you for coming up with it. Believe me, I'm grateful for everything you're doing."

As he hung up, Mark made a mental note to call the phone company. The *clicks* on his line, a recurrent joy of country living, had become annoying.

5:35 P.M.

Snowflakes the size of cotton balls floated onto Lucy's black hair, where they sparkled like points of a tiara before vanishing. "Battle stations," she said to Mark under her frosty breath, a gleam in her eye as they climbed the freshly shoveled steps to where Charles Braden stood just behind his butler, who'd swung open front door.

"Lock and load," Mark muttered back at her.

In seconds they were shaking hands with their host, and the butler took their coats.

Lucy looked stunning in a floor-length, black, body-hugging sweater. "Good evening, Dr. Braden," she said. "Thank you for inviting me along."

"Lucy O'Connor. Why, I had no idea you were the beauty the whole town's been talking about. What a pleasure to see you again."

"You already know each other?" Mark asked.

"Yes," Braden said quickly. "I had the pleasure of chatting with Lucy shortly after her arrival at NYCH. A year ago, wasn't it?"

"Yes, it was."

"My, how time flies. Now come on in, and meet my other guests." He took her arm and led her into the living room.

Mark followed, surprised at the exchange and wanting a chance to ask why she hadn't mentioned meeting Braden Senior before. At the same time he was overwhelmed by the memories of arriving here as a small child, with Kelly greeting them at the door and leading them in to meet the guests.

"I didn't think my having met Braden was important," Lucy whispered, apparently reading the puzzlement on Mark's face.

They entered a massive room full of young and middle-aged men. Braden introduced them to the nearest group and beckoned to one of the numerous waiters circulating through the room.

Lucy requested champagne.

Mark asked for a beer.

Within moments they had their drinks in hand and Lucy was receiving the lion's share of attention from the men around them. She acted fascinated with every single one.

Mark recognized the names of at least four or five heads of the Fortune 500 whose firms were headquartered in New York. The ingrained resentment he'd always had for the silver-spoon set stirred deep within him.

Other men walked over to introduce themselves. He barely paid attention, until:

". . . Freddy Lawler II, and this is my boy Ronald . . ."

Mark started at this name, and found himself staring at a small-statured man with delicate features and short-cropped blond hair. He reappraised his audio impression of the kid's mother, downsizing his mental image by about 50 percent. But he wasn't curious enough to go over and ask Ronnie if he carried a picture of the woman to be sure. He did wonder if this well-heeled son ever visited Diane Whigston in her trailer park, and if he drove up to her front door in whichever fancy car parked outside was his, or arrived in a taxi to save them both embarrassment at the difference in their economic stations.

He slipped away from where Lucy continued to hold court and parked himself beside a table of hors d'oeuvres, making it a point to be alone and accessible.

He and Lucy suspected Braden wanted a private word with Mark, perhaps to suggest subtly that it would be wise to leave Chaz alone during the investigation. But while Mark went one-on-one with Charles, she would work the crowd, and perhaps succeed at prompting somebody to make a slip about Chaz's real whereabouts at the time of the ambush. Judging by how readily they fell under her spell, Mark figured she just might pull it off.

At least that had been their plan.

"And you all hunt, do you?" Lucy asked the men arrayed around her. "I have a huge weak spot for venison. My four brothers used to bring in enough to feed our entire family for a winter, and nothing, but nothing, could surpass the taste of that meat prepared in my mother's marinade . . ."

Her enthusiasm was so convincing that Mark figured her every word to be true. In any case she had her audience eating out of her hand.

". . . so if any of you gentleman are willing to share some of your catch with me, I'd be pleased to remunerate—"

"Love to, Doc!"

"How much do you want?"

"I've got a dozen steaks in the freezer with your name on it—my gift to you . . ."

Mark chuckled at how she'd captivated these weekend hunters.

". . . why, thank you gentlemen," Lucy continued. "But which of you has bagged the most? I wouldn't want to deprive someone of their sole catch?"

"We could show you later."

"Yeah, it's all down in the meat locker."

"Just at the foot of the back steps."

"Really? It isn't bloody, is it? I can't stand the sight of blood."

"Oh, of course not," reassured a very earnest young man with blow-dried black hair. Chipper he'd said his name was. "It's all been cut into steaks, just like at the meat market—"

Lucy burst out laughing and, laying her hand on his, gave him a wink. "Chipper, you forget what I do for a living."

He flushed.

The rest roundly laughed.

"Now you quit teasing me, Doc," Chipper said, breaking into a good-natured smile.

Mark looked around, but Charles didn't appear to be in the room. Spotting a group of men in a small parlor with sliding doors, he thought his host might be there, and sidled over. As he drew near, he picked up snatches of the conversation.

". . . shareholders will bale at the slightest rumor . . ."

". . . exercising my options . . ."

". . . if it gets public . . ."

But no Charles.

Nevertheless, he strained to hear, thinking he might at least get a tip on which stocks to dump.

". . . other CEOs have had worse problems . . ."

". . . the SEC filed charges against Bob last week . . ."

". . . Christ, everyone's going down like flies these days . . ."

At that moment Charles appeared out of nowhere, stepped over to the doors, and drew them closed. He turned around and, seemingly only then, spotted Mark. He smiled, and shrugged, almost apologetically. "Business-men are like doctors," he said, walking over to take him by the elbow and lead him away. "You can't even invite them to a party but they clump to-gether and talk shop."

"Well, I guess that's true—"

"I wonder if you and I could have a word in private?"

Here we go, Mark thought.

"Of course."

"Perhaps you'd be kind enough to wait for me in the library. I have to speak with the caterer, but will be along in a minute. You remember the way, don't you? You used to play there as a child."

*   *   *

The double wooden doors of polished mahogany were as high as the fifteen-foot ceilings. They opened as soundlessly as he remembered, admitting him to the silent interior. Overhead chandeliers suspended from dark wooden beams cast a dim golden glow over the thousands of book spines that lined the shelves along the walls. Though the room seemed smaller than before, it remained impressive.

Perfect, thought Mark. With the two of them alone, Braden would be more likely to start in with his refined arm-twisting techniques. There'd be no need to keep it polite. That might be more revealing about any family secrets Braden wanted to keep hidden than the nuanced exchanges they'd had thus far in the middle of crowds. Mark might even press him a little— make him defensive about Chaz.

As Mark waited, the soft pungent smell of leather mixed with the caramelized odor of varnish. Closing his eyes, he could have been back in that time when the three people he loved most in the world were as close as the next room, all happily, he'd believed, laughing, eating, and drinking together. Then he felt all the more desolate for the reminder of what he'd lost. "Goddamn it," he muttered, starting to stroll and read the titles, anything to prevent the past from reinvading his memory. He resented such incursions at the best of times. Somehow, in this house, thoughts of his mother, his father, and Kelly were unseemly fresh and doubly painful.

Yet he found himself heading for the corner he'd liked best—the place where he had curled up on one of the big leather reading chairs with books on travel adventures that were full of wild-animal pictures.

On the way he passed entire sections of medical works, and quickly appreciated the extent of the collection. Interested, he took a closer look.

Initially he saw worn, faded books on obstetrics, some of them almost historical records exhibiting how crude and primitive the profession once was. Others documented more recent history. He pulled down an old leather-bound text dated 1930 and, flipping through it, shuddered at the realities of infant and maternal mortality in the era when his own parents had been born. Ether had been the only anesthetic, sulfa the only antibiotic for infections, and neonatal care for any compromised infants amounted to little more than keeping them warm and hydrated until they died or revived on their own.

The next shelf over contained more up-to-date texts on both childbirth and neonatology, some of them real doorstoppers. Mark remembered his OB rotation under Charles Braden—it had been the man's last year before retirement—and, whatever he thought of him personally, begrudgingly admitted how excellent he'd been as a teacher. Always on top of current practices, Braden had a wonderful knack for putting those techniques and advances in the context of how things were before.

A few steps farther, he found a whole section of completely contemporary editions, including the latest works on high-risk births, neonatology intensive care, and the management of congenital birth defects. There were scientific publications as well—molecular biology, DNA, the human genome—and tucked alongside them were reprints of articles that Charles Braden coauthored six years ago outlining the potential of screening amniotic fluid for mutated genes to diagnose genetic abnormalities in utero. Handwritten notes in the margins outlined the commercial possibilities of marketing kits to make doing the job easier. Well-thumbed journals with the latest studies in theoretical applications of gene and stem cell therapies completed the collection.

This was not a person who had slipped into retirement and let his profession pass him by. He'd kept up.

On the adjacent shelves, he found the other end of the spectrum—the less noble records of the profession, including yellowed tracts from the thirties and forties that were little more than fascist rants on eugenics. Filled with crude caricatures of Africans pointing out their Negroid features and accompanying texts that were outright racist in attributing inferiority to such physiognomy, these were published in both Boston and New York. Other paperbound manuals hailing from the University of Berlin spewed similar filth about Jews, but had been translated into English by a well-known Manhattan publishing house better known these days for bestsellers by lawyers. Still others were journals that tried to argue the superiority of the white race through exhaustive measurements of cranium sizes on cadavers.

"I see you found my hall of shame," Charles Braden said from the doorway.

Mark gave a start. He quickly slid one of the works he'd been perusing back into its slot.

"I remember poking through books in here as a kid, Dr. Braden." He gestured to the room as a whole, hoping to draw attention away from that particular section. "Except I obviously didn't appreciate then the extent of the medical collection. It's very impressive."

"Please, continue to browse. And don't be embarrassed. Most doctors are drawn to those particular writings. They're both fascinated and repulsed." He started toward him, and pointed to the shelves near the end of the wall. "Down there are the big results, the global offspring of these poisonous tracts"—he hooked his thumbs at the odious titles Mark had been looking at—"if they are allowed to bear fruit. Come, take a look. The legacy of hate."

Not sure what Braden was getting at, or why the man would even collect such despicable material, he hesitated.

"Don't be shy." Braden walked to the next set of shelves and ran his hands over the half dozen maroon spines of what resembled an encyclopedia set. "These are bound articles related to war crimes of doctors in Germany and Japan during World War II." He pulled one out and handed it to Mark. "This author actually does a good job at explaining why genocide occurs."

As Mark glanced at it, he recognized the name of a Pulitzer Prize–winning journalist whose work he still read regularly in the *Herald*. Braden had tagged some of the more insightful pieces, often the same ones that Mark remembered clipping and saving when he needed a little extra help sorting out the latest ethnic cleansing on the planet.

Braden moved on to less-weathered volumes. "The study of how our profession has strayed into evil is a pursuit of mine," he said. "We should all be forced to read the obscenities of science, in order that none of us drift into a similar arrogance."

Mark picked up the top sheet of a printout that had obviously been taken off the Internet. It reported on recent war crime prosecutions in Tokyo. Included were photos of a vivisection being done on an unanesthetized pregnant woman in a notorious torture camp during Japan's occupation of Manchuria. *The woman had screamed entreaties that her baby be saved as they cut out the womb,* read the caption quoting one of the witnesses. He shuddered, and returned it to its place. "Strong stuff."

"We have our local brand of monsters." Braden reached up a few shelves and handed Mark a pamphlet written in the early thirties by a Dr. Brown from a town not twenty miles north of Hampton Junction. It argued for the smothering of babies at birth if they have obvious physical defects.

The back of Mark's throat closed as he tossed the paper onto the nearest shelf. "That's hideous!"

"Don't think this guy was that far off the thinking of the time, at least in small places like this."

"What do you mean?"

"It was the depression. The good Dr. Brown and every other GP in impoverished, isolated parts of the land would look at a severely deformed baby they'd just delivered and think, What about the family? Barely able to survive now, how will trying to care for this hapless creature sap the little energy and money they have for the healthy siblings? Most doctors might just despair, but some might act—think the right thing to do would be protect the other children from even more abject poverty than they already suffered. Haven't you ever wondered why there are so few older adults with severe disabilities in the little villages of rural America?"

"You're kidding. You don't believe doctors actually smothered infants."

"And you don't believe it ever happened."

Mark felt too startled to speak. He'd heard stories from long ago about midwives doing that kind of thing, but not doctors. "Surely that's the stuff of rural legends."

"I think you're hopelessly naive."

"Hopelessly naive to say most doctors draw the line at murder."

"Yes, it is about drawing lines. Except those lines—between right and wrong, life and death—change with the circumstances and the times. Look how blurred it's getting these days in ICUs with all the high-tech advances we have in keeping people alive."

Even though Braden's tone was quiet and polite, almost professorial, Mark felt uncomfortable. Why was the man going on about this? It certainly wasn't what he'd brought him into the library for. And right now, that was all Mark had an interest in. "Why did you want to see me, sir?" The question sounded more impertinent than he intended, but it got to the point.

The landscape of Braden's features shifted slightly, from pensive to thoughtful. Not different in a way he could describe, but different.

"I wanted to thank you for the discreet way you've been handling your investigation into Kelly's murder," he said.

The compliment caught him by surprise. "I haven't done anything special."

"That can't be true, not for Mark Roper. You're too much like your father. Best damn mind. Inquisitive as hell. That's what made him such a great doctor. Could have been a leading specialist in any field he chose."

"He was. He chose to be a country doctor, and was the best at it."

"Well, yes . . ."

"Dr. Braden, why did you invite me here?"

"Who do you think killed my daughter-in-law?" he answered without missing a beat.

Mark didn't reply, beginning to feel all the digressions in their conversation were deliberate, meant to throw him off.

Charles looked him right in the eye. "Your asking around after the memorial service, did it give you any idea who the mystery man was?"

"No."

"You looking for him?"

"I'm looking at all the possibilities of who her killer might have been."

"Including my son?"

"To be frank, yes."

"Who else?"

"That's not something I'd discuss—"

"The mother?"

"As I said—"

"Any other leads?"

Mark sighed. "No."

"No? My sources at the hospital tell me you've recruited a former classmate of Kelly's to snoop around for you. Earl Garnet. I looked up his record. Pretty smart. But he seems to be asking the same stale questions you are."

"As I said, all possibilities—"

"I'm disappointed, Mark. Going after my son is an old idea already pursued to a dead end by the police. And having had Samantha thoroughly investigated by private detectives without results, even I have to admit that going after her is an old idea, too."

So much for putting Braden on the defensive about Chaz, Mark thought, irritated he hadn't managed his host the way he'd planned. He could either walk out, or stand here and defend himself. "It's fresh ideas about old suspects that I'm after," he finally said, and started for the door.

"What if I told you *I* had a fresh lead?" Braden called after him.

"Yeah, yeah."

An insinuating silence worked on Mark's back until, halfway to the exit, he turned and asked. "Okay, what is it?"

"I might be able to give you a new suspect, somebody who no one else has thought of."

"Who?"

"I can't tell you right now. But I'm working on a promising idea. Just give me a few days to verify what I've found. All I'm asking in the meantime is that you hold off on any move against Chaz."

Mark slowed. He finally had the opening he needed to put Braden on the defensive. Wheeling around, he jabbed his forefinger at him. "So your privileged, fiftysomething brat can take another shot at me? There's a fresh idea for you!"

Braden frowned. "I'm afraid I don't have any idea what you're talking about."

"Oh yeah? Monday night someone fired a bullet through the window of my Jeep, remember? Dan Evans questioned you about it."

"Why, yes. I knew that. It was a terrible incident. But you can't be suggesting Chaz had anything to do with it."

Mark said nothing.

The pleasantness on Braden's face withered a shade. "Of course you know the penalty for libel, defamation of character, and unprofessional conduct."

"Are you threatening me, Charles? You did tell me to call you Charles, didn't you? Well, Charles, some people might construe that kind of language as an attempt to intimidate me while I'm doing my duty as coroner."

The older man's eyes seemed sad. "What I'm doing is trying to tell a young hothead whose father used to be a guest here, at Kelly's insistence, by the way, that if he picks too much at a scab, he's liable to find unexpected pus."

"And what the hell's that supposed to mean?"

"It means sometimes we're forced to face unpleasant truths, aren't we?"

"Oh?"

"Did you ever wonder why, when your family visited here your mother looked so unhappy? Of course, maybe you were too young to notice that sort of thing. But she used to hang around in the background, scowling, all while your father laughed and enjoyed Kelly's company."

Mark felt as if a snake that had long lay sleeping deep in his subconscious suddenly stirred. "If you must know, she despised how you and your friends treated my father." His throat tightened on his words as he spoke.

"But that's the reason she'd give, isn't it?"

A terrible coldness formed in his chest. "What are you getting at?"

"Just remarking on how lonely your father must have been during the years after your mother died. He and Kelly spent a lot of time alone during that period, didn't they?"

"Son of a bitch!" Mark started for the old man.

"Are you menacing *me* now, Mark?" Charles said. His voice rose only a shade louder, but it reverberated with authority.

Mark checked himself, his fists clenched.

"Innuendo can be so damaging, almost as much as the lies that have been told against my son."

"Is there a point to this, Charles?"

"Only that this case could get a lot messier than you ever imagined unless you slow down. What'll happen to your credibility once the press gets even a whiff of the possibility you could be covering up an indiscretion on the part of your father with the victim?"

"What!"

"It's not me you have to worry about. I already told you, I may have the evidence to hand you Kelly's murderer in a matter of days and end this nastiness for all of us while protecting the reputations of the innocent, your dad's included. So in the meantime, back off, young man."

Mark stood still, his insides tightening as he contained his fury. He'd been outflanked and trapped.

He pivoted on his heel and strode down the corridor back into the salon, unsure how long he could keep from throttling the manipulative bastard.

Lucy was still surrounded by her newfound admirers. He walked up to where she held court. "Sorry to interrupt," he announced, "but Dr. O'Connor and I have to leave. We've got a patient in the oven that needs basting."

She looked startled, but said lightly, "He just means my turkey."

"By the way," Mark continued, "I hope you boys are more careful with your rifles than the asshole who took a shot at me two nights ago. It happened on a country road not twenty miles from here."

The men fell quiet.

"What are you saying, Dr. Roper?" Braden asked, having rushed in a dozen seconds behind Mark.

"Oh, I think you know. Just some of my 'fresh thinking' again. Since you already told Sheriff Evans that Chaz was sick and headed back to his New York apartment that night, I thought I'd ask a few of his friends what happened. Maybe they know something about it."

Braden stiffened. "I'll have you know that my guests are all excellent marksmen." His normally genial tone had turned to ice. "Harrison here is even a regular participant in the Marlborough hunt. Besides, these men didn't arrive until Tuesday. So if you're suggesting any of them could be part of that unfortunate incident, you're not only unforgivably rude, but sorely mistaken."

"Really? I'm merely advising everybody with a gun to be careful. Very careful."

Before anyone could say a word he took Lucy's arm and walked out of the room.

"You sure do know how to start a war, Mark Roper," she said once they were out on the highway. Her tone sounded more amused than critical.

He could barely speak, still shaken by the slimy insinuations Braden had made. Of course they weren't true, he kept telling himself. But the press would have a field day with that kind of salacious garbage. And he'd better improvise something to explain himself to Lucy. She was looking at him expectantly, obviously awaiting an explanation for their abrupt departure. "Sorry for losing it back there. I just wanted to shake their above-it-all, smug-assed attitudes. And that house, it stirred up a lot of memories, from when Mom and Dad were alive."

She didn't reply, but he could feel her studying him as he drove. His knuckles hurt, he gripped the steering wheel so hard, and his clenched teeth made his jaw ache. "So what did you learn from the boy's club?" he asked, her silence getting to him.

"You mean besides the fact they're sexist, racist, xenophobes?"

"That deep, are they?"

"Creeps are the same the world over—desperate to find like-minded creeps. They throw out their filth like feelers. And once Braden went off with you, they became outright talkative. I'd say that your investigation of Kelly's murder doesn't faze any of them. It's amazing what men will tell a woman if she shows the least interest in their work or hobbies and comes across just the tiniest bit slutty."

"You acted slutty?"

She cut the darkness with a grin. "Just a little. Purely to get information."

"Such as?"

"Three of them gave me their private cell numbers."

"I'm not surprised. Those young bucks couldn't take their eyes off you."

"I'm talking about their fathers."

He forced a chuckle. "You learn anything more useful?"

"Not much. Like they said, they're here to hunt, though they seemed more interested in talking about their financial empires. One thing's clear. They're all pretty enthralled by their host. Especially how he greases the chute for them when it comes to medical matters."

"Greases the chute?"

"They kept bragging how, thanks to Charles, they had access to the best specialists in New York. That's something I notice a lot in Manhattan— people boast about their doctors with the same passion they show for cars, houses, or favorite baseball teams. Trouble is, they can't all be right."

He chuckled easier this time. "Did any of them let slip they'd been up here before Tuesday?"

"They were too busy asking if men minded when I checked their prostate. Told them I had guys lining up for a second opinion."

He laughed and felt the coiled spring in his chest unwind a turn or two. "Did anyone say anything about Chaz being there?"

"I was roundabout in asking, so as not to put them on guard. Told them I knew him through my residency, which is true, and that I wanted to say hello. To a man they said he was in New York, down with the flu."

"Did you believe them?"

"I think *they* believed it."

More Braden alibis, he thought, sinking back into the driver's seat. They passed the floodlit grounds of Nucleus Laboratories. The sodium lamps cast the swirling snow in a giant web of yellow light, at the center of which sprawled the darkened building.

He'd phone Victor Feldt in the morning, although he wasn't optimistic about finding any leads there. But the prospect of calling up the list of doctors Victor had provided him with seemed a tad more interesting now. They were an *A*-list, the kind of physicians, apparently, that Charles Braden referred his friends to.

*   *   *

Victor heard the car drive up.

He switched off his computer screen and peeked out the window.

Four men in bright ski outfits got out of a red sedan.

Lost tourists? He opened the front door before they came all the way up the walk. "Evening. Can I help you—"

That's when he saw the black stubby cylinders two of the men carried at their sides, muzzles pointed to the ground.

Chapter 15

Victor slammed the door shut, snapped the lock, and ran for the phone. He'd barely dialed nine when the line went dead. He raced for the rear of the house. In seconds he was through the kitchen and out the back entrance. A fifty-yard sprint through a half foot of snow and he'd be into the forest. Moonlight glinted off the snow, revealing the black line of trees. The shouts of the intruders indicated they were still at the front of the house.

"Unlock the door."

"We'll go easy on you."

"Liquor and money's all we want."

Yeah, sure.

The terrain sloped upward, and the leather soles of his shoes kept slipping. After a dozen paces he already gasped for air. He tried to accelerate, only to send his feet flying out from under him, catapulting to his hands and knees. The icy surface of the snow abraded his wrists. Sliding in every direction, he finally managed to get up and look over his shoulder, expecting to see that the four men had realized he made a break for it and were coming after him.

Not yet.

He started off again, still struggling to get some traction and gulping for air. By two dozen paces, he sobbed every time he exhaled, his chest burning as it heaved in and out. He continued on, choking, gasping, weak with fear, but halfway to cover. Once in the trees, he'd at least have a chance to dodge a bullet.

His feet slipped again. He pitched facefirst to the ground. Bits of slush filled his mouth, stuffed his nose, and dripped off his glasses. He spit and wiped his lenses so he could see. Panting fast and loud, he rose, then stumbled ahead. The shouts from behind grew louder.

"Stop!"

"We just want to talk with you."

"Come here."

He turned his head, straining to see where they were, but could only make out watery shadows.

He moved faster now, taking longer strides, the extra effort exacting its toll. Fatigue seared the front of his thighs until he could barely lift them. The incline steepened, doubling his workload.

He never once wondered why his pursuers were after him. Gay-bashers were a constant threat anywhere. Someone in town probably told these clowns about "the queer" living on Route 9, and this was some sick fuck's idea of how to end the hunting season. But how far would they take it? That was the life-or-death question. That they had guns didn't look good.

The shouts grew closer.

A tightness ripped through his chest.

"Oh, God, no," he whimpered.

By the time he reached the forest's edge he felt squeezed in a vise from the neck down and was staggering, his torso heaving, his heart hammering the inside of his ribs. He ducked behind the first tree he fell against and doubled over to get his breath, at the same time trying to make out the men.

A collective smudge jogged toward him through the gloom, at thirty yards and closing. He took extra big lungfuls of the cold, but couldn't relieve the smothering sensation. Waves of nausea lapped at the back of his throat, and cold sweat soaked his shirt.

Something zinged by his ear and embedded itself in the bark above his head with a loud *thwack*.

No question now, this pack was out for slaughter.

He pushed off from the trunk he'd been leaning against and lurched deeper into the woods.

Angry cries ordered him to halt.

Panic drove him. He repeatedly churned up muddy snow, getting nowhere; the clamp that had locked around his chest grew tighter. Yet he fought to move forward, crawling and pulling himself along, grasping at any root or bush to get a handhold.

"Give it up, asshole!" More bullets hit the snow around him.

He knew he was doomed, but his instinct to survive wouldn't let him yield. Even as they encircled him, stood over him, taunted and goaded him, he writhed to gain a few inches, to breathe a few more breaths.

"Hey, he don't look so good."

"Maybe he's having a heart attack."

The pain grew as if his heart were ballooning out of his chest, ready to burst, and the agony became unbearable. Yet he could still see their boots at his head, hear their voices.

"This is better than any accidental fire."

"He won't have a mark on him."

"I better go back and reconnect his phone line. The snow will cover the tracks. Nobody will even know we've been here, let alone look for bullets."

Why didn't they kill him? Have done with it. He found himself begging that they end it. But as he tried to speak, his lips, embedded in snow, barely moved, and he had to lick them free.

"Hey, he's trying to say something."

One of the men bent down, removing a ski mask and placing his ear near Victor's mouth. "Wants us to finish him off," he announced after listening to his whispers.

"Give him your cock to suck. That ought to do it," one of them added.

More cackling came from above as the kneeling man slowly got back on his feet. "I'll give you a gun barrel to suck on, you make another crack like that," he said, obviously not amused.

Victor hadn't the breath to cry or the strength to budge. Sinking into a delirium of pain and asphyxia, his mind still flickered with life, firing out fragments of thought, the last dispatches of a dying brain.

They weren't gay-bashers. Hadn't once called him a fag.

He'd spent a lifetime dealing with that kind of insane fury. These men were more callous and calculating.

So why were they here to kill him?

Because he'd discovered the secret?

But how could they know? He hadn't told anyone yet. Only left a message on Mark's answering machine, saying to call him, that he had the answer.

His mind downshifted again, losing the function of logic forever. Only memories swept through his neurons now, unlocked from one cell after another as they winked out.

* * *

The aroma of turkey greeted them when Mark opened the front door.

Lucy busied herself with the bird while he stoked the woodstove and opened a bottle of white wine he'd put in the refrigerator before they left.

"It'll be another twenty minutes," she announced, holding out a pair of beautifully tapered glasses she'd gotten out of the china cupboard.

He filled them, then raised his in a toast. "Here's to the first Thanksgiving dinner I've had at home in years," he said, determined not to let his state of mind ruin her efforts at providing a nice evening.

She smiled and curled up in the captain's chair at the head of the table. She seemed to like that spot. After a few sips of her drink, she said, "Was it your plan to stir up a hornet's nest tonight, or did those people really get under your skin?"

He didn't want to talk about it. "Bit of both, I guess. Mostly I'm frustrated at how Braden has outfinessed every official attempt to get at Chaz since 'seventy-four, mine included. And all that politeness as he pulls it off, I just couldn't take it—wanted to throw it back in his face. At least now I've made the smooth-talking son of a bitch take his fight with me out in the open."

"You did that all right."

Not to mention he'd also assured any attempt by that same son of a bitch to drag Cam Roper's name through the mud would now look like payback. "For what good it will get me," he muttered.

"What do you mean?"

"We're no further ahead in what we know."

She watched him across the top of her glass. "But there's more than that bugging you."

Dammit, didn't she realize he really didn't want to have this conversation. "Look, Lucy, like I said, the place revived a lot of personal issues for me. Let's just leave it at that, okay?" He'd sounded far testier than he intended. At least she'd get the point and back off.

To his surprise she laughed, reached across the table, and patted his hand. "Looks to me like it's you who can't just leave it at that, judging by the way the Braden bunch gets to you."

She managed to make them sound like a cross between a popular TV family and a gang of outlaws. It was his turn to laugh. "Sorry, I didn't mean to take your head off."

"Purely understandable." She took another sip of her wine. "My brothers say I'm like a tank when it comes to butting into their private business. Though I am a good listener, and you could do worse than talking to me about that kind of stuff. Believe me, I'm an expert on how the past can come out of nowhere and bite you on the bum."

She didn't offer to elaborate, and he didn't ask, welcoming the light mood she'd created. To his surprise she sustained it throughout the meal and the rest of the evening, engaging him in a relaxed easy exchange of anecdotes about medical school, residencies, and the slapstick side of life and death as it's sometime seen from inside a white coat.

They moved into his combination living-waiting room, and he lit a fire. For a while they sat quietly side by side on the floor, watching the flames. He felt comfortable with the silence. So comfortable, he decided, it was time to clear up at least one of the many unknowns that worried at him. "Lucy, what were you on the verge of telling me last night, before you left to buy a dress?"

He felt her stiffen. After a few seconds she said, "I haven't been entirely honest about why I took my elective here."

He didn't reply, wanting to hear more, but not about to extract it piecemeal.

"You see, I've got ghosts here, too, just as you do," she continued, "but I'm trying to find mine, not run from them. So what I'm about to say might be upsetting to you."

The same feeling he'd had two days ago while they were talking in her car, that she was about to cut very close to a vital organ, crept through him, and once more he grew still.

"Where I've worked the last seven years, all that sudden death, families ripped apart, and the life-and-death struggles so many thousands went through to reunite with their blood kin, it awakened a similar hunger in me. When I came back, Mom and Dad were great and gave me all the papers they had.

"I'd been adopted from an orphanage in Albany. But after I got my original birth certificate unsealed, the father was listed as unknown, and all attempts to locate the woman registered as my birth mother came to a dead end. The people I hired to find her told me she didn't exist, that a false name must have been used. They suggested I contact the place where I was born, that the birth records would be more extensive and might give an indication who my mother really was. That led me to Hampton Junction and Braden's home for unwed mothers. But all my attempts to get the original records from Braden Senior failed."

She paused and took a sip of wine, keeping her eyes on the flames. "First I went through legal channels. Apparently the records room burned just prior to the place shutting down. Then I went to Braden himself. He apologized, but said essentially the same thing. He even had affidavits attesting to the fire, as others had been looking for records before me. When I asked him to refer me to people who had worked in the place on the off chance they could help me, he said he'd have his secretaries try to find some of his old staff, but in the end told me they hadn't been able to locate anybody who'd worked there the year I was born. Now maybe I've been working around war criminals for too long, but when record rooms catch on fire, or nobody can find the people who worked in a place, that's when I begin to get a little suspicious."

Another pause, another sip.

Mark didn't budge.

"So I moved on to Plan B. Since I was going to do a residency in family medicine anyway, I chose the teaching hospital that offered rural electives up here, intending to find out what I could from the local residents."

He felt incredulous. He'd been dreading something sinister, yet here was an innocent story that he could hardly believe. "How could that help you?" he asked.

"One thing I did know. My records at Albany were in a red file. The other dossiers were mostly green. The administrator there said she thought the red folders designated a mother from the Hampton Junction area, the color signaling the need for special precautions regarding confidentiality so no one living nearby would learn who in town had been a patient . . ."

He immediately thought of Nell's friend. There couldn't be too many local women who went there. Not that she necessarily might be Lucy's mother, though that was a possibility. But she might know who else from the area had been in the place. What if Nell were to ask her—no, he mustn't let his imagination run wild. It was too great a long shot.

". . . Now don't get me wrong. I would have chosen you as my first pick for a rural rotation anyway. The residency program rates a stint with Mark Roper as their top elective, and being here with you and your patients—I adore it. But I also hoped working with you would give me a quick way into the community. I thought that maybe I could find something that would lead me to my biological mother. When I heard about the discovery of Kelly's body, and that you were investigating her murder, I changed my schedule, bumping my rotation ahead. I figured there'd be no surer way of finding out what I wanted than by getting myself into the middle of what would probably be a major gossipfest, everyone talking about the Bradens and that era, then take advantage of it by steering conversations toward the subject of the home. So here I am. I didn't tell you because I didn't think my own quest would make any difference to my doing a good job working with you. And I couldn't be sure you would accept me if I told you my story outright. I hoped after a week or so, once you were satisfied with my performance, I'd be able to confide the rest, and it wouldn't make a difference to you. And if in the process of trying to find my mother, I helped you dig up something on the Bradens that would help you, so much the better."

She fell silent and just kept staring at the fire.

His initial relief gave over to feeling a little uneasy at how calculating this all sounded. Strip it down, and she'd basically come here to use his patients and the investigation to pursue her personal agenda. But she was also a legitimate resident and damn good doctor who had provided first-rate care to the people he'd entrusted her with. So was there a problem here?

For one, he'd shown her evidence in a coroner's case. Should any of those files ever add up to charges against Chaz, the fact they'd been in the hands of someone who had her own issues with Chaz's father might give the Braden lawyers yet another conflict-of-interest gun to hold over his head. He couldn't believe she hadn't thought of that.

She turned her head and gave him a contrite smile as if she sensed his discomfort with what she'd done. "I would have told you all this by next week. Events just started to roll faster than I expected, and you got the jump on me. Our first day together, when you said how everyone would let me in on the seamier sides of Hampton Junction, I nearly 'fessed up then and there. I hope you can forgive me."

Forgive? His instincts leapt to point out the potential problems she'd caused, but in the firelight her dark eyes emitted a sad warmth that laid a calming hand on his concerns. "Of course," he said, deciding against saying anything for the moment. It was too late to do anything about what had happened anyway.

They remained where they were for a while, sipping wine, Lucy talking about the service industry that had sprung up for people trying to find a biological parent—everything from detectives to tracking programs on the Internet—and how none of it worked for her. To Mark it sounded as if she was still trying to justify her subterfuge. In any case, the openness between them from before dinner was gone.

Before going to bed, he took his messages.

". . . Dr. Roper, it's Victor. I think I've found what had companies using Nucleus Labs so jumpy. Also, I got to wondering about the group of New

York doctors and, being in a suspicious frame of mind, figured I ought to check if there were anything in the test results themselves to warrant someone wanting to store them separately. I hacked into the terminal we forward them to, and there's a peculiar little something there as well. Give me a call . . ."

Instantly he felt wide-awake. He was dialing the number when the next recording sounded.

". . . Mark, it's Earl. I'm in the hospital, admitted as a patient. We have to talk . . ."

Holy shit! he thought. There was no answer when he got through to Victor's. "Maybe he's out somewhere for Thanksgiving dinner," he said to Lucy, who had appeared at the door to his office. She must have overheard the messages.

He was already dialing the number for NYCH.

"I'm sorry, sir, but all calls to that number have been blocked. I can give you the nurse's desk."

"Are you a relative?" said the woman who picked up.

"No, I'm his colleague, Dr. Mark Roper. He and I are working on a coroner's case together. I must talk with him."

"Dr. Garnet has been sedated, sir, and Dr. Collins has left strict orders he not be disturbed."

"Then connect me with Dr. Collins's home."

"One moment."

"Mark!" Melanie greeted him. "I'm sorry, I guess I should have informed you about Earl's admission. Apologies."

"What happened?"

"Looks like he picked up a bug from our fair city's fine cuisine. I'll have preliminary cultures in the morning."

"But is he all right?"

"Sure. I mean, he's got a lot of discomfort, but vitals are fine, lytes et cetera check out okay, and believe me, he's well covered in the analgesia department."

Mark's heartbeat ticked up a notch. He hesitated to ask his next question, thinking it would sound crazy, but went ahead anyway. "Melanie, I know you're going to think I'm nuts for even suggesting this, but is there any way Earl could have been deliberately poisoned?"

"You mean by the likes of Chaz Braden?"

"My God. Earl told you?"

"Only about your suspicions over what happened to Bessie McDonald. As for him, his case seems bona fide. Certainly Earl didn't say anything to make me think differently. But don't worry. I'm hovering over him like a mother hen. Chaz Braden, or anyone else I haven't personally authorized, won't get near him."

That's a pretty big promise, Mark thought, knowing perfectly well how staff could come and go as they pleased on a busy ward, whatever Melanie might order. Nevertheless, he thanked her, asked that she phone him if there were any changes in Earl's condition, and hung up.

Quickly telling Lucy what had happened, he tried Victor's number again.

Still no answer. "I guess we'll have to wait until morning. He's obviously got a better social life than I thought."

"Let's hope he's getting laid," she said with a wicked grin, and walked over to where she'd left the boxes of birth records she'd been going through. "As for me, I'm going to work on these a while. You, mister, better go to bed. You look tired."

Mark felt a flash of alarm, his concerns about the integrity of evidence resurfacing. Then he thought, *What the hell.* She'd already been through them once. From his own look at them, they didn't seem to have a bearing on the case anyway. And somewhere in there should be her own birth record. Maybe she'd find something useful in that regard. Who was he to stand in the way of a woman's search for her mother?

As she spread out some of the papers on the kitchen table, he saw large sheets that looked like accounting ledgers with reams of handwritten numbers on them. "What are those?"

"A summary I'm making of all the statistics. I got pretty good at spotting trends on spreadsheets like these in the refugee camps. I thought I'd give it a go here."

Impressed by her diligence, he wished her good night, and went upstairs to bed.

But as he tried to fall asleep, his ugly confrontation with Braden crowded in, hanging over everything like a cold shroud. Damn the man to hell for suggesting such muck about his father.

He eventually drifted off.

Bad dreams ambushed him throughout the night. The one that brought him fully awake found him in the cold water where they'd found Kelly with her killer out in the blackness, circling him, drawing closer. He struggled to reach the surface, but his limbs moved in agonizing slow motion as he sank deeper, and the dark liquid congealed around him with the smothering slipperiness of blood.

**That same evening, Thursday,
November 22, 11:30 P.M.
New York City Hospital**

Earl's eyes shot open.

He lay motionless, peering through the darkness, wondering what had awakened him. He heard a soft click, the sound of his room door swinging shut.

Someone must have been in to check on him and just left.

Probably a nurse.

Mentally he felt wrapped in cotton from the morphine he'd gotten during the day, but for the moment he didn't have any pain. He definitely didn't want another shot, not the way it turned his brain into cream cheese.

When the first dose wore off, he'd managed to phone Janet and explain what had happened, trying to minimize his symptoms. "Don't worry, you know these things are usually over in twenty-four hours. I'm just sorry I can't have Thanksgiving dinner with you and Brendan."

"Dammit, Earl, be straight with me."

"I am, I swear—"

"You wouldn't let anyone drag you into a hospital bed unless you were half-dead. Now tell me what's going on—really."

"Everything's fine, Janet, just fine . . ." As he'd talked, it became all he could do to keep his voice from giving away the sheer agony in his stomach. He didn't want her jumping on a plane, bringing Brendan, and having them both fretting at his bedside. He finally convinced her to stay put.

"But if you're not telling me something, Earl Garnet, I'll doctor you myself, starting with the biggest colonoscopy tube I can find—"

"Of course I'm telling you everything."

"You lie like a pirate."

"Me?"

"When it comes to whether you're sick or in trouble, you do."

To Brendan he'd said, "Just a sick tummy, like you get sometimes."

"Drink Seven-Up," his son had advised.

He'd also tried to reach Mark, got his answering machine, and left the number.

Then he'd requested a nurse to contact Melanie. "Ask her to please change the order to Demerol or codeine—something that won't put me so out."

A matronly red-cheeked woman wearing granny glasses had cheerfully spiked another needleful of morphine into his IV line. "No such luck. Dr. Collins says you need your rest." She relaunched him to the other side of the universe.

The soft squeak of crepe soles approaching his bed snapped him into the present, and a white shape glided toward him in the darkness.

"Who's there?" he yelled, jackknifing upright.

"It's Tanya Wozcek, Dr. Garnet. Quiet down. I shouldn't even be here."

"Tanya?"

She snapped on his bedside lamp. The light caught the bristles of her short hair and turned it into a silvery brown aura. "I heard you were admitted. All the women on my floor are talking about what a weird coincidence it is, you getting sick after asking all those questions about Bessie. I had to make sure you were all right, so I slipped away."

"I'm okay," he said through gritted teeth.

"Chaz Braden hasn't been near you, has he? I mean, is there any way he could have made you ill?"

Whatever he suspected Braden of doing, the last thing he needed right now was an outlandish rumor casting himself as the man's latest victim. Should he or Mark ever find enough evidence to lay charges against Chaz, he could just imagine what a defense lawyer would say. "So Chaz Braden, in addition to murdering Dr. Kelly McShane, making Dr. Bessie McDonald slip into a coma, and firing a shot at Dr. Mark Roper, also managed somehow to poison Dr. Earl Garnet, even though no one can tell us when or how. Is there an MD in Manhattan he hasn't attacked?"

"No, I haven't even seen him since last Saturday. And though I appreciate your concern, I insist you don't go spreading—"

"That doesn't mean he won't take advantage of your being here."

"Tanya, don't get carried away—"

"Dr. Garnet, for God's sake, he got to Bessie. He could get to you the same way, or have someone sabotage you for him."

That gave him pause. Still, such talk had to stop. "No way," he said, even as he began to wonder about whom Braden might have hired to poison him. "There hasn't been anyone near me, and if we go around making unsubstantiated allegations, no one will ever believe us once we do get evidence—"

"Dr. Collins has got you on morphine, for Christ's sake. A squad of Marines could march in here, and there'd be times you wouldn't know." As she leaned in to speak with him, the illumination from the lamp caught her face from the side, exaggerating the shadows around her mouth and eyes. "So tell me, how do you feel?"

"Crappy." He grinned at his choice of word.

Her worried expression continued to hover over him like an over-wrought half-moon. "But are your symptoms what they should be, or has he done something else to you?"

Let's see, he thought. *Excruciating pain, nausea, a bellyful of writhing snakes, and soon to come, promising more delights. Maybe vomiting, most certainly the runs. Yeah, Tanya, that seemed exactly right. What a relief. I've only got one thing wrong with me, with or without any help from Chaz Braden.* Clenching his jaw even tighter against a new volley of cramps, he muttered, "Of course they are." *Now go away, so I can twist and squirm in peace.*

"What's in here?" She turned to read the label of his IV bag.

"Normal saline, with extra potassium, exactly as it should be."

"And who prepared it?"

"Dr. Collins herself. She did it to save the nurses—Oh, God." All at once he felt scalded inside, as if something were shredding the walls of his intestines.

"What is it?"

"Just please leave. I've got to call the nurse."

"For more morphine?"

"Whatever."

"Why not Demerol—"

At the moment he didn't care. "I'll ask for it. Now, please get out of here."

"Who gives you your shots? Always the same person?"

"Yes! She looks like Santa Claus in drag. Now dammit, Tanya, I'm ringing my buzzer." He flayed at it with one hand, cradling his stomach with the other.

"Okay," she said, pressing it for him, then heading to the door, "but I'm keeping an eye on you."

He let out a long moan, and twisted himself into a pretzel.

Two hours later he fell and cut his head making a rush for the toilet as the remainder of his symptoms, long expected, kicked in.

That put an end to the morphine.

It also earned him a tube down his stomach.

His life became sandwiched between basins at one end, bedpans at the other, and the unremitting agony of a gut on fire in between.

They started giving him Demerol, but it barely muted the pain. A second dose didn't work much better, other than to make him sleepy. He knew not to request a third. It'd have the same effect as morphine as far as suppressing his gag reflex, and he'd be choking on vomit.

"How about we ask Dr. Collins about a tube in your trachea to protect your airway? Then we could knock you right out," the nurse with red cheeks suggested.

He declined. Then he thought, "Wait a minute. Weren't you on the day shift?" he asked, fearing he'd let himself get disoriented.

"Dr. Collins asked that I switch to nights, just so you got the best of care."

Oh, great!

By dawn he felt like an empty husk. "I'm dehydrating," he told Santa, trying to prop himself up on one elbow. He flopped back, unable to bear the weight. "The IVs aren't keeping up with the fluid I've lost. And better check my potassium. My muscles are so weak I can hardly move."

"This isn't a service station, Dr. Garnet." Her icy tone sounded as cold as the North Pole and just as hostile, making it clear he wouldn't be breaching the divide between patient and staff on her watch. But she sped up the IV.

By the end of her shift he could barely hold an emesis basin.

"And how are we today?" Melanie asked, disgustingly chipper as she swept in at 7:00 A.M. on the wings of a crisp lab coat, obviously giving him the honor of being her first case for morning rounds. A semicircle of sleepy residents sporting more wrinkled wear shuffled in after her and formed a small white amphitheater at the foot of his bed.

"As you recall," she began, addressing her entourage without giving him a chance to answer, "Dr. Garnet came into ER over twenty-four hours ago with symptoms of bacterial enteritis characterized by inordinate pain, yet a relatively delayed onset of diarrhea. With this subtle discrepancy, I suspected this might be *E. coli 0157:H7*, rather than the more typical organisms we might expect. Of course I withheld antibiotics pending cultures. As I passed through bacteriology this morning, I picked up the preliminary results. All sorts of normal *E. coli* are being grown as would be the norm, but no salmonella, no shigella, and no *Campylobacter*. That means, I think it's reasonable to assume that hidden amongst these noninfectious *E. coli*, we'll find the infectious strain, or a serotype close to it, that I initially suspected. Of course we'll have to wait a full forty-eight hours . . ."

As Melanie went on and on, Earl felt like a specimen laid out in front of her and began to resent the gleeful way she talked about her probable diagnostic coup, oblivious to the agony he was in. It's not all about you, Melanie, he wanted to yell at her, figuring she must have used the word *I* over two dozen times. He remembered when no one, including her, thought she'd make it through medical school. Well, she might have gotten smarter, but her bedside manner remained the pits.

He curled up on his side again, as red-hot spasms did laps from one end of his gut to the other.

She finished her spiel, told him she'd be back, and was out the door with her posse before he could stop her.

But she had to increase his IVs. Check his potassium. Listen to him lie about not being Kelly's lover. "Melanie!"

No reply.

Son of a bitch!

Minutes later she whisked back into the room, all smiles and shaking a new IV bag with a big sticker on it indicating she'd added a twenty milliequivalents dose of potassium. In seconds she'd replaced the old with the new and had it running into him at a good clip. Turning to his other arm, she produced a rubber tourniquet from her pocket and tied it snugly around his biceps, then gave his veins a swipe with a cold alcohol swab. They bulged, glistening blue, and he shivered, thinking of the toxins coursing through them.

"You always draw bloods and start IVs on your own patients?" he said, trying to make small talk in the face of knowing too damn well the assault that his intestines, kidneys, pancreas, and brain were under. Even if he didn't die, he could still end up with seizures or diabetes or be on dialysis.

"Yeah, I'm known for it," Melanie said, taking yet another tube of his blood. "What the hell, nurses being busy as they are. Treat 'em right by giving them one less thing to do, and they're on your side for life, right, Earl?"

He tried to grin at her in agreement, but it felt more like a grimace. Flippant banter between physicians was how they normally coped with the life-and-death tensions that went with the job—a kind of whistling past the graveyard. But when that grave might be his, the schtick grew a little thin.

She leaned closer. "And in your case, given your suspicions about the cause of Bessie McDonald's coma, I think it best I handle as many procedures on you as is humanly possible. I mean, after our drink the other night, I started to think. Do you know how many ways a doctor could secretly do away with a hospitalized patient, yet never get caught? It's unreal."

With that, she bade him good-bye, and left.

Thanks for the comforting words, Melanie, he wanted to call after her. Instead, he simply lay there, trying to put what she'd said out of mind. Only to end up thinking instead about the surface of his gut shredding itself raw as the *E. coli* bacteria deepened their hold and even more toxins flooded into his bloodstream. He tried to prepare mentally for the hemorrhages that were bound to follow. What lay ahead wasn't hard to imagine. He'd seen too many patients lying in their crimson waste to have any illusions about it. He started to regret having lied to Janet about the seriousness of it all. He wanted to see her, to see Brendan. Especially if—No, he mustn't think that way. Wouldn't, dammit. But another round of pain skewered him so hard he couldn't help but think the worst.

That same morning, Friday,
November 23, 8:05 A.M.
Hampton Junction

Mark navigated the red Jeep by following the loom of the road under a foot of fresh snow.

"Still not answering," Lucy said, snapping her cellular shut.

They'd been trying to raise Victor since seven.

The coffee he'd gulped down before leaving the house seemed to repercolate itself at the back of his throat. Let him be getting wood. Or be gone for a walk. Maybe off on a drive.

But the Victor he knew would not only have been by the phone, eagerly awaiting Mark's call, ready to divulge whatever he'd discovered, but also would have called Mark by now, perhaps a dozen times over.

Ice coated everything, and the frozen world seemed metal hard, cast in silver, gray, and black. Even the shiny surface of the snow had a jagged-ness to it.

Mark's grip tightened on the wheel.

Victor's car stood in the driveway.

A Tiffany lamp glowed warmly behind the front window.

No smoke rose from the chimney.

They walked up the unshoveled steps and knocked on the front door.

No sounds came from inside.

Mark reached for the handle, turned, and shoved the door open.

It revealed a long, dim, central hallway leading toward the back of the house.

Empty.

"Victor?" he called.

No answer.

"It's Mark Roper and Lucy."

Still no reply.

Mark stepped inside, making his way between the antique tables and shelves loaded with porcelain figures that lined the walls. The place seemed cold. "Stay here," he said, continuing down the corridor. A peek through the door on his right revealed a magnificent mahogany dining room table and china cupboard, but no Victor. The door on the left opened into a small living room dominated by a baby grand but otherwise empty.

He followed the hallway toward the back, coming to a swinging door at the end that he presumed led to the kitchen. "Victor?" he repeated, the floorboards creaking under his boots. The air here felt cooler still.

He pushed his way through.

The back door was open. Halfway across the threshold lay Victor, face-down, his legs covered with drifted snow. A half dozen logs lay scattered on the floor in front of him.

Mark swallowed once, walked in, and knelt by his head. The skin was ice-cold. He felt for a carotid pulse, knowing he wouldn't find any.

Whenever Mark found himself alone with a dead body, the absolute si-lence of the corpse unnerved him the most. No soft sounds of air moving in and out of the lungs, no brush of clothing against the skin with each in-halation or expiration, no tiny *cricks* that tendons sometimes make when a person moves, not even a gurgle from the stomach. He instinctively slowed his own breathing, so as not to disturb that stillness, and the world around him seemed to go quiet as well. It was as if all that dead flesh, like a black hole, sucked the sounds of life from the room.

What had happened appeared obvious. An overweight, hypertensive, diabetic man had gone out to get wood in the snow, and the exertion had brought on a heart attack. Except he must have initially fallen outside, Mark thought, noticing recent scratches on Victor's wrists. They were identical to the ones he himself had received the other night while running from his pursuer, his wrists plunging through the icy crust of the snow each time he slipped.

Maybe that outside fall had been a simple slip, or due to the initial symptoms of what killed him, and he'd been able to pick up the logs and continue to the back porch.

He looked around at the once-cozy room where Victor had prepared meals, mostly to dine alone. Brightly embroidered wall hangings offered homespun encouragement for the future, confidently predicting: MY PRINCE WILL COME; A KITCHEN IS THE HEARTH OF A FAMILY'S HOME; A COUPLE'S LOVE IS A FEAST FOR LIFE. Beside these were photos of a young man whom Victor had told him about. His first name was Brad, and he had died the year before Victor moved here. They'd been lovers for over a decade. Victor thought a period of time in the country would make it easier to get over his grief and move on. It never happened.

Mark snapped open his phone to call Dan. Only when he saw the blurry numbers did he realize his eyes were full of tears. He stayed kneeling, wiping them clear, whipsawed between sad and angry, not really understanding why. After all, he'd seen patients die before, even people who had called him friend.

He heard the floorboards creaking. "Did you find him?" Lucy asked from out in the corridor.

He tried to warn her back, but she stepped through the door.

"Oh, no!" Her hands flew to her mouth as she sank to her knees by his head. "The dear, dear man." She reached out and ran her fingers along the side of Victor's face, brushing the tip of his magnificent mustache.

Mark quickly turned away. Victor would never feel her simple gesture, just as in his last years he'd so rarely felt the caress of someone who loved him.

"Let's wait in the car," he said to Lucy. "I'm going to call Dan and treat this place as a crime scene, so don't touch anything on the way out."

"A crime scene?"

Mark nodded. If there was anything to Victor's last message, his death had been damn convenient to someone.

*   *   *

"No forced entry, nothing broken, no suggestive marks on the body. Suspicious as hell, right?" Dan asked when Mark told him to treat the death as a possible homicide.

"I know it sounds crazy, Dan, but humor me. Too many timely illnesses have happened on this case." Mark filled him in on what Victor had been up to and how Earl had to be admitted to NYCH.

As Dan listened, his scowl deepened, but in the end, he pulled out the yellow tape. "You realize I'm on thin ice here," he muttered, cordoning off the driveway.

Within half an hour men and women in dark blue jumpsuits, SARATOGA SPRINGS P.D. written on the back, were crawling all over the house using Ziploc evidence bags and tweezers to collect every stray hair, thread, or broken nail they could find. A pretty blond woman, her regulation peaked cap worn backward, hunched over Victor's computer and carefully covered the keys with a fine white powder. "Look at this, Chief," she said, summoning Dan to her side. "Most of his prints have been partially smudged out."

"Wiped?" Mark asked, leaning in to see.

Dan shook his head. "More like someone's used it while wearing gloves."

"Can I try and turn it on?"

The woman stood aside. "I'm all finished. Be my guest."

Mark pushed the ON button, and the screen flickered to life. Against a background of tropical fish, it requested an access code. "Have you got someone who can hack into these things?"

Dan chuckled. "Yeah. They're called kids."

"Seriously."

"There's a white-collar crime unit in Albany. They've done a few favors for me from time to time."

"Anything quicker?"

"We've got some floppies and CD-ROMs back at headquarters programmed to search for passwords," the woman said as she packed away her supplies. "I could give them a try. But we'd need a warrant."

The prospect of learning what Victor had found out, like scent to a hound, unleashed a rush of adrenaline in Mark. "Great. I'll come with you—"

Victor's phone beside the computer started to ring. They all looked at each other. Mark took the initiative, and picked up the receiver. "Victor Feldt's residence."

"Victor?" It was a woman's voice. She sounded young, but he couldn't be sure.

"Who's speaking, please?"

"I need to speak with Victor."

"I'm Dr. Mark Roper. Can I know who's speaking?"

"Dr. Roper? Is Victor all right?" She sounded alarmed.

"Can I know who's speaking, please?"

"Oh, God, what's happened?"

"Are you family—"

He was cut off by a dial tone.

He tried *69 to get the caller's number.

It had been blocked.

"Don't get too excited about our CD program helping you," the technician said on her way out the door. "Whoever was at the keyboard after Victor might have gotten in and already trashed everything, or worse, substituted new data for old, which means the original is really gone."

3:40 P.M.
Hampton Junction

A low gray sky had slid over the valley, as oppressive as a slab of cement.

"Earl, it's Mark. How are you feeling?" He'd asked Lucy to drive so he could use the phone.

"Mark? Frankly, I don't feel too good."

He sounded groggy as hell. "I'm not surprised. Melanie told me what happened to you. Are you able to talk? It's urgent."

"Talk's about all I can do."

"You're sure you're able? I could call back."

"Now you've got me dying of curiosity. Shoot!"

Mark briefly explained who Victor was and everything that had happened to him.

"You think he was killed because of what he discovered?" Earl asked at the finish. His voice had become hard-edged, with none of its previous languor.

"If so, it was very cleverly staged. Even the lividity matched how we found him." The purplish discoloration where venous blood pooled, then clotted in the lowest points of the body during the first hours after death was an indelible record of the person's position when he died. A pattern that didn't conform to how the body lay would indicate someone had subsequently moved or repositioned the corpse. "I've arranged to do an autopsy on him tomorrow morning at Saratoga General, so I'll be able to pick up obvious signs of foul play. And I'm going to screen his blood for every drug I can think of that could precipitate an MI. The lab people are going to scream, but I'm on my way there now to make sure I'll have everything I'll need. But there may be no signs or drugs to find."

"And you've no idea what he turned up?"

"Nope."

Earl exhaled into the phone. "How can your man and whatever he found have anything to do with Kelly's murder?"

"I've no idea yet. We're going to try and get into his computer."

Silence reigned on the line.

"Earl?"

"I'm here. Just thinking, to see if I can put any of this together."

"What you ought to be thinking about, with opportune comas and heart attacks going around, is if someone made you sick as well."

More silence.

Finally, Earl said, "To be honest, I've started to wonder the same thing. My end of the investigation has sure as hell been sidelined, if that's the motive."

"I'm afraid it might not end at that."

Again more silence.

"Anyone try to get near you who shouldn't?"

"You mean like Braden? No."

"Earl, get somebody you can trust to stay in your room. Can Janet join you?"

"I'm not putting her in danger."

"Then hire a guard. Jesus, man, if we're right, you're a sitting duck."

"I'll take care of it."

"You're sure? Why don't I make the arrangements?"

"I said I'll take care of it. Got to hang up now. Goddamn nature calling!"

The line went dead.

"How is he?" Lucy asked.

"Not so good."

"Hiring a guard, now that's a good idea. Do you think he'll do it?"

"I don't know. But if he hasn't by later tonight, I will."

The Braden mansion came into view, all its parts coated in gleaming white, again reminding him of a bird, but iced over this time, trapped in midflight. And the limousines were gone. The lack of tracks in the drive meant they'd left during the night.

"Hunting season over?" Lucy said.

She drove in silence after that, her lips drawn in a tight line. As he watched her profile in the thin winter light, her skin seemed pale, translucent even. The tiny furrows at the corners of her eyes narrowed. "Mark, may I give you some advice?"

He smiled. Whenever a woman asked if she could give him advice, he inevitably got it, wanted or not.

"*You* better take care," she continued, without waiting for his permission.

"In what sense?"

"You don't get it, do you?"

"How do you mean?"

"If you're right about Bessie, Victor, and Dr. Garnet, you could be next."

3:45 P.M.
New York City Hospital

Mark's phone call and the news about Victor Feldt galvanized Earl, made him realize the extent this business might be a killing game. It sent his mind racing through possible scenarios—when he wasn't writhing in pain.

If he'd been deliberately poisoned, and the bug was indeed *E. coli 0157:H7*, then the normal incubation before the onset of symptoms was three to nine days, but sometimes as short as two. It could have been slipped into his food or drink anytime since he arrived in New York last Saturday up to Tuesday evening.

The reception? Unlikely, since no one else was sick—unless someone hired a rogue waiter to do the job. The same went for the hotel. But why increase the chances of getting caught by bringing in an outsider who might later blab everything to the police? The smart thing would be to act alone.

So when?

In the bustle of the hospital cafeteria? Someone could have been close to him in line, slipped something into his food or drink. But that raised other questions. How would the person have transferred the organism to his food? The easiest way to transport it would have been in water. But he would have noticed if someone had soaked his plate—unless it was added to an already full cup or glass. Or was in such a small quantity he wouldn't have detected it. Still, the pouring move would be tricky, since the person would likely have used a sort of container and acted when nobody was looking. With a lot of people around, somebody else might easily see. No that wasn't it—

"Dr. Garnet?" Tanya Wozcek poked her head in the door, greeting him with a big smile. "How are you feeling?"

The pain only lapped at his innards for the moment, temporarily spent. "Okay, I guess." As she approached his bedside, he tensed.

She eyed his IV bags and checked the rate of flow. "Everything still what you'd expect?"

"Pretty much. Except I'm more goddamned weak than ever."

She frowned. "I peeked at your test results. Potassium, lytes, and hematocrit—they all seem fine."

"Well, I sure don't."

She studied him, her overly intense gaze flicking to the IV bottle and back to him again. The movement made him uneasy, and a chill swept through him. What did he know about her, anyway? He'd taken her word about her devotion to Bessie McDonald. What if the opposite were true? As Bessie's nurse, she'd have had an easy time secretly injecting her with anything, including a dose of short-acting insulin. And what better way to mislead him, loudly voicing her suspicions and concern? No, it didn't make sense. She wouldn't have had to voice anything to cover up what happened to Bessie. Yet Tanya had raised his own doubts about the coma. If she just kept quiet, most likely he would have dismissed it as an unfortunate but plausible outcome for a woman with a history of strokes, exactly the way everyone else had. Then again, that could all have been a clever way of winning his trust, so she could get close to him.

"Results can be wrong," she said, her somber expression still disquieting. She reached for the tray of blood-taking equipment that Melanie had left by his bedside. "Let me check them again. I'll submit the sample under my name, in case someone's been tampering with your readings."

She was as paranoid as he needed to be.

Still not entirely certain he trusted her, he gingerly held out his arm.

Because he'd seized on a strategy that could bring everything to a head. Let whoever it was make a move. Odds were his would-be assassin had some mortal complication from his toxic *E. coli* infection planned for him. That meant sooner or later they'd come face-to-face. So get the showdown over with. The trick? To be ready.

Suspect everyone.

Stay alert.

And keep tucked into his bedclothes a handful of syringes. They had three-inch needles that he'd already stolen off the tray of blood-taking equipment. Weak as he was, he could drive them into an eye of the attacker.

Even Tanya's.

She slid the gleaming tip of her needle into his vein, and he poised himself to spring at the first sign of her doing anything bizarre.

But the woman expertly finished the task, pressed a piece of cotton to the puncture site so it wouldn't bleed, and smiled. Then she rushed toward the door. "I'm taking this to the lab myself," she said. "I'll be back at eleven, when my shift ends."

Earl loosened his grip on the makeshift weapon but remained tense. He couldn't stay awake forever; eventually he'd have to hire a security guard. Even then he'd only be delaying an adversary who had already gotten to him once without his knowing. It would also tip him or her off that he, Earl Garnet, was onto the fact he was a target. Unless Janet hired the people in the guise of a twenty-four-hour nursing service. Still, better to chance luring the killer in now, while this creep still believed Earl to be unprotected as well as unaware. Having already refused any more Demerol, he counted on pain to keep him from falling asleep, at least until morning. If by then nothing had happened, he'd ask Janet to bring on the watchdogs.

As he lay waiting, the afternoon light waned, and a thickening sludge of dirty brown smog nuzzled the window.

Chapter 16

Mark's attempts to reach the doctors on Victor's list had proved futile. All were gone for the day, and he'd ended up talking to machines or leaving messages with tired-sounding operators at their answering services.

The last thing he felt like doing was eating dinner at Nell's.

On the other hand, Lucy was adamant they go. "If the woman knows anything about these places," she said, folding up her spreadsheets of statistics and sticking them in her purse, "I want to talk with her."

"She's not going to look at a bunch of numbers."

"They're for me to use, like notes, to guide me in what questions to ask."

"Such as?"

"I won't know until she talks to me." She slipped the strap of her purse over her shoulder and walked out the front door.

Mark followed her to the Jeep, once more with the uneasy feeling that she was leaving something out. He took a breath of the crisp air, trying to clear his head. Dealing with Victor all day had occupied his thoughts, but now they roamed freely through all the other unknowns that were piling up, as foreboding as thunderheads. He couldn't shake his fear about Earl being in danger, so much so that he'd tried to phone Melanie again, figuring she could ensure a security guard would be at his door. But he'd only reached her answering service. Pulling out of the driveway, he started to call Nell on his cellular, then hesitated, his finger suspended over the number pad.

One way someone could have known that Victor had found something suspicious at Nucleus Laboratories might be a phone tap. Mark recalled that on the night of the break-in, he'd found the clock on his phone stand slightly out of position. Someone could have been trying to place a tap on the line. And how would the person who shot at him know when he'd be driving on the road from Nell's? Maybe those damn *clicks* weren't the usual problem with his line.

He'd check when he got home. And forget using the cellular. Anybody determined to listen in on him could buy scanners for them. Shit! Had Nell been overheard saying she had new information about Kelly's death?

Jesus, he thought, and gunned the car, heading for the nearest pay phone on the edge of town.

"What's up?" asked Lucy.

"I just realized our phone conversations may no longer be private." He explained why in the minutes it took to reach the booth.

To his relief, Nell picked up. "Nell, listen—"

"I know. You're going to be late," she said without letting him speak.

"We'll be there in twenty minutes. But maybe we should rethink this."

"What do you mean?"

"We're going to go somewhere else for dinner."

"Are you crazy?"

"We'll pick you up—"

"Just come on over. I can use the extra time to have a bath." And she hung up.

He tried dialing her back.

Off the hook.

Not this nonsense again.

"Oh, God," said Lucy when he told her.

As he drove, he figured out how to convince her she needed protection. Hell, maybe she'd even get off on the idea. And he'd call Dan. She might listen to him. But listen she would, because damned if he was going to put anyone else in danger. The entire day he'd agonized over the possibility that he'd gotten Victor killed by encouraging him to play computer detective. He remembered his singing at the piano only two nights ago, and the thought of performing an autopsy on him in the morning became unbearable.

Lucy rode staring out the window.

The quiet between them grew suffocating.

"You know, we could both go deaf in this kind of silence," he said.

She gave a small, solitary chuckle. "Sorry. I was just thinking how sometimes in the camps, when I felt most overwhelmed and helpless, I'd take care of some small, personal matter, just to get the world back into perspective."

"Such as?" He welcomed the chance to discuss anything that might get him out of his own head.

"Writing letters home worked best, saying things I hadn't had the chance to say to the people I loved most. Once I did that with each of my brothers, Mom, and Dad, I usually felt better. At least, it seemed less daunting to face the big problems in front of me."

"What would you write about?"

"Usually I'd pick something I really liked about the person I wrote to and let them know. And if there were any unresolved quarrels, I'd try to patch them up. That way if something happened to me, I wouldn't have left precious words unsaid."

"Sounds like a nice kind of letter to get."

She grew quiet again, her gaze fixed on the dark blur of forest at the road's edge. "Would you like me to write one to you?" she asked after a few seconds.

He grew very still. "Yes, I'd like that."

"Because that's what I've been doing, Mark. Sitting here composing a letter to you."

"Really?" He drove the next mile without saying anything. "What's in it?" he finally asked.

"Most I think you already know. How great a doctor I think you are. How much I adore working with your patients and being up here. And how worried I am that I've permanently ruined your opinion of me by coming to you under false pretenses."

She was right. He did know all that. And her failure to be up front with him had stoked his suspicions of her. Once fooled, it was easy to wonder what else she might keep from him. And he still felt a woman as smart as she should have known better, especially about letting her personal issues place evidence at risk.

He was about to tell her so, then suggest they put it behind them and make the best of her time here, when she added, "I don't know if I can ever win your trust back. I'd like to try, but I won't stay if my being around makes you feel I compromised you, your practice, or your investigation. Just give the word, and I'll leave in the morning."

That surprised him. Her words sounded as if she'd been reading from a carefully written note, with the ring of an ultimatum. But he also knew something else. When this case ended, he'd have to come to grips with the fact his ineptness might have cost a man his life. Measured against that, whatever technical dings his reputation as coroner took in the process would no longer matter. Yet going back to his old existence, living alone in the house where he'd been born and practicing medicine in isolation, would be even lonelier than before, entirely because of her having been here. He realized this without having to think about it or put it into words. It came to him the way an animal senses its terrain is no longer hospitable, through a combination of instinct and intuition that reads a warning to move on and find more fertile ground, yet she'd catalyzed the process. All at once he felt cautious about how to handle the next few minutes with this strange, forceful, and disquieting woman who had entered his life.

"Basically I still think you need me around here, and more than just professionally," she continued "You're one lonely bugger."

He gripped the steering wheel tighter. "Any other revelations you'd care to reveal?"

"Yes."

"Oh?"

She held her head a notch higher. The light from an oncoming car caught the fine lines of her nose and jaw, making him think she looked absolutely regal.

He held his breath, and waited for it.

"I don't have a fiancé."

He reacted with a mix of relief, pleasant surprise, and a self-congratulatory he'd-known-something-was-fishy-about-her-engagement-all-along celebration. Where there had been doubt and suspicion seconds before, there was the glimmer of a new possibility here. It had nothing to do with the grim business that seemed to be closing in on them, but a sea change occurred inside his head. As he sometimes did in a tense moment, he laughed. "Why the pretends?"

By the light of the dashboard he could see her face. She pursed her lips, but the corners played at breaking into a smile. "I heard you were a real womanizer and figured it was the best way to avoid trouble."

"Womanizer? Who told you that?"

"The other residents who'd done a rotation with you. All your patients gabbed to them about the string of women you get up here, and how none of them stay. Let's see, there was a theater director, a physiotherapist, and a veterinarian—"

"Jesus Christ."

"Having met you, I personally think they must have been nuts."

"Well, thank you for that at least. Residents should know better than to believe country gossip—"

"Oh, I don't mean them. I'm talking about your lady friends, for not wanting to stay, silly."

He still hadn't come up with a reply to that when his cell phone rang. "Hello?"

"Dr. Roper, you don't know me," a woman's voice said. "I got your number from the book. You answered the phone when I called Victor's house this morning."

"Oh, yes. I recall your voice." He heard her suck in her breath, but she said nothing. "May I know who I'm talking to?"

He listened to her breathing a few seconds. Finally, she said, " I have some documents that belong to Victor. I didn't know what had happened when I tried to reach him. I feel terrible, first the firing, and now . . ."

He slowed, and pulled over to the side of the road. "Let me call you back—"

"No! I don't want anyone to know who I am."

He didn't want to lose her again.

"Then let me give you another number where to reach me." He'd take the call at Nell's. She and Lucy could wait in the Jeep. "In about ten minutes?"

"No. I'm freezing my buns off as it is in a pay phone."

Oh, God. He'd have to risk being overheard. As long as she didn't say her name, at least she'd be safe. "What documents?" He motioned Lucy to slide over and listen with him. She responded immediately, a puzzled expression on her face.

"You mustn't tell anyone about this. We've had orders not to talk with you about him."

"We?"

"The people who worked with Victor at Nucleus Labs."

Her breathing sounded in his ear a few seconds. He could even hear her shivering. She must have her lips pressed to the mouthpiece.

"What do you want to do?" he asked. "We could meet."

"No."

"I could pick these documents up."

More breathing.

"Tell me what you have then." He felt cold just listening to her.

"Maybe I better explain how I got them in the first place. I don't want to get in trouble with the police."

He opened his mouth to stop her, but she pressed ahead.

"Victor programs his PC at home to forward whatever files he's working on to both his and my computer at our offices whenever he shuts down—" She stopped and let out a breath that stuttered into a sobbing sound. After a few seconds, she said, "I mean he used to. I still can't believe he's dead."

She may already be saying too much. "Listen, you should call me on a regular phone before saying anything more. I'm on a cell phone," Mark warned her, all the while worried he might lose her for good.

He thought he heard her swallow. "No, I can hear you okay, and I want to get this over with. He'd set the system up that way so we'd always be sure to have his files the next morning in case he forgot to forward them manually. For a bright man, he sometimes had a mind like a sieve . . ."

She didn't understand. But if he spelled it out that someone might be listening in . . . Christ it was too late anyway.

"He obviously didn't delete that function, because a folder dated yesterday was on top of my e-mail when I got to work. The first pages were nothing special, results of genetic screenings we'd done on various groups of siblings, mainly for different sorts of cancer genes. You've probably seen the type of reports I'm talking about in your own practice."

He had. They were a bunch of spikes along a horizontal line, each peak representing the amount of a particular sequence of DNA, the building blocks of the gene under investigation, including a peak or peaks for the mutated section, if it's present. These defective portions stood out like sore thumbs when compared to a similar preparation of a normal strand, even to the untrained eye. "Victor left me a message saying he'd retrieved some test results that he'd found peculiar. Could they be the ones?"

"Peculiar? Not that I could tell. The only thing odd about them was that they'd been flagged for some reason, yet there were no obvious abnormal spikes. I wouldn't know how to read the finer details well enough to have spotted anything else. Victor could have, though. He had the knack, and the training. In fact I initially thought they were copies he'd been using to practice his interpretation skills on and had simply returned them. It was the next few pages that got me concerned. As soon as I read them, I knew *they* were nothing anyone at Nucleus Labs had been meant to see. When I phoned his house, it was to ask him what he wanted me to do with the file. But you answered. By midmorning word got around that he'd died, probably from a heart attack, and I was devastated. But when we found out the police were all over his house, I got frightened. After all, I know you don't bring out the yellow tape for simple coronaries, and after seeing what he'd been doing on the computer, well, my imagination went into overdrive."

"Just tell me what you have." He could barely keep his voice steady.

Still more breathing. Then she asked, "Do you know how screening for executive health plans work?"

"Sure. I've done my share."

"He's managed to get records from some of our biggest clients documenting when executives' policies were newly issued or terminated," she continued. "This basically reflects who's been hired and who's been fired. I can only guess someone at these companies sent them to him on the QT after he'd twisted their arms. He had that kind of good rapport with the people he dealt with. Word got around like wildfire on the Internet when they learned . . ."

He thought he heard her sob again.

"Sorry," she said. "All those e-mails of condolences, yet outside of office hours he seemed so alone."

Waiting for her to compose herself, he wondered if she knew the half of it.

She sucked in a deep breath. "Dr. Roper, before telling you what he found, I have to know. Did someone kill Victor because of this?"

Mark's official line that he couldn't give out confidential information sprung to his lips, but he didn't speak it, knowing he might spook an already frightened woman. Instead he told her the truth. "I don't know."

"Oh, God! So it's possible."

"Listen. We can get you protection. I'll take you to the police myself, right now if you want. And we mustn't say anything more—"

He was listening to a dial tone again.

As he slowly lowered the phone, he sat staring straight ahead, trying to think what he should do. His gaze swept north, pulled by a glowing orange smudge that pulsed and waned above the trees against the nighttime skyline. It took him a second to realize it must be coming from a huge fire, and a heartbeat more to think it could be near Nell's cabin.

*   *   *

A wall of flames rose above the back half of the structure; smoke engulfed the front.

She lay in the snow before the door where she'd crawled, naked, the skin on her head and the left side of her torso covered in carbon. But within the blackened face, white eyes glittered, alive, the nightmare from his childhood.

He thought her wrist had a weak pulse. As he reached into the flesh of her neck to palpate her carotid to be sure, that same cloying smell that could send his heart pounding came off her in waves and filled him with terror. Swallowing to keep from gagging, he felt the artery fluttering beneath his fingertips. In the headlights of the Jeep he could see the burns weren't that deep. The black was mainly soot.

Her darkened lips parted, revealing a slash of creamy teeth, and she screamed.

"Help me get her to the back of the Jeep," he told Lucy, his voice quivering and barely able to keep from breaking.

Seconds later they careened out of the driveway, Lucy at the wheel as he huddled over Nell's body, muttering words of encouragement, at the same time punching in the number for the fire department, summoning them to a lost cause. Then he called Dan, briefed him on the details, and dispatched him to the scene.

Her screams continued, and her pulse grew weaker.

"She needs morphine and IV fluids, or she'll never make it to Saratoga. Go to Mary and Betty Thomson's," he yelled at Lucy. Then he called their number, told them he'd be there in five minutes and what to have ready for him.

Betty stood at the door with the vials, bags, needles, and tubing in a plastic bag. "I'm praying for her," she told Mark as he scooped up the equipment.

"Me too," he heard Mary call from the back room.

Lucy spun the Jeep back out on the highway and they were off again.

The burns on her head, shoulders, and left trunk were less than he originally thought, first- and second-degree at the most, the same for the side of her face. It puzzled him how she'd protected that part of her body from more severe damage. The mucosal membranes inside her mouth, however, were blackened as well, and he feared most for her airway. The soft tissues there were much more vulnerable, and even with less deep burns, they could swell up to obstruct her breathing. An explosion must have accompanied the flames, as only hot gases would penetrate orifices to damage them like that.

He easily inserted an angiocath needle into her right arm and opened the IV full, to raise her pressure, then adjusted it to replace the bodily fluids that would leak from her charred skin. To quiet her shrieks and cries, he injected half an ampule of Mary's morphine.

To his astonishment, her eyes fluttered open, she moaned, and said, "Some dinner party, eh, Doc?"

"What happened, Nell?"

"The back of my cabin blew . . . where propane tank is."

He reached for her hand, feeling the need to hold it, not just to comfort her, but to keep his own from trembling.

"Was in the tub taking my bath," she continued. "That's what saved me."

Her voice kept fracturing into different pitches, all of them high, as if forced through a strainer. The soft tissues near her vocal cords were swelling closed. She'd need a tube to keep breathing, and fast.

Like a drowning man clinging to a single plank, he focused solely on what he knew best: checking her pulse—weak; assessing her breathing— labored and noisy; fine-tuning her IV—running fine. The routine momentarily kept his larger questions at bay, and all their ramifications. "We'll soon be at the hospital," he said, reassuring her and hitting the numbers for ER on his phone.

She began to moan again, and mutter incoherently.

"This is Dr. Mark Roper, and I'm bringing in an eighty-year-old woman who's been in an explosion and has first- and second-degree burns to the head and trunk, but with more severe airway involvement . . ."

His own voice sounded far away as he continued to brief the triage nurse, kneeling over Nell and watching Lucy at the wheel as they sped along the deserted road. Riddles and ghosts continued to circle, threatening to come in from the darkness.

He continually had to reposition Nell's head to prevent her tongue from falling backward where it might obstruct her breathing; only then did he realize she'd finally worn her damn plate.

* * *

"Roper's special," the triage nurse called into her intercom the minute she saw Mark jump out of the Jeep in the ambulance bay.

Lucy frowned.

Instantly orderlies, nurses, and two doctors arrived to help.

"I thought only doctors who didn't want your patients called them Roper's specials," she said to him as they transferred Nell to a stretcher and raced her down the hall.

One of the physicians, a tall ebony-skinned woman with a long gray braid down to her waist gave her an incredulous look. "Where are you from, gal? In ER it means when Mark sends us someone he can't handle alone, we better be on our toes."

"Dr. Lucy O'Connor, meet Dr. Carla Moore, one of the few in this establishment who don't always consider me and my patients to be a pain in the ass." He tried to sound calm, yet he still quaked inside, trying to keep memory from intruding on what had to be done now.

Nell's respirations were already down to a squeak. "Seems like we need to intubate this one," Carla said, as they skidded into a resuscitation room the size of a shoe box lined with racks of equipment, everything—lines, monitors, IVs—within easy reach.

Carla shoved an anesthetic tray at him. On it were different-sized endotracheal tubes spread out in a semicircle around a laryngoscope. "Will you do the honors? I could use your help."

He nodded, slipped on a pair of sterile gloves, then positioned Nell's head and neck as if she were leaning forward to sniff a flower, maximally opening her airway. He reached for a silver suction probe to clear away her saliva, his fingers fumbling the instrument as he worked.

Stepping to his side, Lucy quickly grabbed a ventilation bag and mask. "Let me help you," she said, handing them to him. For a second, he felt her hands linger on his and give them a squeeze. The orchestrated chaos and noise of a resuscitation swirled about them—people shouting orders, running to draw bloods, sticking in needles, snapping on electrodes.

Her touch steadied him.

He placed the mask on Nell's face and squeezed a few trial puffs of oxygen into the woman's lungs. There was a lot of resistance, the effect of her airway closing off. He scissored her mouth open with his fingers, removing the partial plate. But his thoughts finally slipped his control and streaked unchecked toward reckless conclusions he never would have even considered twenty-four hours ago.

The explosion must have been deliberate, to prevent her from telling him anything, just as someone had silenced Victor Feldt and Bessie

McDonald. What's more, he and Lucy would also have been in the blast had they arrived on time. That couldn't be an accident either.

Lucy handed him the laryngoscope, snapping it open and illuminating the blade.

Taking it with his free hand and keeping Nell's mouth pried wide apart with his fingers, he slid the instrument along the side of her cracked and swollen tongue. This was going be a difficult intubation. As calculating as a computer, his brain flashed to the alternative, a tracheotomy, or cutting a hole directly into her windpipe.

Nell's eyes snapped open, her pupils wide with fear, and she grabbed at his hand. Her lips moved around the blade of the scope as if she were trying to say something.

He took it out.

Her attempts to form words continued.

He bent down to hear, once more fighting back his nausea at the terrible smell.

In a high-pitched whisper no louder than a breath, he heard her say, "What's my chances?"

He involuntarily glanced along a length of her blackened skin where it had split open and glistened in its own juices. The rest remained intact. She might survive the burn, the tub having protected her, but not the ordeal on the respirator that lay ahead, pneumonia being the most likely cause of death. Beyond that, if the burns were truly just second-degree, she'd avoid painful skin grafts and a protracted recovery. Comfort her with a lie, or give her the truth? Or a bit of both. He usually had more time to make such calls.

She seemed to sense his hesitation, widening her eyes and imploring him with her gaze to answer.

Before he hooked her lungs up to a machine, before he submitted her to the indignities of ventilators, catheters, and mind-numbing drugs, before he stole her voice by sticking an tube through it, she'd a right to say "Yes" or "No."

"The skin doesn't appear to be too bad, Nell. Your airway, though, needs help."

"Odds?" she whispered back.

"Four to one against, for most eighty-year-olds. But you're way better than most. And once the swelling goes down in your throat, they get way better."

He wasn't sure she'd heard him as a darkness seemed to gather behind her eyes again. But then she shook her head. "No lingering . . . on a chest pump . . . and don't let me . . . choke to death."

The sounds in the resuscitation room seemed to grow very distant.

"You understand what that means—"

Her stare silenced him.

What she wanted was clear as a shout. To be put out of her misery, pure and simple. He imagined Charles Braden leering over his shoulder. "Nell, I can't do that," he whispered.

She retreated into the black recesses where such final decisions are made, but not before he saw an unmistakable flash of contempt in her gaze.

"What's the delay, Mark?" Carla asked.

"She refuses a respirator, but asks us to keep her from choking to death."

"Wants to go to heaven, but doesn't want to die," muttered a young nurse behind him.

He ignored her and, agonizing over the ordeal he was sentencing Nell to, made his decision. "That means I sedate her with midazolam, we intubate to protect her airway, and you keep her topped off with morphine to combat her pain. Remember, she gets the same compassion you would give your own grandmother . . ."

As he spoke, looks of distaste spread over the faces of Carla and her staff. It was a gray call. No one in ER was ever comfortable with half measures that violated their pull-'em-back-from-the-brink-no-matter-what mentality. Little wonder. They didn't see what some of their successes had to go through once they got upstairs. At the same time Nell would feel betrayed by his sticking a tube down her throat. Yet he wouldn't give in to what she asked. He could no more commit active euthanasia than will his heart to a standstill. So he'd do what he could live with, no matter how anybody else in the business might second-guess him, or his patient despise him on her deathbed. And Charles Braden could go to hell.

"Nell, can you hear me? I'm going to make you sleep. Whenever you wake up, they'll give you more medication to keep you under. But I've got to intubate. . . ."

No response. Whether she ignored him, or had gone beyond hearing anything, he couldn't tell.

He injected the fast-acting tranquilizer, followed by a shot of succinylcholine, a short-duration paralytic. Together they'd make it easier to open her jaw and visualize her vocal cords despite all the boggy swelling in her upper pharynx. Provided this time he could get by her tongue. The paralytic would also stop her breathing. If he bungled the procedure, he'd have precious little time to go in through the trachea, and Nell might end up with what she wanted in the first place.

He navigated around the tongue to where the lining of her throat bulged like a blackened frog belly. Parting the puffy tissues with the laryngo-scope, he slid the endotracheal tube through the V of her cords and at-tached an Ambu bag, pumping hard and sending squeeze after squeeze of oxygen into her lungs until she recovered enough from the injections to breathe on her own.

Now he had Nell in the odd limbo of morality where doctors, himself included, willingly committed euthanasia, albeit the passive kind, with-holding heroic treatment if it's either futile or against the patient's wishes, yet doing what's necessary for comfort. If she continued to breathe by her-self, she'd survive. If in the name of controlling her pain or sedation they suppressed her respiration, unintentionally hurrying her to her death, so be it. The law, most physicians, and he could live with that as well. Such were medical ethics in the "gray" zone. To the layperson it might sound like word games. To the one faced with pushing in the plunger, that nuance of intent meant being able to sleep at night. The best Mark could tell himself as he walked out of emergency? He'd saved her the agony of asphyxiation, and bought her a bit of time to have a change of mind about dying. As for the weeks and maybe months of suffering he'd imposed on her, that's what would keep him awake at night. But for now, perhaps for all eternity, she wouldn't be telling anyone what "tidbits" or "name" she'd claimed to have for him.

"Make sure someone lets me know if she regains consciousness," he called back to Carla.

*   *   *

"You were great back there," Lucy told him.

"I don't think so."

They sat side by side on a soft leather couch in the doctors' lounge at Saratoga General, a room outfitted with tastefully upholstered chairs, pot-ted plants, recessed lighting, and an espresso machine that would have done Starbucks proud. "Those were tough calls, and I doubt even an anes-thetist could have pulled off that intubation—"

"That was how my father died," he said, holding a mug of cappuccino with both hands as he took a sip. The warmth didn't help the icy grip on his stomach any, nor the cold in his fingers, and his insides were still shaking. "Except there was no one there to help him."

She went very quiet. "How did it happen?"

Unwanted flashbacks flickered to life: the boom that he heard a mile away, racing toward the smoke on his bike, the circle of people standing around something.

"It was an accident," he said, trying to shut down the images. "And there's nothing to talk about. I just wanted you to know why I wasn't exactly a rock tonight." The darkest notion of all continued to circle him, but he wouldn't allow it even to take the shape of thought.

She watched him over the white mound of foam while taking small sips from her own cup, her dark gaze giving him the tell-me-your-story look that he'd seen work so magically with his patients.

Well, it wasn't going to succeed with him.

Using a tone intended to be all business, he told her only what had been tumbling through his head while he'd worked on Nell, that the gas tank explosion had been deliberately set, intended to kill the three of them. Yet as he talked, his mind veered to the woman on the phone tonight. Whatever else Victor had found, it was what he discovered about the big companies and their executive health plans that seemed to be important. At least she seemed to think so, enough to believe someone could kill him over it.

His thoughts shifted to Charles Braden with those silver-spooned friends of his from the business elites of Manhattan. Maybe one had nothing to do with the other, but he found it impossible not to think that their corporations might be involved.

So he shared all this with Lucy as well.

It didn't sound so outrageous laid it out in words.

He even talked about his turmoil over how to manage Nell in ER, including the way Braden had intruded on his thoughts because of the set-to they'd had over euthanasia while they were in the man's library. "I thought he played devil's advocate last night. But I'm not so sure he wouldn't have granted Nell's wish and put her out of her misery if he were running the resuscitation just now."

"How do you mean?"

"He pontificated about how the line between right and wrong, even life and death, blurs with advances in technology and the times. To prove the point, he raised some pretty troubling issues about euthanasia. It was chilling, hearing him talk about how, in the past, country doctors had smothered deformed newborns to save the family the hardship of raising a handi-capped child.'"

"What?"

"You heard me right. He's got this weird collection of medical atrocities he calls his 'hall of shame'—twisted eugenics, medical war crimes, that kind of thing—and he uses it to proselytize against deviant science."

Lucy's jaw fell, her eyes widened, and she dived for her purse. "Mark, I know what's wrong!"

"What?"

She hauled out the folded spreadsheets of statistics she'd brought with her and spread them out on a nearby coffee table. "All along you've been preoccupied with Chaz, but what if it's Daddy who has a secret?"

"How do you mean?"

She tapped the papers in front of her. "I didn't want to tell you my sus-picions about what I found here, because they seemed to have no context, and . . ." She stopped speaking, her cheeks flushed.

"Go on."

She hesitated, then said, "It's what we fought about earlier. I wasn't a total klutz when I came here and stuck my nose in your investigation. I ac-tually bent over backwards not to let my issues with Braden cloud your judgment about the man. So when I saw the discrepancy, I figured my own history with him had made me so biased I might be making too much of it, and I didn't say anything."

"Making too much of what?"

"Check this out." She began to draw her finger down the various columns of numbers. "I think I discovered why your father had been inter-ested in Braden Senior's charitable works."

He immediately leaned forward to see what she had.

"These are summaries of the births, deaths, and adoptions at the home; these, births and deaths at the center in Saratoga Springs. Like you, I first looked for the usual indicators of something wrong—a higher mortality-morbidity rate, that kind of thing. But as you said, the statistics are right on the norm for the home, and even lower than normal for the maternity center. In both instances, anyone looking at them would quickly conclude all was well."

"Right."

"So let's say we give the guy credit for superb obstetrical skills on his moneyed patients." Beside the mortality-morbidity numbers she placed yet another paper full of figures in her handwriting. "This is a synopsis of the actual delivery records your father had requisitioned from both places. I totaled all the infants pronounced normal, and here I itemized those with congenital abnormalities—heart defects; urinary tract anomalies; cleft lips and palates; limb aberrations, including club feet; neuronal tube defects of varying severity, some with only nominally open spines, others with fully open cords; and of course twenty-three trisomy where the mongoloid features were recognizable at birth."

"You were busy!" Mark said with a whistle, realizing she must have stayed up most of the nights he'd left her working on them at the kitchen table.

"As I said, I got used to reading mass records at the camps. Now here's the point. The guy's maternity center is short on congenital abnormalities."

"Short?"

"Yeah. Remember obstetrical statistics. Three percent of all newborns have some defect at birth. Out of the six thousand deliveries documented in these records, he should have recorded about a hundred and eighty with some kind of problem. He had barely a dozen. Good prenatal care can accomplish a lot, but change the rate of defects that much, no way. He had to be fudging his numbers. At least, that's what I thought initially, but couldn't see how or why."

"Well, I'll be."

"And I figured your dad couldn't pin him down, or he'd have done something about the place."

He never got the chance, Mark thought.

"Which begged the question," she continued, "why Braden would care about anyone twigging to the discrepancy in his records at this late date, there being no obvious link with Kelly's murder or anything else. At least it seemed that way, which is why I hesitated to even bring it up . . ."

As Lucy talked, the number 180 stuck in his mind. He'd found something of that amount when he reviewed the records himself. But what? He recalled it had to do with the home for unwed mothers, not the maternity center.

". . . I did spot another connection, but it didn't mean anything until just now, when you mentioned eugenics. Look at the total number of adoptions. Braden claimed to have made them directly out of the home for unwed mothers." She flipped back a page and began to scan yet more lists of figures.

Mark reached over and laid his hand on her arm. He knew what the number would be. One hundred and eighty. His breathing slowed.

"Here it is," she continued, obviously too charged up to heed his touch.

"The number of private adoptions arranged from the home—180! See what he might have been doing? Substituting healthy babies from the home for deformed ones at the maternity center. I mean, my God, can you imagine anything so hideous? It might actually have been legal if done on the up-and-up, couples from the maternity center putting their deformed kids up for immediate adoption, at the same time picking themselves up a healthy child from the home. Odious, but legal. The trouble is, there's no records of the abnormal kids at either place. It's as if they disappeared."

Chapter 17

"My potassium's 2.1?" Earl felt a ripple of fear. At anything below 3.0, heart muscle became so twitchy the slightest stimulation could throw it into various sorts of fibrillation. Just like what happened to Bessie McDonald. Except hers had been limited to the upper chambers. His entire myocardium could end up squirming like a useless sack of worms, in other words, complete cardiac arrest. He broke out in a cold sweat that had nothing to do with his gut.

Instinctively he didn't want to move. Any exertion at all could tip him over the edge. Already he could feel his pulse start to pound, the effect he'd expect from all the adrenaline that must be surging through his blood. *Christ, slow the rate down,* he thought, trying to calm himself, but that only made it tick up higher. His intestines kicked in with a snarl, and hinted at sending another wave of cramps his way. "Oh, great," he muttered, pain being another surefire way to get his heart racing. "Tanya, I need IV potassium fast, maximal dose, sixty milliequivalents in a liter, run it in at ten to twenty milliequivalents an hour." The rate had to be exact. Too much too fast could also stop a heart cold.

She grabbed two more vials of potassium from the medication bin, having already added one to the new bag of normal saline that she'd brought with her.

"And I'll need to be on a cardiac monitor, plus you better give me a hundred milligrams of Demerol after all, to at least take the edge off the spasms—"

"Whoa, I'm not even supposed to be here, remember?" She shook up the intravenous solution to mix in the added vials. "What I suggest," she added, her fingers flying as she got the new bag up and running, "is request the Demerol yourself as already ordered, and complain of palpitations or something so they put you on a monitor while they sort it all out. That ought to just about cover your needs for the moment. Just before shift change in the morning I'll phone the result to the floor clerk here, pretending I'm a lab tech reporting an error. She'll tell the nurses, and they'll order a repeat themselves. That way you'll know if more potassium's required."

He felt sheepish about his previous suspicions of her. "You're a wonder, Tanya Wozcek. I don't know how to thank you."

Her weak smile couldn't hide the worry in her eyes as she fine-tuned the intravenous rate. She knew as well as he did it would be very touch and go. "Does that burn?" she asked.

The concentrated solution she'd prepared could strip the lining of a vein, sclerosing it. It already felt like fire going up his arm. "I'll live," he muttered.

She slowed the rate by two-thirds.

What he wanted to know was how his potassium could have been brought so low so fast. The runs? Not this quickly. Something else had to be depleting it. But what?

He glanced toward the IV bag Tanya had discarded. "Did your friend run any other tests on me?"

"Sure. Your white count's up, which is to be expected with the infection, but everything else was fine, except for a high CO_2 which probably doesn't matter." She anchored the tubing to his skin with tape.

CO_2 was an indicator of his naturally occurring bicarbonate level, the base that balances all naturally occurring acids circulating in the body. It also existed as a pharmaceutical preparation. Though rarely used anymore, it was part of the emergency protocol for dropping critically high serum potassium levels, and large vials of it were common in hospitals. The solution itself looked clear as water, and if someone did do a blood test checking the bicarb level, it would normally be to make sure the reading wasn't too low. Nobody would make too much out of an unexplained elevation, just as Tanya hadn't. In other words, it would be a perfect agent to mess up a patient's potassium without raising suspicions, and anyone could have slipped a dose into his IV while he'd been sleeping. It also had another nasty little property, he remembered, a chill slowly creeping up his spine. It could precipitate digoxin toxicity in patients who were already on the medication. "Tanya, quick, please grab a urine dipstick and hand me the IV bag you just replaced."

She frowned, but did as he asked.

He released a few drops of the remaining fluid on the test strip.

The portion measuring acid–base should have remained a neutral beige. Instead it turned blue as a sapphire, indicating extreme alkalinity.

Bingo!

A sickening cold sensation filled his chest.

"Who else would know how to play with potassium like that but a doctor?" she said, once Earl told her what had been done to him. "Chaz still has my vote, or someone he ordered to do it. Christ, forget our other plan. We've got to get you out of here. If they can get to your IV bottles without you knowing—"

"Not just yet."

"Are you nuts?"

"I'll be okay for tonight," he bluffed. "Whoever did this doesn't know we're onto them or that you've changed my IVs."

"But what about telling the nurses, so you get the monitor, and the Demerol?"

"I'll still ask for the Demerol, and make up enough of a story about fluttering in my chest they'll wire me to something."

"Then who'll replace your intravenous with extra potassium when it's empty? I can't keep sneaking in here to do that."

"This bag is good until morning. By then Melanie will be here, and she'll handle everything. You forget, I start walking around now, my heart's primed to break into a jitterbug."

Scowling, she planted her hands on her hips. "I can arrange a wheel-chair. A stretcher even."

"And where would you put me? I need to be in a hospital. The worst of this damn infection is yet to come."

"And you could have yourself transferred, by air ambulance if necessary, back to Buffalo, where you'd be a lot safer than you are here. So quit the bullshit and tell me the real reason you refuse to leave. Are you using yourself as bait?"

Damn right, he thought, more determined than ever to carry out his plan now that he knew what to expect. Logically, the person who'd gotten to his IV before would want to pull a repeat performance, but only after the next scheduled change of the intravenous bag. Since the old one would have run out around 5:00 A.M., that's when Earl expected his would-be killer to come sneaking around. "Of course not," he answered, giving Tanya his most sincere smile, until a new wave of cramps twisted him in two and sent his pulse into triple digits again.

"You are nuts!" Her voice slid a notch higher, sounding frightened.

No fooling her. Worse, he sensed she was going to blow the whistle on him. "Tanya, now don't you tell anyone, hear me? I'll be all right. Whoever added the bicarb probably won't try to slip me another dose until after I'm due to get a new IV bag in the morning. And I'll be ready to raise holy hell the second anyone comes near me. If I haven't got a nibble by tomorrow, I promise you, I'm out of here."

She stared at him with that odd moonlike face of hers, looking skeptical as hell.

It took some arguing, but he finally convinced her that if she made a fuss now about extra security or tried to keep watch over him herself, it would alert his attacker and only postpone another attempt on his life. She reluctantly agreed not to interfere.

"But it's guards, an air ambulance, and home to your hospital in Buffalo if this nonsense doesn't work," she insisted.

"Agreed."

Shaking her head, she turned and left.

He pressed the call button and waited for the nurses, trying to keep a grip on his nerve and ratchet down the drubbing that his heart-turned-boxing-glove continued to deliver against the inside of his chest.

10:30 P.M.
Hampton Junction

It was snowing again, the flakes coming at the windshield like tracer bullets. Mark sat hunched forward over the wheel to see better as he pulled out of the hospital parking lot. "Nell told me recently about a friend of hers who had a baby at the home," he said.

"Oh?" Lucy paused in her attempt to direct a blast of hot air from the heater so it would defog the glass.

"The woman had said how she and other expectant mothers wanted to make a garden as a way to lessen the dreariness of the place, but were refused. Not only that, she complained they only had a half-finished lawn to walk on, even though the place was big as a park. And when I went out there, it seemed that lawn never did get completed. It had gone to seed of course, but I could make out the shape. It looked irregular, the bordering undergrowth from the forest having intruded on areas where the grass should have been. Hard to imagine fat cats like the Bradens unable to spring for a bag of seed or more than a few rolls of sod at a time. Unless someone needed an area that was constantly in a state of being dug up, so he could bury what he didn't want found, then cover it with grass so it stayed put."

Lucy rode with a hand over her mouth, as if trying not to throw up.

"Are you all right?" he asked her.

"No, I'm not."

"Do you want me to stop the car?"

"Won't do any good. I got like this in the camps. All objective when I found the bodies on paper, but ready to upchuck when the reality of them sank in."

They rode in silence.

"Why would he do it?" she asked after a few minutes.

"Who knows? Money maybe?"

"But I thought he was already richer than God."

"He is now. But back then? Sometimes these dynasty families have trouble coming up with the inheritance taxes to pass their goodies from one generation to the next."

She gave a shudder and huddled deeper into her coat.

He thought of the books in Charles's library that chronicled all the times and ways humankind had attempted to rid itself of *others* and protect *sameness*. "Or it could be a new variant of an old disease," he said.

"An old disease?"

"Think about the atrocities you've seen these last seven years. Aren't they committed so that the position of one tribe or group or race might be enhanced over the rest?"

"Pretty much."

"The factions always seem to share the same pretenses, right? Protecting culture, spreading religion, getting an economic edge, creating a nation of superior beings, righting old wrongs—then they outshout each other *trying to proclaim their unique benefit to the world, thereby justifying their own entitlement.*"

"It's sounds like you're quoting a sociology text."

"It's by one of my favorite journalists. He writes for the *Herald*, and I spotted some of his articles glancing through one of Braden's books last night. That particular line came from a series that won a Pulitzer. It always stuck with me."

"Well, it describes a few drunken warlords I met in Serbia to a *T.*"

"I probably still have clippings of the piece at home. It suggests that while primitives use genocide to eliminate outside threats, the sophisticated supremacist prefers eugenics, because that offers the possibility of strengthening the desirable traits of the tribe and weeding out its weaknesses all from within. In other words, improving the species."

"That's Nazi drivel."

" 'Marry your own kind' still holds sway among a lot of non-Nazis."

"What are you getting at?"

"I'm just trying to crawl inside his head to answer your question, 'Why?' "

"You spend too much time inside that creepy place, and you're going to have to hose out your own brain."

"If Braden believes in smotherings, maybe he's also an advocate of other twisted beliefs in that hall of shame of his. He and his cronies are as arrogant a bunch of elitists who think they are the chosen ones to rule their patch—a sizable chunk of corporate Manhattan—as any tribe you ever came across on your travels, and a hundred times more powerful."

"So?"

"So maybe Charles Braden made sure they had more than their fair share of healthy offspring."

"What?"

"Probably some crazy idea to assure their succession—hand off their life works to a generation free of flaws."

"But that's nuts. Sick. Loony!"

"Of course it is. That doesn't mean he didn't do it."

"But if he wanted healthy kids for all his crowd, why not just help the parents adopt? He didn't have to risk committing murder."

"I don't know why he didn't go the official route, but I'm almost certain he didn't."

"Why?"

"Because I don't think the parents knew. At least not the mothers."

"That's impossible."

"Not necessarily. I think I may have already talked to a woman who had her baby switched."

"No way!"

"Someone who gave birth at his maternity center. Nell suggested I get in touch with her. She blew me off—thinks Charles Braden is a god—but a lot of little details add up."

"Such as?"

"She said the baby 'wouldn't breathe when he came out.' What else might have been wrong, I've no idea. But Braden, instead of trying to resuscitate the kid on the spot, ran from the delivery room, giving the infant mouth-to-mouth respirations, and get this, jumped in his car and supposedly raced to the hospital himself."

"That's ridiculous."

"Except a week later he placed a healthy baby boy back in that mother's arms."

"And she thought it was her own?"

"From the description of what happened in the delivery room, I don't think she or anyone else got a good look at the newborn. And Nell told me how both at the maternity center and the home, they never let the same staff work more than a few days a week. I'll bet that was so he could 're-turn' babies when different people were on duty, and he also timed it so the mother went home the next day."

They rode in silence again.

"I can't believe the parents knew about the smotherings," she said eventually.

"Neither can I."

She remained huddled up in the corner of the cab, apparently lost in thought.

He peered into the storm, the downpour having grown so thick he was driving through white streamers.

"Do you think there'll be too much snow once we get there?" she asked.

"Don't know. But I doubt this will keep up. It's too heavy to last long."

"Why would he bury them on the grounds, and not off in the woods, someplace far from any connection to him?"

"Ever try to dig a hole in the forest floor? Around here it's full of rocks and roots. Whenever murderers have made that mistake, even if they managed to scratch out a shallow grave for their victim's body, animals usually dug it up. I know infants are much smaller, but hunters still might spot the remains, or someone's pet might start bringing in the bones."

She fell silent again, leaving him alone with his thoughts.

He'd certainly sewn up Charles Braden, all right. Taken threads of the man's life and tied them together into a nice tight story. Even managed to get him with his own words, quoting from that odd book collection of his. Clever, and no holes. He had an answer for every question or objection Lucy could throw at him, coming up with motive, means, and opportunity.

Yet it almost seemed too neat. Other less macabre explanations were possible. Braden could have been switching babies in secret, but not killing the deformed ones. He might have been turning them over to other orphanages farther afield so the paperwork wouldn't appear locally. That would require documents he wouldn't have, but maybe he'd simply forged the signatures, given fictitious names for the mother, listed the father as unknown. If Braden had been switching babies, phony paperwork was much more plausible than infanticide. Yet after seeing those books he had, and hearing what he said about smotherings . . .

All they would need was one trace of human DNA from the soil and they would have him. But they'd have to get it clandestinely. The minute Braden suspected anyone digging soil samples, he'd have lawyers by the carload sealing up the place.

He glanced over at Lucy. She rode with her face turned away from him. He had to hand it to her, she had quite a talent with spreadsheets. Braden must have figured no one would ever notice the discrepancy with the numbers. Certainly he, Mark Roper, coroner, hadn't, and wouldn't be planning to head off in the middle of the night with a pick and shovel if she hadn't pointed the way.

One thing he hadn't shared with her, had been trying not to think of at all—the similarity in the attack on Nell and—No, he wasn't going to even consider that. Couldn't!

They made the rest of the trip without talking.

As they passed the pay phone near his house, she said, "Maybe you should don your coroner's hat, phone the friendliest judge you know to get a warrant. Violating the rights of a derelict lawn shouldn't be too much of a hurdle for American justice. If we do find anything, we'll want to be able to use it in court." She gave him a weak smile. "See, I'm learning. Then you and I are going to have a bowl of soup—something UN soldiers in Bosnia told me was a necessity for this kind of detail."

He could imagine. Rule number one: Never spend a cold night digging for bodies without something hot on your stomach.

He pulled over and made a call to a semiretired judge living in a cottage nearby who had once known his father.

"Any luck?" Lucy called from the Jeep when he hung up.

"The guy agreed—promised he'd get the paperwork to me tomorrow," he yelled back to her, holding the door to the booth open as he dialed the nursing desk for Earl's floor at NYCH. "If anyone bothers us tonight, we're digging for worms—Oh, hello, it's Dr. Mark Roper. Is Dr. Garnet awake?"

"Awake! He's a one-man, all-night vigil."

"Plug in his phone. I want to call through. It's urgent."

In a matter of minutes he'd told Earl everything that had happened—the explosion, Nell, the conversation he'd had with the woman who worked at Nucleus Laboratories, and that what Victor had found seemed mostly to do with the executive health plans of big corporations. "At least that's what upset the lady who called. Victor had also zeroed in on some genetic screening results he thought were peculiar, but she couldn't see anything wrong with them."

"Who were they of?"

"Siblings with a family history of cancer. They apparently were all negative."

Earl immediately triaged the rest of the information into a series of succinct questions.

"You've still no idea who owns Nucleus Laboratories?"

"No."

"Any ideas about how to track down your caller and this file she has?"

"Not yet. Haven't had a chance to even think of it."

"And Nell never said what she'd remembered."

"No, chances are there never was anything to tell. She could have said that just to get a visit."

"So we've got nothing."

"Not exactly. I think my phone's tapped."

"What?"

"So no more calls to the house, and cell phones are out."

"Jesus Christ!"

"And I got a pretty good idea what was going on at Braden's maternity center and the home for unwed mothers." He spent the next few minutes outlining the implications of the statistics his father had kept, and went on to describe his library encounter with Charles and the hall of shame.

"Mother of God!" Earl muttered at the end of the story. "That's so monstrous it's unbelievable." After a few more seconds, he added, "It could have been why Kelly was murdered, if she found out."

"Exactly."

"Unfortunately, that expands the list of suspects," Earl continued, still sounding incredulous. "We'd have to add Charles, and it could still be Chaz, defending his father. Hell, we might even have to think of Mrs. Charles Braden, wherever she is these days. No one's brought her up, but I remember a rather fierce woman who, back then, certainly seemed capable of taking extreme measures against anyone who threatened her husband. But it's astute work, Mark. Excellent, in fact."

"Oh, it wasn't me. Lucy figured it out—"

"Who's Lucy?"

That's right. Earl didn't know about her. "The wonderful Lucy? She's this miracle resident who's descended into my life and become my right hand at work, who also makes great soup . . ."

As he heaped praise on her, giving her credit for having cracked the secret of his father's files, he opened the doors of the booth again to let her hear. Her cheeks flushing crimson, she waved him to keep quiet from the rolled-down window on her side of the Jeep.

The silence at the other end of the line was total.

"What's the matter, Earl?"

"I hope you didn't tell her about me and Kelly."

"No, of course not."

The silence continued.

"What?" Mark asked.

"Did you check her out?"

"She's all right, I promise you."

"The casualty rate among people who might have helped us has tripled in the last twenty-four hours. At best she's bad luck. You be careful. My advice is turn over everything you've found out to the local sheriff and let him handle it. Don't go doing anything stupid on your own, hear me?"

11:04 p.m.
New York City Hospital

Earl's pulse leapt to triple digits as he watched the cardiac monitor the nurses had provided. Though at the moment the pattern indicated a fast but normal heartbeat, the result of his own anxiety and responsible for the boxing-glove effect, nasty-looking runs of extra squiggles occasionally popped up. Diagnostic possibilities of what they could be the precursors to ran through his head, and a cold sweat crept over his skin again.

He averted his eyes and settled himself back down. Better keep his imagination in check if he had any hope of toughing this out and catching a killer.

Yet he continued to worry. First about the arrival of this resident, Lucy, on the scene. As much as he liked Mark, the guy jumped to conclusions and rushed to judgment about people, for better or worse. His resentment of Chaz had almost led him to exclude other suspects since the beginning of the case. Then he'd been ready in an instant to label Samantha's doings with Kelly as Munchausen by proxy syndrome. What if this time he'd gotten it wrong the other way around, and mistaken a serpent for an angel? He was lonely enough to be a mark for any intelligent, half-decent-looking female. From the way he babbled on about her, he'd been smitten, which meant she could lead him by the nose. What if she were in cahoots with someone who wanted to sabotage the investigation, or worse, lure Mark into danger? And now, apparently thanks to this woman's helpful interpretation of Cam Roper's old files, Mark was chasing a crazy idea that Charles Braden could have been involved in some bizarre scheme involving mass infanticide. At first, he had to admit, when Mark told him, he'd been shocked into at least considering it, but then when he learned its source . . . "Jesus!" he said out loud, his bad feeling about her growing worse by the second.

A fluttering sensation in his chest alerted him to a new round of palpitations, and he lay still, inhaling, exhaling, and getting frustrated as hell.

Tanya slipped in to check on him at eleven as promised.

"All's well," he lied, grateful that his tracing on the monitor happened to be going through a quiet spell.

She left looking as concerned as ever.

His restlessness became unbearable. He rang for the nurse, asked for a pad of paper, sticky tape, and as many different colored pens as she could spare.

"You should get some sleep, not stay up coloring all night," the woman said, not at all as jovial, with her red cheeks and granny glasses, as he'd remembered while loaded with morphine. Her name wasn't much of a yuk either. The tag read MRS. WHITE, as if she'd killed Professor Plum in the library with the pipe wrench.

"What'll it be next," she added, "cutting out paper dolls?"

"Sweet!" he told her.

He proceeded to do what he always did when the complexity of a patient's medical problem overwhelmed him—make a flowchart of all the variables.

At the center he wrote *Kelly*.

Circling her like malevolent red moons he placed *Chaz Braden* and *Samantha McShane*, and in more distant orbits, using a slightly less vibrant orange, *Charles Braden III* and *Walter McShane*.

Closer to Kelly he added *Earl Garnet, Cam Roper*, and *Mark Roper*, all in green—the men who loved her.

Radiating out from *Charles Braden III* he drew two lines. On the end of one he wrote *Maternity Center*, the end of the other *Home for Unwed Mothers*. He also made a horizontal line connecting the two, in red.

Floating above these, suspended in the middle of nowhere, he added the name *Nucleus Laboratories*, and joined to it with a hard black line, *Corporate Executive Health Plans*. With a lighter line, he added, *Genetic Screenings: Siblings with a Positive Family History for Cancer*.

From these he penciled in a tentative line to Chaz Braden's name with a *?* on it.

Finally, he scribbled *Victims with information* at the very top of the page, added *Victor Feldt* as number one with a black line joining him to Nucleus labs, and *Nell* as number two, her black line leading to *Kelly*.

And that was it for Hampton Junction.

Or was it? He added *Lucy*, circled it, and penciled in three faint lines, each marked with a *?*, between her name and his principle suspects— *Chaz*; *Charles*; *Samantha*.

Moving to the bottom of the page he wrote *NYCH*, with four spokes radiating out from it, one to *Kelly*, one to each of the *Bradens*, and one to himself. He added a fifth spoke and on it wrote *Bessie McDonald-Victim?* Finally, he designated a similar *Victim?* status to himself.

At first he felt a sense of mastery, having condensed everything on one page. A half hour later he seethed with impatience at being no further ahead in sorting it all out.

He couldn't pull anything into a coherent whole. The diagram seemed to highlight differences between the various parts of the puzzle rather than link them together. Where were the common threads? He couldn't relate Bessie McDonald to Victor Feldt and Nucleus Labs. He couldn't connect the labs to Kelly's murder. There was even a lack of consistency in the attacks on the victims. At NYCH, the person who had silenced Bessie McDonald and infected him operated like a ghost, attempting to leave no trace of foul play. Such stealth suggested a perpetrator determined to escape suspicion altogether, not just evade capture. In Hampton Junction, however, the attempts to remove people, though clever, were crude. The explosion tonight might silence Nell, yet it most certainly would raise suspicions. As for Victor Feldt's timely heart attack, that, too, could have been achieved with unsophisticated means. Mark had said he was overweight, hypertensive, and diabetic—significant risk factors. Someone with a gun had already chased Mark up a hill. The same thing could have been done to Victor with lethal results. Again, clever, but nowhere in the same league as what had been done to Bessie and him. It was as if whoever carried out these acts felt he or she could withstand doubts on the part of the police and public about there being foul play, so long as the events could also be read as accidental, and there was no evidence to prove otherwise.

He sat scowling at the diagram, wondering how the same scam could include such wildly divergent tolerances to risk.

"Too many players," he muttered.

Yet surely Kelly's murder was at the center of everything.

A sudden pain coiled through his abdomen, once more sending him writhing, his insides on fire despite the Demerol. When it passed he lay drenched in sweat and exhausted, warily watching the monitor while trying to control his pulse. The slightest sound out in the hall set it racing again.

He shakily returned to his diagram, but a single answer to explain the events in Hampton Junction and NYCH continued to elude him. On a whim he thought, *Maybe that's what this crazy picture was trying to tell me.* If he couldn't make sense of it as a whole, what if he broke it down and looked at the parts separately?

He slashed a black horizontal line across the middle of the paper, dividing the two locales and the respective players.

Immediately it simplified things.

Now he could run any number of scenarios to explain the Hampton Junction half of things. Chaz Braden could have killed Kelly because he'd found out she was leaving him, and Nell he tried to blow up because he feared she really did have information that would finally convict him. Simple, straightforward—he liked it. But he still had no idea why Victor Feldt had been killed or by whom. Nor would anyone, it seemed, until they tracked down the woman with the file. And he couldn't even begin to guess how the lab's secret tied in with Kelly's murder. As for the infanticide story, he continued to find that beyond belief.

Again, he wondered about Lucy's role in all this.

Sent to sidetrack Mark?

By whom?

Chaz? But would he incriminate his own father?

No, that didn't make sense.

And Charles wouldn't set himself up.

Samantha maybe?

Well, whoever it might have been, weaving a story of murder from old birth records was preposterous.

Except for one detail.

He circled Cam Roper's name.

The man had been the first to take an interest in the statistics that Mark and this Lucy woman now found so incriminating. Yet he died before he saw fit to do anything about it. Or had his death conveniently stopped him from taking action? He'd have to ask Mark how his father died. In the meantime, he lightly penciled in *Victim?* beside Cam Roper's name.

It was probably another absurd idea. Otherwise, Mark would certainly have seen the possibility and said something.

Or would he?

Earl thought a moment, recalling how Mark had avoided all mention of how his father died. A person could spend a lifetime trying to bury that kind of pain, especially after losing his mom just two years before. Well-ingrained defenses might have kept him from looking too closely.

"Shit!" he said, abruptly folding the Hampton Junction part of the paper out of sight, admitting he wasn't anywhere close to getting a handle on the happenings there.

A faint noise of squeaking wheels filtered through his closed door from somewhere out in the hallway. He stiffened as it drew nearer.

A medication cart? Shouldn't be at this time of night.

It kept coming, the high-pitched sound like fingernails on a blackboard.

Then it stopped.

The sound of a wet mop slapping onto the linoleum floor echoed along the corridor.

Just the cleaner pushing his pail, he thought. But the tightness in his muscles wouldn't go away. He sat listening, hearing nothing else at first, then a soft swishing right outside the entrance of his room and an occasional tap as the handle struck the wall. He held his breath, expecting to see the door push open and someone come lunging in at him.

The tapping passed down the corridor and out of earshot.

He went back to his diagram, this time focusing only on the NYCH half of things. He first considered the three suspects again. Beside their names he printed the word *GHOST.*

If it was either Chaz Braden or Charles, he couldn't see how either one of them could get close enough to him and pull it off themselves. But again the idea of accomplices grated.

A solitary physician working for Samantha? That would be the only way she could pull it off.

There was also another scenario, yet he was reluctant to consider it because it opened up so many unknowns. But to be complete in assessing all the options, as he was always telling Mark, he had no choice. The disparities in "risk tolerance" that he'd noted between what had happened in NYCH and the more blatant violence of Hampton Junction, demanded he look at it.

What if there were two separate processes going on, each with its own players, those players each having his or her own motives, but both people connected to Kelly and her murder?

Or had he missed someone in lining up the suspects?

*   *   *

Mark sat at the kitchen table, halfheartedly spooning down a bowl of chicken and barley soup as Earl's words ate at him. Of course the man didn't know Lucy, so naturally would be suspicious of the way she'd shown up in the middle of everything. Yet as coroner, Mark himself should have been more questioning and checked out her credentials a bit better before taking her so much into his confidence.

As for leaving everything to Dan in the morning, that also would be the smart thing to do. Mark had even spoken briefly with him from the pay phone, but only about Nell and her prognosis. The prospect of slipping out to the home for unwed mothers, grabbing some soil samples from under Braden's nose, and possibly hitting a home run against the man before anyone else got hurt still seemed awfully tempting. But now he wondered if it wasn't too tempting. For starters, why would Braden have talked so openly of smotherings if he had something to hide? It didn't add up.

"You go get the shovels, flashlights, whatever. I'll make the soup," Lucy had said when they'd arrived home. Twenty minutes later he'd loaded the Jeep, changed into warm clothing, and dug out some caving headlamps so they could work with their hands free. As she quickly emptied her bowl and helped herself to seconds, he even started to second-guess her willingness to go out there. *Shit! I have to stop thinking this way.* But once released, his doubts roamed free.

"Why so moody?" she asked.

He filled his spoon and took a small sip. "Like you, I'm drained." He hoped he sounded casual enough. "And I'm beginning to think we must have been crazy to consider doing this tonight. Tomorrow I'll call Dan, he'll provide the men, and we'll do the search properly."

She stopped midway through taking another mouthful. "Are you serious? Somebody will spot us, call Braden, then watch the injunctions fly. Believe me, I've been in court against the kind of legal might Charles can wield. They're masters at delays and stalling. The warrant you arranged for tonight will be shredded. Mark, we could be in and out, get the samples, and maybe it's case closed."

"That's what bothers me, Lucy. Everything points us in that direction. Well, I don't feel like going where I'm pointed anymore. I mean, we almost got killed tonight. Victor's dead. Nell's hanging by a thread. It's time to pause and reflect, wouldn't you say?"

Her expression turned stony.

He immediately regretted the outburst. "Sorry. I didn't mean to take your head off."

She surprised him by removing the spoon from his hand and entwining her fingers in his. "Come with me," she said, and led him to the front room, where she sat him down beside him on the couch.

"What's up—"

She silenced him with a pair of fingers to his lips. "Remember I said you could do worse than talk to me about how the past can bite you in the butt. Well, now's as good a time as any."

"Lucy, what are you—"

Her fingers pressed against his lips again. "Tell me what seeing Nell brought back."

"What's the point—"

"I'm as horrified at what happened to Victor and Nell as you are. It's horrific. Tragic. Shocking. But what you're feeling goes beyond that."

"Now wait a minute—"

"The point is you're obsessed with discovering the secret of Kelly's murder."

"No—"

"I've watched you, Mark. Even when you're not working the case you get a faraway stare in your eyes, and I can tell you're thinking about it. Believe me, I know the look. I've seen it in men on a battlefield who get trapped in what they've seen and can't escape reliving the violence even when everything's over. Except you were a kid—"

"That's nonsense. You're talking about post-traumatic stress—it's something soldiers get—"

"You've never been this wrapped up in a coroner's inquiry before, have you?"

"Well, no—"

"I think you're tangled up in 1974, both chained and drawn to whatever happened back then. I also get the feeling you don't know if you're stuck in this place, mired in some compulsion, or it's really where you want to be, doing what you do so well."

He tried to pull his hand away from hers, but she tightened her grip. Its strength surprised him.

"No, you don't. I'm the best friend you could have right now, Mark Roper, because I'm not afraid to say what you need to hear. Face it! After all these years, you can't afford to let much more time slide before you shake off whatever has sunk its teeth into you."

He felt himself grow sweaty, and the images he'd fought against for a lifetime began to reappear.

He'd jumped off his bike, run up to those people standing in the circle, and pushed through their legs—No he wouldn't do this. He pulled his hand away. "What do you want to hear, Lucy? That I cried, that I felt terrified, that since then I've never stopped feeling there's this cavity inside me I can't fill, and the only way to numb the hurt is to keep busy. Holding hands isn't going to help. There, I've talked about it. You want to know how this let-it-all-hang-out crap makes me feel? Angry as hell!"

She grabbed his hand again, her grip even stronger than before. "Fine. Of course you're angry. Now tell me your nightmare."

Jesus, is there no stopping her? "You really want to hear this? Fine!" Let her have the story with both barrels, he thought, then watch her run for the hills. "I was riding my bike around town one evening, when there was a big explosion. I raced toward the sound, and saw smoke and flames from his office—"

She silenced him with a finger again. "Lose the anger, Mark." Her pupils pulsed wide, filling her gaze with a soft darkness that sucked the fight right out of him.

He took a breath and continued. "I skidded to a stop, jumped off, and ran toward a crowd standing in a circle. They were looking at something. No one saw me or barred the way, and I managed to push between somebody's legs. At first I didn't even realize the black thing in front of me was a body. But then his eyes opened, and they looked right at me. At that instant someone grabbed me, tried to put their arms around me so I couldn't see, and kept saying it would be all right. I think they started to take me away, and I don't know what else I actually saw or only thought I did. But I could still hear. The sounds coming out his throat were the same high-pitched squeaks we heard tonight, except they went on and on, and no one did anything about it. I kept looking around for my dad, expecting him to run up and help. It was only when he didn't come that I realized who . . ." He felt his throat constrict.

"Go on."

Her voice came from somewhere outside what he was seeing. He could never tell if he'd actually witnessed this part, or he'd built it up over the years in his imagination, his mind, his nightmares. In front of him lay his father, straining to breathe. Enough of his clothing had burned off that the underlying skin of his chest, already laid raw with the heat, rippled, then split open to the muscle with the effort. The man arched forward and reached toward him, the whites of his eyes bulging out of his carbon face, imploring him for help.

"Go on," he heard her say again.

". . . I started to scream, broke free, and ran. They found me hiding in the basement of this house. I've been trying to erase that sound, that smell, those eyes ever since. Tonight just . . ." He couldn't talk anymore. The tears he'd fought back while working on Nell met no resistance this time, and a sob, raw and loud as an animal's bellow, broke free from deep within his chest.

Her arms were around him in a flash.

"No one helped," he gasped when he got his breath. "They just stood around and watched him die." He tried to wipe his eyes and stifle his crying, but she kept telling him that it was okay, and her cool fingers stroked the side of his face. She cradled his head so closely that her hair fell around him in a sheltering bower, and the soothing sound of her heartbeat filled his ears.

He looked up and gently cupped his palm over her cheek. She turned her head slightly, brought her lips to his fingertips, and softly kissed them, keeping her eyes locked on his, not allowing him to evade the truth of these seconds. They remained huddled side by side, cocooned in each other's embrace, straddling a distance far greater than the reach of their arms.

He lay back and drew her on top of him, and kissed her, and was kissed by her, a fearless gentle kiss.

*   *   *

A mile down the road a red car stood parked under a grove of poplar trees, its windows well frosted by the breathing of the three men who waited inside.

A fourth carrying night goggles walked up to the passenger side and got in the front seat. The driver finished talking on his cellular and snapped it shut. "No phone calls, neither on the land line nor his cellular. They may have figured out we're listening," he said to the newcomer.

"It doesn't matter. Roper loaded up the Jeep with shovels. Looks like they're going digging."

"He's coming now?" the man behind him asked, sounding surprised.

"All I can tell you is he's ready to break ground. That means we need to get there and wait for him to show up."

The other man in the backseat muttered, "Well, god damn. I didn't think he'd take the bait to that extent."

The driver started the motor and turned the defroster on full blast. "I guess this time we played him just about perfectly."

Chapter 18

The beam from Lucy's headlamp sliced through snowflakes big as polka dots as she followed the road in through the woods. Barely a foot had accumulated on the ground, but the stickiness of it made the trek hard going and transformed the branches overhead into a giant corridor of curved white ribs. It was her first time on the grounds, but Mark had pointed out the entrance several times.

She had awakened about an hour ago, languidly stretched, and left Mark sleeping in their bed—she paused. *Their bed.* She liked the sound of that, and savored the memory of his naked body against hers.

Her feelings for Mark confused her. She'd had lovers before. It had been a way to keep sane at the front of a war zone, losing herself in the embrace of a man she liked and respected, with no illusions about the future. Before that, in medical school, she'd had little time for sweethearts, though sex with the right friend on occasion had been comforting during that ordeal as well. Yet with every man she'd shared her bed, she always knew how ephemeral their affair would be even as they first began to make love.

She'd hadn't felt that with Mark. Nor did his evident experience as a lover remind her of the other women he'd had. Rather the way he gave himself to her so wantonly let her respond in kind and made their love-making all the more special, as if it erased all the times before.

She even liked the edginess she felt in him as he wavered between wanting to bolt from Hampton Junction or staying to practice in his father's footsteps. It excited her, because as he stood torn by those two extremes, he still exuded the aura of a man with a spine of steel in him, and a moral compass that would point true north no matter what.

And when he was ready, they would talk more about his father's death. She'd already decided not to raise the possibility Cam Roper had been murdered until Mark could bring it up himself.

But she had also sensed something else. Afterward, as she lay in his arms, she felt a wariness in him that saddened her, a watchfulness as part of him sealed itself off. He still didn't entirely trust her.

Back in his kitchen she'd made herself a thermos of tea, then, having dressed warmly, grabbed one of the headlamps along with a few other items, switched all the garden tools Mark had selected from his Jeep to her station wagon, and fishtailed out his driveway onto the road.

And here she trudged, having decided to prove herself to him once and for all.

Her frosty breath rose straight up, weaving among the tumbling flakes in the windless night, and the squeaky crunch of her boots on the frozen snow carried in the frosty air. The sound was audible for a long way, which meant she would just as easily hear anyone sneaking around the woods. It reminded her of similar nights in Bosnia, when her medical team had to go out on emergencies, and they knew for sure men with guns were everywhere. Now that had been scary. This felt like a walk in the park. The last thing Braden would expect was for anyone to show up at this hour.

She walked into the clearing and saw the hulking, gray building looming at its center as if waiting for her. It looked exactly the way Mark had described. At least she didn't have to go inside.

She picked her way through the shrub growth until she reached where it bordered spindly stalks of dormant grass. The perimeter of the lawn he'd talked about, she figured. Walking a few dozen yards farther in, she proceeded to tramp down a twelve-foot square. She then selected a half-moon garden edger from the tools she'd carried with her and sliced the area into six-foot lengths of sod. As she'd expected this time of year, the ground hadn't frozen yet. Using the blade to pry up the end of one piece, she gave herself a handhold and pulled. It took some additional cutting and slicing, along with a lot of heavy tugging, but she ripped it out more or less intact. Rolling it up and laying it aside, she got to work on the rest. Within half an hour she'd lifted two dozen rolls of turf, exposing moist black earth underneath. Luckily the flakes dissolved on contact with the wet surface.

She fished a rolled-up newspaper from an inside pocket of her jacket and spread it out where she'd first be working, anchoring the corners with clumps of sod. Using the shovel she turned over a strip of soil, then took a garden variety trowel, got down on her knees, and sifted through the dirt, picking up a small trowelful at time, then feeling through it with her fingers over the paper. She figured she wouldn't have to dig too deep, a couple of feet at most. But it was slow going, and the sweat she'd worked up earlier congealed to her skin, making her all the colder.

She didn't count on finding anything right away. That would be pressing the laws of chance. But if there were anywhere near 180 tiny corpses buried here, odds were she'd eventually come across at least one set of bones. Not that she needed to find even that these days. In Bosnia they'd been able to detect traces of human DNA in soil samples. And if she wasn't successful this time, she and Mark could do a little each night, covering up their work with snow so Braden need never know.

Her world narrowed down to the circle of light in which she worked, the tiny sound of her trowel biting into the dirt, and the patter of soil bits falling onto the newspaper as she filtered them through her fingers. She kept her back to the building, preferring to face the forest and the dark opening where the road led off toward the highway. That'd be where anyone following her tracks would appear. She raised her head and sent the beam of her headlamp sweeping through the gloom along the forest's edge, breathing through her mouth to achieve total silence. Nothing caught her eye in the quiet swirl of the storm, and not a sound reached her ears.

Every fifteen minutes she got up, stamped her feet, and swung her arms in an effort to warm up. The tea helped as well. The first hour passed, and she covered a third of the area she had set out for herself. Not bad, she thought, having no illusions about how long and tedious this kind of work could be.

Then the cold and damp seeped into her marrow, and she took more frequent breaks. By four-thirty she'd covered only half the exposed area. Finishing the last of the tea, she imagined Mark back in bed, cozy and warm. "Bugger," she muttered, smiling to herself, half-hoping he'd wake up, realize where she'd gone, and come join her. He seemed to be a light sleeper, like herself—the legacy of taking night calls.

She went back down on her knees, but her hands shivered so much she couldn't grip the trowel properly. As much as she wanted to keep going, she'd have to return to her station wagon and warm up.

She rose to her feet and started to walk briskly away from the building.

After no more than a dozen steps, she heard boots crunching on snow behind her. She spun around and saw four men in gaily colored ski outfits charging toward her. They must have come out of the building. "Hold it right there, asshole!" yelled the one closest to her.

Lucy turned and ran, figuring she had a twenty-yard start. More than enough.

"I said stop!"

She accelerated, high-stepping along the trail she'd made coming in.

A stuttering, dry, coughing noise ripped through the air from behind her, and spurts of snow flew into the air farther up the trail.

Oh, shit!

She pulled up, turned, and raised her arms.

"One shout out of you, and I'll blow your head off," said the man in the lead, striding up to her and pointing a gun with the stubby cylinder of a silencer right at her forehead. "You've been ambushed, sister!"

The others closed in around her, and she could feel their breath on the back of her neck. She recognized one of them from Braden's party, where he'd served drinks. "What the hell do you think you're doing?" she demanded, as if a show of outrage would stop the attack.

A punch from behind hit her right in the kidney. She bellowed and arched backward, only to have someone grab her by the hair. She managed to stay on her feet, watching for an opening to karate kick the one with the gun.

"We told you to keep quiet," repeated a voice in her ear.

"Search her; find her keys," said the armed man, stepping back out of reach but keeping the muzzle pointed for a shot between her eyes.

The one holding her hair threw her forward to the ground, shoving her face into the snow. He then knelt on her legs and held her arms as the other two roughly groped in her pockets.

"You've been played like a violin, sister," he said. "All so you and Roper would show up here, looking for baby bones that don't exist. People will just think you two were off on a wild-goose chase and had a horrible accident!"

What the hell! thought Lucy, looking up to see the muzzle still directed at her head.

"I found her keys," one of the searchers called out, standing up and dangling them in front of the others. "Remember, when you haul her up to remove the chains, cut off every trace of the tape before you dump her back in, and don't leave any pieces on the ground."

He sounded as nonchalant as if he were organizing the cleanup after a picnic. What the hell did he mean?

"Where are you going?" the man with the gun asked. "I thought we were still waiting for Roper."

"You and I might as well take her car and go get him. He must be asleep back at his house. No way he'd have knowingly let her come here on her own." They started to walk off together, and he gestured at the other two. "Don't forget to break the board so it looks as if they went through by accident."

Oh, God, what did they plan to do?

One of the men holding her produced a gun from inside his coat and grinned as he pointed it at her. "You're going to get cold, real cold now." With his free hand he pulled a roll of duct tape out of his pocket and handed it to his partner, who still had her pinned from behind with his knees. She heard him rip off a piece, and he slapped it over her mouth. Night before last he'd handed her a glass of champagne.

The pair of them pulled her to her feet and twisted her arms behind her back as the one with the tape wrapped a strip of it around her wrists. They then frog-marched her back where she'd been working, the man holding the gun prodding her every few steps with the barrel. Once there, the former waiter who'd taped her up threw her to the ground and sat on her legs as he cinched them together at the calves and ankles. The muzzle held at her head by his friend made her hold off any attempt to kick him where it would hurt. Then he got up and continued on to the building, disappearing around the corner. Seconds later he reappeared, carrying something about four feet long, and Lucy heard the clank of a chain.

Oh, my God!

The shape of an anchor became clearer as he brought it closer.

"No!" Lucy screamed into her gag, and started to buck and kick against her restraints.

For her trouble the armed man shoved the barrel of his gun into her ribs. "Behave!"

Still she writhed and tried to scream.

The man with the anchor dropped it at her feet and wrapped the chains tightly around her ankles over top of the tape. Reaching into his jacket he took out a padlock, secured it through the links, and snapped it closed. He walked back to the building and returned with a coil of rope, which he tied to the anchor. "She's ready," he said.

They left her lying there and tramped off a few yards, shuffling their boots through the snow as if trying to find something.

Lucy increased her struggle to at least free her arms and tried harder than ever to scream,

"Found it," said one, leaning over and lifting a plywood sheet out of the snow. The black mouth of a well yawned beneath it.

Her terror rocketed.

Jesus Christ, stop!

She started to hyperventilate. The tape made it hard to breathe. Her fine-toned muscles quivered the length of her body as she strained to break free.

They returned, picked her up, anchor and all, and carried her with monstrous deliberateness toward the opening.

No! Oh, God in heaven, please, no!

Without so much as a second's pause for a last thought, word, or prayer, they threw her in, feetfirst.

Chapter 19

Mark woke and felt for Lucy in the darkness. His hand patted nothing but a wrinkled sheet.

He sat up. "Lucy?"

The house was silent.

What the hell?

He threw on his robe and ran downstairs. "Lucy—" Through the front door window he saw that her car was gone. So was the warm clothing she'd laid out earlier on the coatrack, and where he'd hung two caving headlamps there remained only one.

His insides turned to ice. In less than a minute he dressed and headed out the door. The headlamp, he remembered, and grabbed it. He also took his bat, just in case. His watch read *4:36*.

Sure enough, all the tools were gone from his Jeep.

He turned the ignition, hit the wiper switch for front and rear to clear away the snow, and accelerated down his driveway. Christ it felt slippery. He braked for the turn onto the road, but too late. He started to skid across it, right into a two-foot bank the graders had left from previous plowings. "Shit, shit, shit!" he muttered as he jockeyed the vehicle back and forth, delicately working the accelerator so as not to spin his wheels.

She's probably perfectly okay, he had to keep telling himself.

By the time he got free, the dash clock read *4:42*.

He forced himself to drive more slowly, peering through the dazzling swirls of flakes highlighted in his low beams. What time she'd gone out there, he'd no idea, but already the storm had filled in her tire tracks.

After five minutes of crawling along, he turned on the radio to keep from screaming in frustration at the slow pace. Normally he would there by now.

"*I'm gonna be all right . . .*" Jennifer Lopez sang.

He had less than two miles to go when he spotted the glow from the high beams of an oncoming car.

*   *   *

Lucy careened once off the stone sides before the anchor crashed through a thin layer of ice and pulled her into the frigid darkness.

The descent accelerated. Water streamed up her nostrils and through the back of her throat. She started to choke and heard bubbles pouring out her nose but couldn't see them, couldn't see anything now. The pressure on her head and ears squeezed in until she thought the end would come when her brain burst. Even greater weight crushed her chest and expelled more bubbles, those in a deafening gargle from where the tape tore free of her mouth. Searing pain burned through her limbs and her mind issued frantic alerts that they were in flames; that lactic acid bathed the tissues inside and out, that she had the the metabolic consequence of no oxygen—the sorts of clinical snippets she might have used to save another, but not herself.

Yet her superb condition prolonged her dying. Her heart, trained to endure on near anoxic blood, continued to beat, her brain to think.

And down she went.

Finally, the inky darkness from without seemed to spill into her mind, and she knew her ordeal would soon end. She felt her entire body stiffen against its restraints and begin to undulate in the jackknife movements of a tonic-clonic seizure, the last bequest from a nervous system gone mad for want of air.

No white light awaited her. No final flash of memories comforted her. Rather the hurt subsided, and she seemed to take leave of her body. But instead of rising peacefully upward, she stayed suspended in the water looking down at herself, watching her remains continue to jerk through the dark in a desperate, never-ending dance.

*   *   *

The white glare hung just over the horizon, the way extraterrestrial events are portrayed in movies, then became very ordinary as the headlamps crested a low hill, and the dark shape of the vehicle drove slowly toward Mark at a cautious speed equal to his own.

Let it be her.

He hadn't met any other vehicle on the road.

Sure enough, as they closed the gap between them, he made out the familiar shape of her station wagon.

Thank God, he thought, relief flooding through him.

He flicked his high beams at her.

And saw two men driving.

"What the hell!" he yelled.

He must have taken them by surprise as well; the night immediately lit up with the red illumination of brake lights, and the station wagon skidded out of control.

Caught in the glare of his lights, they both gaped at him, their features coarse, white, and garish as they glided closer.

He saw the man on the passenger side reach down and come up with a gun.

Mark floored the accelerator. The much-heavier Jeep rocketed forward and smashed into them head-on. For the second time in a week he was surrounded by the impact of crumpling fenders and exploding air bags, but this time he was ready. Gripping the steering wheel, he'd pushed himself well back in his seat and barely felt the blow against his chest. Better still, his windshield stayed intact.

He held his foot on the accelerator. His tires whined, the Jeep shook, but shuddered ahead, pushing the lighter car before it. Not that its two occupants were about to cause him much trouble. They must have been the kind not to wear seat belts. Both looked to be slumped on the dash, asleep on big white pillows. One had blood pouring out his nose.

Mark kept the pedal to the floor, aimed for the ditch, and, continuing to shove Lucy's car until its rear end lifted up over a snowbank, stranded it so nothing short of a tow truck would set it free. Throwing the Jeep into reverse, he shot back to the right side of the highway. Despite the body damage, it still drove fine. Sick with fright over what they'd done to Lucy, he slammed the gearshift into drive, ready to speed away and find her at the home. But wait. She might be in the back of the car tied up on the floor. Or they could have already taken her somewhere else.

Shit!

Grabbing his bat, he jumped out of the cab, ran to the driver's side of the car. A quick glance in the back, and he knew they didn't have Lucy with them. He wrenched open the door. Neither man moved, but both were still breathing. The gun he'd seen before lay on the floor between them. He didn't know what type, but its stubby silencer on the end of the barrel made it look like something James Bond would carry.

He reached across the knees of the one closest to him and grabbed it. Then he went through their pockets. No more weapons, but the roll of duct tape he found would be useful. And in the second man's pockets he'd found what he wanted most of all—a cell phone from the bad guys. It at least wouldn't have a tap on it.

In the minutes it took to bind their hands and feet, the driver started to moan and come around. The passenger hadn't budged, his respirations growing increasingly gurgly, and from the lie of his head, the neck looked a little twisted.

Mark grabbed the driver by the collar of his ski suit, pinched him hard on the earlobe to speed his ascent from the depths, and yelled, "What have you done to Lucy?"

The guy opened an eyelid. "Go see for yourself, asshole."

Mark balled his fists and yanked the creep forward, as close to killing someone as he'd ever been. But Lucy mattered more. He threw the scum back, picked up the cell phone, and roused a very sleepy Dan Evans. "Don't ask questions. Bring the cavalry—"

"Mark?"

"I'm east of the the entrance to the home for unwed mothers. You'll find two of Braden's killers bound and gagged in Lucy's car. One's alive, the other—handle his neck with care if you ever want to question him."

"Wha'—"

"Hurry! They've done something to Lucy." He hesitated. Should he assume the worst? Better safe than sorry. "Get an air ambulance to the grounds of the building, pronto!"

"My God! Right!" He finally sounded fully awake.

Two minutes later Mark pulled his battered Jeep up in front of the gate, slipped the gun into his pocket, and yanked the headlamp over his ski hat. Quietly, he climbed the gate and started to run, entering the darkness of the forest. He didn't turn on his light in case he'd give himself away. His insides seized with dread at what he'd find up ahead. Glancing at the luminous dial of his watch, he read *5:01.*

New York City Hospital

Earl awoke with a jump, and immediately realized he'd dozed off. "Damn Demerol," he muttered, glancing at his watch. Christ, he'd been asleep well over three hours.

Had someone slipped in here during that time?

He quickly eyed his IV bottle and did the calculation to estimate the amount that should remain. The fluid was at the line marked *250 ccs*. Exactly where it should be. But anybody could have injected a needleful of God knows what into him or the bag. Yet he felt the same as before.

His stomach sent a shard of pain from his belly button through to his spine. No change there. Wait a minute. His arms and legs weren't quite so listless. The potassium was kicking in.

He glanced over at his monitor.

The extra beats were less frequent.

If he'd been given something, it hadn't hit him yet.

To keep his mind off doomsday scenarios, he fetched his diagram from where it had slid off the bed and got back to work. Just before he'd conked out, he'd started adding to his list of existing suspects all the people, especially doctors, who either had offered him food or drink between Saturday and Tuesday or come near enough in the hospital to have tampered with his IV, or both. Though he'd accepted the possibility of accomplices being involved, he still didn't buy the idea of his having been contaminated at the funeral or in the cafeteria by rogue waiters or kitchen staff. Too messy.

That meant he started with Lena Downie. She'd brought tea to him a few times on Monday. The woman had no medical knowledge other than what she read in charts, and talked way too much ever to be chosen as an accomplice. Nevertheless, he wrote down her name at the side of the page.

Next there was Tanya, who'd made him coffee Tuesday morning. Of course he'd since put his life in her hands, but he put her down as well.

There were only two doctors he could specifically pinpoint. Again he felt there wasn't much point, but wrote *Melanie Collins* and *Tommy Leannis*.

Except he'd already pegged his drink with Tommy as taking place after he'd been infected.

He added *Samantha McShane* to the list because of the coffee she'd served him when he'd been at her apartment on Wednesday morning. But that, too, had been outside the time frame for the organism to incubate. Besides, he'd already dismissed her as lacking the skills to be The Ghost on her own.

Which left Melanie and her martinis.

Great. He'd landed his own physician.

He pulled the covers around him, finding the air in the room clammy. Whether he was getting a fever, or the heating normally reached its nadir at this hour, he didn't know. It was the quietest he'd ever heard the building, the usual rush of air through the ventilation system having been shut down. Out in the hallway a distant click echoed as if someone had closed a mausoleum door, and the squeak of rubber soles rushed by his room, then silence returned except for his own breathing and the occasional snarl of his intestines.

He doodled on his sheet of paper, making certain he hadn't forgotten somebody who'd slipped him a nibble of food or sip of a drink. He couldn't come up with a single other person. Only Melanie fit all the criteria.

"Yeah, right," he muttered, his sarcasm venting the frustration of having drawn such a blank. She probably infected him with that blue lady she served at her penthouse. Fixed his IV herself, too, so she could add the bicarb. And the bloods, what better way to falsify his results than draw them herself, then substitute them with someone else's.

He liked indulging in irony. It was often the most direct way to show up the absurdity of a bullshit idea and dispense with it—a valuable exercise in a busy ER where fuzzy thinking could be deadly.

Except this idea didn't succumb. Instead of wilting under ridicule, it stayed in his head, nagging at him.

"Don't be absurd," he said out loud, trying to clear his mind and think straight, figuring the combination of pain, weakness, and Demerol were taking their toll.

Yet the notion stuck. Like a bad tune caught in a loop of memory, it kept going round and round. Because none of the other players he'd listed had the means and opportunity to do what had been done to him.

His little ditty didn't ring so ironic all of a sudden.

No, he told himself. To think Melanie could be The Ghost was nuts. Insane. Had to be. For starters, what about motive? Why would she try to kill him? His investigation into Kelly's murder didn't have anything to do with her.

Besides, the reason she had means and opportunity wasn't of her doing.

She'd served him drinks on Tuesday because he'd wanted to see her then. She had access to his IV and took his bloods because he'd insisted in ER that she take care of him. To make anything more of it was plain paranoid.

Unless she'd used the situations he'd given her to her own advantage, suggested a perverse voice from the insolent part of his mind that had first played devil's advocate by questioning the tooth fairy, the Easter bunny, and Santa Claus when he was aged five. It had been getting him to the bottom of things ever since, and he ignored it at his peril.

Melanie had offered him that blue drink, topping his glass off from a separate pitcher, then washed her hands as thoroughly as if she were preparing for surgery. She'd arrived in his hospital room, carrying his IV bag that she'd already prepared elsewhere, despite everything she'd needed, including potassium vials, being in the medication bins at his beside. She took his bloods, slipping the full tubes into her lab coat pocket without labeling them first. All little details, none of which proved anything, but every one of them giving his suspicions free rein.

He sat huddled in the bedclothes, stunned by all the unthinkable things that swept so easily to mind, now that his normal checks against imagining the worst about her were breached.

What about motive—a motive that would make her commit murder to stop his investigation?

It couldn't be because she herself had killed Kelly.

That idea was lunacy. She'd had no reason to murder her. Of course there'd been jealousy on Melanie's part, Kelly being such a star. But surely that wouldn't have been enough to commit murder over. Besides, around the time Kelly was killed, Melanie had already begun to blossom as a doctor. It must have been months earlier when she aced the Bessie McDonald case that started to build up her confidence. So people were well into making a fuss over her and her own work by that summer. He vividly recalled how she'd basked in all the attention. At times she carried it too far, the way she evidently craved and reveled in adulation. Judging from her grandstanding with the residents these last few days, he could see that nothing had changed on that front. But back then, as far as he could remember, after achieving her own moments in the spotlight, she threw off the old resentments about Kelly. If anything, he remembered Kelly growing cool to Melanie. She also seemed to find Melanie's newfound enjoyment of being in the center of things during teaching rounds a bit off-putting. But he'd never heard words about it between the two women.

Yet a vague pattern, a sense of déjà vu, a feeling of being on the verge of grasping an elusive link-it-all-together piece swirled as illusively as smoke through his thoughts.

He stared at the shadows cast by his night-light. They filled the end wall like ink blots, his own shape at their center, but failed to offer the revelations he sought.

He closed his eyes.

Images of Melanie at the foot of his bed putting on her show melded with memories of her strutting her stuff at teaching rounds twenty-seven years ago. They lasted but a second, only to be displaced by scenes of the intrusive Samantha McShane playing out one of her signature it's-all-about-me performances.

"Oh, my God," he whispered.

A dreadful sense of isolation enveloped him and filled his ears with a hollow ringing.

5:02 A.M.
Hampton Junction

Even in the shelter of the trees the snow fell so heavily it practically caused a whiteout, but Mark raced through it, slipping as he went, the previously made depressions in the trail already beginning to fill in. He ignored the noise of his boots crunching on the snow, thinking only of reaching Lucy. His breathing quickened more from fear than exertion, and he sucked in cold flakes with each gasp. They choked him, then burned at the back of his throat. Rounding the bend, he peered ahead to the swirling luminous opening that led to the clearing and poured on the speed.

His eyes accommodated to the darker forest, and he emerged to find the night cast in more visible shades of gray and silver. Immediately he saw two figures huddled side by side near the front of the building. They were peering down at something. His heart leapt.

"What'd you forget?" one of them called. Whether they glanced his way, he couldn't tell. It was too dark to see their faces or clothing.

Which meant they couldn't see his. But they'd obviously heard him coming. His making no attempt to hide his arrival must have inadvertently tricked them into assuming one of their buddies had returned. It gave him an edge. All this he realized in an instant. And his plan to exploit that edge came just as fast.

Bluff and get closer.

He gave a wave, as if signaling them to keep quiet, and started forward, his head down the way a man might walk in order to watch his footing. He had no strategy of attack other than cross the hundred yards and see what they were looking at, then trust to instinct and reflex. He tried to remember how his height measured against the two he'd left in the car. The driver at least had appeared to be tall, but there'd be no mistaking that Elvis suit of his. As soon as Mark got close enough to see details of their outfits, he'd have to make his move.

The pair kept their attention on whatever lay at their feet.

He quickened his pace, pulling the gun from his pocket.

He hated firearms of any sort, but as coroner he'd seen his share— enough varieties of weapons to find the safety on the one in his pocket. Feeling for it with his index finger, he clicked it off.

He'd closed the distance to about eighty yards when he made out a black shape at their feet. It appeared round and far too flat to be a body.

At sixty he could see it was an opening in the ground.

The well.

His stomach clamped down so tightly he almost threw up.

He broke into a run, watching their backs.

At forty he stopped and took aim. "Freeze," he shrieked, all his rage at what they might have done to Lucy funneled into his voice.

The two men spun around.

"What the fu—"

"Shit!"

The one on the left grabbed for the inside of his jacket.

Mark shot him first, aiming for his legs.

The man screamed, grabbed his crotch, and doubled over. His partner immediately took off toward the building, dodging and weaving.

Sprinting forward, Mark fired on the run, still aiming low. Each shot sounded no louder than opening the twist top on a beer bottle, but the pistol gave a heavy kick. He missed every time. "Stop!" he yelled and drew a bead on his quarry's back. Before he could pull the trigger, his target darted around the corner and out of sight.

The man on the ground continued to howl as he writhed in a ball. "You fuck! You goddamned fucking bastard!" The snow under him rapidly turned dark.

Mark knew he wouldn't be causing trouble anytime soon, if ever. As for helping him—not even an issue until he had Lucy safe. He nevertheless paused to retrieve what the guy had been reaching for and dropped—a gun identical to the first—then raced by him. "Lucy!" he cried, sliding to a stop at the edge of the opening. Bits of snow dropped off into nothing as he teetered over the hole, and his stomach heaved to his throat. He snapped on his headlamp. Water gleamed back at him from forty feet below, the surface as shiny and black as oil. A white rope trailed into it from a large coil that lay half-buried in slush. He grabbed it up and started to reel it in, his worst fears lurching out of control.

But it came too freely. There mustn't be anything on the other end. How could he get to her? Or maybe she wasn't even in there—

It snapped taut, and he could barely haul it up any farther.

"Oh, God no." He choked back a sob, tightened his grip, and strained to pull as hard as he could. But his hold kept slipping on an icy film that had coated the water-soaked nylon. He looped the rope around his hands, only to have it bite into his skin and cut off the circulation. Yet he raised the load, hand over hand, the effort making his head spin. Every few seconds he glanced over to the building for any sign of the man who had run off. He kept tabs on the whereabouts of the bleeder by his shrieks, though they were growing weaker.

His forearms vibrated as he taxed the limits of their strength, and he whispered, "Lucy!" over and over, as if calling her name could coax her to him, until the trembling stopped and he managed to pull some more.

Her body broke the surface with an echoing splash and the clink of chains. He didn't dare get close enough to the edge to see her for fear of losing his footing and sliding in himself. He tugged all the harder, but managed only another four or five feet before the weight overpowered him. "Lucy!" he sobbed, irrational with fright, knowing she'd never answer. The noise of water streaming back into the well sounded like a dozen running faucets.

Without buoyancy to help him, he could barely hold her. His finger joints locked with the cold; his arms shook from the extreme effort. The rope started to slip from his grasp.

"No!" he screamed, twisting it yet another time around his arms. Even his feet slid as he tried to get traction to support the weight.

He quickly looked around for something to anchor her to. One of the medium-sized trees stood about twenty feet away. Feeding the rope through his palms, he managed to make his way over to the trunk and, using it like a winch, circled it three times, then tied off on it without letting her drop any lower.

In seconds he was back at the well, peering over the edge with his light. His knees buckled at the sight. She hung by her heels below him, her arms bound, her head trailing lifelessly a foot above above the water, her hair pooled on the surface like black seaweed.

With no thought but to reach her, he straddled the rope with his back to the well, grabbed it with both hands, and let himself over the edge. He intended to rappel down the stone lining, but with the ice he slid most of the way, scraping the walls, abrading his palms, then ricocheting off her legs before plunging into the frigid water. He bellowed at the shock of the cold, but the water closed over him, swallowing the sound.

He had the presence of mind to clamp a hand over his headlamp so it wouldn't come off, and quickly fought his way back to the surface. The beam never so much as flickered. Immediately he saw her face above him, upside down, covered in a silver glaze. He reached up to it, and at his touch thin flakes of ice fell off her like scales. Underneath, her skin taut with the gray-white pallor of a corpse, her eyes looked made of glass and stared off to one side, lifeless as they glistened through the remaining film of frost.

His sobs, unstoppable now, broke from deep within him, like retching, and racked him from head to toe. "Oh, God, please no" he cried, his mind hurtling between praying for a miracle and knowing she was dead.

With one hand he grabbed on to the chain that dangled from her heels into the water. At its lower end, a few feet under the surface, he felt the anchor they'd used as a weight and knelt on its flanges, bringing his head level to hers. With his free arm he clutched her to him. The meaty horror of what he held blasted all rational thought out of his brain, and his thinking collapsed in on itself like an imploding star. Yet a fragment of him still rebelled, refused against all logic to accept the clammy reality in his arms. He summoned enough of his training to slip his fingertips along the side of her neck and push them into skin that had the consistency of cold Plasticine. The vessels within lay lifeless as he counted off the seconds. Just hours earlier he'd felt them pump with excitement as he'd explored every dimple and depression of her with his mouth.

He slammed his fist into the middle of her chest three times, then palpated over the carotid again. Sometimes the impact of a "chest thump" could restart a fibrillating heart.

He knew it to be a useless gesture, but had to try. The desperate ploy extended hope by a few more seconds and kept him in a universe where she might be alive just a little longer.

He'd reached twelve when he felt a solitary impulse.

Could his mind have imagined the absent beat? Perhaps it had been a twitch or throb of an artery in his own finger.

He swallowed his cries, stilled his breathing, and waited, once again counting seconds, the spaces between each number stretching to an eternity.

Another beat.

He waited for a third.

Again a sluggish rise pushed up against his fingers.

Instantly he had his lips on hers. They felt like wet clay, but he molded his to form a seal, and blew. The resistance of her lungs made air squeak out the side of his mouth, but he saw her chest rise. As he continued to give her breaths, he mentally ticked off everything he could remember about hypothermia.

People had survived up to an hour submerged in ice water. He'd no idea how long she'd been under.

That she'd recovered a pulse at all was better than a full-out cardiac arrest. The slow rate might even be protective, reducing her heart's oxygen requirements. And cold could lower the metabolism of her other vital organs so that they might survive the subsequent reduction in blood flow. As for her lungs, her airway ought to have protected them from filling with water, seizing shut at the first influx of liquid, the same reflex that kept fluid out of the lungs in the womb.

His mind raced, dredging up every hopeful scrap he could summon, then clung to the science of it. His teeth chattered, and he shook with such force that all his muscles, including those in his vocal cords, snapped into spasm. Each time he exhaled into her lungs, a plaintive, tremulous moan issued from his throat, the mournful sound filling her chest, then echoing toward the pale, barely visible opening above their heads. He listened for the staccato noise of helicopter blades or the wail of police sirens over his own pathetic keening, but to no avail.

Yet he continued to deliver air to her, puff after puff, settling into the rhythm despite being half-submerged and clinging to the chains with one hand, supporting her head with the other, all the while precariously perched on the anchor.

He paused between breaths to quickly shine his beam of light into her pupils. From the middle of her deathlike stare came a slow sluggish constriction. *Yes!* She still had life in her brain.

He even went so far as to lay out a treatment plan for when the air ambulance arrived: *Intubate and ventilate her. Slowly warm her body core with heated oxygen and warm IVs. Raise her temperature no more than two degrees Fahrenheit an hour as per protocol.* Visualizing this ritual made it seem closer at hand. And at the hospital, if need be, they could even put her on a heart-lung machine to warm her blood directly.

I can bring her back, he told himself. *She can survive this.*

Such were the mental games he played to keep despair at bay and blot out his more objective clinical voice that told him nothing would work.

And I'll protect her from overeager residents, he continued in the same vein, filling his mind with anything to avoid thinking she was finished.

*Keep them from loading her up with adrenaline and atropine, that'll be the trick—*He stopped in midthought.

The water crept up his chest, and the top of her head edged closer to the surface.

They were sinking.

Their weight was stretching the nylon rope.

His panic surged.

Within seconds he felt the icy water at his neck and watched it inch past her hairline toward her eyes.

He got off his knees and crouched on the flanges, then pulled her to him, trying to bend her at the waist so her back was on his lap and she'd be faceup. That way he could keep her head above water and still give her mouth-to-mouth ventilation. He moved her into position, but her entire body, already stiff with cold, wouldn't flex properly. When he bent down to deliver another lungful of air, the waterline lapped over her face.

Where was Dan?

What if the pilots couldn't fly because of the storm, or took too long, or couldn't find this godforsaken place?

Rapidly losing strength, his teeth chattered so fiercely now that they clicked against hers. He tried to recall what his textbooks said about survival times in frigid water as far as staying conscious, but his memory no longer functioned that well, a sign that his body heat was quickly dropping.

Choking, he pulled her higher onto his thighs.

Again he scanned the pale circle and strained to hear the sounds of rotors or approaching sirens.

Nothing—only smaller circles of snow reeling and floating in total silence.

Come soon, he prayed, and filled her lungs yet again.

The ghostly opening peered down on them, offering no more hope than a malevolent, empty eye.

5:15 A.M.
New York City Hospital

Earl had to escape. The one person he couldn't defend himself against was Melanie Collins.

He tried to call Janet. If anything happened to him, he wanted someone to know the truth. But he found his phone line dead.

He immediately summoned his nurse.

"Dr. Collins's latest orders are for complete rest," Mrs. White, his cherry-cheeked angel informed him, delivering the news with an emphatic stare over the top of her tiny square-rimmed spectacles. "She phoned at midnight to check how you were doing. When she learned you'd been making late-night calls and complaining about palpitations, she read the riot act. No ingoing or outgoing communications, period."

"Now wait a minute—"

"Told us she'd put you out and intubate you if she had to, just so you'd get some rest."

"No way!"

"Talk it over with her. She'll be here at seven for morning rounds—you can set your clock by her."

She turned to leave.

And if he told this red-cheeked minder that Melanie Collins might be trying to kill him?

What makes you think a crazy thing like that? she would ask.

Because Melanie Collins may have killed Kelly McShane.

And why would she have done such a thing?

Because as Melanie basked in the adulation she garnered for nailing hard-to-diagnose illnesses, Kelly must have sensed the same all-about-me afterglow she'd seen her mother exude when people gushed over her for taking care of Kelly's mysterious diseases.

"So?"

So Kelly realized Melanie made patients sick for the purpose of playing the hero later.

At which point Mrs. White would report he'd gone paranoid, giving Melanie the perfect opportunity to shoot him full of major tranquilizers and summon six big orderlies to tie him down if he protested.

Better he just walk out the door, then sort out the details once he got beyond her power.

He sat on the side of the bed and gingerly tested his legs.

They wobbled as he stood, but held him.

He took a few trial steps, and they nearly buckled.

No matter.

He turned off the alarms on the monitor, shut it down, and disconnected himself. How long would it take the night nurses to see his screen on their central console had gone blank? A while, he hoped.

Next he ripped out the needles in his arm, the IV bag being almost empty. Hoping he'd received enough potassium to at least stabilize his heart, he pressed on the puncture site with his thumb to staunch the flow of blood and hesitantly walked over to the bureau where they'd put his clothes. He started to dress, first pulling on his socks.

"Going somewhere, Dr. Garnet?" said a man's voice at the door, and Charles Braden III stepped into his room.

Primed on adrenaline, pain, and no sleep, Earl reacted like a cornered animal. "What the hell are you doing here?" he demanded. He backed up to the bed and slid his hand under the covers, his fingers closing around the fistful of syringes he'd planted, needle first, into the mattress. His revelation about Melanie might change some of his ideas about how the Bradens fitted in the picture, but not enough that he suddenly felt safe around them.

Charles started toward him.

"I'd stay where you are!" Earl said.

The man stopped in midstride. "Why, I just intended to sit down—"

"Tell me what you want."

In the dim light, the steel-brush silver of Charles's hair made him seem more formidable, as if he were bristling with quills. "All right, but perhaps *you* better sit down. What I'm going to say will come as a bit of a shock, and you don't look so good."

Earl stayed leaning against the bed, his hand still clutched around his makeshift weapon. "I'm fine where I am."

Braden shrugged, and sank his hands deep into the pockets of the white coat he wore over his suit as if he were still a practicing doctor. "I'm here to inform you that late yesterday afternoon Dr. Tommy Leannis approached my son with the news that you were the man who went off with Kelly in a taxi the night before her disappearance. Is this true?"

Earl felt the blood drain from his head.

He'd end up being handed to the cops for Kelly's murder after all—by Charles and Chaz Braden, goddamn it. Exotic theories about Melanie Collins wouldn't protect him now, especially since he had no proof other than a used IV bag with bicarb in it and a bunch of false-normal potassium readings. The rest was all just speculation.

Instinctively he tried to bluff. "What are you talking about—"

"Don't play with me. I've already heard your denials. Leannis gave my son a tape of a conversation in which you went on at length about it not being true."

Earl swallowed, his mouth going drier by the second, his heart giving the inside of his ribs another going over. Like a man just shot who tries to fathom the damage, he cast about in his mind for what he'd said to that weasel Leannis, dreading he may have let something slip that would incriminate himself.

"Sure you don't want to sit down?" Braden said. "You're starting to look worse than when I came in."

"No, I'm fine, except I can't seriously believe you'd take what Leannis said—"

"I also heard the same allegation from the biggest gossip in the hospital, Lena Downie in medical records."

Earl's face grew warm. If that woman was blabbing about it, he'd be the talk of NYCH in no time. Whether the police believed the story or not, his credibility, especially now when he needed it most, would be toast. "Oh, my God."

"What's even more interesting is who told her."

Earl felt another surge of pain shoot through his gut. He fought to stay on his feet, a prickle of cold sweat sticking his hospital gown to his skin. "Told her?"

"Yeah. Turns out it's the same person who gave the notion to Tommy Leannis."

"But you said Melanie Collins did that."

"Right. She picked him because, as everyone in the hospital knows, Leannis is a brown-nosing fool. He'd try anything to curry favor with our family in the hope our influence might throw some fresh meat to that cut-and-tuck business he has the nerve to call the practice of medicine. She probably figured he'd come running to us in some sleazy manner with the news, and he didn't disappoint. Telling Lena Downie as well would be Melanie's way of assuring a more general distribution."

"You mean—"

"Melanie Collins is setting you up to take the blame for Kelly's murder. Not that I figure she intends to let you live long enough to go to trial. Smear you by innuendo as the killer, I suspect, is her plan, then you conveniently die of some apparent complication from your infection, and the case is closed. Nobody's going to look too closely at loose ends when the prime suspect is dead, especially in a twenty-seven-year-old murder."

Earl wasn't sure he'd heard correctly.

"Setting me up? You mean you don't believe I did it. And you know what she's doing to me?"

"How she specifically intends to make you die, no. But I've been through enough of her charts in the last few days to get a pretty good idea of her repertoire. She's a regular alchemist when it comes to fiddling with drugs and eliciting their side effects, altering sugars, playing with acid–base balance, shifting potassium and sodium levels up and down like elevators—"

"Wait a minute. You make it sound like there's been a lot more cases than the two Kelly discovered."

"The woman's been setting up her 'triumphs' for a couple of decades. Glory-kills, I suppose you could call the ones who didn't make it. Deaths didn't really matter to her, as long as she got kudos for nailing the diagnosis."

"My God. But how did you get onto her?"

"I started with the same two charts you did, and saw the same patterns. I also had access to her student evaluations. I remembered she had been something less than a star during her rotation in obstetrics. My staff nick-named her 'Fumbles' they were so afraid she'd drop a baby. I also looked up the other departmental assessments of her. Borderline. So how does someone so mediocre get so good? I asked myself."

Earl listened with a mixture of relief and wariness. "And what about the rest of the story?" he asked. Braden seemed about to clear him, but would he help Kelly's lover, or make him pay?

"Obviously, Kelly came to the same conclusions about the digoxin cases that you and I did." Braden said with no hesitation. "She confronted Melanie, and Melanie killed her to avoid getting caught." He continued to stand there, his hands in his pockets, white coat immaculate, looking like he'd stepped out of a fashion magazine, at five-thirty in the morning. Something didn't add up. "Why did you tell me this now?"

Braden looked at him as if he were crazy. "Because my son and I only just now finished going through Melanie's files. We've been at it since yesterday morning, and wanted to make sure we were right before saying anything. I came right up because I figured your life might be in danger. And so did you, from the looks of it when I got here. Weren't you about to escape her clutches?"

Sounded reasonable. And he should be grateful to the man. Why didn't he feel that way? Instead, he had the inkling he was being manipulated. "What do we do now?" he asked, playing along while trying to sort out his doubts.

"First thing this morning I'll call the CEO of the hospital and the president of the medical school. This is going to be a tabloid special, and they'll want to get all their legal ducks in a row. Then we'll call the police, and they'll arrest Collins. I want it over with fast, before anything else tragic happens. I tried to warn Mark Roper the other night that I was onto something and requested that he slow down to give me a couple of days. But he's such a hothead, just like his father. Insisted on plowing full speed ahead with his investigation."

The more the man talked, the more Earl grew wary. Charles Braden still had a lot of questions to answer about his role in other matters, from the demise of Cam Roper, whom Braden had just called a real hothead, to a recent gas explosion. And he appeared to be in an unseemly hurry to rein in Mark. In fact, Earl just realized an obvious hole in Braden's story.

"Tell me, Charles, how did you know which charts I first looked at in this case?"

Braden studied him a few seconds, his blue stare now cold as a polar sea. "Why, Lena Downie must have told me. You know what a chatterbox she is."

Really? Earl thought. That would be easy enough to check out. "Why I asked is that Mark Roper said someone sneaked into his house and went through his father's file on Kelly. The M and M reports on those two patients that started this whole paper chase were in there. Would you know anything about that break-in?"

Braden didn't bat an eye. "You, know, Earl, after what I've just done for you, I don't necessarily want a show of gratitude, but I would expect you to have the common courtesy not to make gratuitous insinuations about the whole Kelly affair, especially after all the harm you did to my son's—"

"She told me it was Chaz who wrecked any feelings she had for him."

Braden said nothing this time, but his body seemed to tense beneath the gleaming white coat.

In the menace of that silence, Earl teetered between opposing instincts.

One urged him to probe further. Demand what kind of game Charles had been playing at the birthing center. Shake him up with the fact that Mark Roper had some interesting questions regarding statistics for the place. Confront him about the death of Victor Feldt and what it had to do with Nucleus Laboratories, executive health plans, or genetic screenings on siblings with a family history of cancer—anything to provoke an angry outburst and a revealing slip.

But self-preservation made Earl cautious. Whatever Charles had been up to, trying to spook him with bravado could be very dangerous. Better to outmaneuver him. "Sorry, Charles, I didn't mean to insinuate you had anything to do with the break-in at Mark's, and I'm most grateful for the warning about Melanie, believe me. As for my hurtful comment regarding Chaz and Kelly, it was inexcusable. Please, accept my apology, and put it down to the morphine talking."

Braden continued to watch him.

Earl felt the man see right through his wooden attempt to make peace. "Look, I spoke out of line," he added. "Let me make it up to you by helping out with Melanie's capture. After all, that's the important thing, right? I'll get back into bed, so when she makes her morning rounds nothing will tip her off that we're onto her. You start rousting the administration. With me corroborating what you and Chaz are saying, they'll be more ready to believe us." His real plan? Pretend to cooperate, then, once Braden left, skedaddle the hell out of the hospital to the nearest police station. Now that he had Melanie pegged, let the cops figure out the rest.

The rigidity under the lab coat lessened. Still, Braden seemed to be in the limbo of deciding something. "You're right about going back to bed and Melanie finding you there," he finally said, turning and walking toward the door. "But we both know you don't intend to hang around, and I can't allow that. Better we sedate you." He stuck his head into the hallway and yelled, "Nurse!"

Earl broke into a cold sweat. "Wait a minute! What if Melanie does something to me while I'm under? You yourself said it would take a few hours to convince the police . . ."

Braden looked at him, his eyes almost sorrowful.

My God. He's going to let her kill me! Earl's mouth went dry "I'll tell the nurses what you're doing." His voice sounded like a croak. "You won't get away with it."

Braden glanced back out in the hallway, apparently unconcerned.

"I'll say that you're under investigation for murder," Earl added, judging his chances of knocking him over and making a run for it.

Braden shook his head as if enduring a great weariness. "You must be mad, the morphine no doubt."

"What about Mark Roper? He already thinks you smothered deformed infants and buried their bodies on the grounds of your home for unwed mothers." Earl raised his voice to make sure any approaching nurses would hear the accusations. Whether they believed him or not, he hoped to at least make them pause before carrying out the man's orders. But his own skepticism about Braden being capable of infanticide had vanished. "He's going to the police about it this morning. When he finds out you visited me, he'll suspect you arranged my death."

Braden stared at him in amazement. "The grounds? Oh, my God, Dr. Garnet. Even if I were the monster you're suggesting, I wouldn't be fool enough to leave human remains on the grounds of an abandoned building."

Braden ought to be sweating bricks by now if he'd done any part of what Mark had accused him of, Earl thought. Instead he remained calm, practically purring. Could he have already moved the bodies? Son of a bitch! Or he'd never buried anything there at all. Of course. He'd be too smart to leave that kind of evidence behind.

Mark's account of what happened with Braden in the library flashed to mind, and a sickening realization swept through Earl. Mark had been on the losing end of a game he probably didn't even realize Braden had been playing. Because not only would Charles have been too smart to leave bones lying about where they could be found, he wouldn't have said the suggestive things that he had about smotherings if he'd truly wanted to avoid such atrocious allegations. Instead, it almost seemed he'd invited them. Why?

"Nurse!" Braden bellowed a second time. "Nurse, come quickly."

"Now hold on—"

"Nurse!"

Earl heard the sound of running feet in the hallway.

Mrs. White bolted through the door, her cheeks aflame.

"I'm afraid Dr. Garnet's having a psychotic episode, probably from the drugs—"

"What are you doing out of bed—" she said, striding toward him. "And what happened to your IV?"

"Nurse, I'm fine—"

"I blame myself, Nurse," Braden continued, his voice serene with the quiet authority of one used to being in charge. "I barged in here on a grievous family matter between Dr. Garnet and my son—well, let's just say I was upset."

"He came here to set me up—"

"This is what I mean about paranoia. We had words, but then Dr. Garnet began to spout the most bizarre accusations, about me murdering babies, and burying their bodies—"

"He's lying! The man is under suspicion for murder. Coroner Mark Roper will verify everything I said—" Earl stopped, realizing too late he'd whipped his hand out from under the covers and was brandishing the glinting points of a half dozen needles in their faces.

Mrs. White screamed.

"My God!" Braden said, recoiling in horror.

Another nurse appeared at the door. One glance and she bellowed, "Orderlies! We've got a code forty-four!"

From his residency days, Earl recognized the call. Within sixty seconds a herd of young men wearing white would stampede into the room with enough Haldol and tie-downs to immobilize an elephant.

"Put down the needles, sir!" the nurse at the doorway said.

Braden and Mrs. White backed away from him.

At the very least he had to get to a phone and call Janet.

"Back off," he screamed at the one blocking the way out.

She stood her ground. "Don't do this, sir."

"All I want to do is call my wife. No need for drugs. No tie-downs. Just let me call my home."

"Absolutely, sir. You can make the call as soon as you put down the needles."

He knew the tone and the routine. He'd used it himself many times. When a patient threatens staff, promise him anything, then hit him with everything, all in the name of preventing anyone from getting hurt. There'd be no stopping what he'd set in motion. And no calls.

"I'm getting to a phone," he said, advancing toward her. "I won't hurt you."

She retreated a few steps, the look of terror in her young eyes horrible to see.

He lunged by her and raced down the hall toward a stand of public phone booths.

His legs nearly went from under him.

"Stop!" he heard Braden yell.

Still brandishing his needles, he ran up, grabbed the nearest receiver, and punched in *0* plus his number.

Immediately he was surrounded by a growing group of orderlies, the two nurses from his room, and Braden. They all shouted instructions at him and each other.

"Put down the needles."

"Watch it."

"Who the hell's he calling?"

The phone chirped through the long-distance dialing and rang Janet's cellular.

The semicircle closed in.

He made wide sweeping arcs with his weapon, and they shrank away from him. He was bluffing of course, and ready to drop them the instant anyone rushed him, but they didn't know that.

The yelling continued.

"We got to jump him."

"You jump him. Those needles could be contaminated."

"Why not wait and see who he's calling?"

"I advise you to get him now!" Braden thundered.

The second ring sounded.

Be at home, Janet, and not off in the delivery room.

More orderlies arrived, tie-down straps in hand.

A third nurse appeared with a large syringe.

A shock of red hair made its way through the crowd.

The next ring broke off with a click.

She'd answered. "Janet, help me. Melanie Collins is trying to kill me, and Charles Braden—"

"The person you are calling is not available . . ."

No!

Over that he heard, "You have a collect call from . . ."

"Janet! Help—"

"I'm sorry, but your collect call has not been accepted . . ."

At that second some hero in the crowd dived at his legs. As he tumbled to the ground he dropped his handful of syringes to one side, careful not to jab anyone, and went limp.

His intention was lost on the swarm that grabbed him. They hoisted him on a gurney, held him in place, and tied him down.

The nurse with the syringe approached. The rest hung back, like onlookers at an accident.

Earl seized on an idea. "You can't give me that," he said to the one with the needle.

"And why not?" She lifted a flap of his gown and anointed his butt with an alcohol swab.

"Because I've a critically low potassium."

"What!" She pulled up just before the tip of the needle hit skin.

He was thinking clearly now. "Low potassium and major tranquilizers don't mix," he told her. "Causes cardiac conduction problems, as if I didn't already have enough of those already. Ask any doctor." He hadn't made it up. And in the time it took her to sort it out, he might convince the other nurses not to give him anything.

"He's right, ma'am," said a male voice from somewhere behind her.

Earl recognized Dr. Roy's voice.

Mrs. White appeared at the side of her colleague who had the needle and showed her Earl's chart. "Better listen. There was some kind of screwup with his potassium last night. The lab called about it."

The one with the needle looked disappointed. "Oh, man, I hate it when we have doctors as patients . . ."

As they second-guessed themselves, a new volley of painful spasms erupted in his stomach. Gritting his teeth, he nevertheless pressed his case. "Nurse, Mrs. White, I don't need sedation at all—"

"Will someone medicate this man, or should I do it myself?" Charles Braden interrupted. He stepped up to Mrs. White and took the chart from her. "Here, he's got a standing order for morphine. Give him that."

Oh, God, not again. I'll be a sitting duck for Melanie.

As Charles walked away, Mrs. White readily trotted off to the medication cupboard.

"Please! Call my wife! Dr. Janet Graceton. She's in the case room at St. Paul's Hospital in Buffalo."

No one paid him the slightest attention.

The crowd started to thin out. He saw Dr. Roy's bushy red hair disappearing down the hall. He had another idea. "Dr. Roy. Call Tanya Wozcek. Tell her what's happened. Then do the DONT."

The people who had started to wheel the stretcher back to his room looked at him as if he were crazy.

"Who's Tanya Wozcek?" he heard someone whisper.

"I think she's a nurse up on geriatric?"

"Sounds like that's where this guy is headed."

Twenty minutes later he felt his brain had been packed in a SlushPuppie. He also didn't seem to care.

Chapter 20

Charles Braden stepped outside the Thirty-third Street entrance of CNYCH and dialed Melanie Collins's number on his cell phone.

"Yes," she said sleepily.

"Melanie. It's Charles Braden. I'm sorry to wake you so early, but there's been a problem with Earl Garnet."

"Problem?"

"Yes. I blame myself. My son had just received the upsetting news that Garnet was the man in the taxi with Kelly the night before she disappeared. I went to Garnet's room and confronted him about it. Now I know I shouldn't have, but—"

"What happened?" Her sudden alertness told him he had all her attention.

"He started going on about how you had been deliberately making patients sick so you could then diagnose bizarre syndromes and act the hero. Even said you killed a few, made one of your former victims slip into a coma to silence her, and, get this, accused you of trying to kill him. Now I think it's the drugs, but they had to sedate him—"

"I'm on my way—"

"Melanie, that's not the worst of it. The man has this crazy idea Kelly found out what you were doing, and that you murdered her to keep her quiet."

"Oh, God."

"Fortunately just the two of us were in the room. He's not talking much to anyone right now, but I thought you should know. Even ridiculous rumors like that, once they get rolling, can snowball."

"I appreciate the heads-up."

I'll bet you do, he thought, hanging up.

Now all he had to do was wait. He glanced at his watch and saw it read nearly six. The coffee shop would be open in a few minutes.

He dialed medical records at Lena Downie's extension. Chaz would be waiting there for his call.

"Dad?"

"So what do you think?"

"You were right. She's definitely dirty. I can't believe the woman got away with it for so long."

"Because no one was looking."

"But she killed who knows how many over the years."

"And Kelly, remember."

The silence on the other end of the phone hung between them, pregnant as a held breath. "I guess I thought I'd feel so different finding her killer," Chaz finally said, his voice funereal. "Rage, relief, free—something. Instead, I'm just empty inside."

"That's to be expected—"

"Expected! My life's been chained to her fucking corpse. Now she's turning to dust, and what do I have—closure? What a fucking joke. And you say, 'That's to be expected.' "

Charles winced at Chaz's anger.

"Chaz, why don't you join me in the coffee shop so we can talk. We still have to decide how to proceed—"

"How did Garnet take it when you confronted him?"

"Not well."

"Did he deny it?"

"He went a little wacko, to tell you the truth."

"I'd like to wacko him—"

"Now you stay away from him, Chaz. This whole thing has to be done properly, and legally. Then you'll finally feel free. I promise you."

He could hear his son breathing at the other end of the line. The seething rage in that sound frightened him. "Chaz, promise me you'll stay away."

"Okay," Chaz said, after a few more seconds.

"Now come and have coffee with me."

"I can't. Since I was here all night anyway, I put myself on call. I just got beeped for a cardiac case coming in by air ambulance."

"You?" His son never took weekend calls. Considered excusing himself from it the privilege of being chief.

"Yes, I know. But a couple of loudmouths in my department started to complain about my never putting myself on the schedule. This'll shut them up for a while."

Charles walked over to the Starbucks on the ground floor and ordered an espresso. He needed to clear his head after practically having to guide Chaz through Melanie's files most of the night. His son might not be the dimmest light on the board, but he was a far cry from the brightest.

He found a chair in the corner where he could be reasonably sure of not being disturbed. The place would soon fill up with people on their way to the seven o'clock shift, and he needed to think.

It had been a long road.

The evening when he'd killed her twenty-seven years ago burned as fresh in his mind as the night it happened.

When she'd called the maternity center that morning, he had no idea it would end that way. She was so abrasive, insisting he keep Chaz from trying to follow her and threatening vague revelations that would ruin their name. He had to find out what she knew, and convinced her to meet him one more time that evening. She took the last train to Albany, and he picked her up at the station, then drove her to his office. It was deserted at night.

She'd initially limited her threats to what Chaz would be blamed for— "failing to properly supervise a resident in a case where the patient died." She hadn't provided details, and he practically laughed at her, saying, "I'm afraid that happens all the time in a teaching hospital, dear. If that's all you have to threaten me with, you're out of luck." He wanted to goad her, find out if she'd discovered more deadly secrets.

Provoked, she let slip she also had something on him—the odd irregularities about his records—and that Dr. Cam Roper knew, might even investigate the maternity center and the home.

He'd known at that instant she'd have to die, and Roper, too. Once either of them found out the gravity of his secret, there would be no bargaining. The two of them were too straight for that.

The nearest weapon he'd had on hand were the heavy metal stirrups his pregnant ladies put their feet into when he examined them. He grabbed one, came up behind her, and smashed her in the temple. She was unconscious but not dead.

He'd stripped her, tied her up, and taped her mouth in case she woke up. Putting her in the trunk of his car, he drove to his house, where he burned her clothes in the basement incinerator. In the boathouse he found an old anchor, chain, and padlock. After midnight he drove to Trout Lake and commandeered an old rowboat from one of the cottages. As he'd attached the anchor and chain with the lock, she'd started to regain consciousness. She cried as he rowed her to the middle of the lake, and he never forgot the terror in her eyes as he dumped her in.

He shuddered.

Now all he had to do was catch Melanie Collins in the act of finishing off Earl Garnet. Actually, a little after the act, then let Chaz present the evidence of what she'd been up to all these years. Thankfully, Kelly's letter to Cam Roper suggested she'd found out about Melanie's first two victims and intended to reveal her discovery. It would be an easy sell to convince the authorities she'd confronted Melanie, and that Melanie killed her to keep her quiet.

Too bad Earl had to die. It would have been possible to convict Melanie without having her kill him, useful even, if he had bought the idea of her guilt so completely he'd have been willing to declare far and wide that her conviction cleared the Braden name. But that had been naive. He obviously still harbored deep suspicions, starting with the break-in at Mark Roper's house and ending God knew where. It became necessary to change strategy on the spot and goad Earl into yelling the same paranoid-sounding accusations that Mark Roper and Lucy O'Connor had been led to make—to help ensure he'd seem as off base as the other two and that anything any of them had said would be easier to dismiss in the aftermath—then serve him up to Melanie.

He took a long sip of the hot drink.

It scoured his esophagus and ignited a small fire in his empty stomach.

As for Mark and Lucy, they'd be frozen corpses by now. "So tragic," he would say to reporters. "If only the man had listened to me. I tried to tell him just two days ago to be patient, that there appeared to be new evidence pointing to Kelly's real killer, but obviously he barged ahead on his own. From the start he seemed obsessed with blaming her death on our family, to the point he began making up the most fantastic stories. That he lost his life trying to find nonexistent remains to support these allegations is a waste beyond words. And what did his futile search prove? Simply how wild and baseless his accusations were. That his resident died trying to save him makes it a doubly senseless loss. Two young lives gone for nothing!"

He smiled at how easily he'd sent Mark rushing off half-cocked. A carefully staged mention of smotherings and eugenics, combined with the young man's lifelong resentment of all things Braden, and he assumed the worst, taking Lucy with him. Such a hothead, just like his father.

What better way to deflect an investigation that might discover his former baby business—purely a commercial venture, albeit illegal—than have his chief accuser run around making the charges so extreme no one would take them seriously? Just imagine, Charles Braden III as some crazed fanatic who had murdered deformed newborns, then buried them under the orphanage lawn. He chuckled at the outlandishness of it.

Of course, setting Mark up like that had been risky, but after O'Connor arrived on the scene he'd had to take the chance. A more sober questioning of the birth records might have revealed the truth.

Still, as much as it might be a masterstroke luring them to their deaths the way they had tonight, everything would have been over and neater had they died in the blast. For one thing, they couldn't have saved the talkative old crone. Fortunately, she still didn't pose much of a threat. According to one of his cronies at Saratoga General, she was a "likely," as in "likely to croak."

One reassuring fact—there would be such a media furor in the wake of charging Collins with so many murders, including Kelly's, none of the recent events in Hampton Junction would garner much scrutiny anyway. His past secrets, and the present one at Nucleus Laboratories, should be safe.

As long as his men found the woman with Victor's files. They'd been damn lucky to overhear that conversation.

He took another sip of espresso.

As he waited for the buzz to hit, he heard the thud of heavy rotors arriving over the hospital and raised his eyes.

Must be Chaz's case, he thought.

* * *

Chaz huddled in the doorway leading to the heliport on the hospital roof. The blast of the rotors stirred up clouds of dust and debris, making it necessary for him to turn away, protect his eyes, and cover his mouth. Beside him the men and women of the ER team did the same. He stayed apart from them a little to keep out of their way as they would be the first to the helicopter. However, they were all puzzled by how little advance information they'd been given. All they knew from dispatch: they were receiving two hypothermia cases, a man and a woman, one of them a near-drowning victim in critical condition. Normally they would get vitals, names, and circumstances. Nobody liked surprise packages in this business.

The craft rocked to a landing on the pad, the rotors whined down, and the ER people, crouching low, ran for the doors. The crew already had them open and slid a stretcher halfway out the craft to their waiting hands. As nurses, residents, and orderlies crowded around their charge, Chaz, still hanging back, couldn't tell if it was the man or woman. He was able to see that IVs were up and running through warming coils, that one of the attendants was ventilating the victim, that the oxygen passed through a tube immersed in what he assumed was a basin of hot water, a pretty good improvisation. Wires lead to an O_2 saturation meter, a catheter bag dangling from a side rail indicated urinary output—*Jesus,* he thought, *everything's been done. There must be a doctor on board.*

Someone still inside the ambulance handed out a half dozen tubes of blood, then a syringe wedged in a styrofoam cup overflowing with crushed ice, the standard way to preserve serum slated for acid–base testing. No doubt about it, a physician had gift-wrapped this case so it could bypass emergency and go straight to intensive care. Chaz stepped forward to take charge when a nurse lifted down a portable monitor that beeped out a very slow pulse. As she moved to secure the piece of equipment at the foot of the stretcher, the victim's face came into view.

"Lucy O'Connor?" Chaz said, so stunned he waded into the throng of people who were beginning to wheel the woman into the hospital, getting in their way.

"Hold it right there, Chaz!" said a man's voice over the noise of the helicopter. "Your services won't be required."

He looked up to see Mark Roper, wrapped in blankets but standing, being helped out of the passenger compartment. Stunned, Chaz yelled, "What the hell's happened?"

Mark brushed off supporting hands and walked right by him, leaving the ambulance attendants shaking their heads in dismay.

"He ought to be on a stretcher," one of them said to Chaz.

"Yeah," echoed his colleague. "Instead, he took care of her the whole way."

"I'm fine!" Mark yelled over his shoulder. "First I get Lucy to ICU." He swung his gaze to Chaz. "Then you and I are going to talk."

*   *   *

Melanie Collins ran across the parking lot toward the front door. She could still make this work. Her gaze traveled up to the floor where Earl lay sedated and helpless. Acutely psychotic patients had been known to possess super-human strength, enough to smash a window despite being drugged, and jump. An early-morning haze of dust, exhaust, and grime blurred the outlines of the building and would provide her with the cover she'd need to break the glass with a chair and shove him through. *He overpowered my attempt to stop him,* she could claim, appearing suitably shaken and distraught, maybe even verging on hysterical, after screaming for help.

But high overhead, a streak of azure showed through tattered gray clouds and tried to pin a blue ribbon on the start of an otherwise mediocre-looking day. It just might succeed, judging by how quickly the smog seemed to be dissipating. By the time she got to his room, there'd not be enough mist to conceal her from the street.

No, better stick to her original plan. She slipped a hand into the pocket of her lab coat and fingered the loaded syringe of short-acting insulin. It might take an hour to produce seizures, perhaps longer, but in the end would be neater. Convulsions were a natural complication of the *E. coli 0157:H7* organism; it accumulated on receptor sites in the brain as well as in the kidney. And she'd be at the resuscitation stressing that fact, loading him up with antiseizure medication that wouldn't work and dismissing the need to give him sugar if anyone suggested it. She didn't necessarily need to kill Earl, just let the seizures knock off enough neurons that he would never talk again. Like Bessie.

Still, having to rush a case like this made her uneasy. She usually took days to plan her approach and pick her times. Even with Bessie, rushed as that was, she'd prepared carefully, substituting the contents of a multidose heparin bottle with just enough insulin that the nurse would draw up the shot, then throw the bottle away. The result—someone else gave the agent and disposed of the evidence. That's how she liked doing things—cleverly, cleanly, and at a distance. Earl would be a hands-on operation.

At first the corridor was empty when she arrived, it being another twenty minutes before people would begin to show up for shift change. Then halfway down the hallway a nurse emerged from a patient's room carrying a flashlight. She'd be conducting the last bed check before going off duty. "Body search," the residents called it, since this was when the people who'd died in their sleep were usually discovered.

"Morning," said Melanie. "Dr. Braden phoned me about Dr. Garnet. How is he now?"

"Out like a light," said the woman.

"I'll just peek in on him."

"Want me to come with you?"

"No, I'm fine."

The nurse shrugged and went on with her work.

Melanie paused outside Earl's door, checked that no one else was near, and went in.

*   *   *

Charles Braden finished a second espresso and glanced at his watch. What was taking Chaz so long? He must be having trouble with his case, but they ought to be spending this time mapping out the best way to approach the dean.

Charles knew he'd have to coach his son through it, without appearing to do so. There couldn't be any mistakes in explaining how they knew to suspect Melanie, such as the one he himself had made with Garnet—practically admitting he'd had access to Mark's files. However, Chaz and he would now be able to claim that Roper and Garnet had showed them those reports during the investigation. There'd be no one to say otherwise, once Melanie took care of Garnet.

He glanced at his watch again. She must be in the hospital by now. How she'd get rid of him he had no idea. Any number of the tricks in the arsenal she'd built up over the years ought to do the trick. But he hadn't heard a code blue over the PA system yet. Maybe she'd arranged for him not to be disturbed, and they wouldn't find him for hours. Should he go back upstairs and recheck on Garnet himself, pretend he'd just dropped by, show concern after the man's psychotic episode this morning—

The door to the coffee shop opened and in walked Chaz.

Good, thought Charles, until he saw the look in his son's eyes. Even from the other side of the room he could see the pupils were far too big, the whites far too wide, the circles far too large. The rage in them pushed aside the rest of his face. "Chaz, what's the matter—"

Mark Roper stepped into the room wearing OR greens. Behind him were three uniformed policemen.

The five of them marched forward, but Charles saw only his son's horrible gaze as he descended on him. *Oh, Jesus, he knows.*

"Now, Chaz," he said, getting up out of the chair. There had to be a way he could still bluff himself out of this, at least for long enough to make an escape. He didn't know how Roper had survived, but there was nothing to implicate him, Charles Braden III, in what went on tonight. Ironically, all those wild accusations that he'd primed Mark to make might save him now, make the police hesitate. "Son, tell me, has something happened?"

Chaz's hands shot out, his fingers splayed wide as if he were holding a basketball. "You! You took her from me. The one love I had." He started to run. "I could have kept Kelly. You ruined that. Destroyed me. Let everyone think I did it."

Charles stood his ground, certain he'd be obeyed. "Chaz, you stop this nonsense!"

"Oh, it's not nonsense," Mark said, his voice filling the room. "Sheriff Dan Evans has your men. The two that can talk are telling everything. Not just what they did on your behalf this last week. Seems they used their special skills at procuring information to ferret out all your past secrets, including the fact that you murdered Kelly and why, as insurance—in case they ever had to bargain their way out of a tight spot."

"No!" said Charles. "They're lying—"

Chaz leapt at his throat.

They crashed over backward as his son's fingers closed around his neck. Charles tried to yell, but already the thumbs were crushing his windpipe. He attempted to claw them off.

"You never had faith in me," Chaz screamed. "Never. You ruined everything I ever tried to do. But Kelly! How could you ruin Kelly?" He broke into a wail as raw and screeching as a wounded animal's.

Charles struggled to draw breath and couldn't. His hands pried and twisted at the fingers, but didn't budge them. If anything they squeezed harder. A loud ringing filled his head, drowning out the shouts that rang through the room. His vision grew dark around the edges, and his son's terrible, pained eyes, circles within circles, spiraled him toward two black pits.

*   *   *

Melanie found Earl lying flat on his back, the IV in his arm, a cardiac monitor attached to his chest. The latter surprised her. Had he already started to complain of palpitations? Deplete his potassium and give him a lethal arrhythmia—that had been her original plan. Too bad she couldn't wait.

She walked over to the bedside and stood over him. His face hung slack, his mouth drooped open, and his respirations were shallow, the way she'd expect to see any patient who'd been brought down with a major tranquilizer. It gave her a sense of total control over him.

So look how we ended up, Earl. Couldn't have guessed this when we were classmates, could you? Who's the hotshot now? You'll be remembered as Kelly's killer, and I'll be wringing my hands and saying, Who would have thought it?

She pulled out the syringe, uncapped the needle, and jabbed it into the side portal of the plastic tubing.

Still, you very nearly got me.

She pushed the plunger all the way down and opened the intravenous valve wide, flushing the solution into his vein.

Except it wouldn't run through.

The normal stream of drops that should be dripping from the bag into the plastic tubing wasn't there.

Was the line blocked?

She bent down to check where the tubing joined the angiocath that had been inserted into the vein. Usually the first sign of obstruction would be a backup of blood.

It looked clear.

Then the problem had to be the angiocath itself. It might have torn the vein, and the IV was simply seeping into the tissues of his arm, not through the bloodstream where she needed it.

Damn.

She'd have to change it. But most of the insulin would still be in the tubing. In a few minutes she could make the switch, run it in, and be out of there.

She quickly found an equipment tray on the counter, located a new angiocath, and broke it out of its package.

Then she stooped over Earl's arm, removed the bandage anchoring the old one to the skin—and stared.

It had never been inserted in his vein. It lay taped to the surface of his skin, the needle capped.

"What the hell . . ."

She looked up, and saw Earl staring at her, eyes wide-open and alert.

The bathroom door opened, and out stepped a resident with red hair and the short-haired nurse who'd been taking care of Bessie.

Melanie felt warm, as if the room had gone on fire. "What are you doing here?" She mustered her most imperious tone, intended to make underlings out of anyone she used it on.

"They came to do the DONT on me, Melanie," Earl said, before they could answer. "You remember. N is for narcan, as in reversing the effects of narcotics, such as morphine. Then, after they brought me around, they heard what I had to say about you."

Earl's quiet voice cut into her like a scalpel. It became hard to breathe. She cast around for some way to regain control. "What are you talking about, Earl? Now you let me restart your IV before I call a code forty-four." She looked over at the others. "He had a psychotic episode this morning, and his infection is getting worse." She'd adopted her confiding manner, the one used to bring friends and families over to her side and away from the patient's. She also scanned their name tags. "So Tanya, and Dr. Roy, I know you two meant well, and if you will just get back to your business, we'll say this little episode never happened—"

"You know, I talk to Bessie McDonald every day," Tanya interrupted, speaking so softly it might have been a whisper.

Melanie's fright escalated. "You what?"

"When I brush her hair and clean her nails—she used to be fastidious about that. Oh, don't worry, she can't speak back. Never will. I do it in case she can somehow hear or sense that I'm there, caring for her."

"Well I'm sure that's very commendable—"

"How could you have harmed her so?" Tanya continued. Her voice floated across the room. It made Melanie shiver.

Dr. Roy took a step toward her. "And I want to know if I'd given her sugar when we found her, would it have made a difference?" He had a harder edge to him. "That will haunt me until the end of my days."

Testosterone defined an adversary so much better; it made him far easier to deal with. "You come an inch closer, Dr. Roy, and I'll lay charges of intimidation and menacing behavior, not to mention libel—"

The sound of ripping tape cut her off. She turned to see Earl holding up the tubing that had been attached to his arm. He'd wound it into a loop. "You won't be laying charges, calling any code forty-fours, or doing much of anything once we analyze what you injected in here."

Her mouth went dry, and her insides felt trapped in ice. The coiled green plastic caught the light like an emerald ring. She fought the urge to make a grab for it. "I'm sorry, Earl. You leave me no choice but to get the orderlies." She spun on her heel and walked out of the room.

She heard Tanya and Dr. Roy offer to stop her.

"Don't bother," Earl said. "She's finished, and knows it."

The day before Nixon left the White House and Kelly gave her the ultimatum leapt to her mind.

Go to the dean and confess what you've done within twenty-four hours, or I'll do it for you.

At Kelly's insistence they'd met around noon by the southeast entrance to Central Park—the place across from the Plaza where horse-drawn carriages waited for tourists. Melanie had felt as helpless to save herself then as she did now.

The fear had only worsened as the deadline expired and she waited for the police to knock on her door. Just as the fear would build and eat into her now. Except this time there would be no reprieve.

She walked briskly toward the nursing station, and right on by to the exit.

*   *   *

Thirty minutes later Melanie sat in her penthouse sipping coffee. It had turned out to be a pleasant day after all. The sunlight crept across the white birch floors on schedule, illuminating her trophies one by one. The designer kitchen, the living room ensemble, the four-poster bed.

She watched the edge of its shadow reach the glass-topped table in front of her and slowly pass by the items laid out on it. She adjusted her gaze to the southwest, looking out the windows toward the Statue of Liberty and to the sparkling water beyond. A cruise ship glided by the lady, bound for who knows where. She'd known the excitement of that moment, embarking on a Saturday morning, leaving New York and work behind, anticipating what adventures lay ahead.

Those trips didn't hold a candle to where she'd be going now.

There would be plenty of time. At least an hour. Probably double that. No one would believe Earl at first.

"The drugs—they've made him hallucinate," everyone would say.

Testing for insulin would also take a while.

He wouldn't have the cops at her door anytime soon.

And she'd be long gone when they did arrive. But then he'd probably known that, too. Otherwise, he wouldn't have let her go.

Another sip, and she savored its bittersweet bite, tempered as it was by cream and sugar. Normally she used skim milk and sweetener, but what the hell. Today was special.

She downed the remnants and poured herself a second cup.

What would her patients think when they found out? Her colleagues? The residents? She couldn't stand the thought of being ousted as a fraud, exposed as something less than the smart, quick, concerned physician she'd craved to be seen as. Now, instead, she'd be made legend, right up there with other doctors who killed, like Cream, Swango, Shipman. They'd have experts on Larry King, Connie Chung, and Barbara Walters dissecting her place in that particular constellation of the murder universe. But she wasn't like those creeps. She hadn't set out to kill anyone. She'd tried her hardest to save them.

One thing she felt in her bones. There were others out there making themselves shine as physicians the same way she had. It was too tempting a scam for there not to be.

She poured herself a third cup.

By now the departing ship was but a dot on the horizon.

She began to feel sleepy.

Good.

The first of the several vials that now lay empty on the table had started to kick in. She wanted to be out cold when the other ingredients took effect. Seizures, arrhythmias, and cardiovascular shock—the symptoms wouldn't be pleasant once they began. And there would be no remedy. She'd chosen the makings of her drug cocktail too well for that. No one, not even a bright boy like Earl Garnet, would ever be able to resuscitate her.

Denouement

Mark looked up from the flowchart Earl had handed to him. "So Melanie intended to kill you and set you up as Kelly's murderer, all to stop you from finding out what she'd done."

Earl nodded, but said nothing.

From his grimace and the sheen of perspiration on his face, Mark knew he was in pain. "But Braden, starting with the M and M reports from Kelly's file, had followed the same same paper trail you were on, reached the same conclusion you did, and realized he had his own scapegoat. He spurred Melanie on to kill you even sooner, intending to set her up as Kelly's murderer, all part of his master plan to wipe out anyone who could expose him." Mark glanced up from the flowchart and regarded its author. "Is that it?"

"That's it," said Earl.

Mark considered the idea. It seemed straightforward enough, but something niggled at him. "Wouldn't it have been safer for Braden to just stand back—let Melanie carry out her plan to finish you off and make you the fall guy? Kelly's murder would still be closed, unofficially maybe, but no one would be looking anymore."

Earl smiled at him. It seemed forced. "Because serving up a proven se-rial killer as Kelly's murderer would be a lot more convincing than leaving people shocked and incredulous that I'd done it. Hell, over the years I've even heard rumors that some people call me Goody Two-shoes Garnet be-hind my back."

In spite of everything, Mark chuckled.

"He needed a definitive scapegoat," Earl continued, "and he needed it now, the more sensational the better. Otherwise, he couldn't hope to pawn off what he'd set up for you and Lucy as the freak accident he intended everyone to take it as. The same went for the explosion at Nell's. Even then some people would still be suspicious, but there'd be no proof of foul play, and the flaming fact of Melanie Collins being in all the headlines, murderess extraordinaire that Charles Braden had helped bring to justice, would blunt whatever a few naysayers might mutter to each other. Hell, if you hadn't played it smart and resisted going body-hunting last night, he might have gotten away with it."

Mark's face went warm.

Instantly Earl's expression changed. "Sorry, Mark. I never meant to im-ply Lucy—"

"It's all right," Mark said. "If you hadn't told me to play it smart, I might have gone out there with her. I owe you my life for that, and what-ever chance Lucy has." But if he hadn't let what Earl said stir up his own suspicions about her, Lucy might not have gone at all. Instead, she'd proba-bly sensed those doubts, and felt the need to prove herself trustworthy to him. Mark's instincts knew this about her as surely as she now lay on total life support twelve floors below with a coma score of three, equal to Bessie McDonald's.

"Get back to Lucy, Mark," Earl said. "Above all, don't lose hope. The re-coveries from hypothermia these days can be nothing short of miraculous."

He tried not to show that he knew Earl had half-lied to him. Mark had already gone on MedLine, as soon as he'd gotten Lucy settled in ICU, and checked the literature, confirming what he'd already known. Success stories about hypothermia were based on single best cases. The over-all statistics were grim, especially for adults. He nodded, and turned to leave.

"And talk to her, Mark," Earl called after him. "Leave tinkering with her biochemistry to others. Every minute you're at her side, talk to her."

That made him pause. "What good will that do?"

"She'll hear you. I'm certain of it. Talk to her and help bring her back."

As he hurriedly returned to ICU he thought, sometimes even bossy people who treated him like an intern could give good advice.

**Ten days later, Tuesday,
December 4, 10:00 A.M.
Seminar Room, Fifteen East,
New York City Hospital**

Mark glanced at the faces of everyone in the room from where he sat at the head of the long table. Nearly all the people whom he'd invited had arrived.

But he quickly turned his attention back to Lucy, who sat at his side. She'd been given permission to get out of bed for the proceedings, though still in a hospital gown and tethered to an IV pole. "Just in case," her doctors had said in the ominous shorthand physicians use with each other.

"Don't look so glum, Mark," she told him. "You and I both know the score. I'm fine."

Yes. He knew the score. She had already beaten incredibly long odds. She'd been in a coma for three days. From what she remembered before going in the water, Mark estimated her submersion time had been ten minutes. When Dan and the air ambulance arrived, he had been in the well giving her mouth-to-mouth ten minutes more, though at the time it felt much longer. Even now her myocardium could overreact to the electrical impulses of its own conduction system and fly into overdrive. PAT, atrial fibrillation, ventricular tachycardia—everything Earl had had to watch out for—could now be hers, including the possibility of cardiac arrest.

"I've made it over the hard part, right?" she cheerfully insisted, reaching over and patting his hand as if he were the patient.

"Absolutely," he said, forcing himself to give a delighted smile. Still, her condition worried him.

Earl himself, a few seats away, looked gaunt, his cheeks and eyes sunken from the ordeal of his infection. Cleared to go home later today, he'd be leaving fifteen pounds lighter, but with kidneys, pancreas, and brain intact. Janet leaned close to him, her hand resting protectively on his arm. A suitcase stood at the leg of his chair.

Opposite Janet, Dan Evans reclined comfortably, a slight smile on his face. It had been there for the last week and a half. He'd been the center of attention for every paper, news reporter, and talk show in Saratoga Springs, and one headline in the *New York Herald* read: *Country sheriff and small-town coroner crack murder that stumped the NYPD for twenty-seven years.* Mark had gladly let him make all the public appearances and deal with the media, Lucy being his sole concern.

A woman occupied the seat to Dan's right. She had come forward in response to all the media coverage. In her late twenties, she wore a stylish gray business suit and had black hair drawn back into a single long braid. From time to time she'd laugh at something Dan said and touch his arm. Dan's smile would widen, the way it usually did when someone appreciated one of his jokes. Mark had never met her before, but instantly recognized her voice when Dan introduced her.

Beside her sat Tanya Wozcek, dressed in jeans, opposite Dr. Roy, in whites as always.

Hunched over by himself a few places away, Detective William Everett, pasty-faced and sullen, played with a paper clip.

There were two no-shows—Walter and Samantha McShane.

Mark had expected as much since this wouldn't be all about Samantha.

The one whose presence surprised everyone—Chaz Braden—occupied the far end of the table. Mark hadn't faced the man since they'd hauled him off his father in the coffee shop. But he looked different somehow. The circles under his eyes sagged less heavily, but the change seemed more substantial than that. He possessed a steadiness in his gaze and a stillness in the way he sat that Mark didn't remember seeing before.

Time to get under way. He snapped on the portable tape recorder he'd brought with him and placed it on the table. "Thank you for coming everyone. I remind you that what is discussed here must remain confidential, and it will be entered as part of my final report on the murder of Kelly McShane. I've already talked to you individually and gone over what each of you knows. I've also collaborated with my colleagues, Sheriff Dan Evans and Dr. Earl Garnet, to piece together the findings. What we ended up with is a story of murder and how trying to find out old secrets uncovered a trove of current ones. This meeting will give all of you a chance to correct any omissions or errors. I caution that for some, the testimony will be painful."

He paused and glanced around at his audience, paying particular attention to Chaz. No signs of anger. So far so good. "Dr. Garnet will begin."

Earl leaned forward, clasped his hands on the table, and looked around him with the easy assurance of a man used to addressing large groups.

"As most of you have seen in the media, I met with Kelly on the eve of her disappearance. While she had already confided in me her intent to end her marriage and drop out of sight, she kept the specifics of her plans private, other than mentioning she had some matters to take care of first. Such secrecy you may find strange, but she didn't want me or any of her friends to search for her, in case we unwittingly gave away her hiding place."

Prior to the meeting, Earl had indicated a willingness, albeit reluctantly, to explain his relationship to Kelly for the record, "So as to avoid any claims later that I've been less than forthright. Otherwise, some idiot's liable to say I compromised the credibility of the whole inquiry by covering up my own role in what happened."

"Don't feel obliged to bring it up unless someone else does," Mark had advised. "But anybody who can read a newspaper has already guessed the truth."

Nevertheless, Earl paused, giving his audience every chance to question him, his gaze tactfully fixed on Janet, presumably to avoid the appearance of trying to stare down whoever might feel inclined to request that he tell all.

Janet gave him a smile of encouragement, as if whatever he had to say would be all right with her.

Chaz seemed to be holding his breath.

No takers.

"So despite her furtiveness, what do we know about Kelly's actions on the last day of her life?" Earl continued. "Direct testimony gave us some leads, we deduced a great deal more from the evidence we gathered, and speculation will have to fill in the gaps." He glanced toward Chaz. "One of those 'matters' she mentioned, we subsequently learned, involved a confrontation with her husband, Dr. Charles Braden IV, when she announced her intention to leave him. The encounter occurred in the street outside his office."

Chaz didn't so much as flinch an eyebrow at the disclosure. He'd been the source of this information, including it in his statement to the police. Everett then passed it along to Mark as a professional courtesy.

"By our investigation of phone records for that day we were also able to determine she'd made a call to Charles Braden III at his maternity center in Saratoga. Presumably at the time he convinced her to come and meet with him in the evening. She did, and, we think, confronted him about the irregularities in his statistics for the facility, specifically the impossibly low number of newborns with congenital defects."

There'd been no statement out of Charles since his arrest other than asserting his right to remain silent. The only information Everett had been able to provide about him—"The son of a bitch sure looks good in an orange jumpsuit."

"We also think it's safe to assume that Kelly did not leave New York without confronting Melanie Collins . . ."

Earl went on to recount the saga of the digoxin toxicity cases.

Confront your fears, went the pop jargon, Mark thought, half-listening to the familiar account. Yet here a woman who'd run from confrontation all her life finally stood her ground, and got killed for it.

". . . Knowing Kelly, however, my own opinion is that she probably intended to give Melanie the chance to do the right thing by turning herself in, and hadn't told anyone the full extent of her suspicions. If she had confided in somebody, it most likely would have been to Dr. Cam Roper, Mark's father and her mentor. But if he'd known the whole story, wouldn't he have acted on it after Kelly disappeared? Instead, I think she may have only asked his opinion on the files, without naming the culprit, but promising to take care of the problem before her departure. When no headlines to that effect appeared, I think Cam Roper tried to check it out himself, following the same paper trail I did and going after the original charts. Except he never got a chance to finish . . ."

Mark had gone very still at the mention of his dad. Ironically, he'd talked to Lucy a lot about him as he kept a vigil at her side, not sure if she could hear but driven to try and reach her. And as he talked, he eventually admitted what he hadn't been able to face before. That in seeking justice for Kelly, he might also be tracking his father's killer.

". . . However, Melanie Collins's suicide means we will never know for certain what happened between her and Kelly on that day." Earl looked over at Dan. "Sheriff Evans will now outline the reason Kelly, and possibly Dr. Cam Roper, were killed."

Dan reflexively looked toward the end of the table where Chaz remained motionless, face calm, eyes steady.

Mark couldn't tell for sure, but Chaz seemed to give Dan a nod to proceed.

Dan nevertheless took a few seconds to scan some notes that he had in front of him. "I've spent the last week taking statements from the bankers, family solicitors, and tax accountants who have managed the Braden fortune for years. It seems they would rather testify under oath than be considered in cahoots with Braden Senior. I also took statements from families whose babies he delivered in his Saratoga maternity center. And have contacted at least twenty orphanages. It soon became abundantly clear that Charles Braden III did what he did for money, pure and simple." He stopped and took a sip from a bottle of water he'd brought with him.

Mark could tell he was nervous.

"In the midfifties, stock market reversals and heavy inheritance taxes on Charles Braden's various properties put him in a precarious financial position. I won't go into the details of how he reversed this situation, but in short, he exchanged healthy babies for deformed ones at twenty-thousand dollars a child, for a total of three and a half million, tax free, over twenty years. In most cases only the fathers knew, and the only crime committed by them had been to forge the mothers' names placing the babies for adoption. So far I've managed to turn up records of 171 children with congenital defects that Braden placed in orphanages throughout the state during that period, and I still have several more institutions to check." He paused, and slid Mark a glance this time. "There were no smotherings. I think he created that rumor himself, to make any accusations against him seem over the top and therefore unbelievable. But as Dr. Roper will now explain, there were bodies."

Mark jumped right in. "Some of these infants were bound to die in transport. Not many, but more than the mortality rate for healthy newborns at the time. While it would be possible to explain live deformed infants to state authorities with incomplete documents, dead ones were another matter. Those, I believe, he did bury on the grounds of the home, probably no more than three or four. Sheriff Evans found a few locals who remember him finally finishing off the lawn after shutting the place down, replacing a few truckloads of topsoil and bringing in a complete order of sod, something he never managed to do while the place was in business."

He cast his stare the length of the table at Chaz. "So why did Charles Braden III kill in 1974? Even if his baby racket were found out, he wouldn't have been guilty of murder at that point. And if manslaughter charges were laid against him for the few infants who perished, I doubt any court would have convicted him since those newborns might not have survived anyway. But he most certainly would have been ruined, professionally and financially, and probably gone to jail—income tax evasion figuring prominently in the charges. For that reason, he murdered Kelly, and, most likely, my father."

The room had fallen silent.

Chaz didn't avert his gaze, but looked desolate, as if his mind were in some private wasteland.

Mark, feeling a sudden urge to move, pushed out of his chair and started to pace. "After closing both the maternity center and the home, Charles Braden III confined himself to legitimate medicine and research, carving out a distinguished career over several decades. He also prospered in the business world. The Manhattan corporate elite who were beholden to him for healthy offspring rewarded him with appointments to their boards of directors and offered him stock options, further increasing his wealth and prestige.

"Charles realized, however, that he was still vulnerable, that his baby swapping and tax evasion could still catch up with him through something as simple as incidental blood work prior to a surgical procedure on any of the substituted children. Some of the fathers Braden conspired with have come forward and given us valuable testimony about the measures he took to prevent that from happening. Like the family accountants Sheriff Evans mentioned before, these men didn't know they'd been in league with a murderer and were just as eager to distance themselves from him by coming clean. 'Charles warned me that should the daughter he'd given us ever require an operation and undergo blood typing, an alert doctor with access to the rest of our family's medical files might spot that she couldn't be progeny of me or my wife,' one of these men told me. 'So he instructed me that should any serious health issue arise requiring a possible transfusion, I should let him recommend a specialist who had never cared for me or the rest of my family.' I heard this story over and over.

"Obviously, the issue could be managed easily while these individuals were young and, odds were, healthy enough that they wouldn't fall sick with a serious illness anyway. Once they grew old enough to leave the nest, those who moved away were no longer a problem, their medical files now far from those of siblings and parents.

"For the ones who stayed in Manhattan, Braden, under the guise of providing the best care, referred them only to doctors who had contracts with labs that were part of the Braden business empire. Why? Another of these dads explained, 'As early as the late eighties, when DNA testing first began to have forensic and commercial applications, Charles anticipated that sooner or later genetic screening for abnormal genes might become a routine part of medicine. When that happened, he wanted to be in a position to flag and intercept any test results that reported my son wasn't our biological offspring.' Others told a variation of the same story, all of them painting a picture of Charles Braden being smug in the certainty that he'd taken account of all eventualities.

"So for twenty-seven years he believed that he had successfully covered up his crimes and gotten away with murder. I can only speculate as to his thoughts at the time we discovered Kelly's body. As you may have guessed, Charles himself isn't telling us anything. But his initial actions suggested a willingness to let the current investigation run its course. Probably he expected it would come to a dead end, exactly as it had twenty-seven years ago. My poking around evoked little more on his part than a few subtle attempts to misdirect suspicion toward Kelly's mother, Samantha McShane, and organizing a break-in at my house—his henchmen gave statements that he'd demanded they place the tap on my phone and get copies of my father's file on Kelly.

"Even when Charles saw those papers, including a letter from Kelly that implied she'd been having an affair, his plan of action appeared limited to finding a fall guy on whom he could pin the murder. According to those same henchmen, their only instructions at the time involved monitoring my calls and keeping an eye on me in the hope I'd discover the identity of Kelly's lover. Again, a careful, shrewd approach, calling for subterfuge rather than violence. And as soon as he rooted out the secret behind the mortality-morbidity reports, he had an even better scapegoat at hand in Melanie Collins. So why would a man supposedly intent on a nuanced, sophisticated strategy to conceal the truth once more resort to the clumsy art of murder?"

He glanced toward the woman sitting beside Dan. "Talk of killing, Braden's thugs told us, came only after Charles listened in on the last phone conversation I had with Victor Feldt." For those who didn't know, Mark quickly outlined the events leading up to Victor's firing and followed them through to the fateful call. "Victor couldn't unravel all the corporate layers that we now know were Charles Braden's doing to keep his role as CEO from becoming public knowledge. And what Victor thought he'd found—hiring and firing irregularities at companies where the executive health plans subjected employees to genetic screening—had nothing directly to do with Braden. It was Victor's interest in the few dozen New York physicians who used the lab for their private patients that meant trouble for him. For here Victor drew perilously close to the very pieces of evidence that Braden knew would reach back over twenty-seven years and point at his baby-swapping business.

"So when Victor later left me a message, stating that he'd hacked into the computer where the results sent to those New York doctors were stored and found something peculiar, well . . ."

He had to stop and compose himself. "Tragically, I didn't realize the danger he'd put himself in until it was too late. But thanks to a very special friend and colleague of Victor's, who came forward with the files he'd entrusted to her, I finally pulled everything together."

Dan's dark-haired companion flushed deeply.

Mark opened a briefcase at his feet and pulled out three folders. From each he took out several lab reports that included graphs with numbered vertical spikes of varying heights along a horizontal line. "For those of you who are interested, these are the results Victor found." He stood and spread them over the table.

Roy and a few others picked them up, studying them with puzzled expressions.

"You're looking at genetic screening on three pairs of sisters, all with a positive family history for breast cancer. To a trained eye, differences in the DNA reveal that none of them are biological siblings—Braden's prediction that the coming age of genomic medicine would mean a whole new level of headache for him made manifest. And over time, as more of the individuals he'd substituted underwent screening for one reason or another, there'd be increasing disclosures of nonsiblings, all involving so-called offspring whom Charles had supposedly delivered. Obviously, he couldn't allow that to happen."

"Were these other doctors in cahoots with his cover-up?" Roy asked, laying aside the graph he'd been studying.

"No, they were unwitting dupes."

"Didn't they miss the reports Braden intercepted?"

"Oh, they got a report. Braden's flagging these results was part of a program where the computer would then generate simple typewritten responses stating whether the genes that had been tested for were present or not, then eliminate the graphs. We checked the other labs he owned and found similar systems in place. The doctors weren't aware they'd missed anything. Most only want the final answer of a test anyway—less paper."

"Why did they all use his labs in the first place?"

"As one of them said to me, 'We didn't know they were owned by Braden. Representatives approached us offering first-rate, competent service at a special price, then delivered—an offer too good to refuse.' "

Mark waited for more questions. No one had any. He glanced once more toward the end of the table. Chaz retained the quiet equilibrium Mark had noticed at the start of the meeting. Maybe witnessing a public dissection of his father's crimes would help him get out from under the weight of the old man's legacy. In fact, maybe it had already started to happen, and that's what seemed different about him.

Mark knew that he should now state for the record the events leading to Victor's death: That Charles Braden III, having learned Victor gave Lucy O'Connor a tour of the genetic-screening facility, must have seen her as a special threat. That Charles knew she already suspected he had something to hide about the home for unwed mothers because of all the records he'd so conveniently lost in a fire there. That finding her nosing around the laboratory, he probably jumped to conclusions. Assumed that she'd somehow found out about the screening results. Mistakenly concluded that she knew they would unmask his secret and had set out to get her hands on them.

So Charles cut off her access to the place by having Victor fired.

Then Victor found the reports, and paid with his life.

But looking at Lucy's frail face, Mark hadn't the heart to make her hear those words.

Wednesday, December 5, 4:00 P.M.
Hampton Junction

Mark turned left at the end of his driveway and settled into an easy stride. He hadn't had a decent run since Lucy went into hospital. The air in Manhattan saw to that.

Dusk hung over the hills, the sun already behind them, and the late-afternoon light had a blue quality to it, typical for the end of day during the weeks leading up to winter's longest night. In the distance toward town he saw tiny clusters of reds, greens, and amber where people had already hung their outside decorations. He smiled, having just dug out of the basement tree lights and ornaments that he hadn't bothered with since Aunt Margaret died. The boxes lay stacked in the living room, ready for the weekend. That's when Lucy would be discharged from hospital, an early release into his care.

His house would soon be a busy place. Lucy's parents and brothers were coming for the holidays. It had been impossible to reach any of them until she'd recovered enough to provide e-mail addresses. They'd literally been scattered all over the globe, and all were ready to run to her side the instant he reached them, but Lucy insisted they hold off until the holidays, "Now that the worst is over."

Mark turned west onto the uphill portion of his route. Traces of woodsmoke wafted through the twilight.

Lucy and he had discussed other plans as well. Again he smiled. As things stood, she would join him in Hampton Junction when her residency ended in June.

"Wonderful," Janet Graceton had said when, as they made their goodbyes after the meeting yesterday.

Earl had asked, "So what are you two going to do?" and Lucy told him. He couldn't have looked happier for them, or congratulated them more enthusiastically.

Janet had chuckled. "Two doctors living under one roof? Believe me, it's a hoot making that work." She gave Lucy a hug. "If you need any advice, call me."

He increased his speed, making his calves burn.

This morning he'd visited Nell in Saratoga General, the first time he'd seen her since that terrible night.

She'd been off the respirator for over a week, and her skin, though it had blistered here and there, confirming his initial impression of first- and second-degree burns, bore none of the deeper, third-degree damage that he'd hoped she would be spared. Most important, she escaped the need for painful skin grafts entirely.

Even with the upper side of her body still swathed in protective dressings, she'd managed to look indignant when he showed up, giving a haughty sniff. "Look at me. I'm done up like some a damned mummy."

"Not for long, Nell. The nurses tell me you'll be out of here in another week and a half—off to stay with your daughter in Florida."

"Christmas in Florida! There's no snow!" she'd huffed, and tried to stay annoyed, but couldn't hide an upward flicker at the unbandaged corner of her mouth.

"I guess you've read and seen on TV all that happened."

"Some."

"Tell me, Nell, when you said you had come up with some other tidbits and a name related to Kelly's murder, was that just a come-on to get me out to your place?"

Her icy silence had told him he'd hit the truth.

"You want to hear the inside stuff the media didn't get?" he'd asked, trying to warm things up between them again.

The flicker at the side of her mouth had shot north for a second, and her eyes showed interest, but she just as quickly continued to look cross. "Don't think tempting me with that sort of thing makes us even. I'm still mad at you."

"For saving your life?"

"For putting that tube into me."

"Same thing."

She glared at him. "You think you're so smart."

"Well, if you don't want me to tell you the good stuff, or about what's happening with Lucy and me—"

"What about Lucy and you?"

He'd told her. All about Lucy. Including where she'd been born.

She'd studied him in silence almost a full minute when he finished.

"And you say the mother registered under a false name, but had a red file?"

"That's right. And the year would be 1969, the date, March 7."

She'd studied him some more.

"You think I might be able to figure out who it is?"

He'd nodded.

From the way her gaze had suddenly intensified, he could tell the wheels were already turning. "Perhaps it would help if you saw her. There might be a physical resemblance," he added.

That had evoked a completely unchecked smile of delight.

He passed the place in the highway where he'd rammed Braden's killers. Minutes later he put the gate to the home behind him. The land-marks had made him tense up inside.

Up ahead stretched open road, steeper, but unencumbered with any bad memories. He picked up the pace and felt himself relax. He got into the familiar rhythm of his body adapting to the change in grade and let it carry him along.

Time would expunge the hold that place had on him. Just as other memories would no longer encumber him. He felt certain of that.

Mark started to sprint, and soon found himself thinking of the wonderful things that lay in store rather than the past. His feet seemed to glide over the gray pavement, and a full moon peeked up over the horizon. Running straight at it, he headed for the summit, grinning all the way.

The Aztecs